THE BODY AT THE AUCTION

I reached in my purse and fished around for my wooden troll talisman. "Something isn't right." I stood and we excused ourselves down the row. "We gotta go. Grover Prickle is AWOL, no one can find Auggie, and I'm in the room. You know what comes next."

Aunt Ginny got up behind Gia, grabbed his elbow, and shuffled along with us.

I clutched my troll and tried to escape as fast as my feet would take me, but two men were coming up the aisle with the armoire I had placed a bid on. *Oh no. No no no.* I looked left and right but I was blocked on every side.

One of the furniture movers stumbled. The man lost his grip on the heavy furniture. It teetered, then slipped out of his hands. The front leg of the armoire banged on the ground causing the door to swing open. A body rolled out and fell to the floor wrapped in Grover Prickle's prized regimental flag soaked in blood . . .

Books by Libby Klein

CLASS REUNIONS ARE MURDER

MIDNIGHT SNACKS ARE MURDER

RESTAURANT WEEKS ARE MURDER

THEATER WEEKS ARE MURDER

WINE TASTINGS ARE MURDER

BEAUTY EXPOS ARE MURDER

ANTIQUE AUCTIONS ARE MURDER

Published by Kensington Publishing Corp.

A Poppy McAllister Mystery

Antique Auctions Are MURDER

LIBBY KLEIN

Kensington Publishing Corp.
www.kensingtonbooks.com

KENSINGTON BOOKS are published by

Kensington Publishing Corp.
119 West 40th Street
New York, NY 10018

All Kensington titles, imprints, and distributed lines are available at special quantity discounts for bulk purchases for sales promotion, premiums, fund-raising, educational, or institutional use.

Special book excerpts or customized printings can also be created to fit specific needs. For details, write or phone the office of the Kensington Sales Manager: Attn.: Sales Department. Kensington Publishing Corp., 119 West 40ᵗʰ Street, New York, NY 10018. Phone: 1-800-221-2647.

The K and Teapot logo is a trademark of Kensington Publishing Corp.

First Printing: March 2022
ISBN: 978-1-4967-3314-6

ISBN: 978-1-4967-3317-7 (ebook)

10 9 8 7 6 5 4 3 2 1

Printed in the United States of America

For Georgina, who was a good sport and continually tries to grow and change in small ways.

And for my real mother-in-law, who has always been a wonderful friend, and has actually worked as a chambermaid and was fabulous.

CHAPTER 1

"Why is it every time a body drops in this town I gotta be questioned by the police?"

"It's standard operating procedure." The walkie Velcroed to the shoulder of Amber's police uniform squawked and she twisted the volume down.

I took a sip of the coffee I'd brought outside with me. "Since when?"

"About two murders ago. Also, since Captain Kieran Dunne took over as acting chief of police and strapped me to a partner who watches my every move like a stalker."

A slim African American woman in uniform stood at the bottom of my porch steps. She folded her toned arms across her chest and her golden-brown eyes assessed my front yard. She frowned at Amber. "And you're such a delight."

I gave the new officer a smile. "Hi, I don't think we've met. I'm Poppy."

Her eyes lolled my way and she scanned me from toe to head. "I know who you are."

I glanced back at Amber and she gave me an eyebrow raise that bobbed her blond top bun. "You see what I'm dealing with here?" She held a photo out for me to examine. It was an older man with a pot belly and a steel-gray comb-over.

He had a face like a bulldog and a tattoo of a snake over his left eye. "Nope. Never seen him before. Who is it?"

"Mitchel Maloney, age fifty-seven, down from Yonkers. He was found under Morey's Pier. Strangled with a macramé plant hanger. I don't suppose he's one of your guests?"

I handed her the photo back. "No. And all of mine are currently in-house getting ready to check out. Sunday morning is a big turnover time for us."

Amber slid the photo back into her front pocket. "Alright. Keep your ears open and if you hear anything, you let me know."

The officer behind Amber sighed loudly, took the few steps up to my wraparound, and fished a business card out of her front pocket with her active-length gold glitter nails. "You got no business being involved, but if you do see something, I want to be in that loop. Here's my card and the number to the station."

I glanced at the white cardstock with the county insignia. I could have told Sergeant Viola Washington that I already had the police department number memorized, but I sensed that would only elicit another eye roll and I was already on shaky ground with her just for existing.

What a pair they made. Amber, a former cheerleader for Cape May High, who was just barely tall enough to ride the Wild Mouse roller coaster on the Wildwood Boardwalk; and her new partner, who looked like a founding member of the Gorgeous Ladies of Wrestling. Amber dropped her mirrored sunglasses to her nose and both officers made their way down the sidewalk towards the police car. I returned to the front desk to finish checking out the Applegates.

"Our whole vacation was ruined. I really don't think we should have to pay for the days it rained."

I handed Mrs. Applegate a copy of our terms of service. "I'm very sorry that you had to miss the beach, but as our policy says, we have no control over hurricane season."

She was a sour one. Cracking a smile might ruin the lifetime she'd devoted to wallowing in bitterness. She'd already turned in a daily comment card complaining about our tea and jam selection. Now I was being punished for low quality weather.

Mrs. Applegate gave me a disapproving sniff. "I still think we should get a discount. It's not my fault it rained."

I was about to remind her and her husband that weather fell under our Act of God policy and we had supplied free umbrellas for their stay, but I spotted Mrs. Newman slinking down the stairs with a distinctive package tucked under her armpit. *Oh heck no.* "Joanne!"

My high school nemesis turned part-time pastry chef emerged from the kitchen wiping her hands on a tea towel. Her brow crinkled as we made eye contact.

"Could you please finish checking out the Applegates? I believe Mrs. Newman needs my attention."

Joanne swiveled to see Mrs. Newman and her souvenir selection. The whites of her eyes popped, and she gave me a nod.

While she took over checking out the third set of guests in a row to attempt to shake us down for a rain discount, I caught up with the little old lady from Piscataway who was trying to steal something from her room. "Mrs. Newman."

The woman jumped when she saw me, and her face blushed a shade of pink that matched the roses in my front yard. "Oh. I was just taking my things to the car."

"Yes, ma'am, but I'm afraid you'll have to leave the painting here."

Her eyes softened like a bloodhound. "Oh, is this your painting?"

"Yes, ma'am. That's why it was hanging over the dresser in your suite."

"Well, couldn't you just look the other way this one time? I'd be happy to give you twenty dollars for it if that would make you happy."

I put my hand on the corner of the gilded frame. "I'm sorry, Mrs. Newman, but this is a painting of my great-uncle Rooster. It's a family heirloom."

Her lips rolled down to a pout. "But he looks just like my Roger."

I didn't see how that was likely since Uncle Rooster had flaming red hair peeking out from under a leather helmet and was wearing aviator goggles that gave him bug eyes. It was a hideous portrait, but he was still my family. I eased the painting from her arthritic death grip. "I'm sorry, ma'am."

Mrs. Newman let the painting go and let her wheelie bag drop with an irritated *thump thump thump* down every step to the front door. Whoever said "Summertime and the livin' is easy" didn't know what the monkey foot they were talking about. They had clearly never worked in Cape May during tourist season.

I said goodbye to the Applegates and returned to the kitchen to bask in the best part of the week. The quiet in-between. Whether guests came for a romantic weekend or an entire week of sun and sand, most everyone checked out on Sunday afternoon laden with boxes of taffy and fudge, to return to wherever they called home and ease back into their normal routines.

Joanne slumped down at the kitchen table with an iced blackberry tea and played a game on her phone. We sat together in silence—our weekly agreed-upon ceasefire from the mutual animosity that was forged in adolescence, lugged through the past twenty years, and thrown into overdrive at one disastrous high school reunion.

I stared at the blinking cursor on my laptop screen. I'd promised a friend I'd write a post for their blog. "What it's like running a bed and breakfast at the shore?" I was afraid that if I told the truth no one would believe me. The last thing I felt like putting up with was a bunch of comments telling me my post was ridiculously far-fetched when I knew every word of it was true. I closed the laptop. This would have to be a problem for another day.

I let the fleeting quiet wash over me before Joanne started on this afternoon's check-in cookies and I began the muffin brigade for La Dolce Vita.

The Butterfly Wings Bed and Breakfast was far too busy for me to spend several hours each day flirting—I mean baking—at the coffee shop. No matter how badly I wanted to spend time with my gorgeous Italian boyfriend. I felt giggly just thinking the word. *Boyfriend.* Like I was some frisky teenager and not a middle-aged widow in a plus-sized sundress. The stakes were so high that I was checking for gray in my natural auburn every day.

My naughty Persian, Sir Figaro Newton, pushed his foofy black smoke face through the swinging door that led from the kitchen to the dining room, making his orange eyes bug out. He spotted me at the table and forced his way in through the crack. Trotting over with his flat nose in the air, he jumped onto the bench seat next to me to see if a snack might be in the works.

The back door cracked open on the other side of the kitchen and Aunt Ginny stuck her L'Oréal Hot Tomato–hued red head through. "Are they gone?"

I stretched my arms over my head. "Yep, it's just us for a couple of blissful hours."

"Thank God." Aunt Ginny sashayed across the gray porcelain tiles in a breeze of piña colada tanning lotion. She tightened the strap of the red and white gingham halter bikini she'd had since the fifties when she worked the lifeguard stand just a block away. She removed a red straw sun hat the size of a beach umbrella, and large white-rimmed sunglasses and threw them both on the island before pouring herself a tall glass of iced tea. "Has Victory come down yet? I've been waiting for this all day."

Victory, my Ukrainian chambermaid, shot through the pantry doors where the spiral staircase led up to the third floor. "I breing box. Eis time!" She threw a bag of dirty linens into the mudroom by the washer, and hoisted the Amazon box full of lost and found trinkets on the kitchen table to start lining the contents up for consideration.

We had decided on a one month waiting period for forgotten items to see if they were claimed before putting them up for grabs. Victory and Aunt Ginny had been chomping to rifle through the box, convinced that guests had abandoned priceless treasures in order to make packing room for fresh-roasted cashews and Swedish fish. Figaro jumped to the table to get a better view of the bounty in case there was anything he wanted dibs on.

One turquoise toe ring; one purple velvet push-up bra—size thirty-six B; a *Fifty Shades of Grey* audiobook on CD—missing CD number three; a tube of Shayla Rose eye cream; a pair of rhinestone bejeweled strappy sandals—size eight; a Hogwarts leather-bound journal; and a bright red satin hair scrunchy.

Victory held up half a tube of mangled dollar-store sunblock. "I want thees. Wednesday ees day off and I go to beach."

"Fine by me." Aunt Ginny reached in the box and took the purple velvet bra. She folded it up and stuffed it in her sun hat. "What? I already have the matching bottoms."

Joanne choked on her tea.

What do you say to an eighty-something-year-old, who has been the single most important role model for your entire life, when she wants someone's left-behind sexy underwear? *You might want to run it through the washer first.* I started setting out ingredients for gluten-free saltwater taffy muffins when the front door chime sounded in the kitchen.

"Hellooo." Mrs. Davis's voice floated down the hall.

Aunt Ginny slid the strappy sandals off the table and held them behind her back. "In here, Thelma."

Thelma Davis was one of Aunt Ginny's oldest and silliest friends along with two other biddies who were mysteriously missing from this social call. They had lived in Cape May so long they remembered when the Welcome Center was a train station, and you could drive down the middle of the Washington Street Mall in a Ford Model A roadster.

"Where are Mrs. Dodson and Mother Gibson? I thought you ladies traveled in a pack in case one of you needs an alibi."

Mrs. Davis headed straight to the table of assorted treasures. "They're coming along in a bit. Ooh, what's this?" She held up the toe ring.

Aunt Ginny was trying on her new sandals since no one had called her out for taking them. "You can have it. We're going through the left-behinds."

Mrs. Davis slipped it on her pinky finger. "Nice. I just wanted to remind you to be at Courtney's at six for his annual snowbird show-off."

Joanne had commandeered the KitchenAid to make a batch of pecan sables, so I dug out the handheld mixer from the bottom drawer. "How'd he do?"

Mrs. Davis shrugged, and her pink perm bobbed like fresh spun cotton candy. "Blue ribbon. Again. He wins every year. I don't know what the big deal is at this point. You'd think he'd let someone else have a chance for Pete's sake."

Joanne looked up from the recipe card she was holding. Bright green reading glasses perched on the end of her nose. "Blue ribbon for what?"

Aunt Ginny was doing a runway strut back and forth in front of the table, trying out her new sandals, while Figaro was trying to capture the red scrunchie with his paw.

"Annual garden show." Mrs. Davis poured herself a glass of tea. "Courtney holds the record for most wins with tomatoes and kohlrabi in an heirloom garden."

Victory wrinkled her nose that was now covered in blue sunscreen. "What eis cowld robbee?"

Mrs. Davis shrugged. "It's like a German turnip."

"Eww." Victory was so overcome that she immediately fell asleep, landing on the tube of sunscreen where an inch of blue paste splotched out.

I was thinking the same thing but didn't put it as delicately as my narcoleptic chambermaid. "How upset would you be if Gia and I missed the party? We've hardly had a minute alone together since we started dating."

Mrs. Davis pointed her toe-ring bejeweled pinky at me. "Absolutely not. You can make out on your own time. I need you both to be there as my buffer. Edith and Lila came up with excuses faster than I could trap them into going. I think they had it on their calendars from last year, so they'd be ready."

I started unwrapping peanut butter saltwater taffy. "What are you not telling me about tonight?"

"My sister-in-law is the most unpleasant woman you'll ever meet. She's conniving, she's sneaky, she has no sense of style, and she's been stealing from me for thirty years. If you're not there I'm likely to put Josephine in a headlock."

Aunt Ginny struck a pose from across the room. "We aren't due another senior citizen brawl until the Methodist Craft Bazaar in December. This would really throw off our pacing."

Figaro had captured the prized scrunchie and rocketed from the kitchen with his illicit treasure in his mouth.

Victory's head shot up. "Eet sound desgoosteeng."

I stared at her for a beat, trying to decipher which conversation she was in the middle of, then turned my attention back to Mrs. Davis. "How do you know your sister-in-law is stealing from you?"

Mrs. Davis cocked her head at an angle and narrowed her eyes. "Oh, you'll see."

CHAPTER 2

I had just poured myself into my new navy skater dress when Aunt Ginny hollered up the steps, "They're here!" I frowned in the mirror. All the weight I'd lost in the spring while worrying over Gia working out his family drama, I'd gained back as soon as I binged on my first lettuce leaf. I slipped on my wedges and headed downstairs.

Joanne was checking in some new guests. She passed me a note when I hit the landing.

> *Two of our bikes are missing again. Your system isn't working Buttface!*

Our loaner bikes were on the honor system. Guests checked them out and failed to return them at least once a week. Now I had to call around town to track them down. We needed a better system. People weren't stealing them.

They were abandoning them on the side of the road when their bodies reminded them that they'd been sitting at a desk for thirty years and they'd rather pay someone fifteen dollars to Uber them back from the winery on the other side of the island.

"Call Kim at the Laughing Gull and tell her to be on the lookout. Nine times out of ten that's where we've found them."

The front door swung open and a six-foot-tall, bronzed god stood in the entry wearing black slacks and a crisp pinstripe dress shirt. "Are you ready, *cara mia?*"

My face split into a grin and I suddenly didn't give a flip about the missing Huffys. I abandoned Joanne's note and let it flutter to the desk. "Hey, you."

"Gorgeous." Gia took my hand. He kissed the back of my knuckles and I giggled.

Joanne cleared her throat. The guests checking in were staring openmouthed and I whispered, "We'd better go."

Aunt Ginny was already out front with Royce, her dapper boyfriend who'd recently retired to Cape May, and she was getting into the back of his sister's gold Lexus. His nephew Iggy was wearing a driving cap and dressed in a chauffeur suit for some reason. He touched his brim in way of a formal greeting and gave me a sly grin.

I didn't have time to decode the conniving in his eyes because Gia was holding the door of his Alfa Romeo open for me. I slid onto the creamy leather passenger seat, chilled from the air conditioner, and Gia shut me in. When we pulled away from the curb, the words started spilling out of me. "Who did you get to babysit Henry?"

"My sister, Teresa. He asked if you could send him some *cuppycakes* since he has to *stays* home."

My heart felt like it would burst. I loved that little four-year-old like he was my own.

Gia and I laughed and chatted the few blocks to Mrs. Davis's family Victorian. He drove with one hand on the wheel and one hand in mine. "What is this deal tonight and can we sneak out early?"

My face warmed at the thought of time alone with him. We'd had very little since tourist season had exploded into full swing the minute we officially became a couple last April. It was a long, painful road to get here, but my life hadn't been the same since. "Mrs. Davis said her brother, Courtney, and his wife, Josephine, are snowbirds."

Gia glanced at me with narrowed eyes. "Shoobies?"

"Not exactly. 'Shoobie' just means tourist. Snowbirds come up every spring and move south for the winter. The Whipples are originally from Cape May, but now they live in Jupiter Island, Florida, four months of the year."

Gia gave a slight shrug. "And why are we doing this instead of . . . anything else?"

"Aunt Ginny's friends have been very good to me since I moved back. I can't say no to them."

"Maybe you just need more practice."

"Plus, we're supposed to help keep the peace between Mrs. Davis and her sister-in-law. They don't get along. Like your mother with . . . everyone else." I caught Gia's roguish grin from the corner of my eye and smiled to myself.

We turned down a quiet, tree-lined street and parked in front of the huge Victorian built in the French Second Empire style. It was custard yellow with a tan mansard roof trimmed in cast-iron cresting. The front steps and recessed entry were painted with a cherry-red lacquer that sparkled over the white ornate gingerbread trim. Three gabled dormers peeked down from the third story in the midst of decorative coral and beige slate tiles. I stepped out onto the brick walkway and shielded my eyes from the evening sun. "Wow. I've passed this house hundreds of times. I had no idea Mrs. Davis grew up here."

Gia eyed the second-floor balcony. "With this much old money you would expect her to tip the barista better."

Iggy pulled up behind Gia and got out to open the door for Royce.

Royce held out some bills. "Thank you, driver."

Iggy pulled at the brim of his cap. "At your service, Mr. Hansen."

Aunt Ginny came around the back of the sedan and gave Royce's middle-aged nephew the stink eye. "He may have dementia, but my mind is just fine." She put her hand out and Iggy frowned. Then he fished out the few dollars from inside his suit jacket and turned them over. Aunt Ginny stuffed them into Royce's breast pocket.

The front door opened and a thin man with sunken gray eyes and wisps of steel-gray hair trotted down the front steps. He was wearing white linen slacks and a pale blue resort-wear button-down. Well-tanned arms reached out to embrace Aunt Ginny. "Welcome, welcome, Ginny. You get prettier every time I see you."

Aunt Ginny smoothed the back of her hair. "It must be the salt air. Do you remember Royce Hansen? He was in the class with Thelma and me?"

The man put his hand out. "Yes, you made quite a name for yourself on Broadway, I hear. Courtney Whipple."

Royce took Courtney's hand. "Tis a pleasure, fine sir."

Courtney turned towards me. "And who is this gorgeous young thing? Ginny, is this your granddaughter?"

Aunt Ginny ran her hands down to her hips. "No, Courtney. You don't keep a figure like this and have babies. This is Poppy, my great niece. She's my late brother Ernest's granddaughter."

Courtney took my hand and held it while he gazed into my eyes. "She looks just like you when you were a girl."

Aunt Ginny gave him a wry grin. "Yes, well, we're a good-looking family."

"Oh, I know." He winked at Aunt Ginny, and Royce reached his arm across her shoulders and pulled her close to him with a quiet grunt.

Courtney held his hand out to Gia. "And this must be your husband?"

My heart sped up with a mixture of thrill and panic. "No, no. Just my boyfriend. I mean he's not *just* my boyfriend. Gia's not really a boy but no one says man friend, do they? Adult friend? He's not my husband. Not yet anyway. Not that he will be!" I was spiraling. "We're not engaged. It's way too soon. We're just two single people on a date. What did you ask me?"

Gia chuckled under his breath. "Okay, Bella, calm down before you have the stroke."

Aunt Ginny slowly nodded. "Mmm. Smooth."

The front door flew open again and a wild woman with a platinum wave of hair launched herself onto the front porch. She was wearing a hot pink caftan with gold trim and what must have been every piece of jewelry in the house. "For God's sake, Courtney, bring them inside. It's so humid they'll have to wring out their clothes.

Thelma is already in the kitchen and I can't leave her for long." The woman locked her fluorescent-purple-lidded eyes on Aunt Ginny. "Hello, Virginia."

Aunt Ginny stiffened. "Josephine."

"I hope you're not planning to put anything of mine in that giant purse you've brought with you."

Aunt Ginny patted my leather tote bag that she was apparently borrowing. "Of course not. Some of us are just more fashion forward than others."

The woman played with three competing strands of beads that were draped around her neck. "You look like you've been unwell, dear. How are you feeling?"

"Fit as a fiddle. But I'm worried about you. You don't look like you've seen a ray of sunshine in months. Have you been stuck over your cauldron all summer?"

Josephine laughed in an unconvincing way that sounded like a lawn mower engine trying to turn over. "*Mmmhnhnhnhn.* And who have you brought with you?"

Courtney put one hand on my shoulder. "This is Ginny's grandniece, Poppy, and her beau, Gia, darling."

Josephine gave us a saccharine smile. "Gia? What a beautiful name. You usually hear that on a girl."

Bold talk from someone whose husband's name is Courtney.

Aunt Ginny sighed, stiffly. "It's short for Giampaolo, Josephine. It means John Paul in Italian. Gia's family is from Italy."

Josephine waved her hand. "Well, welcome to America. We're not fascists like you Italians, but I think you'll learn to accept us anyway."

Gia flashed her a tight smile, and I could tell he was holding back a laugh. He put on his thickest accent. "*Grazie, signora.* I am sure I will learn to love *América.*"

Aunt Ginny snorted. "Well, if your citizenship these past twenty-odd years hasn't done it, I don't know what will."

Josephine circled both her hands in the air and her rows of bracelets clattered against each other. "Come on in, everyone. I've got to check on Thelma before she turns out the house. She's like a sneaky pink magpie. Ginny, why don't you join me. Maybe you can keep her from rifling through the cabinets."

The garden party was not off to a great start and we weren't even inside yet.

Courtney led us up the brick walkway that divided the manicured yard into two beds filled with flowering shrubs and late summer bulbs edged by a cast-iron fence. I would have to pay for a full-time landscaper to make my yard look this amazing, but Courtney proudly exclaimed that he had done all the work himself. "Gardening is a Whipple family tradition."

The inside of their home was like a china outlet store. My stomach gave a flutter as I looked around at the delicate and expensive treasures on every corner within reach of my elbow or derriere. Courtney had a wealth of antique furniture, but there was refreshing lack of lace and chintz found in so many of these Victorians.

A polished dark wood staircase graced the front foyer. A blue damask living room was to the right. Across the hall was a spiced-peach sitting room where a man and woman sat drinking cocktails like they were posing for the cover of *Collector's Quarterly.*

They were about my age. The woman was thin and shapely with a pixie cut of ash-blond hair and an air of confidence like she had never had a day of self-doubt.

She wore a silk sheath dress that matched her cornflower-blue eyes.

The man was a touch taller, with dark brown wavy hair that would be unruly if he let it get any longer, a slight trimmed beard like he had forgotten to shave for the weekend, and the same blue eyes as the woman, but with a little more mirth to them. He had an infectious smile that said he would be the life of any party if given the chance—just ask his fraternity.

Aunt Ginny and Royce followed Josephine down the center hall towards a massive dining room while Courtney introduced us to the handsome couple.

"Poppy, I want you to meet my daughter June and my son Augustus. There is no July. My first wife wanted to be clever with the birth names. We were planning to hit a few more of the months but she took ill and we only have the summer represented. June has come down from Cherry Hill to help me celebrate my big win."

"It's nice to meet you. This is . . . Gia." After that crash and burn outside I wanted to play it safe. *What am I supposed to say? Paramour? Soul mate?* Everything sounded weird all of a sudden. I tried to gauge Gia's reaction to my introduction to see if this one went better. Nothing.

The man shook Gia's hand. "Call me Auggie. Augustus sounds like the fat kid from *Willie Wonka*." June shook Gia's hand and held it long enough that I wanted to smack her wrist. *Next time I'm saying "boyfriend," so there's no confusion.*

Courtney headed out of the room. "My stepdaughter will be here shortly. I think she and her husband got bumped to a later ferry. I'm just going to check the marinade. June Bug, get them a drink."

Gia agreed to a glass of pinot and I accepted an iced peppermint tea. Then we sat in awkward silence until June returned and Gia broke it. "Are you two also the snowbirds?"

Auggie reached his arm across the back of a vintage golden tufted sofa. "No, I live here. Someone has to keep an eye on the place while Dad's in Florida. I've been running Whipple's Antique Emporium on the island since my father retired in 2010."

June sat back in a white wing chair with a pastoral pattern in pumpkin-colored toile and lazily crossed one leg over the other, showing how long and toned they were. "I've escaped. I put Cape May in my rearview mirror as soon as I filed for divorce last year. I can't stand the beach. I only came down this weekend to celebrate Dad's blue ribbon."

Auggie snickered. "His twenty-third blue ribbon in as many years. Don't worry. You're going to hear all about it whether you want to or not."

Gia gave Auggie a polite smile. "You own antique store?"

Auggie nodded but June answered. "We both do. Auggie works locally and handles sales and customer relations. I've moved on to evaluation and procurement. I don't like to be trapped behind a desk."

Auggie rested his ankle on his knee, showing a bright pink sock. "Are either of you going to be at Cold Spring Village next week?"

Cape May had a series of theme weeks throughout the summer. We'd just survived the Fourth of July celebration. Then it was on to Pirate Week and the Annual Garden Show. Now we were full steam ahead for the Annual Antique Show and Auction.

Auggie grinned in a very impish way. "I have something dangerously unusual to auction off—if the authenticity can be verified in time."

My ears perked up at the promise of something intriguing. "Ooh, what is it?"

Auggie grinned. "It's top secret, but why don't you two come out and see the unveiling? I think you'll be impressed."

I took a sip of my mint tea and immediately realized we had had an error in communication over how much alcohol belonged in mint tea. I thought none. June had not mentioned that the mint would be coming in the form of schnapps. I strangled back a choke. "What is procurement?"

June shook her ice and her chunky silver bracelet clanked against her highball glass. "I visit estate sales and buy items of value at a fraction of their worth for Auggie to resell at Whipple's. Although this last item he found all on his own somehow."

"That sounds interesting."

Auggie gave his sister a defensive look. "I don't just resell things. I rescue and restore them too. And I search for hard-to-find items for collectors."

June shrugged. "I'm rather tired of it all, to tell you the truth. I just want to get home to my Jack Russells. I would have brought them with me this weekend, but Josephine is afraid they'll ruin the hardwood floors. It would kill her to let someone enjoy themselves here."

The schnapps was firing up a hot flash and I had to fan my face with my cocktail napkin.

Gia took my iced tea from me before I hurt myself and placed it on a coaster. "How long have your father and his lady been married?"

June and Auggie looked at each other, mentally calculating. Auggie answered. "Twenty-five years?"

June nodded. "Sounds right. We weren't yet teenagers when they met. They waited a while to get married."

Gia raised his glass. "To second chances in love."

Josephine's voice rang through the house like a car alarm. "Tildy's here! She's here! Hands where I can see them, Thelma!"

June sighed.

Auggie stood and downed the rest of his drink. "Well, buckle up."

CHAPTER 3

Josephine's daughter was an adorable brunette with soft curly hair and giant green eyes behind tortoiseshell glasses. She rested her hand on the belly of her flowy bohemian maxi dress while a lanky young man with curly hair reclined next to her on the sofa, his arm around her shoulders. He pushed a pair of purple glasses higher up on his nose. "And we had to wait for the next ferry. That's the last time I don't reserve ahead."

Auggie poured the man a glass of rosé. "I told you to reserve this time of year. Especially on a Sunday."

Josephine massaged the girl's shoulders from behind. "Poppy, this is my daughter Matilda."

The girl held her hand out to me and kept the other across her belly. "Call me Tildy."

Josephine flicked her hand in the direction of the man chugging the rosé. "And her husband, Spencer, who is a bit overdressed for the occasion."

Spencer picked awkwardly at a thread hanging from the frayed cuff of his tuxedo jacket. He offered Gia his limp hand. "Hey, man. I hear you own a bed and breakfast in town."

Gia shook his hand and nodded in my direction. "The *love of my life* has the bed and breakfast. I run the espresso bar on the mall." Gia turned his head and gave me a lopsided grin.

A very uncouth giggle erupted from my throat and ended in a snort, making me appear to be slightly demented. *Okay, hint taken.*

Spencer eyed me with greater interest. "A bed and breakfast? I would love to hear more about that. Like did you keep the Victorian authenticity, or did you refurbish? And is there a lot of competition with the other bed and breakfasts or is there enough business to go around?"

"Spencer!" Tildy made a face at him.

He looked at his wife and shrugged. "Maybe we can chat after dinner. I'd love to pick your brain and get every inside detail about the biz."

I nodded politely. "Of course." Who wouldn't want to talk about work the first night they have off in weeks? *Mrs. Davis, you owe me.*

Courtney came in carrying a large paper bag with both hands and gave a nod to the newcomers. "Glad to see you could make it." He handed me the bag. It was full of warm vegetables. "Just some produce from my award-winning garden."

"Thank you. I will be sure to put this to good use." I looked around for somewhere to set the bag. Every table space was covered in priceless objects I didn't dare move, and the rug looked very expensive, so I kept the bag on my lap.

Courtney made small talk with Tildy and Spencer. I didn't see Mrs. Davis anywhere. Aunt Ginny and Royce were huddled tightly on a corner love seat looking even more suspicious than usual. There was something going on, and I was beginning to feel like the bait in one of their traps.

While Spencer regaled the room with stories about his drive up from Delaware, Gia leaned into me and whispered, "What is around Spencer's neck?"

I giggled softly. "I think it's a ladies' scarf made to look like an ascot. I've only ever seen Mr. Howell and Fred from *Scooby-Doo* pull that look off."

Gia's eyes crinkled at the corners and I felt his hand brush across my neck. "Are you going to hold that bag of tomatoes all night?"

"I don't know what else to do with it."

He snickered under his breath and took the bag out of my lap. When he crossed the room to put it by the front door, I couldn't help but notice June's eyes never left him, like she was appraising his value.

Courtney announced that dinner would be ready in twenty minutes and asked if we'd like a tour of the house. "I've spent a lifetime collecting antiques and have a few pieces I think you'll really appreciate."

Josephine scrunched up her nose. "They don't want to see your dusty old collection, do you?"

Aunt Ginny and Royce jumped at the chance, probably to irritate Josephine. "We wouldn't miss it."

Josephine sucked her teeth. "Be careful where you swing your pointy elbows, Ginny. Some of those ancient pieces are almost as old as you are and they're worth a fortune."

Aunt Ginny hooked her arm around Royce's. "What can I say? Some things get better with age, and others compensate with cheap costume jewelry."

Royce snickered and gave me a wink. "'Though she be but little, she is fierce.'"

The line between Josephine's eyes deepened. "And just where is Thelma!" Josephine shot from the room and Aunt Ginny grinned in triumph. Royce patted her hand.

Courtney led us through a dining room and a spacious white kitchen, and back to a paneled library off the break-fast nook. There was a beautiful blue clock on the mantel with an intricate face and golden cherubs playing harps on either side. "This is one of my prized possessions. My great-grandfather brought this home from France. This nineteenth-century French portico clock is made from Bleu de Savoie marble and the angels are gilt bronze."

Auggie set his drink on the mantel and pointed to the ornate piece. "The clock face is Sèvres porcelain. And as you can see here, the only flaw is the intricate, broken second hand. I've tried to repair it, but I can't seem to get the springs right, so it just dangles there in a dramatic corkscrew of ebony."

I wanted to ask how much it was worth, out of pure fascination, but there was no way not to sound rude and money grubby, so I kept the question to myself.

"How much is something like that worth?" Aunt Ginny was not bound by the same social anxieties that I was.

Courtney winked. "Let's just say if it was up for auction at Christie's, it would be more than either of us could afford."

I gave a look of horror to Aunt Ginny that only she could see. "Wow, it's really lovely."

Courtney nodded appreciatively at the clock and continued with the history lesson.

Tildy sidled up to me and grinned. "Don't show too much enthusiasm or he'll never let you go."

"I'll try to control myself. Which is more than I can say for my aunt."

Aunt Ginny crept up on the other side of me and craned her neck. "It's good to see you again, Matilda."

"Likewise, Mrs. Frankowski. How have you been?"

"Just ducky. When are you due?"

Tildy's hand shot up to her belly. "Oh, I'm not pregnant."

Holy cow, Aunt Ginny!

Josephine entered the room, the clacking of her many beads announcing her presence. She looped her arm through Tildy's. "Well, not yet anyway. But hopefully soon. Come help me with the squab, darling."

I felt a twinge of sadness for Tildy. She was closer to forty than twenty. There was something off about that whole exchange. Maybe they were having trouble conceiving. That was a heartbreak I understood too well, and I didn't wish it on anyone.

They retreated from the library arm in arm, and Spencer took Tildy's place at my side. "Don't worry, if Tildy ever is pregnant, her mother will know before I do. They're thick as thieves, those two. They tell each other everything. So which bed and breakfast is yours?"

"The Butterfly . . ." I didn't get the full name out.

Courtney had finished giving us two hundred years of history that felt like it was told in real time, and took the clock off the mantel to show us the mechanism in the back. There was a small white sticker attached to the frame and the name *Auggie* was written on it in blue ink.

June huffed. "I told you I'm getting the clock, Auggie."

Auggie returned the clock to the mantel "Well, my name's on it."

"We had a deal. You're getting the house. You know I want to come here as little as possible."

Courtney's look brought them to silence, and we were on the move again.

Gia whispered, "Please tell me squab is a kind of hoagie."

I giggled in return. He was being so patient. "It's like chicken, but tiny."

He frowned. "How tiny?"

Courtney showed us an S-shaped Victorian love seat and launched into a new speech. "My father started Whipple's Antique Emporium. When he retired, it passed down to me, and when I retired it turned over to Auggie and June. June Bug has an expert eye for quality. She found this tête-à-tête at an estate sale in Berkshire. This girl can spot the difference between genuine and fake in a heartbeat."

June put her hand on her father's shoulder. "You taught me everything I know."

I glanced at my phone to check for messages behind the tête-à-tête.

Courtney peeled a sticker off the back of the settee and held it at arm's length to read it. He stuck it back on the fabric. "Auggie's talents flourish in the more practical side of the business. He has a degree in finance from Rutgers University. He keeps all the books and makes sure we turn a profit."

Auggie raised his glass to his father. "Learned from the best."

As we walked away, I noticed the sticker had "June" written across it. Courtney tromped us around the house twice, showing us porcelain statues, lamps with stained glass shades, and an eighteenth-century end table he said was once owned by Thomas Jefferson. We received a history lesson on each piece. Every item was stickered by either June or Auggie. June peeled the Auggies off as she passed them.

Gia's stomach growled and I put my hand in his. It was nearly eight o'clock and we'd not had so much as a cracker or a wedge of cheese. He gave me a serious look. "I'm about to get a tomato and eat in the car."

Thankfully, that's when Josephine called us to the dining room, and we found our name cards placed around the table. June gave Gia a conspiratorial grin as she took her seat on the left of him. He grabbed my hand under the table and squeezed it. Spencer picked up Auggie's card and swapped it so he could sit on my right.

Josephine carried in a tray of roasted squab and Tildy followed with a plate of vegetables and they set them on the sideboard. Mrs. Davis placed two baskets of warm rolls on the table and took her seat. All my senses were pierced with the smell of rosemary and thyme and roasted fowl. I'd burned through my protein shake before these vegetables were harvested.

Josephine took a large silver bowl with a stag on the lid off the sideboard. "Since we're showing off the family treasures, Courtney and I met at an antique auction in Crumpton, Maryland, of all places, where I was getting this appraised. It was my grandfather's." She opened the lid to show us the interior. There was a sticker that had Spencer's name on it. Josephine frowned, peeled it off, and stuck it on his hand.

"What? Auggie and June have claimed everything else," Spencer said.

"This goes to Tildy," Josephine muttered angrily. "God knows she isn't getting much of anything else."

Tildy blushed and gave us an apologetic smile.

We heard Courtney chuckling before he appeared from the sitting room, giddy and glowing, holding an ornate silver and blue box the size of a toaster oven. As soon as she saw it, Josephine gasped. "I told you not to bring that out!"

Courtney snapped back at her. "I want to show Poppy and Gia. They'll appreciate it." He placed the box on the table like it was made of eggshells. "This was my great-grandmother's. The blue is lapis lazuli, and these pink stones are rose quartz."

Aunt Ginny folded her hands demurely in her lap. "Why, Thelma, isn't that yours? I believe I've seen that in your home over your fireplace."

Mrs. Davis narrowed her eyes at Josephine. "You better believe it is. My mother gave it to me."

Josephine moved to hover protectively over the jewelry box.

Courtney began opening drawers and latches revealing empty compartments while he told another story about his grandmother. "She was an amazing woman. Salt of the earth. An angel come from heaven. She's the one responsible for the heirloom garden. I didn't know my grandfather, he died in the First World War, but my grandparents' love was legendary."

Auggie, June, and Josephine all chimed in with Courtney, ". . . and rivaled the greatest love stories of all time."

Courtney snapped at them. "Well, it did! My grandfather wrote home to my grandmother every week and she said she kept all his love letters, but we've never found them."

Royce and Gia were passing silent messages to each other over the rolls. Royce cleared his throat. "'What say you to a piece of beef and mustard?' Heh. That is from the Bard's masterpiece, *The Taming of the Shrew*."

Gia nodded appreciatively.

Mrs. Davis rolled her eyes. "No one wants to read smutty letters written to our grandmother, Courtney. And you know that box belongs to me. Your wife keeps stealing it from my house."

Josephine snatched the box from Courtney's hands. "You keep your hands off, lady. There was nothing in the will about this box."

Mrs. Davis's face became pink and splotchy. "Because she passed it down to me while she was still alive, you greedy twit."

Spencer leaned in and whispered in my ear. "So, what's it like running a bed and breakfast? How many rooms do you have? Do you live there or just go in for work every day?"

Oh my god, what is his deal about bed and breakfasts?

Tildy tilted her head and looked at him over her glasses. "Stop bothering them, Spencer. They're our guests."

Gia pulled his phone out and said he had to take a call.

Aunt Ginny reached across the table and grabbed his wrist. "I didn't hear your phone ring."

He leveled his eyes at her. "It is on vibrate."

Aunt Ginny gritted her teeth. "I know what you're doing, and you'd better not try it."

Gia sullenly shoved his phone back into his pocket.

Courtney sat at the head of the table. "Thelma's going

to get it eventually, dear. We're getting on in years. Who else is going to appreciate all the things we've collected?"

Spencer leaned forward to look down the table. "This house would make a perfect B and B. Tildy and I could run it for you."

Ah, there it is.

Auggie shook his head. "No way. B and Bs are so tacky, no offense, Poppy."

How is that no offense?

Auggie peeled a June sticker off the chandelier. "I don't want weird randos sleeping in my bed."

June ran her finger around the rim of her glass. "That never stopped you before."

Tildy spoke in a soft voice. "I think the food is getting cold. Maybe we should start."

Spencer put into motion a practiced sales pitch. "Bed and breakfasts are a great industry in this area. You already own the house, so we would make instant profit. Just think, you could get other people to pay your taxes while you retain the property value to pass down to the next generation."

Auggie growled. "Where would I live, Spencer? You want me to move out of my home just so you could try to dig yourself out of bankruptcy?"

Josephine sighed loudly. "Go dress the salad, Spencer."

Oh my god. The salad isn't even finished.

Gia's stomach growled again, and he dropped his chin to his chest and heaved a sigh.

Spencer shoved his hands in his pockets and stomped himself to the kitchen.

Aunt Ginny leaned across the table and whispered, "Did we have instant profits?"

I forgot where I was for a second and snorted. "We're hanging on by a thread."

No one moved to serve the food and Royce cleared his throat. "As the Bard says, 'I almost die for food, and let me have it.' You may recognize that line from *As You Like It*."

Gia raised his empty glass. "Cin cin."

Aunt Ginny patted Royce's hand. "That's very subtle, dear."

Auggie reached over and tapped his father's shoulder. "If you want to cover the taxes, I say we put the French clock in the auction. It would bring a fortune. I may already have a buyer lined up."

June threw her napkin on the table. "The clock is mine, Auggie!"

Courtney slapped the table. "No. Absolutely not."

While they were arguing, Royce snaked his hand out and snatched two rolls from the basket. Tildy's eyes grew wide but she didn't say anything. Royce's hand disappeared under the table and his shoulder jerked. A few seconds later, Gia was pulling pieces of dinner roll apart and sneaking them into his mouth.

I gently pinched his arm and whispered through clenched teeth, "Are you going to share that?"

He shook his head. "Sorry *lady friend*, no gluten for you."

"I'm starving. I'll take a pill at home."

"No way. At this speed you won't get that pill before breakfast. It is every man for himself." He popped another piece in his mouth with a grin.

Josephine's voice broke. "Neither of you appreciate the history of this family and what your father has worked for. Always trying to auction off the heirlooms. Putting your names all over everything like you're at a hillbilly yard sale. You should be ashamed of yourselves. My Tildy would appreciate these things and yet she gets nothing!"

The room erupted in a mushroom cloud of awkward, and no one moved during the fallout. Then there was a loud clatter of utensils landing on the kitchen floor followed by a few expletives.

Spencer returned with a giant bowl of lettuce and slammed it down on the table. "I hope you're happy. I overdressed the salad. It's not even edible!" He stormed from the room in a fit.

CHAPTER 4

"Bella, I do not care if I need a kidney and that woman is the only match. I am not going there for dinner again."

We had excused ourselves after Spencer returned to apologize for his tantrum and it was decided that a fresh salad should be made, and the squab should be warmed again. That's when Gia stood and thanked our hosts and said he only had the sitter for a couple more hours, so we needed to go home. He was officially hangry.

Now we were in my kitchen rifling through the fridge for anything we could get our hands on. I took out lunch meat and cheese from Westside Market and grabbed the loaf of rye bread. "Okay, settle down."

Gia got the glasses from the cabinet and filled them with ice. "Who invite you for dinner and not let you eat? It is after nine." He got the blackberry iced tea and poured for us while I made him a ham and Swiss on rye with Courtney's tomatoes.

"That was a disaster. They should have abandoned the salad and moved on to the entrée. No one really wants the salad anyway. It's the obligatory course so you don't feel guilty about having dessert. I'm the one who's usually stuck eating it because I can't have anything else. And that tantrum. I've never seen a grown man cry over vinaigrette before."

"That was not a man. That was child. And he has serious anger issues. Where is the gluten-free bread for your panini?"

"I probably shouldn't have the bread this late. It will go right to my thighs."

Gia gave me a piercing stare. "I bet you have not eaten all day."

My stomach growled. "There's a loaf in the freezer."

He took out the bag and put two slices in the toaster. "I do not get enough time with you to spend it with crazy people who put sticker on furniture and fight in front of guest."

"I don't know, June seemed to like you." I gave him an evil grin and spread mayonnaise on his bread.

Gia sliced the tomatoes. "I was afraid she would rip my clothes off if you left the room."

"Maybe that's why she gave me the tall glass of liquor. So she could have her way with you after I passed out." I put the tomatoes on the sandwiches and cut them in half.

Gia took my hand and gently pulled me into his chest. "I do not want anyone to have their way with me but you."

Well, we agreed on that. Finding time to make it happen was more difficult than expected. Of course, that was a line I hadn't crossed in a long time.

Gia leaned in and kissed me senseless. "Maybe we should skip dinner and take advantage of time alone." He started to lead me out of the kitchen.

My heart was pounding. I heard bells ringing. *No wait, that's the front door chime.* I froze. "Maybe it's a guest coming back from dinner."

Gia listened. "Do you have a guest who sounds like a mob of old busybodies?"

Old lady voices came cackling around the corner. "No, I'm sure they aren't doing anything important. See, they're just about to eat a sandwich." Aunt Ginny and Royce apparently left the party soon after we did. And the biddy bat-signal had been lit because Mrs. Dodson and Mother Gibson were trailing right behind them.

Gia released me. "It was too much to wish for."

I squeezed his hand and took our sandwiches to the table. He brought our teas, and we ate side by side while Aunt Ginny took out vanilla ice cream, peanut butter, and Hershey's chocolate syrup.

"How did you and Royce escape?"

Aunt Ginny opened the container of ice cream and unloaded half the bottle of chocolate syrup over it. "I said Royce had gout and had to rush home to take his medicine."

Royce gave me a grin and a shrug.

Mother Gibson took several packages of McDonald's crushed sundae peanuts from her purse and emptied them over the lake of chocolate. "I'm so glad you called, Ginny. Edith and I were about to give up on you and head over to late-night canasta."

Mrs. Dodson sidled up to Gia with a wicked gleam in her eyes. "How was dinner with Josephine?"

Gia rolled his eyes up to the stout matron. "We did not get that far."

She saw his expression and chuckled. "We were there around Mother's Day, weren't we, Lila?"

Mother Gibson clamped her lips shut and shook her head. "Mmm-mm, child. Next time, eat before you go."

Gia muttered. "I doubt there will be a next time."

Royce stared so longingly at Gia's sandwich that I felt sorry for him. "Would you like a sandwich, Royce?"

He rocked back on his heels and ran a hand over his flat belly. "I wouldn't turn down a little ham on rye."

I took out two more pieces of bread and sawed off a couple new slices of tomato.

Figaro trotted into the kitchen following the crinkle of cellophane, his snack senses on high alert. Wheezing, his flat nose poked through the center of the red scrunchie held in his mouth.

Aunt Ginny dropped dollops of peanut butter over the ice cream. "Can you believe that Iggy has been taking tips from Royce? I put a stop to that, you better believe."

I placed the sandwich on the table in front of Royce and snuggled back into Gia's side. Figaro dropped the scrunchie and squeezed in next to me so he could pat me on the leg and beg for bites.

Aunt Ginny pointed a fistful of spoons at Gia. "You need to get a bigger car so we can all drive together."

Gia choked on his sandwich and I put my hand on his knee under the table.

Mrs. Dodson fished around the refrigerator and pulled out a can of whipped cream. "Is this for anyone?"

I nodded and she shot out a mountain of Reddi-wip over their sundae trough.

The front door chimed again, and Mrs. Davis entered

triumphantly, holding my tote bag over her head. "Mission accomplished! I snuck it out while Josephine was reheating the vegetables for the second time."

The biddies cheered and passed around spoons while Mrs. Davis took the ornate jewelry box out of the bag.

Gia paused with his sandwich halfway to his mouth and stared. "You stole it?"

Mrs. Davis gave him a tart expression. "No. I reclaimed what is rightfully mine that had been stolen from me by that harridan. She discovered it under my bed a few weeks ago when they stopped by to bring me fresh asparagus. I won't fall for that diarrhea ploy again."

Mother Gibson and Mrs. Dodson oohed over the jewelry box as Mrs. Davis polished it with the purple velvet bra Aunt Ginny still had not put away. "My great-grandmother smuggled this out of Russia in 1917 while being chased by the Bolsheviks. It's been passed down from mother to daughter for generations. One day, I'll pass it down to my Tina Louise as long as I can keep Josephine's claws out of it."

I eyed the jewelry box with interest. "Is there a sticker on it anywhere?"

Mrs. Davis grunted. "I already pulled it off. Auggie tried to claim it."

Aunt Ginny unloaded the rest of the chocolate syrup over the ice cream. "You've got to move fast; those kids are already laying stakes to their territory."

Mrs. Davis grabbed a spoon and plunged it into the center of the carton. "This is my territory they're claiming. And Auggie will put my grandmother's box in that auction if he gets it away from Josephine. My nephew's a good boy, but he always was bad with money."

Gia took a long drink of his iced tea. "I thought he had a degree in finance."

Mrs. Davis scoffed. "Knowing how to balance a ledger and having the temperament to control your spending are two very different things. That's why Courtney sent him to a fancy university. Auggie's always thrown his money around like it was burning a hole in his hand. You two sure are wolfing down those sandwiches."

I reached for my tea. "We're starving."

"I told you my sister-in-law was a flake. I've never had a single dinner there that didn't take a few laps around the microwave first."

Mrs. Dodson held her spoon like an exclamation point. "One must go into dinner plans with Josephine knowing she runs about a meal behind schedule."

Gia wiped his mouth and set his napkin down. "Where was that information four hours ago?"

I drained my glass and watched Mrs. Davis gingerly polish the jewelry box. Figaro patted me on the leg and I fed him a bite of ham. "What's the chance those letters to your grandmother are hidden in the house somewhere?"

She nodded. "We've been looking for them since she passed away. I know in my bones they're in that house. I'm sure the Smithsonian or the History channel would be very interested once we locate them. My grandmother used to tell us that when the time was right, we would find the letters and we would know just what to do with them. Courtney wants them in a museum—he says they're a piece of Early Americana, but I always thought she wanted them published in a book."

Aunt Ginny added some more whipped cream to their sundae. "I bet the Hallmark Channel would make their love story into a Valentine's Day movie."

Mother Gibson reared back in her seat at the bar. "I would watch that. Girl, you better get busy finding them. We aren't getting any younger."

Aunt Ginny licked a glob of peanut butter off her wrist. "Speak for yourself."

Figaro patted my leg again and snagged his last bite. Then he jumped down and slid through the kitchen, batting around the red scrunchie, playing defense with the biddies' legs.

Gia took my hand and rubbed it with his thumb. "I am sorry I was cranky. I hope I did not ruin our date. Why don't we go in the other room to be alone?"

I grinned at him and put our plates in the sink. Then I got out a cotton candy unicorn cupcake for Henry and boxed it up. We slipped through the dining room door while the biddies discussed the reclaimed jewelry box and the missing letters and headed for the front parlor.

Gia pulled me into his lap. "Do you know how much I love you?"

He ran his lips across my neck, and I giggled. "I have an idea."

He pulled me into a kiss and my heart threatened to beat through my chest. His cell phone rang. Gia pulled it out of his pocket, sighed, and rolled his eyes to mine. "*Ciao*, Momma." He listened for a minute. "*Sto arrivando adesso.*" He hung up. "I have to go."

"What is it this time?"

"Momma says she cannot breathe."

Again? That's the third time this month. Does she have a proximity device on Gia? I put my hand on his cheek. "Don't worry. I'm sure she'll be fine as soon as you leave."

CHAPTER 5

I put a pitcher of watermelon-infused ice water on the tray table in the library next to a plate of lemon short-bread. We had two rooms of guests checking in today and I set out welcome treats to make a good first impression. Since Aunt Ginny was walking around dressed as Elly May Clampett, and Figaro had taken a shine to bringing all my socks and hair ties to the middle of the foyer, I also needed to lay a distraction when greeting the arrivals.

"Oy. Oy. Oy. Oy."

Oh yeah, and then there was Victory. My chamber-maid hobbled around the corner with her arms sticking straight out and her legs wide like a zombie. "I weill sue sunscream companee. I am shreemp."

"I think you mean lobster. At least you know to avoid expired discount-store sunblock in the future."

Victory leaned to her left and gingerly lowered a stack of fancy paper napkins to the tray table. "Oy. Oy. Oy."

"Are you sure you don't want to go to urgent care? I can drive you. You look dangerously red."

"No. I jus need cowld shower an aspreen. I go make bed now. Oy. Oy. Oy."

There was a knock on the front door and Figaro galloped down the hall with the red scrunchie in his mouth to greet the newcomer.

I found Spencer standing on my porch holding a giant bowl full of tomatoes and a vegetable that looked like a miniature purple bagpipe. "Courtney says I have to apologize for my tantrum the other night. He sends these from his garden as a peace offering. We are all so ashamed over our behavior. Especially my wife. Tildy embarrasses easily."

She's probably had the most practice with it. "Oh, this is too generous of you . . . really." I took the bowl of vegetables and set them carefully on the front desk.

Spencer followed me in and shut the door behind him. "It's the least we could do. We aren't usually like that. Well, Josephine is—but the rest of us are mostly house trained."

Oh, so you're staying. I tried to force a smile. "It's no problem. Really. I'll just add these to the vegetables from the other night."

Figaro jumped on the desk to examine the guilt offering, reared back at the bagpipe, swatted it with his paw, then hauled fluff down the hall.

Spencer looked around in a big arc, taking in as many rooms as he could from where he was standing. "Your floor plan is similar to ours, I see."

"Our houses were built roughly at the same time."

"Really?"

"Well . . . yes. Most of Cape May was rebuilt in the

late eighteen hundreds after a big fire destroyed a lot of the original buildings."

Spencer started an unsanctioned self-guided tour of my first floor. He looked around the library, running his hand over the bookshelves, then ran across the hall to the sitting room. "Like the fireplaces on both sides of the house? What do you think they were for?"

"Heat. Central heating was a luxury not wasted on summer homes."

"Well, what do you know. When did you get the idea to make this a bed and breakfast?"

When we realized we might lose the house. "This is our first season."

"I bet you're on track to make a bundle this year."

"Not really. Running a bed and breakfast is hard work with high overhead, and there's a lot of competition in this town. The taxes on these historic houses are higher than the average mortgage. And there's a lot you can't do to your own home because it's on the National Register of Historic Places. You want to really think long and hard before you make an investment like this."

Spencer was busy examining the plaster cornices in the sitting room. "Yeah, but Courtney already owns the house, so I should start out in the black my first year."

"It's none of my business, but I got the impression that Courtney wasn't interested in turning his home into a bed and breakfast. Auggie was certainly against it."

Spencer stuck his head in the fireplace to look up the chimney. His voice came out tinny and muffled. "Don't worry. I can handle Auggie."

I was tempted to flick the damper to see what would happen. "What exactly are you looking for?"

Spencer pulled himself upright. He had soot on one

cheek, and he shrugged. "Nothing. Josephine won't let me look around their house."

I checked the time again. "I don't want to keep you if you have somewhere to be." *Please have somewhere to be.*

Spencer wiped his hands on his cargo shorts and worked his way through the sitting room and into the dining room, examining Aunt Ginny's antique sideboard and china hutch like he was the next contestant on *Fake or Fortune?* He put his hand on the kitchen door right under the employees only sign. "I don't have anywhere to be."

God help me. "Well, I have guests checking in any minute . . ."

But I was too late. He pushed his way into the kitchen. When I caught up to him, a very irritated Joanne was about to swat him with a whisk.

"Who are you?! What are you doing in here? Didn't you see the sign?"

Spencer was oblivious to being scolded. I suspected he'd built up an immunity. He adjusted his glasses and looked around in wonder. "You gutted the kitchen and started over with all the mod cons. Are the guests disappointed with that?"

"The guests aren't allowed in here, so they don't really have an opinion about it."

Joanne was still in swat mode. "And what in god's name is a mod con?"

Spencer had the audacity to open the oven door and look inside. "Modern conveniences. This is really remarkable, Poppy. How long does it take you to make breakfast in the morning?"

Joanne and I stared at each other, openmouthed, on the same side for a change.

The front bell rang, and I knew I had to get him out of here. "Spencer!" It came out a little sharper than I intended. It was also a lot gentler than I felt, so . . .

Spencer looked at me with wide eyes and adjusted his glasses. "I'd love to see a menu."

I took him by the elbow. "Why don't we get out of Joanne's way. She's very busy. As I'm sure you are too."

"I could come back."

"Call me and make an appointment. You can ask me everything you like when I have more time." I grabbed a business card on my way to the door just as the bell went off again.

"Awesome!" Spencer tucked the card into his pocket. "I'll text you later to set that up."

Is it too late to give him the number to Angel of the Sea?

I pulled the front door open to a little elderly couple on the front porch carrying a cat carrier, and ushered Spencer out with a wave. "Hello, you must be the Grabsteins."

The woman was small and birdlike with a tuft of white hair poking up on top of her head. She wore giant black-rimmed glasses that made her look like an owl in Ruby Slipper lipstick. She was dressed to the nines, as Aunt Ginny would say. White summer slacks and a black and white sleeveless silk blouse with ruffles at the collar. She blinked twice, her coated eyelashes like tarantulas through the thick lenses, and croaked in a low voice, "Hey, doll. I'm Elaine and this is the hubs."

Her partner was a round little man in a gray porkpie hat with a fluffy white beard and eyebrows. I knew in my heart he was asked to play Santa every year for Christmas. He gave me a giant smile and his eyes crinkled at the corners. "How do. I'm Burl and this here's Cleo." He held up the cat carrier and a pair of green eyes blinked at me through the screen. She pushed her head against the carrier door and purred.

"Oh, she's lovely. Come on in, I'll get your bags in a minute."

"Oy. Oy. Oy. *Ded Moroz*! Eis Grandfater Frost!" Victory was at the top of the stairs holding a basket of towels.

I cleared my throat loudly. "*Unhuh* Victory! This is Burl and Elaine Grabstein and their cat Cleo."

Elaine waved her hand. "That's okay, doll. Burl gets that a lot. Sometimes kids'll wander up an tell 'im what they want for Christmas."

Burl smiled and shrugged, his pink cheeks puffing in amusement.

Victory looked to me like she wanted to give Burl her list, so I shook my head no and sent her slowly down to the kitchen to get her usual soda before leaving for the day.

Elaine watched her totter from foot to foot. "Oh, the poor dear. She shoulda worn sunscreen."

Figaro trotted down the hall, requisite red scrunchy in his mouth, and Elaine squealed as much as I assumed an eighty-year-old woman with a two-pack-a-day voice can squeal. "Look at this handsome guy, Burl. What is the fella's name?"

Figaro sensed he was the center of attention and sat tall at their feet. He wrapped his bottlebrush tail around his front legs, which was the equivalent to a gentleman's bow.

Elaine bent to let him sniff her hand, which came out like a wheeze through the scrunchie.

"This is Sir Figaro Newton, he's a black smoke Persian with a pedigree, as you can tell by the damp ratty hair tie clamped in his jaws."

Figaro's ears flattened and he glanced my way.

There was a curious little meow from the carrier in Burl's hand. He looked inside. "I think our Cleo wants to say hello."

"Fig is usually pretty good with other cats. We had another Persian visit a few months ago who he took a shine to. He was devastated when she left us."

Burl put the carrier on the floor. Figaro eyed it warily. Probably having flashbacks to vet appointments. When Burl flicked the latch, the crate door swung open and a slinky little black cat minced out. She stopped to rub her head against the crate door, then licked her paw. Her green eyes turned to Figaro and she started to sashay towards him, her snowy whiskers twitching in curiosity, her tail dancing as if to a snake charmer's flute.

Figaro's eyes opened wide and his ears stood at attention. The red scrunchie fell out of his mouth and landed at his feet. He took off like a shot and ran down the hall with his tail dragging on the floor and disappeared into the kitchen.

Elaine croaked, "Aww. I guess he doesn't like our Cleopatra, Burl."

Burl appeared to be laughing. His body shook like he had the giggles, but he wasn't making a sound.

Cleo sat in front of the scrunchie and gave it a sniff. She made a polite little meow.

I took a breath. "I'm sure they'll be fine. Figaro usually warms up." *Usually.* I certainly hoped so. We could not afford to give any more discounts to disgruntled guests.

"Our Cleo is a lover just like her namesake, isn't she Burl? She'll win Sir Figaro over. Wait and see."

CHAPTER 6

The Grabsteins were tucked into the Purple Emperor Suite and the next guests weren't due for a couple of hours. I had to remake the beds in both of the suites Victory had cleaned this morning. They looked like she'd jabbed the sheets over the mattress with a coat hanger. I also had to re-clean the top third of the glass shower in the Swallowtail and both of the mirrors in the Adonis and Monarch Suites since she couldn't raise her arms above her head. Then I separated the beds in the Monarch Suite from a king into twins in preparation for sisters checking in tomorrow.

I stopped in my room to freshen up, and Figaro's flat face poked out from inside the closet.

"What are you doing in there?"

The barest hint of a flop sounded from behind the door. "Oh, don't be that way. I know you still miss Portia, and Cleo comes on a little strong, but this is your house. You don't have to hide. Any lady of quality will take the hint that you're not interested and back off."

Figaro sneezed, or hissed, it was hard to tell which, but his meaning was clear. He rejected everything I'd just said.

I sprinkled a few catnip treats on the floor to help him relax. "I'm going to the coffee shop. I'll be back soon. We have more guests coming tonight, so try not to be naughty."

He peeked out and eyed the treats, then eyed the door, checking for would-be slinky seductresses.

I sprayed a de-frizz mist on my hair and touched up my makeup. By the time I pulled the door to a crack I could hear the lippy-smacky crunchy sounds that meant the playboy had given in to the siren call of Whisker Lickin's.

I opened the door down the hall and descended two flights to the kitchen pantry. Joanne jumped when I popped out on the other side.

"Gah! Cut it out, Buttmunch. I hate it when you do that."

"I'm sorry, did I startle you?" I was not even a little bit sorry. Joanne was so mean to me, scaring her was one of the perks of my job. I grabbed the containers of muffins that I had made earlier for the coffee shop and snagged my keys on the way by.

Joanne hung up her apron. "The Martins are checking in tonight. Try not to mess that up. I was in the middle of *90 Day Fiancé* when that family called me last week to come check them in."

"I'll be right back. I'm just dropping off. I doubt anyone will need to use the emergency number while I'm gone."

I opened the front door and was smothered with a blast from hell. The air was thick, giving me instant asthma. I started to sweat through my blouse and the charmeuse clung to my back like I was being shrink-wrapped in a camisole. *Why do I even bother putting the clothes in the dryer this time of year?* Normally I would walk to the Washington Street Mall since it was so close and there would be nowhere to park, but it was ninety-two degrees. I'd look like I took a waterslide to La Dolce Vita by the time I arrived.

On my way out the door, I grabbed the giant bowl that Spencer had used as a Trojan horse to get into my house earlier. If I didn't return it today, I had no doubt he would use it as an excuse to come back in the morning for another interrogation.

I lifted the garage door. Aunt Ginny had given me her classic red and white Corvette after my Toyota was totaled by vandals at Convention Hall. Four boxes of muffins safely nestled next to the spare whitewall tire, and I started Bessie up and let her growl.

A few minutes later, I pulled into Courtney's driveway, relieved to see a white Lincoln with the license plate that said COMPOST. Someone was home. I grabbed the bowl and said a prayer that it wasn't Spencer. I didn't have time for an inquisition even though I thought his wife Tildy could use a friend.

I rang the doorbell, but there was no answer.

A voice behind me called, "Well, howdy." Courtney was dressed in dirty green jeans and a white T-shirt. He took off a wide-brimmed hat and ran a hand through his wispy hair. "What brings you by, girlie?"

I held out the bowl. "I just wanted to thank you for the vegetables and return this."

He waved his hand towards the front steps. "Put that down over there and I'll give you the grand tour."

Didn't I already have the tour? It ended about as well as the three-hour boat ride on Gilligan's Island, *as I recall.*

Courtney led me around the side of the house and through a gate to the garden. A wooden privacy fence bordered the yard with a row of fruit trees on the west end. Both sides of the yard held long rows of corn, and in the center was a gorgeous design of flowers, vegetables, and herbs that would put any English garden to shame. Courtney's entire face lit with pride. "My grandmother's masterpiece. It's the same design as the vegetable garden at Fontainebleau, except in miniature."

I took a couple steps towards the center. "It's amazing."

Courtney was chattering on about soil samples and pH. I was starting to sweat like my camisole was made of Kevlar.

He held up one of those miniature purple bagpipes. "And of course, my kohlrabi wins first place at the Annual Garden Show every year. The secret is in the soil. I rotate the kohlrabi with the peas and runner beans, and dear God keep it away from cabbages." He laughed at a joke only he appreciated.

I wiped my forehead with the back of my hand and pointed to a cluster of tall vines on trellises in the center of the garden. "I've never seen such beautiful tomatoes."

Courtney beamed. "My grandmother planted the first heirloom tomatoes in the center of this garden right after my father was born. We've kept the tradition of harvesting the seeds to keep the same stock growing year after year. We've never bought seeds from a catalog."

A movement to my right caught my eye and I spotted a floppy purple hat floating above the fence in the yard next door.

Courtney picked a few tomatoes and handed them to me.

"Oh, I couldn't possibly."

"Nonsense. You can never have too many. The secret is to surround them with basil and marigolds. I've been proud to carry on the tradition my grandmother started. I guess that tradition will end with me. Auggie and June aren't the least bit interested in gardening. They'll probably patio over the entire yard after I'm gone."

"What about Tildy?"

Courtney made a face like he didn't take my comment seriously. "She has enough to deal with."

The purple hat moved down the fence and half a face appeared. Pinched and disapproving. The neighbor looked from me to Courtney and her eyes narrowed even more.

Courtney pulled a few of the purple kohlrabi bagpipes from the dirt. "I'll send your bed and breakfast some of my blue-ribbon produce. You can tell your guests they won first place at the Annual Garden Show. Won't that be a pip?"

The next-door neighbor choked like she may have swallowed a tomato worm.

"Oh, um . . . sure. That would be very nice. The guests would enjoy that." *God knows I'd be the only bed and breakfast in town to serve kohlrabi for happy hour.*

I shifted my weight as a trickle of sweat ran down the center of my back.

The neighbor's back door slammed, and Courtney chuckled in delight. "Don't worry about her. She isn't very friendly. Garden envy. She's a little bitter because she's never beaten my tomatoes and she's dying to know my secret."

CHAPTER 7

My lovely little jaunt to Courtney's had turned into a field trip to Mount Vesuvius. Bessie's air-conditioning kit was doing her best, but I was stuck to the leather seat and peeling off was going to hurt—there was no way around it. My face was blotchy, my hair frizzy, my mascara running, and I had to stop several times for tourists crossing the street, thinking about crossing the street, taking pictures of houses across the street, and a horse-drawn carriage giving a tour down the street, before I finally turned into the parking lot behind La Dolce Vita. An old lady with a walker could have lapped me.

I parked behind a car with Pennsylvania tags that had pulled up to the No Parking sign in Gia's reserved spot. Threats didn't work on tourists. They were always going to be "just a minute." Tickets weren't a deterrent. By the time the cops arrived they'd be gone and someone else would be parked there anyway. It was a never-ending game of spin the violation, and it just wasn't worth it. The bad review on social media overshadowed the five minutes of righteous indignation getting an open spot brought you.

The back door opened, and Gia appeared, pulling me against him into a passionate kiss. There was a series of hoots and applause from a group of shirtless young guys walking through the parking lot, looking for love or trouble, whichever presented itself first. I couldn't blush without fear that the extra heat would send me supernova, so I just closed my eyes and smiled. "Hey you."

"*Ciao,* Bella." Gia took the boxes from the trunk and held the door for me. I stood under the air-conditioning vent and let it blow on me like an arctic turbine until you could no longer fry an egg on my face.

Gia waited for me to relax and give him a smile. "Better?"

I nodded and he kissed me again. Then we went through to the dining room past the coffee bar and the espresso machine. "You want iced doppio?"

"Does Henry say 'pasketti'?"

"Cameron, iced doppio for Poppy. One stevia."

Cameron was a new hire for the summer. A recent graduate from Cape May High. He was a somewhat dorky-looking kid with curly hair the color of gingerbread and an infectious smile. He would leave us in a few weeks to start the fall semester at Seton. He tamped down the ground espresso in the portafilter. "Why don't you ever get iced Americano?"

Before I could answer him, Gia's other young employee, Sierra, bumped him out of the way and took over pulling the shot. "Because she doesn't like her espresso that watered down. Duh."

Cameron's eyes lit up. "Yo dawg. You need help pulling that shot? I'm really boss at it."

Gia and I stared for a moment, then giggled. Cameron's thug research sounded like it had come straight out of a nineties hip-hop movie.

Sierra's lip curled. "I got it. Why don't you go help Poppy stock the desserts for tonight?"

"Your wish is my command." Cameron shot Sierra a flirty grin that she shut down immediately with a scowl. He didn't take his eyes off of her when he was coming around the bar and he slipped on a spill. He flailed his arms and caught himself on the edge of the counter, gave us a huge grin of relief. Then he lost his grip and went down hard.

Gia laughed and I elbowed him in the side. He laughed harder. "What? Is funny, no?"

I went over and helped Cameron up. "Are you okay?"

"Pssh." He glanced back to Sierra. "Just a small tibial fracture. No biggie."

She rolled her eyes and placed my iced espresso on the bar. "You should clean that up before someone important falls and gets hurt."

Cameron went to the back to get the mop and I grabbed my espresso to cover my giggle. I almost lost it when I looked into Gia's face and saw he was biting his lip. We'd been watching these two all summer, and it was not going well for Cameron. I didn't blame him for having a crush on the twenty-one-year-old strawberry blonde. She was a cross between girl next door and swimsuit model.

I snickered behind my coffee. "Someone's still playing hard to get, I see."

Gia placed the last of the muffins in the case and whispered, "He gives her nothing to work with."

Two women came in wearing towels, and I hoped to god there were swimsuits under them. Sierra was taking their drink orders while Gia and I arranged the pastries. Cameron was trying to get the mop as close to Sierra's feet as possible to irritate her into noticing him.

I moved a cotton candy cupcake to the front. "She has no idea he's flirting with her right now."

Gia closed the case and turned to face me. "I know someone else who does not see when man is flirting with her."

"Who?"

"Who?" Gia mocked me. "You. No matter what I try to get you interested, you do not notice me. You ignore all my moves."

"You had moves? While I was here? What moves did you have?"

Gia's eyes sparkled. "What moves? I flex my muscles carrying heavy bags of coffee beans. I give you the sexy eyes that look like this." He wiggled his eyebrows. "I did my best flirting and still you ignore me."

I giggled. "Oh, were you flirting with me? I thought you had a stye."

His eyes grew in mock horror. "Mamma mia! I install a brand-new kitchen to get you here every day, and still you have no idea."

I shrugged. "I figured it was because you don't know how to bake your own muffins."

He advanced on me until my back was against the pastry case. "Is that what you think of Giampaolo? I could make a muffin if I want to."

I was full on laughing now because he was nuzzling my neck like it was some kind of Italian torture, when Sierra cleared her throat loudly.

We looked over at her. "What?"

She pointed to the sunburned lady in a tie-dye sarong. "She wants to know what this is."

I looked in her hand. "Banana Fanna Taffy Muffin. Peanut butter saltwater taffy baked into a gluten-free banana muffin."

The woman bit into the little cake, her eyebrows lifted. "Give me six."

I turned back to Gia. "I'm going to need more taffy."

"That remind me. I have a special order for a gluten-free anniversary cake on the desk."

"I'll grab it on my way out." I gave him a kiss. "I love you."

He swatted my butt. "I love you too. Henry and I will see you tonight for dinner."

I downed my iced espresso, waved goodbye, and handed my keys to Cameron, who had offered to watch my car in case the blocked driver returned. I whispered some parting encouragement to him. "Quit saying 'dawg' for a start and she might come around."

I walked down the brick-paved shopping area to Fralinger's Saltwater Taffy and was just checking out with my wholesale discount when my cell phone rang. The picture that flashed up looked like Endora from *Bewitched*. I stared for a second, confused as to how Endora would be calling me, then realized it was Aunt Ginny standing too close to the camera. "I see you changed your contact photo again."

"Hee hee. How do you like that one?"

"You hardly ever see anyone wear that much blue eyeshadow anymore."

"I was going to dinner with Royce."

I took the boxes of taffy from the cashier and thanked her, then went back to my call as I exited the shop. "What's up?"

"When are you picking me up?"

"What do you mean? Where are you?"

"I'm home . . . Waiting for you . . . We promised Auggie we'd go see his big surprise reveal for the auction this afternoon."

Aw, man.

"Courtney called to say *The Press of Atlantic City* is there and apparently one of their competitors is making a big stink. Accusations are flying."

"What does he want us to do?"

"Be ready for anything."

CHAPTER 8

"You forgot about me, didn't you?"

I pulled up next to the mailbox to get Aunt Ginny on the curb. "I forgot we were suckered into doing this."

"Well, you were light-headed from hunger. You may have blocked it out."

"Do you have any idea what this big reveal is?"

Aunt Ginny pulled down the passenger-seat visor so she could apply another layer of Princess Peach lipstick to coordinate with her lemon-yellow pedal pushers. "No. But Thelma said Auggie is so excited about it he called her to make sure we were still coming."

"What did I do to deserve this special treatment from the Whipples?"

"Thelma may have told her brother's family that you were a local celebrity with a lot of influence around town."

"Why in the flippity-flop would Mrs. Davis tell them that?"

"Because she wanted you invited to dinner to run interference with Josephine. Besides, she couldn't tell them the truth. If Jessica Fletcher has taught us anything, it's that no one invites a *death magnet* to a garden party."

I stewed in aggravated humiliation while I drove down Seashore Road. We turned into Cold Spring Village, a twenty-two acre Early American living history museum much like a small version of Williamsburg. It was devoted to the cultural heritage of eighteenth- and nineteenth-century farm life. At least that's what the brochure said. I thought of it as that place I took a tractor-drawn hayride in seventh grade and held hands with Harry Chiswick under the flannel blankets.

We passed the two-story Grange with its white clapboard and black shutters—originally a meeting hall, now a restaurant—and began the search for a parking spot. I did two laps around the small lot and was about to call it off and go home when a dad carrying a toddler having a Chernobyl-level meltdown came puffing around the corner. We hovered and waited the amount of time it could have taken him to buckle in twenty-six kids and hit the road. Then we claimed the spot.

Cold Spring Village had a variety of historic outbuildings arranged on two parallel, crushed-clamshell-strewn lanes, like a guitar neck with five cross-street frets between the main thoroughfares.

Antique dealers had lined the streets with rows of tents displaying Civil War artifacts, Depression-era glass, pottery, collectibles, ancient tools, and period furniture.

We groused to each other about having to pay for admission just to fulfill our social obligation, and took the offered map of the property with the vendor booth locations. Whipple's Antique Emporium's tent was past the blacksmith and in between the woodworking and pottery shops. We passed a booth selling antique poisons being run by an elderly woman in a leather biker vest who sat on a camp chair knitting, and a booth full of very creepy porcelain dolls with blank stares coming from dead eyes that sent a shiver down my neck.

The next tent was completely enclosed. A wooden sandwich board sign with handwritten curly script read Good Luck Charms and Talismans. Aunt Ginny clapped her hands. "We have to go in. We have to."

"Okay, but just for a minute." I didn't want to let her down, but I had a lot of cupcakes to bake at home.

She put her hand on the blue canvas flap. "Get ready for maximum weirdness."

There is no way this ends well for me.

Our eyes took a minute to adjust to the darkness. A tiny round woman with a craggy face sat behind a white plastic folding table. She didn't say a word but grinned, causing deep trenches to form around her mouth and eyes. She looked like an old potato that had taken its dentures out.

The voice of a five-year-old child asked if we needed any help. Both Aunt Ginny and I looked around to see where it had come from. Aunt Ginny looked back at the little lady and narrowed her eyes. "Pardon?"

"I said do you need any help?"

There was the voice again. I was stone-cold stunned.

Aunt Ginny cleared her throat, seemingly unsure of her senses. "Er . . . We were wondering what kind of wares you sell."

"I have powerful charms and protective talismans to ward off evil."

"Well . . . That. Is." Aunt Ginny looked around in wonder. "Something."

What a bunch of hooey. Have you ever heard anything so ridiculous? "Do you have anything to break a curse for finding murder victims?"

The woman blinked at me, all her creases drooping.

"It's for a friend."

Aunt Ginny gave me some side eye but clamped her lips shut.

The woman smiled and her eyes disappeared to slits. "I'm sure it is."

I was deeply regretting coming in here when she pulled out a hand-carved doll about four inches tall. It was brown like a clod of dirt and had beady eyes. It had pasted-on bushy white hair and looked uncomfortably similar to the woman holding it.

She shook it and the hair frizzed out from the humidity. She placed the wooden talisman in front of me. "The hair is genuine Tibetan yak. I think this is just what you need."

I have made a horrible mistake.

Aunt Ginny coughed in attempt to choke back a laugh. "We'll take it."

"We will?"

Aunt Ginny held out the money the woman asked for, with an evil gleam in her eye. "It can be for your friend's birthday. She has one coming up soon. I think it's really close to yours."

I gave Aunt Ginny what I hoped was threatening side eye, but she just laughed at me.

She dropped the powerful talisman in a used ShopRite

plastic bag. "Tell your friend to be sure to sleep with it under her pillow."

Fat chance of that.

Once outside the tent, Aunt Ginny wanted to see the talisman in the light. "Oh, it's horrible."

"Then why do you sound so gleeful about it?"

"'Cause it's horrible."

Aunt Ginny was shoving the troll into my hands and I was trying my best to shove it back at her as we left the tent and almost knocked over a young couple walking past.

"Oh, excuse me, ma'am. Tildy?"

"Poppy, hi." Tildy gave me a broad grin. "Fancy running into you here."

"We're here to see your brother's antique reveal." Tildy's gaze landed on the troll and I shoved it back in the bag and in my purse. "It's a . . . gag gift."

Spencer pointed finger guns at me. "Don't forget about that coffee you owe me. I'm free right now if you are."

Tildy's smile disappeared. "You said we could look for items for a nursery. The catalog says there is a dealer with hand-carved mahogany cradles over by the weaver."

Spencer put his arm around her. "We can, honey. I just have to make sure I pump Poppy for information while I have the chance."

Tildy closed her eyes as a pink sheen flushed over her face.

I see another giant bowl of apology vegetables in my future. "Well, I'm afraid I can't talk right now, Spencer. But maybe later this weekend."

Spencer nodded. "Understood." They took off up the side street, and we headed further down the lane.

There was a crowd of people standing around Whipple's Antique Emporium's booth, excitedly taking photos. Auggie's Aunt Thelma—or as I knew her, Mrs. Davis—waved madly when she caught sight of us. She pointed at the table in front of Auggie and mouthed, "Right here!"

There were two official-looking men standing behind the table. One was bent over with a magnifying glass. Auggie stood back with his arms folded across his chest and his grin about as broad as his shoulders.

Aunt Ginny shook my arm. "Well, I don't know about you, but I can't wait to see what it is. Aren't you excited?"

I rubbed my shoulder. "The yak troll took all the excitement out of me."

Aunt Ginny grunted. "I didn't come all this way to stand out here and bake while we wait for this riffraff to disperse."

"What do you mean 'all this way'? It took us ten minutes."

Aunt Ginny didn't hear me. She was elbowing her way into the throng. I knew she'd reached the front when I heard her say, "What the heck is that supposed to be?"

Auggie was more wound up than the first kid who discovered that Mentos makes soda explode. "It's a very rare, genuine nineteenth-century vampire-hunting kit!"

The audience broke into a round of applause. *Oh, this I gotta see.* I followed Aunt Ginny's path through the crowd taking photos with their cell phones. Mrs. Davis waved me over to her side to get a better view. There, in a hand-carved, red-velvet-lined box, was an ivory cross, a small Bible, a very sharp-looking, silver-tipped wooden stake, a tiny finger-trigger crossbow with miniature silver-tipped bolts, a vial of holy water, rosary beads, and a shriveled black lump that was supposed to be garlic. Auggie lifted out the top tray to reveal another chamber underneath that held a row of glass bottles filled with various herbs like wolfsbane and belladonna, an ancient pistol, and several silver bullets. I looked Auggie in the eyes to see if he was laughing at us.

Aunt Ginny reached for the wooden stake. "Is this thing real?"

One of the official men intercepted her. "Please don't touch that, ma'am. I assure you it is very real."

"And stolen."

I followed the voice to an older man standing in the shade of the tent next door. His gray hair was shaved on the sides and combed straight back and gelled into a pouf. His eyes narrowed under bushy dark eyebrows and he had a dark mustache over a close-cut snowy-white beard. He was putting off a *Sons of Anarchy* vibe if *Sons of Anarchy* ever guest hosted the *Antiques Roadshow*.

The official cut his eyes to the other tent. "Ladies and gentlemen, as the foremost expert in European antiquities in the tri-state area, it is my pleasure to confirm that this Edwardian era vampire-hunting kit is authentic."

Another round of applause erupted and the man in the tent next door let out a few choice expletives. "It's also stolen from my store!" He shoved his hands in his pockets and disappeared through the flap into his own tent.

Auggie shook hands with the antiquities expert and the other official, a very fit-looking man of about the same age, with a five o'clock shadow on his face and most of his shaved head. They posed for more pictures, then the antiquities expert left the tent, and the other man made an announcement.

"Thank you. Thank you so much for coming, everyone. I'm Blake Adams with Adams Galleries." He paused to wink at an attractive brunette in the crowd. "This item, as well as many that are displayed in the dealers' tents, are open for previewing. Please join us at Adams Galleries just across the street on Saturday night for what will be a very exciting auction. The details are in the complimentary catalogs displayed in each tent. We hope to see you there."

He took a step to the side and I had to edge out of his way. He whispered to Auggie, "If I find out you're up to your old tricks, you're banned from my auction house for good."

Auggie laughed. "Dude. Relax, okay. Grover is a miserable old man with no one but his six parakeets to keep him company. He's been jealous of us since Dad ran Whipple's. I don't know why you put up with him."

Blake Adams stepped down into the crowd and personally invited each of the women to come to the auction. The rest of the crowd dispersed, but not before cleaning out Auggie's stack of auction catalogs.

While Aunt Ginny fussed over the vampire-hunting kit, I inched to the tent next door to see if the surly accuser had a catalog I could covertly appropriate.

The banner at the back of the booth said Prickled Curiosities. It was full of Civil War artifacts and a beautiful antique armoire that I knew instantly would be perfect for the Scarlet Peacock room. It was one of my biggest rooms and it was underappreciated because the bathroom was out in the hall. Running my hand over the sculpted arch, I opened the door and checked the interior for signs of damage or repair. "How much are you asking?"

The man considered the armoire for a moment, then called over his shoulder. "Pauline!"

A cute little thing flew in through the back flap of the tent. She couldn't have been more than twenty-five. With her cinnamon hair flowing wildly around flawless skin and bright blue eyes, she gave me a shy smile. "Yes?"

"Pauline, how much are we expecting for the Louis the Fifteenth?"

She consulted a ring-bound notebook and turned it to show me the appraised value.

"Oof. Is there any wiggle room in that price for a local B and B owner?"

The man appraised me like a china buffet. "Fill out the pre-bid offer and I'll see what I can do."

"That is very generous of you . . ."

He put out a hand. "Grover Prickle."

We shook hands, and Pauline handed me the sheet for the pre-bid offers. My heart fell when I saw an M. Humphries had already listed a sizable bid for the armoire. I filled in my own offer of just five dollars more, felt pathetic about it, and gave a smile to Grover to cover my embarrassment. "You have some interesting items in here."

Grover nodded and looked around his booth. "I take my collection very seriously. It's not a job, it's a calling. Unlike some people." He rolled his eyes in the direction of Auggie's tent.

"I thought I heard you during the reveal next door. You think the owner stole that vampire-hunting kit from you?"

"I don't think, young lady, I know. I found that item on a recent trip to Boston and now it's missing from my stockroom. It was going to be my window display for Halloween."

Pauline turned scarlet.

"Did you tell the police?"

"Of course, I did. But I have no proof that it was stolen. Until it showed up here today, I thought it was gone forever. What can you expect? His father was the same way. Cut your throat for a nickel."

I couldn't imagine Mrs. Davis's brother Courtney cutting anyone's throat for a nickel, but I wanted that armoire, so I let it go. Pauline raised her eyes to me through long lashes and looked away immediately.

I spotted a framed needlepoint sampler with the date 1864 sewn in black thread. "You have a very impressive collection of Civil War items."

Grover gave me a hint of a smile and took down a glass-topped display box. "This is a New Jersey regimental flag circa 1861 in near pristine condition. I'm unveiling it this weekend. It should have been the star of the show, but it isn't getting the attention it deserves because it's being overshadowed by that vampire-hunting kit that probably isn't even real."

"I thought you bought it in Boston?"

Grover's jaw clenched. "I bought it from a junk shop and hadn't had it authenticated yet. It disappeared too fast."

"Oh. I'm sorry. And it turns out it's genuine."

Grover gave me a slow blink and put his flag away. "Yes, well. I use a different expert than the one on Whipple's payroll. You can get a lot of questionable items authenticated for the right price over there."

Auggie walked into the tent and Pauline knocked over a stand of brochures and tried to pull them into a quick stack with trembling hands. She looked like she wanted to scatter, but her black pencil skirt held her knees tight behind the table and she could only shuffle.

"Aunt Thelma says they want to show you something." He gave Grover Prickle a smug look. "Hey, sorry about all the press here earlier."

Pauline gripped her binder against her chest like a life vest keeping her afloat. "Congratulations, Auggie. You must be very pleased."

Auggie gave her a slight nod before turning back to Grover. "Fair warning, I have two photo shoots lined up this weekend. The *Press of Atlantic City* is covering the auction, and Whipple's Emporium is going to be on the cover of *Antique Alley Magazine* next month. They want an exclusive interview."

Pauline's eyes were begging Auggie to notice her, but as soon as he'd glance at her she'd look away.

Grover's lip curled in disgust. "And where are you going to tell them you found the thing? Because you and I both know it was in my storeroom until you broke in and stole it."

"I've never stolen a dime from you, Prickle."

Grover's lip curled in a sneer and he grabbed a polished saber. "Liar! If I ever catch you on my property, I'll show you what this was used for." Grover brandished the saber and his footing slipped. He missed Auggie's ear by inches. A couple shoppers dropped the knives they were perusing and backed out of Prickled in search of safer venues.

Auggie slapped the saber from Grover's hands. "Curb your jealousy, old man, before you get hurt." He called to Pauline over his shoulder. "Later, little pea."

Pauline's eyes filled with tears and she squirmed out through the back of the tent.

I gave Grover a wan smile. "I hope this doesn't influence your decision to sell me the armoire."

I followed Auggie through the flap back to his booth.

"Don't worry about him. He's full of spite because he's never been as successful as we are at Whipple's."

"I take it your families are rivals?"

Auggie nodded. "We're the oldest antique stores in the area. I wouldn't put it past Grover to try to sabotage my vampire kit. He's seething with envy over it."

"Where *did* you get it?"

Auggie shrugged. "Not important."

We entered Auggie's booth and Mrs. Davis took my arm. "I was just telling Ginny that if we're going to the auction together, we have to register for paddles."

"Is that right?" The vision of the biddies buying a sarcophagus flew into my mind. "Maybe you could share one paddle. And I could hold it for you."

Mrs. Davis waved across the road. "There's Tildy and Spencer. Let's go say hello."

She and Aunt Ginny took off after the couple, who appeared to be having a fight. Tildy looked on the verge of tears.

Auggie shook his head. "That poor girl. She could have done so much better for herself."

I followed his gaze. "They seemed happy the other night. Aren't they trying to get pregnant?"

Auggie snorted. "Everyone knows Spencer has no interest in starting a family until he strikes it rich."

"Your stepmother seems to think it's happening soon."

"Josephine is dreaming. Spencer does just enough to keep them on the hook without actually committing to anything. They couldn't afford the medical bills to get pregnant anyway."

"If they're having fertility issues, there are places they could go for help. It's nothing to be embarrassed about."

Auggie cut his eyes to me and laughed. "Spencer won't spend that kind of time or money unless it's on himself. He was status shopping when he met Tildy. He only married her for the family money. That's why Dad isn't leaving her anything in his will."

"Nothing?"

Auggie shook his head like I'd asked to make that holy water into lemonade. "Not a dime. If she inherits anything, Spencer'll rob her blind."

"Tildy must be very hurt by that."

"What difference does it make? It's not like my dad is dying anytime soon. And if he goes first, Josephine will probably sell everything out from under us."

That seemed an odd statement from someone who'd claimed his inheritance with an ironclad bequeathment plan of sticky notes.

Auggie wasn't paying attention to me anymore. He was watching a beautiful woman with long green hair staring at him from across the lane. "If Tildy needs money she'll just have to beg, borrow, or steal it like the rest of us."

CHAPTER 9

Aunt Ginny and the biddies went to the Grange for a celebratory dinner. They didn't invite Auggie, so I guess they were celebrating being eighty and still able to chew a steak. Which now that I think about it, does sound like something worth celebrating.

I rushed home to get dinner ready for two of my favorite men in the world. Figaro met me at the door, his tail flicking like an irritated sky dancer. "What's the matter, baby?"

He let out a low moan that he was feeling sorry for himself. A pair of green eyes peeked around the corner from the library. Cleo slinked into the foyer and dropped the red scrunchie at Figaro's feet. Then she waited to be praised.

Figaro's ears flattened and he looked the other way.

"I think someone is trying to make friends, Fig."

Cleo swatted the scrunchie closer to Figaro, then lay down to wait for his return swat.

Figaro looked at the scrunchie, looked at Cleo, and walked away through the sitting room.

Cleo gave me a look that said, *Men!*

I rubbed her head and scratched her under her chin before heading to the kitchen to marinate shish kebabs for the grill. I made Henry a dairy-free mac and cheese out of butternut squash and cashew cheese. It looked delicious but I was more than skeptical. Macaroni and cheese was sacred. You don't ruin it with vegan cheese unless you have to. This poor baby was allergic to dairy, so it would be a treat for him.

The front door opened, and a herd of buffalo thundered down the hall in the form of one four-year-old little boy. Henry threw his arms around my legs. "Poppy!"

"Hey, sweets. Have I got a surprise for you tonight."

"What is it?"

I pulled the DVD out of my purse on the counter. *"Paddington."*

Henry's eyes grew to the size of quarters behind his glasses and he danced around with the DVD. "Can we watch it now?"

Gia gave me a kiss hello. "After dinner, Piccolo."

"All I have left to do is to grill the meat and set the table."

Gia put his hand out. "I can grill for you. Grilling is the man's work."

"That's a horribly sexist thing to say. I'm surprised at you. You know women can grill just as good if not better than men. Some of the best pit masters in the country are women. One thing you need to know is that you should never underestimate me." By the time I was done with my soapbox speech I had the apron around his waist, the tray of kebabs in his hand, the tongs in the other, and I was holding the side door open for him.

Gia raised his eyebrows and gave me a smirk. "Uh-huh."

I flashed a grin. "The button to ignite is on the side." *I'm just as good at it, but it's also a hundred degrees next to that grill and my hair frizzes in the steam.*

Henry and I set the table while he told me all about something called the Octonauts and Captain Barnacles saving a sea cucumber. I wasn't sure if this was a real thing or if he was making it up. Our only hiccup of the night was Gia's lack of a poker face over the mac and cheese. He frowned at an orange noodle on his fork. "What is this?"

"That is gluten-free, dairy-free macaroni and cheese and it's the very best you've ever had in your life, isn't it?" I made my eyes the size of saucers and he followed my hint to Henry, who was happily scarfing his macaroni and cheese down while looking back and forth between us trying to figure out what was going on.

Gia made a crooked smile at Henry and forced a swallow. "Yeees. Is *squisito*."

Henry looked at me and giggled. A noodle fell from his fork and hit the floor. Figaro sniffed it and walked away.

Gia poured me some more iced tea. "How was the antique show?"

"You'll never believe what Auggie's big reveal was."

Gia grinned. "An iron maiden?"

"Try silver bullets and a wooden stake."

Gia's face froze and he blinked a couple of times. "No."

I told him about the box, using select words to avoid

explaining what a vampire was for the giant eyes watching me from behind a Fred Flintstone jelly jar full of apple juice. And all about Grover Prickle and the dustup between him and Auggie. "But you know who I didn't see there at all? Courtney or his daughter, June."

Gia nodded. "After the fuss they made about it being for family, you would think everyone would be there for big moment."

"I was thinking the same thing."

We cleaned up and moved to the sunroom across from the kitchen. It was a beautiful back tower room and where we put the TV and DVD player for the guests to use. The furniture was less fussy than in the rest of the house, but we still had to update it to be bed-and-breakfast-level schmancy. Aunt Ginny's ancient recliner and TV tray table had to go, along with Grandma Emmy's pea-soup-colored rocker. I'd had my handyman, Smitty, paint the room pewter and I found a comfy gray sofa and two white leather wingback chairs. Aunt Ginny found the black and white fleur-de-lis rug online. It was one of her few purchases that didn't end in disaster. I'm still not allowed to bring up the Victorian tilt table that was "a steal." It was also for a doll house.

Gia and I snuggled down on the couch and Henry sat on the floor at our feet to watch *Paddington*. We asked him if he wanted to join us on the couch, but he said he had to keep Figaro company. I leaned to look over the edge of the sofa and caught Henry placing small pieces of popcorn on the floor next to him. Then a gray fluffy paw reached out from under the sofa, snagged the popcorn, and disappeared again.

"What is he doing, Henry?"

Henry's eyes were on Paddington. He placed another

piece of popcorn in front of the sofa. The gray paw came out and snatched it. "He's hiding from the black kitty."

Gia and I looked out in the hall and Cleo walked past, looked around, meowed, and kept going.

Gia kissed me. "Maybe Henry will fall asleep."

"I wouldn't count on it. Paddington is a very naughty bear."

"What is your fascination with things that are naughty?"

"*Paddington* was my favorite book as a child. He's always sticky with marmalade and covered in some kind of mess from a disaster of his own making."

That's when Aunt Ginny walked in, covered in mud, and dropped her purse on the floor in the hall. The similarities to the naughty bear did not escape me.

"I'm fed up!"

"What happened?" Gia asked.

Aunt Ginny frowned. "Pottery class."

Gia shook his head. "It did not go well?"

"No, it was great."

"But you had accident with the mud."

"Don't be ridiculous."

I'd had these conversations with Aunt Ginny before. Gia was on his own.

Gia waved his hand up and down. "Then how this?"

"Josephine is a big baby."

Gia blinked and cocked his head.

I leaned into him. "Wait for it."

Gia narrowed his eyes. "How did you get the goop in your hair?"

"Thelma started it." Aunt Ginny walked into the kitchen and came back with a can of Fresca.

"She threw it at you?"

"She wouldn't dare!"

Libby Klein

I giggled to myself.

Gia took another run at it. "Are you and Thelma having a fight?"

Aunt Ginny looked at him like he'd just asked if they were cannibals. "Boy, what is wrong with you?"

He thought for a moment. "I give up."

"Thelma accused Josephine of stealing the jewelry box."

Gia's hands flew over his head. "And she did."

I whispered to Gia, "You're getting close, don't screw it up now."

"Josephine threw clay at Thelma and it hit her pottery wheel a little wonky."

Gia nodded. "Mm-hmm."

"Then it spun off her wheel and hit the fan in front of me."

I whispered, "There it is."

Aunt Ginny held up her soda. "Then it got ugly."

Gia's eyes popped in surprise. "*Then* it got ugly?"

Aunt Ginny nodded. "This is war." She took a drink of her Fresca and looked at Henry. "What's going on there?"

Henry looked at Aunt Ginny with a very serious expression. "Figaro doesn't want a girlfriend."

Aunt Ginny nodded. "Fair enough."

I looked in Gia's eyes. "Welcome to the family."

The front doorbell chimed, and I got up to answer it. An African American couple I assumed were somewhere in their forties stood on my front step. The woman was beautiful, with golden-brown bangs swept down and around her head in a tiny ground-floor beehive. She was wearing a tight yellow sleeveless dress and had the look about her of being a woman who was constantly putting up with something. And what she was putting up with, was standing right next to her. He was chubby, with close-cropped dark hair and a mustache-goatee combo. He had a mischievous twinkle in his eyes that said he was a perpetual comedian. I couldn't help but smile.

The woman held out her hand and her bright red nails were a mile long and covered in crystals. "Hi. We're Kevin and Shondra Martins. I'm so sorry we're late. Someone had to stop for a chili dog, and we missed the ferry."

Kevin made a face of indignation and his eyes grew very wide. "Did you know you could just drive around? What kind of racket is that ferry?"

I laughed. "Well, I'm glad you're here now. Come on in and we'll get you settled."

Gia came down the hall with Henry and they had matching frowns of disappointment on their faces. Gia held up his cell phone. "Momma has broken water pipe. She need me to come immediately."

Out of the corner of my eye I saw Shondra tip her head towards Kevin and mutter, "Mm-hmm."

I wanted to tell her, "You are not wrong," but the woman in question was Henry's Nonna, and he was like a little sponge who would report on me to the commandant. I told Henry they could come back, and we'd finish the movie later. He wanted me to commit to an exact day and time, so we made a date. I kissed them both goodbye and watched them leave.

Shondra put her hand over her heart. "I'm so sorry. We arrived at a terrible time, didn't we?"

I tried to give her a comforting smile. "No, of course

not." *It's not your fault that old woman whacked her own pipe to end my date.*

"Before we go up to our room, are you aware there is an old lady in her pajamas sitting in the middle of your yard?"

I looked out the window. Elaine Grabstein was sitting next to the squirrel feeder having a conversation. She was completely alone.

CHAPTER 10

"What in god's name are you making?" Joanne took a tray of bacon out of the oven and slid a tray of scrapple in its place.

"Strawberry funnel cake muffins." I poured gluten-free funnel cake batter in golf-ball-sized swirls into the deep fryer. "It's part of my summer theme I'm calling Boardwalk Sweets."

Joanne tried to roll her eyes in disgust, but I could tell a big part of her was intrigued. "Well, you ruin everything by making it gluten-free."

Silly me . . . always wanting to avoid stomach cramps and swelling. The funnel cake had puffed to the size of a flat baseball. I flipped it over, revealing the tan underbelly. "Once I put this on the vanilla bean muffin with strawberry compote and top it with powdered sugar, I don't think anyone will care that it's gluten-free."

Joanne narrowed her eyes and looked in my deep

fryer. She turned her nose up and grunted for lack of a comeback and went back to her Denver omelet quiches with Courtney's tomatoes. Aunt Ginny hired her to help me in the kitchen. Her delicate biscuits and pastries kept me from letting her surly mood dig an icepick into my brain, even though we'd never be friends. In her olive bike shorts and camo tank top she had the look of a lady drill instructor on her day off. And she loved barking orders at me.

"You'd better take that out before you burn it."

Aunt Ginny appeared in the kitchen, dressed in a faded vintage Mama's and Papa's T-shirt from the sixties and pink terry cloth shorts she'd pulled on in such a hurry they were backwards. "Where's the bacon?"

I took my miniature funnel cake out of the oil and set it on the rack to cool. "Good morning to you too, sunshine. I see you got the clay out of your hair."

Aunt Ginny sniffed around until she found the bacon Joanne had hidden under sheets of paper towels. "Stupid Josephine. If you're gonna start slinging mud, you'd better have good aim."

Joanne's eyebrows shot up and she glanced at Aunt Ginny, but she didn't comment.

I took a piece of bacon from under the paper towels and Joanne almost flipped her wig. I squatted down in front of the cabinet under the island. "Come here, baby. Bite."

A gray fluffy head pushed his way through the opening and licked his chops. I broke off a piece of bacon and fed it to his Royal Scaredy Pantsness.

Joanne pointed a spatula at the cabinet. "How long has that cat been in there?"

A soft *merrroww* lilted down the hall and Cleo slinked

into the kitchen. Figaro disappeared back into the cabinet, the door shutting with a thud.

"Since Cleo snuck up on him while he was taking a very intimate bath and he lost one of his lives."

Cleo sauntered over to my legs and pushed her head against the cabinet, purring. I fed her a little piece of bacon, hoping Figaro wouldn't notice.

Aunt Ginny poured herself a cup of coffee. "That cat's putting on the full press and Fig's not having it."

I finished eating the piece of bacon and sprinkled powdered sugar over my mini funnel cakes. "He'll survive. She's only here for a week."

Joanne took the tray of scrapple patties from the oven and flipped them. "What are you going to do when the other one arrives?"

"The other one what?"

Her head lolled to the side when she looked at me like I was slow. "You really have no idea what's going on here, do you?"

I considered the fact that I had a cat hiding in the cabinet, a great-aunt who'd been in a pottery brawl a few hours ago, and a narcoleptic chambermaid who I'd already woken up in the broom closet this morning, and I thought I was doing pretty good. "What do you mean?"

The doorbell rang and Joanne set her spatula down. "I'll let you go see for yourself. They're right on time."

Well, this can't be good. Joanne looks like she just won a round and I didn't know we were in the ring. I took off my apron and headed down the hall to the front foyer. Figaro loped past me like a baby bear. He kept one eye on his tail, he was so afraid Cleo would jump him and force him to commit to a relationship.

I opened the door to a small couple in their sixties with

matching cropped hairdos of solidarity. They were dressed in blue and white striped shirts and red shorts. The man put out his hand. "Hi. We're the Robbinses. I'm Paul and this is my wife, Marty. We have an early check-in."

"Well, you sure do. Come on in." *We need a better system for Joanne and Aunt Ginny to tell me when they do stuff like this. Check-in at eight o'clock in the morning? I don't know which one to blame, but they are the broken sides of the efficiency triangle.*

Paul Robbins bent over and picked up an enormous cat carrier that was almost big enough for a child to sleep in. I jumped forward to help him and the crate rumbled. It wasn't a tiny little Cleo meow. It was a German weight-lifting meow. I took a step back and counted my fingers.

Marty grinned and reached forward to open the front door of the supersized crate. "And this is our precious little baby, Sveltelana. She's a Maine coon. Come say hello, baby."

Marty pulled a toddler-sized orange cat from her Volkswagen-sized carrier and cuddled her. Sveltelana meowed again and a thud reverberated off the wooden floor behind me. I looked down and Fig's eyes were the size of walnuts. Cleo spun in tiny little circles on the floor next to Fig and made kneading motions with her paws on the hardwood.

"Sweet Jesus, what is that?" Aunt Ginny came around the corner and stopped by the front desk, afraid to come any further.

"Aunt Ginny. This is Paul and Marty Robbins, and Sveltelana."

Aunt Ginny eyed me. "Svetlana?"

"No. *Svelte* Lana."

Paul lowered the carrier to the floor and rubbed his arm. "And in this corner, weighing in at twenty-three point eight pounds of orange fur, Sveltelana the marshmallow."

Marty giggled and shifted her weight. She set Sveltelana gently on the floor. I had to snap my mouth shut. Sveltelana looked at Fig and chirped a friendly hello. He, being the gentleman that he was, tucked tail and shot down the hall like he was being chased by an orange rhino.

I gave an apologetic smile to the Robbinses. "Sorry. I'm sure he'll be back."

Aunt Ginny was, as always, a paragon of tact. "No, he won't. He's terrified that she'll eat him."

Sveltelana gave me an angelic blink of her golden eyes.

Cleo took in the other woman and arched her back. She hissed, but Sveltelana ignored her like a trucker being honked at by a moped.

I put my hand out to take the crate. "Why don't I show you to your room and you can join us for breakfast once you're settled in? Joanne can check you in after you eat."

Marty bent over and picked up her baby. "Ooh, yes please."

I took the Robbinses to the Scarlet Peacock, gave them their keys, and showed them their bathroom across the hall. They were over the moon with the room. Sveltelana made herself right at home in the middle of the king-sized brass bed. From the corner of my eye, she looked like a mountain lion. I wasn't sure where these two would sleep. "Please let me know if there is anything else you need during your stay."

Marty pulled the curtain aside and she looked out the window. "We'll be fine. This week will be good for all of us."

When I returned to the kitchen, three sets of eyes were glaring at me and a giant bowl of kohlrabi sat in the middle of the table. Aunt Ginny said dryly, "Spencer was here. I told him you were tied up with guests."

Joanne pointed to the bowl of mutant turnips. "Just what do you think we're going to do with all these? How many things do you think I can make out of kohlrabi?"

I sighed, trying to come up with some way to get out of this apparent produce contract with Courtney. "At least there are tomatoes."

Victory was sitting at the banquette, glistening and slickery head to toe, with a gauze bandage wrapped around her forehead. She slid off the vinyl seat and landed on the floor.

"What do you have all over you?"

She tried to pull herself up by the edge of the table. "Eis aloe verra for some sunburns."

Aunt Ginny ran her finger down Victory's arm and rubbed the gelatin between her fingers. "Are you sure this is aloe? It feels like Vaseline."

Victory looked at her arm. "Eis from dollar store. They give me to say sorry for sunscreem. I complain but never tell them about lost and founds bein."

Aunt Ginny wiped her hand on my apron. "We can't have her cleaning the guest rooms while slipping around here covered in goo. What are we going to do?"

The front door chimed. I thought it was one of our guests moving out to the front porch to enjoy the rocking chairs in the cool morning mist. Then the hair on my arm stood up and the temperature in the kitchen dropped. An unnatural silence descended on the room. The blood drained from Aunt Ginny's face as an eerie clacking echoed down the hall like the staff of the grim reaper counting the final heartbeats to death.

Joanne shook out her hands. "What's happening? I don't like this."

With a breeze of Aqua Net and a whiff of Chanel number 5, our fate was sealed. "Surprise! I'm baa-aack!"

CHAPTER 11

"What do you mean you don't have a room available? I'm an owner."

"You have a ten percent share, Georgina. And it's the busy season until Labor Day. You should have called first. We're booked solid."

"Well, what am I supposed to do?"

Aunt Ginny picked at one of the funnel cakes I'd made. "There's a lawn chair out back."

I shot Aunt Ginny a reproving look. "You can sleep in the spare bedroom next to me on the third floor."

Georgina blinked and sputtered like a hard drive with a processing error. "In the attic?"

I moved the funnel cake away from Aunt Ginny and started topping my muffins with the ones she hadn't picked at. "It's not an attic. It's the third floor. They're finished bedrooms and bathrooms. They just aren't fancy like the guest suites. The room over the Swallowtail is beautiful."

Georgina blinked. "Aren't those the servant's quarters?"

Aunt Ginny rolled her eyes and snagged one of the finished funnel cake muffins before I could stop her. "This isn't *Upstairs Downstairs*, Georgina. There haven't been servants in this house in my entire lifetime. And if I remember correctly, my father's bedroom when he was a child is on the third floor over the Adonis Suite."

Victory crept over to the island and snagged a funnel cake muffin. Her arm left a gooey trail next to the platter.

Georgina looked her up and down. "What happened to you?"

"Do not trust lost and founds."

I picked up a tea towel and wiped Victory's aloe goop off the countertop. "You know what, Georgina? I think you're here just in time to help out and put some sweat equity into your ten percent investment."

Aunt Ginny took a giant bite of the funnel cake muffin and strawberry compote oozed onto her chin. Her eyes grew twice their size.

"Are you making that face because of the muffin or because you know what I'm going to ask Georgina?"

Aunt Ginny swallowed. "Both. Wow. Wait till Lila tries these."

Georgina's face paled, giving her rouged cheeks the look of being applied in a mortuary. "What do you mean sweat equity? What do you want me to do?"

"Victory is too badly sunburned and greased up to clean the rooms for the next couple of days, and Joanne . . . How's that muffin, Joanne?"

Joanne had her back to me, but she'd forgotten the microwave was reflective. I caught her eyes rolled back in her head while she was elbow deep in one of my funnel cake muffins. "What? I'm not . . . It's just okay."

I turned the oil back up to fry more batter. "As I was saying, Joanne is too busy in the kitchen and the front desk, so we really need someone to help clean the rooms."

A snort escaped Georgina's perfectly lined mauve lips, and her hand flew up to cover the unladylike outburst. "Poppy, you can't be serious. Why don't you just call the service and hire a new maid? I can do *that* for you."

I faced the insane woman who happened to be my very wealthy former mother-in-law. "Are you kidding me? It's August in Cape May. The height of tourist season. There isn't a service within fifty miles that has a chambermaid available. Are you saying you're not *able* to make a couple beds to protect your investment?" I took out the gluten-free flour. "Would you rather do the baking and I'll do the cleaning?"

Georgina looked like she was about to have a fit of the vapors. She fanned herself with a potholder. "Certainly not. Don't you know who I am? My ancestors came over on the *Mayflower*. I don't know how to wait on people."

"You've had sixty housekeepers."

"Yes, but they weren't any good."

Aunt Ginny gave her a droll look. "Then this will be a walk in the park for you. Just do what you wanted them to do for you but were too incompetent to pull off. Unless you don't think you can hack it. I could do it, but then I am pretty flexible."

Georgina took two steps backwards and sat heavily on the banquette bench, her chest heaving with panic. She rolled her shoulders back and steeled herself in her most comfortable position with her nose in the air. "Of course, I can hack it. I have a degree in literature from Smith, I think I can handle making a few beds."

"Good. Then it's settled." *I give her six hours.*

"I just need someone to show me how to do it."

Four hours.

The guests in the dining room were milling about around the coffee, so I took the plate of funnel cake muffins out before any more disappeared to the peanut gallery in the kitchen. Burl and Elaine were introducing themselves to Paul and Marty while their cats sat at the foot of the china hutch looking towards the ceiling. I followed their gaze and caught Figaro sitting on the high shelf lurking down like a buzzard on a branch.

Elaine in her round black glasses grabbed my elbow. "Hey, doll, I think ya have a problem."

My eyes flicked up to Figaro. "I'm sorry. I think he's trying to avoid the girls."

Shondra and Kevin came through the sitting room and said hello to the other guests. Kevin stopped short when he spotted Sveltelana. "Whoa. What is that? A cougar?"

That's what Figaro said.

Elaine waved her hand at the cats. "Not them. I think ya have an evil presence in the house. I could sense it this morning."

"That's just my mother-in-law."

"No, honey." Elaine continued. "I mean a spirit from beyond. I could perform a seance and cast it out for ya if you'd like."

"Um . . . I'll get back to you." *Let's see how well she does cleaning the rooms first.*

Aunt Ginny and Joanne brought in the pitcher of juice and quiches, along with the plate of bacon and scrapple.

By the time the other guests took their seats, Burl held up the empty plate from the funnel cake muffins and grinned.

I took it from him and assured the guests, "It will take just a few minutes for me to make some more." *The spirits in the kitchen ate a few too many of them before you all came down.*

A couple hours later, I packed up the nine funnel cake muffins I had left, along with a dozen saltwater taffy muffins and a dozen apple pie caramel corn cupcakes that had just finished cooling and getting drizzled in caramel, and headed over to the coffee shop.

Four girls in bikini tops and handkerchiefs that were masquerading as cover-ups were hanging around the granite-topped walnut bar, flirting with Gia.

Gia was polite but aloof, something I now realized had the opposite effect. It didn't dissuade these girls; they took it as a challenge.

The one with the cup size to match her ego made a big show of dropping her debit card and bending over to pick it up. Cameron's eyes practically popped out of his face like a cartoon wolf.

Gia turned on the foaming wand to the espresso machine and filled the back bar with steam. Cameron jumped back, startled, and Sierra laughed out loud. "It serves you right."

Cameron raised his hands in surrender. "What? You're better looking."

Sierra rolled her eyes and groaned.

Gia turned to head back to his office and realized I was standing there. His face broke into a grin so wide I laughed in spite of myself. He took the boxes of cakes and handed them off to Sierra and Cameron so he could greet me properly and shocked the self-esteem out of the bikini girls.

Once Sierra had filled the pastry case, and the bikini girls had said they didn't want anything except skinny frozen lattes because they were all on diets, then one by one bought apple pie caramel corn cupcakes and ate them while their lattes were being whipped, Gia and I retreated to the kitchen.

After a few snuggles, I filled him in on the happenings at the B&B. "I have an old lady who wants to cast evil spirits out of the house."

Gia laughed hard. "You want me to get you Saint Juanita medallion?"

"What's that for?"

"Protection from crazy people."

"You're making that up, aren't you?"

He grinned.

"You'd better not. Aunt Ginny would have to move out." *Speaking of crazy*. "Whatever happened with your mother's broken pipe?"

Gia shrugged. "I screw it back on."

"Wow. How very frightening. Did FEMA have to set up a tent?"

Gia knew he was being teased and he advanced on me with a wicked gleam in his eye.

"Did the coast guard send in a rescue boat for the survivors?"

He caught my hand and pulled me against him while tickling me. "You think you are funny, don't you, Bella? So naughty."

I couldn't stop laughing and wiggling to get out of his grasp. "I'm just glad she lived through the ordeal."

"*Ahem.* Giampaolo Matteo!"

Gia snapped to attention.

Momma stood in the doorway. Her steel-gray bun pulling her eyebrows into perpetual surprise that fought against her continual disappointment in me.

"Momma. What is wrong?"

"*Ho bisogno di aiuto.*" She also said a bunch that I didn't catch in Italian then made a face at me.

Gia sighed and kissed my forehead. "She says the stove is not lighting in the restaurant. Can you wait for me? I will not be long."

My phone buzzed from Joanne and the screen read 911. "I have to head back to the B and B for some emergency. Plus, I have two sets of guests coming tonight and I have to check the banister for aloe schmears."

He raised an eyebrow then kissed me goodbye, which was incredibly awkward with Momma glaring at me. They left through the dining room to her restaurant across the courtyard. Momma frowned at me behind Gia's back before going through the door.

Is it too late to contact Saint Juanita?

CHAPTER 12

"What is the emergency, Joanne?"

Joanne pointed her scowl to a produce box full of tomatoes and kohlrabi. "Courtesy of Courtney Whipple."

"Oh no. What am I going to do with all this?"

I could feel my approval rating with Joanne dropping to a new low. "You need to get this under control."

"Isn't there a food bank we could donate to?"

"I already called them. They said no thank you."

I stashed the box in the mudroom sink and told myself I'd come back later to take care of it.

Joanne did not appreciate my plan. "That isn't a long-term solution."

I was mercifully saved from listening to the many ways I was a loser when the doorbell rang. "That's our four o'clock. I have to get that."

Burl and Elaine were in the sitting room putting together a puzzle. At least Burl was. Elaine was leaning back with her hands in the air like she was tuning a cosmic radio. Burl saw me look at Elaine and gave me a grin. "Looking for spirit guidance."

It was hard not to smile back at Santa. "Are you enjoying your puzzle?"

Burl gave me a grin and a nod, and his white beard puffed a little. Elaine blinked behind the giant black glasses. "Yeah, doll. Ya wanna join in?"

The doorbell rang again, and I pointed to the foyer. "Maybe another time. I think some guests have arrived." *It better not be Spencer.*

It wasn't. It was a gorgeous young couple who were in the middle of a passionate embrace when I opened the door. Wade and Jenna Foubert had come down from Canada for a romantic getaway. She was beautiful in her flirty little sundress with her long legs and blond hair braided across her temple down to a loose side ponytail. He was tall and broad shouldered and couldn't keep his eyes off of her. I checked them into the Swallowtail Suite with its elegant round sitting room in the back and told them happy hour would be set out shortly. I had the impression that I would not be seeing them for the rest of the afternoon.

I placed a wedge of Gruyère and a cheese knife next to a bunch of purple grapes for the guests. It gave them something to nibble on before they went to their dinner reservations around the island. I took it into the library and set the tray on the coffee table along with an open bottle of chardonnay and pinot. I returned to the kitchen to get the small plates and napkins. When I got back to the library, the entire wedge of cheese was gone. Like completely disappeared. Figaro peeked his head out from under the couch and blinked.

I whispered to him, "What happened?"

He disappeared back under the couch, no help at all.

I peeked in the sitting room where Burl and Elaine had been working on their puzzle, no Burl or Elaine in sight. No trace of the cheese. *It's gonna be that kind of week, is it?* I took the tray through to the kitchen, passing Cleo prowling around the dining room, sniffing around the chairs for Fig or crumbs. I took out another hunk of cheese for the happy hour tray.

Georgina limped into the kitchen and slumped at the table. She groaned pitifully.

"Tired?"

Her head in her hands, she mumbled something I couldn't make out and ended it with a deep sigh.

"Where'd you get that outfit?" She looked like a 1950s sitcom maid in a black dress with a starched white cap and apron.

Her head jerked up and she squeaked. "Ginny said I had to wear this. She said it was the appropriate uniform for the chambermaid."

"I see." Aunt Ginny, meanwhile, had worn satin booty shorts and a Beach Shack T-shirt to our last Innkeepers Association meeting. "Don't you have better shoes you could wear?"

"What's wrong with my shoes?" Georgina was wearing her usual three-inch Louboutin pumps.

"Do your feet hurt?"

"They're killing me."

"Well, there you go."

She looked at her shoes and grimaced.

I reset the grapes and arranged them in an arc. "How far did you get?"

"That enormous Emperor room."

I paused, my hand hovering over the block of cheddar. "That's it?"

She blinked at me in horror.

"I'm just saying, you've been at it for hours." Thank god there were only two rooms to clean today.

"Are you kidding? It took me twenty minutes to get the vacuum cleaner down to the second floor."

"Why didn't you just use the one that was already there?"

Her mouth popped open.

"There is a vacuum on every floor in the supply closets."

"Why didn't you tell me that in the first place?"

"I thought Aunt Ginny showed you where everything was . . . oh."

Georgina's face pinked, making her look like an ad for Good & Plenty licorice.

"Let me put out the tray for happy hour and I'll meet you upstairs."

Georgina gave me a very un-high-society-like huff and stormed from the room.

Figaro crept into the kitchen, pried the cabinet door open with his paw, and disappeared under the sink. A few seconds later Cleo and Sveltelana both appeared around the corner, sniffing.

I took the refilled tray out to the library. Paul and Marty were sitting in Burl and Elaine's places, shuffling a deck of cards. "Do you have dinner reservations for tonight?"

Marty grinned at me as she dealt. "Oh yes. We're going to the Lobster House."

Paul fanned out his cards. "Sveltelana will be thrilled. Marty always saves her a little something."

Sveltelana looked like she could crack her way through an entire lobster if left to it, but I kept my thoughts to myself. A crash overhead followed by Georgina's squeal caused me to cut the chitchat short. "I'm sorry . . . let me just go check on whatever that was."

I rushed up the stairs to find Georgina lying at the foot of the third-floor steps. She had a bucket and rags scattered around the landing. "What happened?"

She twisted herself upright. "I fell over this rope coming from upstairs. I've been struggling to get around it all day. Why is that even here?"

I unclipped the rope and helped her to her feet, then lowered my voice. "Georgina, the stanchion rope is to keep the guests from venturing to the third floor where our rooms are. I have to leave the door open for Figaro and I don't want people wandering around my bedroom. Why aren't you using the hidden staircase?"

She swept the hair out of her eyes and patted her bob back into place. "What hidden staircase?"

Aunt Ginny! "Come here." I reclipped the rope and picked up the cleaning supplies, then led Georgina down the hall to what looked like a closet. There was a sign on the door that said, "Private—No Entry." I checked up and down the hall before opening the door to reveal a spiral staircase.

Georgina stepped back. "What the devil?"

"Shh." I pointed up the steps. "There's a door just like this on the third floor where our rooms are." And then I pointed down. "And that way takes you to the pantry in the kitchen. These houses were built so the wealthy didn't have to pass the servants on the stairs carrying buckets and rags."

"Well, I definitely see the appeal of that." Georgina craned her neck to look up the shaft. "I don't want to go up there. It's like a spiral coffin."

"Oh, it is not. And if you don't go up this way, you'll never see what one of my great uncles hung on the wall halfway to the landing."

She wrinkled her nose as she considered my words. The doorbell sounded below, and I checked the time on my phone. "The sisters are here. Can I trust you to get downstairs by yourself?"

Georgina looked down her nose at me. "Of course, you can. I'm not helpless."

"Good." I started to leave the closet.

"Where is the light for this death tunnel?"

Sigh. I reached my hand back and flicked the light switch on the wall inside the door, illuminating the stairwell.

"I would have found that."

We don't have that much time. I took the main staircase to the foyer, glanced in the library, and saw that the wine was missing. *Are you kidding me?* I opened the front door and took a minute to stare at the ladies before me.

One of them said, "Yep. We're twins." Then the other one said, "And yes, we are identical."

They were flipping adorable little old ladies with matching wooly white hair and pink YOLO T-shirts.

"I'm Grace and before you ask, I'm older by four minutes."

The other one nodded. "And I'm Faith, and no we can't feel each other's pain, but yes we have switched places."

I had to hold in a giggle. "Well, come on in, ladies." I shut the door behind them, and Figaro ventured out to the foyer and flopped. He quickly jumped up and checked behind him.

The ladies laughed in unison. "Oh, how adorable."

"Funny. That's not usually the reaction he gets."

"Well, we're used to being stared at for being unusual."

I looked in the sitting room and saw that Paul and Mary were gone. *Who is stealing my happy hour?*

The front door opened, and Aunt Ginny came in. "You will never believe what happened." She saw the twins and stopped short. "Whoa. Look at that."

The ladies smiled at her and I made the introductions. "Grace and Faith Padawowski." Then I gave Aunt Ginny a warning look that said, "No questions."

Aunt Ginny gave me a slow nod. "Okay. Well, I'm just back from Cold Spring Village and it's crawling with whackadoos."

"Even now that you're gone?"

Aunt Ginny narrowed her eyes and swatted me. "Don't be fresh. Edith and Lila wanted to see Auggie's vampire-hunting kit before it gets seized by the police."

Grace and Faith Padawowski's eyes sparkled in interest. One of them said, "Seized by the police?"

"After all that hoopla, it may not even make it to auction. There was a huge argument. Grover Prickle filed a lawsuit against Whipple's Antique Emporium, blocking the auction of the box until ownership can be established and his claim of theft is satisfied. Then Auggie accused Prickled Curiosities of sabotage. He threw a case of Civil War medals and threatened Grover that he'd better watch his step or else."

"Or else what?"

"That's what we were waiting to find out when the police shut the whole thing down."

CHAPTER 13

"I'm not going to breach the perimeter in this heat unless I'm guaranteed the vampire box is a go. I already spent the morning at Qigong on the beach and I'm not getting sweaty again." Aunt Ginny had been on the phone with Courtney, Thelma, and Blake Adams of the auction house since returning home this morning, while Joanne and I made BLT quiches with Courtney's tomatoes—the "L" in this case stood for leeks—and blintzes with fresh berries.

I yawned and poured myself a third cup of coffee. Today was going to be a struggle. Someone rang the doorbell last night at midnight. By the time I had dressed and made it to the front porch there was a wrapped Italian hoagie sitting on the welcome mat with a receipt billed to the bed and breakfast. Joanne promised to call the deli this morning and tell them they'd made a mistake.

Victory came through the back door covered in aloe and wrapped in bandages like she'd just escaped the Pyramids. Since she couldn't help clean the rooms, she'd come in early to help eat the breakfast. So far, she'd consumed three blintzes with a half-gallon of mango juice and Aunt Ginny had re-wrapped her.

Something thudded overhead causing the pendant light over the stove to sway. We all paused for a moment and listened. It scraped across the kitchen ceiling like a slow T. rex dragging its kill through the Adonis Suite. A few seconds later it tumbled down the pantry steps like a boulder. We heard cursing, and eventually, Georgina opened the pantry door and stumbled into the kitchen. Her hair was disheveled, and her lipstick smeared in such a way that she wouldn't be caught dead in front of the Junior League. She had a full laundry basket, and she was kicking it forward a few inches at a time with a *thump— screeecht*.

I knew my face was giving away my irritation, but I was too tired to fight it. "Georgina! What on earth are you doing?"

"Do you have any idea how heavy wet towels are? I can barely move. Every muscle hurts." She looked at Victory. "How do you do this every day?"

Victory shrugged, winced, and grabbed a piece of pork roll off the platter. "I stretch feirst."

Aunt Ginny marched back and forth in front of the oven, causing three of us to repeatedly duck under the coiled cord from the ancient landline telephone. "I'm going to hold you personally responsible if I don't get to bid on that half-naked-centaur lamp I put a pre-show offer on."

Georgina got clotheslined with the cord and shot Aunt Ginny a hostile look.

Aunt Ginny was oblivious to the havoc she'd caused. She pointed to the phone and mouthed, "Auction house."

I freshened up her coffee. "Which half of the centaur is naked?"

She stuck her tongue out at me.

I carried the warming tray of blintzes into the dining room and put it on the sideboard. Joanne was right behind me with the quiches.

Elaine Grabstein clutched my arm as soon as the door swung back and hit me in the butt. "Hey, doll, I wanted to let ya know that I don't think your chambermaid knows what she's doing."

I know for a fact she doesn't. "Why? What's wrong?"

She led me away from the kitchen by the elbow. "Well, it's no big deal or nothing, but I think she cleaned our mirrors with furniture polish. Burl thought his cataracts were back until I was able to buff some of it out."

Burl was dressed for the beach in a bright red T-shirt and shorts. He grinned and his belly jiggled. The kids were going to go nuts today. Santa's day at the beach would be all over Instagram before lunch.

"I'm sorry about that. I'll fix it this morning."

"Thanks, doll. Also, I tried talking to that spirit last night. I could hear her clattering around the floor above me, moaning. I think she needs help crossing over."

On the other side of the door Georgina was busy complaining about how fast the Lemon Pledge came out of the nozzle. I narrowed my eyes at Elaine. "Well, she definitely needs help with something, I'll give you that."

Back in the kitchen, Figaro was having his morning

crab feast when Cleo came in and dropped a Q-tip at his feet. He looked her up and down while licking his whiskers, then dismissed her and went back to his crystal pedestal bowl. A few minutes later, Sveltelana came in and lay down next to him to watch him eat. She batted a dice of onion she found on the floor in his direction. His ears flattened and he moved to the other side of the bowl with his back to her.

Georgina moaned. "I can't do it today. Those twins asked me for more towels and by the time I'd returned with them they wanted more washcloths too. Why are these people so demanding?"

I knew for a fact that Georgina had once fired a maid because the flowers on the bathroom wallpaper looked "wilty." I swallowed the temptation to hand her a mirror and hid behind my coffee.

Victory reached for another blintz. "Oy. I forget to tell you. Beicycles are back. Kim say hello."

I nodded. The Laughing Gull Winery was the Bermuda Triangle for our loaners. Every once in a while, one popped back out and was returned. I would have to send the staff a thank-you basket of cupcakes at the end of the season.

Aunt Ginny hung the phone up. "The auction house opens in an hour for the noon preview. Blake Adams assured me the brass centaur lamp would be on the list."

I handed her a plate with a blintz. "I thought you were calling about the vampire-hunting kit."

"Oh. I forgot about that." She shrugged. "Oh well. I did what I could. All we can do now is wait and see."

"Gia is picking me up at one thirty to go to the auction. How are you getting there?"

Aunt Ginny grabbed a circle of pork roll. "I'm riding with Edith. She has more room in the minivan for purchases."

I had visions of an entire yard sale coming home with Aunt Ginny. "Remember to pace yourself. We're hoping to close the B and B for January and we can't do that if you go crazy at the auction."

Aunt Ginny waved her pork roll in my direction. "When do I ever go crazy?"

CHAPTER 14

We survived another breakfast service, and I was showing Georgina for the third time in twenty-four hours how to work the washing machine. She had never done laundry in her life and we'd spent the afternoon mopping up suds and having a little talk about why more detergent wasn't better.

"I just don't see why we have to do the laundry at all. Isn't there a service that can come pick it up and do it for us?"

"Not without charging us a fortune, and we need to watch our overhead. Remember, you get ten percent of the *profits*."

Georgina examined her hands. "Do you have a spa that takes emergency appointments?"

"Georgina, I'm not sure there *is* a salon that considers chipped polish an emergency."

"Well, I've got to do something. I'm going to see my

little man tonight and he can't see me with washerwoman cuticles. You're lucky your boyfriend doesn't care about how you look."

Ouch. Georgina's boyfriend was my handyman, and I had it on good authority that Itty Bitty Smitty's favorite things in life were Eagles football, salt-and-vinegar potato chips, and the Three Stooges. I doubted Georgina's Tickle My France-y nail lacquer made the list for number four.

"Besides, I've got to treat myself to a little spa day. These spoiled rich people are exhausting. Nothing is good enough for them. First, they want extra shampoos, then fluffed pillows and little chocolates, and where did you hide the remote? They want me to jump through hoops to come as soon as they call, and they always want to be first like they're special. When does it end?"

"Yeah. Spoiled rich people are the worst."

She gave me a hard look, trying to determine if that comment was meant for her, then gave up and took herself to the nail salon for an urgent walk-in appointment "like the peasants do."

After she left, Joanne and I had to remake the beds because Georgina didn't understand that sheets were not one size fits all.

Now it was a quiet afternoon and most of the guests were out shopping, biking, and beaching. No one had seen Wade and Jenna Foubert, which as far as romantic getaways go, meant they were doing something right.

Gia pulled up at half past one and beeped. I thanked Joanne again for covering the front desk so we could go to the auction. "Hopefully M. Humphries won't attend, and I'll win the armoire for the Swallowtail."

Joanne sneered. "You sure you got armoire money?

We're going through the wine and cheese like this is a menopause conference in Napa Valley."

I took my purse out of the desk drawer and put my sunglasses on. "When Georgina gets back, ask her if she found any wine bottles in the guest rooms."

I slid in the seat and kissed Gia hello. "Who's watching the shop?"

"My sister, Karla, is there for rest of the day. I am all yours."

"Ooh. Why don't we skip out on the auction after I bid on the armoire? We could go watch the sunset at the point."

Gia kissed my wrist. "How about the sunrise?"

I can't breathe.

The auction house was across from Cold Spring Village in a long white building that used to be a Church of the Nazarene. Before that it was an auto repair garage. The main doors opened to a small vestibule with a long hallway to the right, and double doors on the left that led into a very large room filled with metal folding chairs. A dais down at the front held a wooden podium. Eight industrial-sized ceiling fans whirred overhead, writing checks for cool air that they couldn't cash in the ninety-five-degree weather. We had a little time to walk around the long tables against one wall and take a last look at some of the smaller items up for bid before the event started.

Gia bought us both lemonades. Aunt Ginny sensed money was being spent, appeared out of the ether, and Gia bought a third lemonade for the wily opportunist.

An unseasonably cool breeze blew across my neck.

"How did your friend like her protection talisman?"

I looked behind me for the small child and then down

into the face of the old woman who had sold me the curse-breaking troll. "Oh, I almost didn't see you there . . . So far so good."

The woman smiled in a cryptic way. "I hope it brings her what she's looking for."

I cast a look at Aunt Ginny. "I'm sure it will."

Gia's eyebrows flicked together when she toddled off. "What was that about?"

"Nothing." I felt my face get hot.

Aunt Ginny, the sneak, was still glued to my hip. She started to belly laugh. "Poppy got the ugliest good luck charm that is supposed to ward off evil and undo her curse of finding dead bodies. Show him, Poppy."

"No. It's nothing." I tried to shrug it off.

Aunt Ginny pulled on my purse handle, laughing harder. "Show him."

Gia raised his eyebrows in amusement. "*Si*, show me."

I sighed and dug around inside my purse until I found the brown little troll the size of a large avocado. I pulled it out and held up my embarrassment.

Gia's eyes widened. His mouth dropped open then immediately his lips clamped shut. He tipped his head to the side and tried to blink the laughter off his face, but it didn't work. "I see."

I frowned. "It's ridiculous."

Gia's lips twitched and he looked at the ground. "Let us not judge it yet. Maybe it works. It could be powerful magic. We should see if it let you in the graveyard."

I made a face at him and shoved the troll down in my purse under my hairbrush and in-case-of-arrest emergency Juicy Fruit gum. Then I made a face at Aunt Ginny for laughing at me, which made her laugh harder.

Grover Prickle's assistant, Pauline, ran by us in a fluster. I called out a hello, but she just raised a hand and waved behind her. "Sorry. Can't stop. Boss is missing."

Aunt Ginny snorted. "Someone's busy."

My phone received a text from Joanne. I heaved a sigh and my shoulders drooped when I read it.

Gia put his arm around me. "What is wrong?"

"Georgina doesn't know if there are any wine bottles in the rooms. She says she didn't know it was her job to take out the trash." I texted Joanne and asked if she could take out the trash while the guests were at dinner. She replied with an emoji giving me the finger.

We signed in, collected our paddles, and found five folding chairs together. We needed a sixth, so Aunt Ginny moved some lady's orange purse to the row behind us. "What? If your butt isn't in the chair it isn't yours."

Mrs. Davis entered the room down at the front, wearing a bubble-gum-pink dress to match her hair. She looked around, spotted us, and speed-walked up the aisle. "Have you seen Auggie?"

I shook my head. "No. Is he across the street at Cold Spring Village? Maybe he's in his booth?"

Mrs. Davis dropped into the chair that had previously held the orange purse. "No, and Courtney is just frantic with worry. Some reporter came for an interview this morning and no one could find him. The auctioneer had to do the interview himself."

A woman with a pinched face not used to smiling came down the aisle in search of her saved seat. She wore a brown flowered suit that I would be sweltering in, with an orange flowered hat that matched the purse Aunt Ginny had moved.

Gia whispered, "Uh-oh."

"Don't make eye contact. If she gets mad, we'll say we don't know these people."

The woman stopped in front of Mrs. Davis. "You're that cheater's sister, aren't you?"

Mrs. Davis kept her stony face looking straight ahead. "My brother doesn't cheat. His garden is just better than yours."

The woman sneered and looked down the row. Gia and I snapped our heads forward. "I know he's using banned fertilizer. I can smell it in my yard. Chemicals are forbidden in the competition."

"He doesn't use banned anything, Madeleine. Our grandmother would roll over in her grave. You need to get over it. They're just tomatoes, for pity's sake."

The woman leaned down until she was pointy nose to nose with Mrs. Davis. "I know he's up to something. No one is that lucky to win twenty years in a row."

Aunt Ginny obviously felt like poking the bear. "Actually, it's been twenty-three years in a row."

The woman straightened up. "I will find out how he's cheating and make sure he is stripped of his ribbons. You have my word." She stood even taller and then counted the rows. "And that's my chair!"

Mrs. Davis snapped at her. "Well, my derriere isn't moving, so sit somewhere else."

The woman harrumphed and snatched her purse from the next row, then stormed off down the aisle.

I looked from Aunt Ginny to Mrs. Davis. "Friend of yours?"

Mrs. Davis blew a raspberry and gave me a thumbs-down. "That's Madeleine Humphries, Courtney's next-door neighbor. She's been bitter rivals with Courtney for years over those stupid heirloom tomatoes. No matter what she does, her tomatoes are never as good as my brother's. She wants to win so badly she's drooling."

Oh no. I didn't recognize her without the privacy fence and the purple hat. "M. Humphries. She's bidding against me for the armoire."

Aunt Ginny frowned and Mrs. Davis gave me a look of sympathy. "I'm sorry, honey. Maybe there's another armoire you'll like."

Gia patted my leg and kissed me on the side of the head. "It is not over yet."

Blake Adams was dressed in a sea-green golf shirt to match his eyes. He took to the podium and greeted a couple of the women before tapping the microphone. "Thank you for coming to Adams Galleries, ladies and gentlemen. One quick announcement: Grover Prickle, if you're in the house, please come to the front and check in. Now, I've been told the air-conditioning is doing the best it can. I've also been told to remind you not to use your auction paddle as a fan or you'll go home with much more than you planned this evening."

The crowd tittered at his joke while Mrs. Dodson and Mother Gibson made their way down the row and took their seats in between Mrs. Davis and Aunt Ginny. "Still no sign of Auggie."

Blake gave a brief explanation about how auctions work and how his staff would bring the items in when it was time for their lot number to be auctioned off. Then he started the bidding on a black and gold early-twentieth-century matador uniform called a *traje de luces*. The black silk jacket and breeches were covered in gold brocade and sequins. It came with a cape of embroidered blood-red roses and blue hummingbirds. They were edged in gold fringe and the moment I saw them I knew they would be going home with us. I leaned over and whispered, "Remember they have your credit card on file for anything you win. You can't take it back if you change your mind."

Aunt Ginny didn't hear me. She had sequins in her eyes and her paddle was hoisted in the air so fast it created more of a breeze than the ceiling fans. I was very lucky, and not at all surprised, that she was the only bidder. One of the auction house employees brought her a receipt after Blake slammed his gavel on the podium. "Sold!"

Courtney hurried over between lots and squatted down in front of his sister. "Have you seen Auggie yet?"

"No, Courtney. Maybe he got tied up in beach traffic."

Courtney shook his head. "He left the house hours ago. He said he had to do something important before he met with the reporter. No one has seen Auggie or June. They should both be here by now. He's supposed to introduce our lot."

Mrs. Davis patted her brother's shoulder. "I'm sure he'll turn up."

Courtney ran his hand over his head. He nodded at her before he rushed away.

Aunt Ginny bid on an English apothecary case and a porcelain vase before I threatened to take her paddle away. The biddies got so caught up in the excitement, at one point they were bidding against each other for a silver snuff box. "You ladies don't even use snuff," I hissed at them.

Mother Gibson wrinkled her nose. "I thought he said it was a stuff box."

Gia was no help at all. An auction aide brought out a

gilt-framed picture of Elvis on blue velvet and he told Aunt Ginny it would look perfect in the TV room.

There was a flurry of activity by the auction house staff and notes were being passed to Blake between each sale. Eventually, he covered the microphone with his hand and had a conversation with one of the aides. Then he came back and announced, "Has Grover Prickle arrived? His lot is next. Grover Prickle? Has anyone seen Grover tonight? I don't think he's ever missed an auction in all the years I've been doing this. Pauline, gorgeous, can you take over for Grover?"

Pauline was down in the front twisting her hands into knots. She nodded.

Blake waved his hand. "Okay. Bring in lot three forty-seven. What?" He muffled the microphone with his hand again, but we could still hear him. "No, that's the vampire-hunting kit. That one's tied up in legal. Plus, we need to hold off until we find the missing—you know. Right." He addressed the audience. "I'm sorry. We aren't usually this disorganized. We seem to be missing dealers tonight and items have walked off. I'm sure we'll get it sorted soon. Bear with us. Bring in three forty-eight."

The hair on the back of my neck started to feel like ants were marching towards my scalp. My stomach did a flip-flop. I turned to Aunt Ginny. "We need to go. Now."

"What? But the centaur lamp hasn't come up yet."

I tugged Gia's hand. "I have to get out of here. Come on."

He started to rise. "What is the matter?"

I reached in my purse and fished around for my wooden troll talisman. "Something isn't right." I stood and we excused ourselves down the row. "We gotta go.

Grover Prickle is AWOL, no one can find Auggie, a piece of that vampire kit is missing, and I'm in the room. You know what comes next."

Aunt Ginny got up behind Gia, grabbed his elbow, and shuffled along with us.

I clutched my troll and tried to escape as fast as my feet would take me, but two men were coming up the aisle with the armoire I had placed a bid on. *Oh no. No no no*. I looked left and right but I was blocked on every side. The men started pushing us towards the stage to get the armoire placed for bidding.

Gia put his hand on my arm to edge me back the way we came, but I was trapped between the armoire and a bottleneck of biddies trying to follow me out.

One of the furniture movers stumbled. The man lost his grip on the heavy furniture. It teetered, then slipped out of his hands. The front leg of the armoire banged on the ground causing the door to swing open. A body rolled out and fell to the floor wrapped in Grover Prickle's prized regimental flag soaked in blood.

The woman in the aisle in front of us screamed, "It's a body!"

Aunt Ginny leaned into me. "I bet there's wiggle room in the price now."

I shook the curse-breaking talisman in my fist and hurled it into the nearest trash can. I couldn't escape it, this was my life.

Pandemonium erupted in the auction house. Some tried to scurry as far away as possible. Others rushed the aisle wanting to get a closer look. People on the left side of the aisle had a full view of the body. Many started to scream and back away. The other furniture mover dropped the back of the armoire. It cracked against the floor, causing the corner of the flag to billow off the victim's face. I grabbed Aunt Ginny's hand. "Oh my god. No!"

It was Auggie. And someone had driven the vampire stake through his chest.

CHAPTER 15

Mrs. Davis clutched her heart and stumbled backwards. The other biddies were right there to pull her into their arms to comfort her. Blake turned Courtney away from the sight. He had to be led to a chair and forced to sit.

Aunt Ginny caught my arm to steady herself. "Dear Jesus, not Auggie."

Madeleine Humphries rushed the stage. "I rescind my bid for the armoire!"

I stared down at Auggie lying at my feet. His shirt was soaked in blood and he had a black eye. I took a deep breath. My hands were shaking. *Why would someone do this?* Gia pulled me against him, and his whiskers scratched against my cheek. "I am here. What do you need?" I buried my face into his neck and a tear escaped.

Blake held up his cell phone and ordered the doors to the front and back of the room to be shut. He grabbed the microphone. "I'm so sorry, ladies and gentlemen, the police are on their way. They've asked everyone to stay where they are and not to touch anything. And please back away from . . . from the armoire. Thank you for your cooperation."

That sent the room into a new direction of chaos. Aunt Ginny started to hyperventilate. "There must be a hundred people in here. We'll be stuck in this madness all night."

Courtney and Mrs. Davis held each other and sobbed. My heart broke in a hundred different pieces. "Watch Aunt Ginny for me."

Gia nodded and I walked to the front of the room and caught Blake Adams by the sleeve. "Hey." I gave him a timid smile that I hoped would put him at ease. "Do you think you could take Auggie's family to a private room to wait for the police? They shouldn't have to be in here with all of this."

Blake's eyes were red and glassy. He wiped them and nodded. Then he gathered Courtney and Mrs. Davis and led them out.

When I returned, Gia took my hand in his and led me a few feet away to some abandoned chairs. "You are always so thoughtful."

I gave him half a smile. "This shouldn't have to be any harder on them than it is." My cell phone rang, and I dug it out of my purse. "Amber?"

"McAllister. Please tell me you're not at Adams Galleries."

"Why would you assume I'm at the auction house?"

"We're en route to respond to a possible homicide."

"That doesn't automatically mean I'd be there."

"But are you?"

I took a deep breath and let it out very slow. "Yes."

There was silence followed by some expletives. "Keep an eye on the body and don't let anyone near it until forensics can determine the cause of death."

"You don't need a CSI team to know a wooden vampire stake through the chest isn't natural causes."

There was more silence. "We're ten minutes out." Amber clicked off.

I looked at Gia. "Why doesn't anyone ever say goodbye?"

He ran his hand down the back of my hair. "What did she want?"

"She wants me to keep an eye on the crime scene until she gets here." I spotted Pauline across the gallery, pacing back and forth, on her cell phone. She looked furtively around the room then slipped out into the foyer. "Whoa. Where is she going? Make sure no one touches anything. I'll be right back."

I rushed to the back and shot out the door where Pauline had escaped. *They really need better security.* She'd gone outside and I saw her fast walking around the building towards a row of cars.

She looked over her shoulder, spotted me, and sped up. "Pauline!"

She stopped and her shoulders drooped.

"You can't leave."

"Why? I didn't kill Auggie." Her voice broke into a sob.

I caught up to her and put my hand on her arm. "Someone is bound to tell the police you were here. If you leave now, you'll shoot right up to suspect number one. Do you really want that?"

Pauline's chest heaved. She shook her head no.

I put my arm around her and turned her towards the door. She was shaking. "Then let's go back inside before they get here."

She whimpered and let me lead her.

"What happened to your boss tonight? The auctioneer said Grover never misses an event."

"I don't know. I've been calling him all afternoon. He isn't answering his cell phone."

"When was the last time you saw him?"

"Last night. We brought a few of our items from across the street to lock in the storage room for today's sale. He was fine when I left. He said he was going home to have a glass of port and read a book."

We entered the building just as two police cruisers pulled into the lot. "The police will want to get your statement. Don't leave anything out, okay? Even if you think it looks suspicious. It will look more suspicious if they find out later—and they will."

Pauline nodded and we slipped back into the gallery.

I wove through the chairs back to Gia, who was holding down the fort by the armoire.

A handful of auction-goers were trying to get selfies with the body and Gia was trying to keep them back. "What is wrong with you? A man is dead. Back up."

Amber and her new partner hit the room to the unnerving crackle of police radio chatter. Officers Consuelos and Birkwell came in right behind them. Since Amber had seniority, she was on point.

"Ladies and gentlemen, I'm Sergeant Fenton. My team and I will need to get statements from each one of you. It looks like it will be a long night, so please, take a seat and try to be patient."

Amber looked for me next to the tipped armoire and headed my way with a scowling Sergeant Washington in tow. She sighed and shook her head. "What have you gotten yourself into now?"

While Viola cordoned off the crime scene with bright yellow police tape, and hovered to observe Amber's investigative technique, I filled Amber in on what we knew, while the other two were taking statements. Officer Consuelos was across the room trying to take Pauline's. The young woman was a puddle of emotion.

The coroner arrived with crime scene technicians who began taking pictures and examining the body. They pulled a fancy-looking set of keys out of Auggie's front pocket and dropped them into an evidence bag.

Amber took her notebook out. "Don't leave. I'll need an official statement from both of you as soon as I'm done here."

I took Gia's hand in mine and we stepped back to let the medical examiner's team through. "Well, this date is terrible."

He squeezed my hand. "I would rather be here with you than anywhere else alone. Uh-oh. Don't look now."

I felt a tap on my shoulder and turned around to find Officer Birkwell handcuffed to a very petulant Aunt Ginny. "I need you to keep an eye on her."

"What did you do?"

Aunt Ginny narrowed her eyes at the blond cop. "He's just being unreasonable. He knows I didn't kill Auggie."

Officer Birkwell fished out a small ring of keys from his pocket and released the handcuffs. "I found her sneaking out of the bathroom window."

"If I have to stay locked in this sauna until you lot take

down all these statements, I'll dehydrate. You don't want a frail old woman passing out from heat exhaustion on your conscience, do you?"

Shane, as he'd told me to call him, put Aunt Ginny's wrist in my hand. "Just give me a few minutes and I'll be back to take your statement. Then I can get you out of here."

Aunt Ginny rubbed her wrist and handed out a little sass. "Alright. Why aren't you back yet?"

I mouthed an apology, and the officer returned to whatever was his most pressing task at the moment. I was left in charge of a renegade senior citizen who knew how to get her own way even if she had to circumvent the law to make it happen.

Aunt Ginny jabbed me in the side. "You know who I think killed Auggie?"

I shook my head. "No. Who?"

She swept her arm across the room. "Who isn't here?"

Grover Prickle.

"Right. His sister."

And her.

Aunt Ginny poked at Gia's chest. "You heard Courtney. June was supposed to be here hours ago. Whipple's is her business too. There's no way she would miss this thing unless she's in hiding."

Gia considered her words. "Maybe something came up to detain her."

Aunt Ginny's mouth slid to a slant. "Yeah, like she's too busy removing all those stickers from around the house now that everything's hers."

Officer Birkwell returned with a bottle of water and handed it to Aunt Ginny. "I see you survived."

She took the water from him and slugged back a mouthful. "Let's do this."

While he was taking her statement—God help him—I spotted Blake Adams talking to one of the auction aides on the other side of the gallery. "Pauline said something outside that I'd like to ask Blake about. Do you mind?"

Gia stood. "I am all yours. You want to talk to Blake; I want to talk to Blake."

We crossed the room and I caught Blake's eye. He held his hands up to shield himself. "I'm sorry, but no one can leave yet."

I gave him a sympathetic smile. "I understand. I was hoping I could ask you something."

Blake looked wary when Gia put his hand out to him. "Giampaolo Larusso and Poppy McAllister. We are friends of the Whipples'. We were here tonight to see Auggie auction his vampire box. It is very sad what has happened."

Blake shook Gia's hand and relaxed. "Tragic. That poor family."

I gave him a nod. "It's awful. Who could have wanted to hurt Auggie?"

He rubbed the corner of his eye. "I can't imagine."

I took another shot at Blake. "What about Grover Prickle? I know they were competitors. You said it was very unusual for him to miss an auction. Have you checked to make sure he isn't hurt somewhere? Are there—other armoires?"

Blake's lips were thin and tight. "No. This was the only large item in the storeroom for auction today. Grover doesn't appear to be on the premises. It is highly unusual."

"Pauline said she hasn't seen him since they were here last night. Something about putting their auction items in storage?"

Blake nodded. "I let Grover and Auggie lock their sale items in my secure storage room before each event. It makes the auction day run smoother and gives me access to items that I might want to take another look at as I prepare. My staff brings the sale items into the gallery when their lot numbers come up."

Gia rubbed his chin and the stubble made scratchy sounds. "Where is storage room?"

Blake stared at him. "Down the hall. But that part of the building is off-limits."

I nodded. "Mm-hm. Did you see Grover last night when he and Pauline locked their items in storage?"

Blake chewed his lip. "No. I must have been in my office getting ready for today. They have their own key to the room."

Gia crossed his arms over his chest. "Who else has a key?"

Blake's head gave a tiny shake. "Just me, Grover, and Auggie."

Gia nodded. "You are not worried they will steal from each other?"

"Not from my auction house. If they're putting something in storage, it's because I've already appraised it and logged it into my records." He paused. "Although Grover did make a big stink about taking his regimental flag home with him last night."

I nudged my head towards the crime scene. "Then how did the flag end up in the armoire?"

Blake made a face like he hadn't put that connection together earlier. "I have no idea."

"Did Auggie lock his box in storage here last night?"

Blake crossed his arms over his chest. "Yep. I had to stay late because he wanted to be the last one to get into the storage room and I had to lock the building after him."

"Grover was already gone? So, no one else was here but you and Auggie?"

Blake's eyes widened. "Yeah, but he was alive when I left him."

Gia gave Blake a comforting smile. "Of course, he was. You stay with him the whole time?"

Blake shifted his eyes left and right. "Not exactly. I had to do some more research on that matador uniform. He said he could lock the room when he was done. We've done this a million times."

"Is that the last time you saw Auggie?"

Blake's shoulders drooped. "I'm afraid it was."

I glanced across the room at the armoire. "You're saying he used his own key to lock the storage room when he was done?" *The one they just fished out of his pocket.*

Blake shrugged. "He would have to have. The door doesn't lock itself. All I know is the room was locked when I checked it on my way out. Look, why these questions? Auggie was a good guy. Everybody loved him."

I glanced at the team from the coroner's office wheeling the body out to the van. "Well, not everyone. Obviously."

Blake paled, which was quite an achievement in this heat. "Who would want to hurt him?"

"Probably the person who gave him that black eye."

Blake cleared his throat and looked for a way to escape us. "Look. Me and Auggie go way back. He had a big personality and not everyone can deal with that. He made some enemies, but I'm not one of them. Auggie and I were close. I think his sins just finally caught up to him."

"The kind of sins that could get him killed?" I asked.

"I shouldn't have said anything. I don't want to speak ill of the dead. I'm sorry, I think someone needs me." Blake tore away from us and headed to the first person who would make eye contact with him.

I looked at Gia. "He's awfully nervous."

Gia stared across the room at the auctioneer. "He says there are three people with keys to that room the armoire was in. Two of them are here."

"Yeah. And one of them is mysteriously missing."

CHAPTER 16

We were at the auction house giving statements until much longer than anyone wanted to be there. When I returned home, all the guests were already turned in for the night. I turned out the lights and climbed the stairs to my room, anxious to put the vision of the crime scene out of my mind for a few hours. Figaro flopped on the pillow next to me and started a long scrub session when someone below us yelled, "SHAZAM!" There was a terrible commotion like a boulder rolling down a waterslide and crashing into a china shop. Figaro shot across the bedroom and dove into the closet—another of his nine lives was gone for good—while I sprang out of bed and threw on my robe inside out.

Georgina ran into the hall, her hair wound in pink curlers and her face covered in cold cream. "What was that?!"

I shook my head and ran down the main stairs. I hopped

the velvet rope on the second floor and flew around the corner. People were coming out of their rooms in various stages of undress looking disheveled and confused. There at the bottom of the steps, Kevin Martins lay splayed out in the foyer, in his Captain America boxer shorts. A broken vase lay in pieces on the floor next to him. I reached out to touch his shoulder. "Mr. Martins? Are you alright?"

"Oh, good gracious, what did he do?" Shondra thundered down the stairs after her husband. Her hair wrapped in a red sleep scarf. "Kevin! Kevin, wake up!"

Aunt Ginny appeared next to me. "What the devil is all that racket?"

Kevin Martins sat up and rubbed his head. "Oh, hey, this isn't Uncle Bill's Pancake House."

I put my hand behind his shoulder to help him. "Are you okay?"

The eight-guest pileup on the steps behind Shondra were doing their best to offer unsolicited first aid advice for everything from seizures to diabetes.

Kevin put his hands up. "I'm fine. Y'all can go on back up to bed. My mission to wake up the house and break a priceless work of art has been accomplished— with help from none of you, I might add."

Shondra thrust her hands to her hips. "Just what were you doing? Were you sleepwalking?!"

Kevin mumbled, "I don't know. I'm just confused."

The doorbell rang and Aunt Ginny made a face. "Who has the nerve to ring my doorbell at midnight?"

Kevin struggled to his feet. "Oh no. Someone called the cops."

I looked out the side window. "No, it's Brother's Pizza." I opened the door. "Can I help you?"

The man pulled a brown pizza box out of a red warming bag. "Someone ordered a large pepperoni?"

I turned to look at my row of guests in question.

The guilty party became clear as soon as Burl Grabstein's whiskers turned the pink shade of shame.

Elaine squinted. "Oh, that's probably ours. Burl sleep orders takeout."

Burl's eyes crinkled and his neck disappeared into his red satin pajamas.

Elaine waved in my direction. "Can ya spot me, doll? I left my cash in my room, seein' as how I had no idea this was happening. I thought your trapped spirit was trying to cross over. Ya can put it on my tab."

Ten sets of eyes followed me to the front desk a little way down the hall. I took some money from the lock box in the bottom drawer, which I would now have to move to a new hiding spot—not that it was a great spot to begin with. I walked back and traded cash for pizza from the delivery man and gave him a tight smile. Then I shut the door and handed the pizza to Elaine.

"Burl don't usually eat what he orders, we just find it in the door when we go get the paper in the morning. Does anyone want a midnight snack?"

Burl looked the most surprised to hear that he wasn't going to eat the pizza.

Kevin raised a hand. "I'll take a slice." Now that he was fully awake, Shazam had to refuel.

Shondra smacked him on the arm. "Really, Kevin?"

Kevin flinched. "What? My momma said it's a sin to waste food, and I ain't no sinner."

The guests meandered their way back to the second floor while divvying up the pizza. The Fouberts noticed

Grace and Faith for the first time, since they had not been seen out of their room before now. "Are you twins?"

"Yes." They replied in unison.

"Are you identical?" Jenna added.

"Yes."

"Oh my gosh, that's amazing. Can you feel each other's pain?"

"No."

Aunt Ginny and I looked at each other without speaking until all five bedroom doors had closed. Then I asked her, "Are you sure you don't want to move into Sunset Valley Assisted Living?"

"Girl, I will knock you flatter than a flitter."

CHAPTER 17

If the shock of seeing Auggie murdered wasn't stressful enough, the Shazam fiasco sent me around the moon. It took me hours to recover from the adrenaline rush and fall asleep.

Figaro did not reappear until sometime in the middle of the night. I woke early with his orange eyes glowering at me while he screeched like a baby pterodactyl. I checked the alarm. I didn't have to get up for twenty minutes yet, and my day was already ruined. Figaro screeched again. "Is this your official complaint for being disturbed last night?"

"MerrOOOww."

"Mm-hmm. I'm sorry, sir. You'll have to tell it to Yelp like everyone else."

Fig let me know what he thought of that by sneezing in my face.

By the time I was showered, made up, and in the

kitchen, Joanne had arrived and was just hanging up her fanny pack by the mudroom. "You look a mess. Did someone tarnish your tiara, Princess?"

Joanne had been pushing my buttons since 1984. She was lucky she could cook because I was in no mood for her bullying today. I'd spent half the night obsessing over how Auggie ended up dead inside a locked room with his keys in his pocket. To add to my displeasure, Joanne's professional uniform of choice was cargo shorts and a blue tank top with a giant talking banana that said, *There's always money in the banana stand.* I leveled a glare her way.

She held her hands up in surrender. "Whoa. Maybe you need a Midol or something."

I'll give you a Midol. Figaro was doing frenzied figure eights between my ankles while I opened a can of trout with catfish. The beige goo flopped into his lordship's crystal pedestal bowl with a squelch. I placed it on the floor just before his begging brought on apoplexy. He purred in ecstasy while snarfing down the pureed mush like it was his last meal before starting Jenny Craig. And then it was all shot to Hades.

"Meow." A black seductress had tiptoed into the kitchen and had her eye on my plus-sized feline for breakfast. Cleo purred loudly and pushed her face into Figaro's neck for a flirty little nuzzle. Figaro shot straight up to the top of the counter without bending his knees and hissed.

Three lives down, six to go.

Cleo sat daintily at the foot of the cabinet and delicately licked her front paw in a come-hither way with her eyes fastened on my baby.

Once he'd stopped spitting and complaining, and his fur unspiked, I moved his breakfast up to the counter and prayed the health department would not make a surprise visit this morning.

Joanne and I worked on a batch of Swedish crepes with blueberry lavender compote, chicken apple sausages, and cheesy potato puffs until they were ready to go into the dining room with a plate of sliced tomatoes.

The guests were already hitting the coffee urns and discussing the events of last night.

Cleo's owner, Marty, grinned at Kevin over her coffee. "You were dreaming you could fly when you threw yourself down the stairs, weren't you?"

Kevin sunk lower in the chair. "I don't sleepwalk. Maybe there's a carbon monoxide leak in my room."

The twins, Grace and Faith, were also extra peppy this morning. "It was a lot of excitement. We thought it was an earthquake."

Shondra made *I told you so* eyes at her husband. "An earthquake, Kevin. You're going on a diet as soon as we get back to Arlington."

Kevin looked like he'd rather eat a hand grenade than go on a diet. "Why am I being punished for having an active imagination? Is it my fault I can't turn my awesomeness off at night?"

Aunt Ginny whispered, "I'll have to remember that one."

I whispered back. "You'd better never hurl yourself down the stairs or so help me God."

Shondra tsked. "Carbon monoxide. I think it's more like all the wine you drank yesterday."

Kevin pouted a little bit. "I'm on vacation, woman."

Jenna Foubert was sitting in Wade's lap drinking her coffee. "I'm just glad you're not hurt."

Shondra shook her head. "If only we could say that

about the vase. How much is that going to set me back?"
She narrowed her eyes at her husband.

I didn't want their holiday to be ruined over one random incident. I could probably replace the vase. "You don't have to worry about that. I think Aunt Ginny bought it locally."

Aunt Ginny was caught filling a crepe with a river of whipped cream. "Oh, I bought that old vase at a yard sale in ninety-three."

"See." I nodded to them.

"I also think I sold it in a yard sale in eighty-seven."

Okay, back to the kitchen before you remember it was Grandma Emmy's and it really does cost me a fortune.

The orange giantess, Sveltelana, had joined the bachelor's entourage, and was pacing in a circle around the island, trying to figure out how to get up to Figaro. She'd get close to Cleo, who'd hiss and swat at her tail, then she'd pivot and go the other direction. Figaro hadn't touched his breakfast since the girls had come in. His eyes followed Sveltelana back and forth like he was tracking a moth. He lifted his paw and swatted the pepper mill off the counter. It landed on Sveltelana's head.

"Fig!"

Sveltelana thundered from the kitchen since the sky was falling, and Cleo was right on her heels. Figaro was so overcome with anxiety he had to choke down his Fancy Feast just to calm his nerves.

Georgina was sitting at the kitchen table still dressed in the black and white uniform Aunt Ginny had conned her into wearing, her head in her hands, a cup of black coffee resting nearby. "I'm so exhausted, I can barely function. I had to call Victory in to assist me in my chambermaiding duties today."

"Trouble falling asleep after the Shazam incident?"

Joanne raised an eyebrow. "The what now?"

Aunt Ginny nudged her. "I'll tell you later."

Georgina heaved a sigh. "No, the couple in the Scarlet Peacock, the ones with that chow puppy."

"That's a cat, Georgina."

"There is no way that's a cat."

Aunt Ginny was appalled. "It was just in the kitchen a minute ago. You heard it meow."

Georgina puckered her lips like she was sucking on a lemon. "Well, whatever it is, it's making a frightful mess with its fur all over the room. Its owners complained that my vacuuming was not up to snuff."

I forced the grin off my face. "Well, after all the maids you've had to fire over the years, it's obvious that you would know better than anyone when the carpet is not up to snuff."

Georgina grabbed her coffee. "That's what I told them. All they did was stare at me like I was a common servant."

Joanne gave Georgina a narrow nod. "And you were wearing your best dress too."

Georgina missed the sarcasm completely. "I had half a mind to tell them that I owned a tenth of their room."

Aunt Ginny sucked her teeth. "That'd teach 'em."

A small knock came on the door from the dining room. I opened it to see one of the twins—I didn't know which one. I smiled at her. "Hello there."

She wrung her hands together. "I am sorry to bother you, but I just popped back up to my room to get my book, and there is a very sunburned young woman fast asleep in my shower under the cold running water. I'm not sure what to do with her."

Aunt Ginny stuck her head under my arm. "That would be our quality control officer. If our shower isn't comfortable enough to fall asleep in, we'll take twenty dollars off your stay."

I smiled at the twin and slowly nudged Aunt Ginny back into the kitchen with my hip. "I'll be right there."

CHAPTER 18

"But Georgeena say I haf to clean room todaee or git fire or somesing."

I handed Victory a towel. "You're not going to get fired. And you're clearly not in any condition to clean anything."

"But Georgina say she weill not share teips wis me."

"I'll take care of Georgina. Don't worry about the tips. Besides . . ." I lowered my voice. "No one is checking out until next weekend after Georgina leaves. So, Georgina isn't getting any tips."

Victory's face split into a grin and her forehead crinkles made white stripes across the pink landscape.

My cell phone rang, and I fished it out of my back pocket. "Hey, Amber."

"I hate to ask you to do this . . ."

I doubt that's true. I grabbed a used towel to mop up

the water all over Grace and Faith Padawowski's bathroom floor. "I'm listening."

"My new partner is making a big stink about your statement."

"Why?"

Amber sighed heavily. "She says your witness interview was compromised."

"Compromised how?"

"Because it was taken by me, and it's missing key information."

"I told you everything I know. What does she think is missing?"

"The crime techs came up with some suspicious evidence at the scene with your fingerprints on it. I didn't even know about it before today. Now she's accusing me of sloppy police work."

"So, who cares what she thinks? Don't you outrank her anyway?"

"I don't outrank Captain Dunne, and that's who she's been moaning to all morning. I've got to get her off my back before this turns into another Internal Affairs crapshoot. I need you to come to the station and go over your statement with the captain."

I led Victory through the twins' room and out to the hall. "I'm really busy here. Is it necessary that I do it today?"

"Only if you want to be cleared as a suspect."

I pulled into the Cape May police station twenty minutes later. I would have been there in five, except I had to dig Figaro out from behind the dryer. Cleo had sat on patrol at the mudroom threshold and he wouldn't come out as long as she was there. I gave Georgina a list of chores to tackle while I was gone. It was the same list she was already ignoring, but I reworded the tasks to make them sound more fun.

> *1. Walk the vacuum back and forth like you're on the pageant stage. The vacuum should be on at the time.*
> *2. Clean the mirrors with Windex like you're waving from a parade float.*
> *3. Make the beds like they are giant tablecloths at a hundred-dollar-a-plate charity dinner to raise money for the disadvantaged.*

I sent Victory out of the house to keep Georgina from pressuring the girl into doing her work. I needed some peanut butter fudge from Douglass for the cupcakes I was making later, and some more saltwater taffy from Fralinger's.

I went through the police station check-in procedure, signed in, and handed over my ID and cell phone. Then I was led towards the interrogation room I had sat in just a few months earlier. My heart started skipping like a baby rabbit. My hands became hot and clammy and I wished I had reapplied my deodorant before leaving the house. And why was the collar on my blouse suddenly so tight?

Captain Kieran Dunne was impeccably dressed in a sharp pinstripe suit. Probably to distract from the fact that he was no taller than five foot five. He intercepted the officer guiding me to the dark room. "I'll take it from here, Welkens." He led me past the room, further down the hall, and around to another interrogation room I had never seen before. Same metal table and benches bolted to the floor.

Same one-way glass. "Thank you for coming down. We just have a couple of things to clear up and you can be on your way. Coffee?"

"No. Thank you."

Amber entered the room followed by Sergeant Washington, who was carrying a manila folder she seemed to think was a smoking gun. Viola slapped the folder on the table. "Here she is. Cape May's own resident sleuth."

My stomach twisted into a knot and I shuddered. *Like the trauma of seeing someone brutally murdered is somehow a fun little hobby of mine.*

Kieran took a seat and flipped the folder open. "It seems there is some question that protocol may not have been followed during last night's incident."

I refused to look at Amber. I knew her history with Kieran Dunne—onetime IA officer now the station captain—was not pretty. Any glances between us would be interpreted as collusion and only serve to complicate matters. "What seems to be the problem?"

Viola tipped her head, her lip curled at the corner in distaste. "Sergeant Fenton was instructed not to take your statement . . ."

Amber cut in calmly, "Instructed by you, my subordinate, who I don't answer to."

Viola ignored her. "As relayed by Captain Dunne, she was to leave you to me. I just want to make sure everything is done by the book with this investigation."

I nodded slowly while considering my words. "I was under the impression that Amber is a highly decorated member of this precinct. I believe I've even read in the paper that she has solved some very high-profile crimes in the past year."

I had read no such thing. I got all my news in the headlines scrolling over my email. But judging from the way the tip of Sergeant Washington's tongue poked through her puckered lips like she was sucking a pit out of an olive, I'd say I hit a nerve. Viola leaned one arm on the table. "We have protocols. They need to be followed. Even by the glorious Amber Fenton."

Okay, that time I did look at Amber. Under other circumstances I would have laughed out loud at her being called *glorious*, but this was hardly the time.

Amber's eyebrows flicked up and dipped down as she looked to the side. I'd been the cause of that move enough times to know she was trying to stay professional.

The captain ignored both officers. "Sergeant Fenton's report says that you didn't touch anything at the crime scene."

"That's right."

"Then why were your fingerprints on the armoire?"

"I previewed it on Friday in the Prickled Curiosities tent. I examined it then, and opened the door. I was going to bid on it at the auction but then . . . you know . . . a body fell out of it."

Sergeant Washington slapped the table in front of me. "Why are you at so many of Sergeant Fenton's crime scenes?"

"Bad luck."

"Your name is all over her reports."

I locked my eyes on Amber's new partner who seemed out to get both of us. "Wouldn't that prove she's following protocol?"

Kieran turned a page. "Did Sergeant Fenton call you the night of Mr. Whipple's death?"

"Yes."

"Why?"

"She had been dispatched to the auction house, and she called to see if I was there."

"Why would she suppose you'd be there?"

"The odds were good?"

Officer Viola pointed one of her gold-glitter nails at my face. "Do you think this is a joke?"

"I wouldn't put it in an opening monologue . . ."

Out of the corner of my eye I saw Amber's lip twitch and she had to lock it down.

Kieran closed the folder in front of him. "Did you at any time, on the day in question, have contact with Sergeant Fenton before the call came into the police station? Perhaps to tip her off privately that a crime was in progress?"

"No. But wouldn't that be a good thing for a citizen to do?"

"Did she send you to the auction house to look around before she arrived?"

"No."

"Did she ask you to hide any evidence for her eyes only?"

"No!"

Kieran tapped the folder with his index finger. He pulled a plastic bag out of his suit jacket. "Can you explain what this is? It was found at the scene and it has your fingerprints on it." My stomach bottomed out and that funnel cake muffin threatened to spring back up. He pulled out the horrid wooden troll I had thrown away and placed it before me. It taunted me with its evil grin inside the evidence bag.

I felt my face heat with the fire of a thousand suns. "That's just a little trinket I bought as a joke." *It turned out the joke was on me . . .*

Viola leaned across the table with her elbows up like a praying mantis in striking distance. "Then why did you throw it away?"

"Buyer's remorse."

Kieran tried to peer through my soul with his intense blue eyes. "Ten feet away from where the deceased was discovered in the armoire you were planning to bid on?"

"Yep. Would you want to keep a souvenir from that memory?"

Kieran crossed his arms over his chest and sat back.

I was getting a little agitated. "Why is that even in here? Is it the murder weapon? Did you bring my empty cup and gum wrapper too?"

The captain held up a hand. "Okay now, settle down. We check everything suspicious."

I may not have historically been the most willing participant, but I had helped the police of Cape May with more than a couple murders. "Am I a suspect?"

Amber snorted. "No."

But Viola nodded emphatically. "Oh, most definitely."

I looked from her to Kieran. "I'd known Auggie Whipple for less than a week. Why would I kill him? How did I get into the locked storage room of the locked auction house to steal the murder weapon? Sneak up on him, stab him, then hide the body in the one item that I had bid on for the following day? Then return to the auction and put suspicion on myself when the body was found? And why would I answer my phone when Amber called, and admit that I was at the crime scene not three feet away from the victim instead of being on the next flight to Mexico?"

The three of them remained silent, then Kieran looked at Amber. "I see what you mean."

Amber returned a slight nod. "Mm-hm."

I was fired up and couldn't stop myself now that I had the floor. Plus, I wanted to say just about anything to distract them from asking follow-up questions about my phony magical curse-breaking troll that looked like it would come to life under the next blood moon. "The questions you should be asking are how did Auggie's body end up in a locked room with his key still in his pocket? And where is Grover Prickle?"

After a moment of reflection, Captain Kieran snapped up the manila folder and stood. He handed me the awful troll doll that was now cleared to be mine to take home again. "Ms. McAllister, thank you for your time. I'm sorry for any inconvenience we may have caused you. We take our code of conduct very seriously and some changes have recently been implemented. We still have a few growing pains. Sergeant Fenton, please show Ms. McAllister out. Sergeant Washington, you're with me."

When he and Viola had left the room, Amber and I stared silently at each other. *Whoever thought in a million years that one day we'd be here?*

"So, how are things going with the new partner?"

Amber's face remained impassive. "Peachy." She led me through the door and towards the exit. "Thanks for coming down. I know during our investigations in the past you've been very . . ."

"Helpful?"

"I was going to say intrusive."

"Well, that's just rude."

Amber ignored me. "But Captain Dunne has Viola stationed so far up my . . ."

"Assault and battery." Officer Welkens handed Amber a new folder as he passed us in the hall.

"I see." We were back at the front desk and I was collecting my personal items.

Amber handed me my ID card. "One more thing before you go. How well did you know Auggie Whipple?"

"Barely. He's Mrs. Davis's nephew. I just met him at a dinner party I was forced to go to with his family."

"How were they?"

"Weird. There were a couple squabbles over some of their antiques, and dinner never actually materialized, but other than that they seemed like a normal loving family."

Amber raised an eyebrow. "Hm. In my experience, that's how you know they weren't."

CHAPTER 19

Aunt Ginny and I stood on Courtney's front porch holding a cherry pie. I pressed the doorbell and blew out a nervous breath. "Are you sure we should be doing this? We aren't family."

"We're Thelma's family and that's good enough."

The door swung open and Josephine met us in a floor-length black satin gown, her face covered in black netting from a slim fascinator clipped in her stiff hair. "Virginia, Poppy, so good of you to come."

I handed her the condolence pie. "We're so sorry for your loss, Josephine."

The black veil nodded. "We're all just heartbroken. Auggie was such a good boy. He was like the son I never had. Who would do something so malicious?"

Aunt Ginny cradled Josephine's hand and gave it a little pat. "Is there anything we can do, dear?"

"No. We have everything we need. Why don't you come in? I'm sure Courtney would love to see you."

Courtney was slumped on the sitting room couch next to June. The same spot where Auggie had sat just a week ago, inviting us to the auction where he died. My throat constricted just stepping into the room. Courtney struggled to his feet to receive a hug from Aunt Ginny.

We took seats, and Aunt Ginny said a few things that we all knew would bring little comfort considering the long road of pain that was before him, but Courtney received them in the spirit with which they were intended.

"He was a good boy. Never gave anyone a bit of trouble, my Auggie." Courtney choked up and could say no more.

June reached up and took his hand. "He was the best brother a girl could have."

Are we talking about the same Auggie I met the other night? 'Cause he had claimed most of the items in the house to take them from you when his father died.

Tildy came in with a tray of cookies and stopped short when she spotted us. "Oh, hello again." She placed the tray on the coffee table in front of Courtney and June.

Josephine sat on the other side of June and put her hand out to Tildy. "Come on in and sit down, honey. You've done enough."

Tildy took a seat on the ottoman. "I made oatmeal chocolate chip, your favorite, Courtney."

Courtney gave his stepdaughter a tremulous smile. "Thank you, hon. I don't think I could eat a thing just yet."

Josephine turned to me and Aunt Ginny. "Tildy deals with pain and stress by baking."

Aunt Ginny nodded. "So does my Poppy."

Josephine looked me up and down, pausing at my midsection. "Yes, I figured as much."

Ouch. What did I do? Now I want my pie back.

Tildy gave me a timid smile. "Spencer will be so sorry he missed you. He had to go out for a bit of air."

Josephine was a woman obviously not used to tact and once again it seemed to elude her. "This is no time for his ridiculous schemes. He should be here with you right now. Your brother was brutally murdered by some madman. You're in mourning."

A sharpness fell on the room and both Tildy and Courtney teared up.

Tildy's lip trembled and she stood up so quickly, the edge of her polka-dot skirt brushed the cookies and dragged a trail of melted chocolate across the table. "Excuse me, please." She ran from the room with a sob and disappeared down the hall.

June shook her head in disgust. "For god's sake, can't you be civil for one day?" Then she stood up and strode out the front door.

Josephine's hands shot in the air. "Now what is wrong with those two?" She scooted towards Courtney and put her arm around his shoulders. "Darling, do you need anything?"

He patted her on the knee and gave her a tremulous smile. "No, honey. I'm fine."

It was an awkward family moment and I found myself looking around to avoid looking right at them. My eyes fell on the mantel over the fireplace. *What the . . .* I immediately looked away, then glanced back again.

Aunt Ginny narrowed her eyes and gave me the tiniest of head shakes. She mouthed, "What?"

I made sure Courtney and Josephine were still distracted, then cast my eyes back to the mantel. There in the center, in pride of place, was the antique box that Mrs. Davis's great-grandmother had schlepped out of Russia in a sack under her dress or something like that.

Aunt Ginny's eyes followed mine. She gasped and started to choke. We had just seen that box in our kitchen a few nights ago after Mrs. Davis stole it from the garden party in my big leather tote bag.

Courtney's attention turned to Aunt Ginny. "Virginia, what's wrong?"

Aunt Ginny was patting her chest. She looked at me with wild eyes.

I jumped to my feet. "I'll just get her some water from the kitchen if that's okay?"

Josephine waved her hand behind her. "Yes, of course. I don't need a second death in one week. Especially not on my Persian rug."

You gotta have your priorities . . .

Aunt Ginny gave me a piercing look as I passed her. She croaked out a couple fake coughs and jerked her head towards the kitchen for me to go check on Tildy.

I found Tildy spooning out another batch of cookie dough with a shaky hand. She sniffled. "Baking relaxes me."

I leaned against the counter. "I know what you mean. My former mother-in-law inspired many loaves of bread."

Tildy smiled. "Are you divorced?"

I shook my head. "My husband passed away."

She paused with the cookie scoop hovering over the tray. "Oh. I'm so sorry. That was thoughtless of me."

I shrugged it off. "No, of course it wasn't. You didn't know."

She put the scoop in the bowl. "How long did it take you to . . . get over it?"

"I'm still working on it. I don't know if you ever get over the loss, but you make peace with it. John has been gone over a year and a half now. Aunt Ginny helps. And Gia. He's brought a lot of joy into my life."

Tildy bent and put the tray of cookies in the oven. "I'm worried about Courtney. He's having a rough time."

"That's to be expected."

She lowered her voice. "His last conversation with Auggie was an argument."

"Oh dear. When was that?"

"The night before Auggie disappeared. He came home a little after midnight after he'd been out drinking. Mom has strict rules that we need to be in by eleven or stay somewhere else so we don't disturb her, since she's a very light sleeper. He left the next morning before anyone was up."

"That's going to be rough to get over. Do you know what they argued about?"

She shrugged. "Something about the antique store. I don't think things were going as well as Auggie said. I don't know what the problem was, but Courtney was very disappointed that Auggie had been hiding something."

"That doesn't sound good."

"I know. They were so close, it wasn't like Auggie not to ask Courtney for advice when he had a problem."

"What will happen now? Will you take over running the store?"

Tildy spoke through a laugh. "What? Me? I don't know anything about antiques. I'm a children's librarian.

Ask me anything you want about the Newbery Medal, but the family business was just for Auggie and June."

"I was wondering why I didn't see you at the auction."

"Auctions are not my thing. I found the cutest little shop on the mall called Petit Pois and I was shopping for baby clothes all morning. For someday." Her voice quivering at the end.

I wanted to ask her more, but Josephine swept into the kitchen and pulled off her mourning veil.

"We were out shopping all day. We found the most darling little onesies, didn't we, love?"

Tildy smiled dreamily. "One has a little duck face on the heinie flap."

"You should go get it and show Poppy." Josephine dug out a chunk of chocolate from the cookie dough and popped it in her mouth. "We didn't even hear the dreadful news until Courtney called from Blake's. Poor Courtney was all alone."

"Well, his sister was there."

Josephine made a face that squished her lips and eyebrows closer together. "Thelma doesn't count."

I wanted to say something in Mrs. Davis's defense, but under the circumstances it seemed inappropriate.

Tildy looked at Josephine. "Did you need something, Mom?"

Josephine took a seat on the barstool. "I came to check on Poppy. It sure is taking you a long time to get that glass of water. I thought Virginia was about to pass out."

"Oh, I almost forgot. Is she okay?" *And has she finished her snooping?*

"Courtney's getting her a tea and bourbon from the liquor cabinet in the living room. She's fine."

We heard the front door open and shut, and a few seconds later Spencer entered the kitchen and dropped a stack of real estate fliers on the island. "Awesome! Poppy's here. I want to get your opinion about a house on Hughes, since you'd have the inside scoop."

Do I look like I work for RE/MAX?

Spencer took down a glass and filled it with water. "I was canvassing the neighborhood yesterday morning looking for a good site for a B and B and I think this place would be perfect."

I know everyone deals with grief differently, but this just seems cold for a brother-in-law. "Did you call a Realtor?"

He took out his cell phone and started swiping through his photos. "Naw. I wanted to get a feel for the neighborhood by myself."

Tildy turned to the sink and started washing the dishes. Josephine spread out the fliers Spencer had brought home and rifled through them.

Spencer turned his phone to my face. "This one. I talked to the owner for a while, but they seemed put off by my questions. Do you know how much they want for it?"

I pushed the phone away from my eyes to get a look at a lovely Queen Anne I'd passed many times on my exercise route. "Is this on the market?"

Spencer took a long drink from his glass. "No. Do you know the owners? Do you think they'd be interested in selling?"

"I rather think if they were interested in selling—the house would be for sale, Spencer."

Josephine swept the pile of fliers into the trash. "You need to quit this foolishness and get a real job. You're never going to make this work, any more than that pudding-truck fiasco. Stop these get-rich-quick schemes and start a family. For cripes sake, you've been married for ten years now. Tildy's clock is ticking so loud it's keeping me up at night!"

Tildy had tears in her eyes. "Mom, please."

Spencer's face turned scarlet. He threw his glass across the room and it shattered against the door that led out to the garden.

Tildy ducked and covered her head even though she was nowhere near the door.

"You don't know anything! I am successful, and I already have an investor lined up for my B and B. You didn't know that, did you?"

I looked for any path of escape that didn't take me through the field of broken glass. I excused myself and slipped into the breakfast nook and out the back door onto a screened porch. I pulled out my own cell phone and checked the time. I had way too much to do to be spending my day with this insanity. *Maybe I can get Sawyer to call me with a fake emergency. She owes me a BFF coffee anyway.*

"They finally got to you in there, didn't they?" June was lounging on a round wicker sofa off to my side, her feet up on a floral pillow.

She'd startled me so badly that my phone slipped, and I accidentally opened Angry Birds. I was so relieved that I hadn't called Sawyer to complain about the Whipples. If June hadn't spoken, I might be neck deep in humiliation right now. I tucked my phone back into my pocket. "Oh, hey. This porch is beautiful. I bet you spend a lot of time out here."

June had her phone up to her ear. She lifted a finger.

"Yeah, it's me. I'll be delayed a few days. I have to bury my brother. He was murdered. We don't know yet, but I'll fill you in when I get back. Believe me, I don't want to stay in this hell hole one minute longer than I have to. I just want to make sure Sam and Dianne are okay. Give them kisses for me." She clicked her phone off and tossed it away from her on the sofa. "My dog sitter. Have you ever hated a place so much it made you physically ill to be there?"

"Yes." *This house. Right now.*

She indicated for me to sit across from her. "Where was it?"

"Cape May. I still can't believe I've moved home again. I spent the last twenty-five years in Virginia."

She nodded vigorously. "I can't stand the beach. It brings back too many bad memories. Were you cheated on?"

"Uh. Not exactly." *But awfully close.*

"How can you stand to come back? And you live here year-round."

"Everything changed when I met Gia and fell in love again."

June crossed her arms and looked out the window to watch the hummingbirds. "I don't believe in love. I almost let my guard down, but not anymore. People don't really change. Even when they try to convince you otherwise."

The screen door opened, and Courtney stepped in from the garden with a giant basket of vegetables. "There you are. Look what I got for you here. Some of my heirloom tomatoes, some kohlrabi, there's even a melon in there. Ginny asked me to find you and tell you she has your purse and she's waiting by the car."

I took the offered basket and forced myself not to groan. "Thank you. You've been much too kind with your garden. Really. If there is anything you need, please give us a call."

"I will. You're a good girl, like my June Bug."

I waved goodbye and exited into the garden. When a purple hat shot up from behind the tomato plants, I got startled, and a kohlrabi launched from the basket. Mrs. Humphries dropped a scoop of soil from her garden spade into a Cool Whip container. She scowled at me, daring me to challenge her. Then she held her hat and scuttled through the fence and back to her own yard, her flowered garden apron billowing out a cloud of dirt around her.

CHAPTER 20

"I thought I would black out from all that fake coughing before I could get everyone to leave the room in search of water. You better believe I checked out that jewelry box."

"Is it the same one?"

Aunt Ginny pursed her lips and gave me a nod. "The nerve of that woman."

I turned the corner for home and found our driveway blocked by a yellow convertible. My orange traffic cone was sticking out from under its front tire. "I wonder if Mrs. Davis knows it's missing yet."

Aunt Ginny waved her cell phone. "She does now. I just sent her the picture."

"Don't you think it's odd that Spencer doesn't seem to be mourning his brother-in-law? Or do you think that temper is misplaced grief?" I parked in Mr. Winston's driveway until I could get into mine. He would recognize the Corvette and be able to call me to move it if he needed to leave. I'd have to take him some of my peanut butter fudge cupcakes later to say thank you.

Aunt Ginny waved the question off. "Beats me. That whole family has always been odd."

By the time we got through the front door, Aunt Ginny had called the dowager network and they were making plans to meet later to strategize.

That sounds ominous. I don't want to know.

I looked into the library and didn't see the happy hour tray set out and it was already a quarter past four. Joanne was snapping her fanny pack into place as I entered the kitchen. "Did you put out the wine and cheese?"

She was rocking her usual vibe of irritation. "I put it out and ten minutes later it was gone off the face of the earth. I have no idea what happened to it."

"Well, who's in the house?"

Her lip curled and she snarled at me. "I don't know. I'm too busy doing the job Ginny hired me to do to babysit your thieving guests."

That's it. I'm making a sign. I let my frustration propel me to the front desk while I planned my scathing note for the happy hour tray. *If Santa is stealing my wine and cheese I may just go to my room and stay there until they check out.*

There was a message on the yellow pad by the phone.

Marty Robbins wants you to schedule a parasailing lesson for them. Also, someone named Pauline called to say she has to talk to you down at Cold

*Spring Village, but you have to be there before six
when she packs up.*

I hollered down the hall. "Joanne! Why didn't you call
me about this?"

Joanne threw some vinegar on her reply. "Because I'm
not your secretary." She walked past me while she put on
her sunglasses. "And I'm not your friend. Answer your
own phone." She shut the front door behind her so loud
that Figaro ran down the hall to investigate.

The girls trotted after him with toys in their mouths.
Cleo twitched her nose, crinkling a velvet mouse with a
feather tail and Sveltelana meowed through the giant
Chewbacca mouse in her jaws. They dropped the gifts at
his feet and waited to see which he would accept.

Figaro appraised the mice like Caesar debating whether
to give thumbs-up or thumbs-down to the gladiators. He
went with the passive-aggressive cold shoulder and walked
away. Cleo picked up her mouse and trotted after him.
Sveltelana looked to me.

"You don't want to be a doormat. Make him come to
you."

She squinted at me and curled up on my feet.

"But for future reference, his favorite is the ratty little
chicken with the catnip inside."

Since I was pinned to the floor by a mountain lion, I
took out my cell phone and called Gia. "Hey, I have to
run to Cold Spring Village to look at something. Wanna
come along?"

"For you, anything, *cara mia*. Cameron! Leave Sierra
alone." Gia chuckled. "He was about to snap a towel at
her."

"What lady doesn't love a good locker room welt?"

"I asked her if she wanted me to make him stop and she said she would handle it. I think she likes making him suffer. I also caught her putting mint syrup on his pizza he brought for lunch, so I think she's teasing him as much as he's flirting. I will pick you up as soon as I get the *tourist* blocking me in to move."

I made the parasailing reservation and put a new platter of fruit and cheese in the library. I considered adding a LoJack to the platter, but that would probably disappear too. I grabbed my purse and went outside. The twins had come down and were sitting on the rockers chatting away about the mysteries of life and Ryan Gosling. I asked them how their day was going, and they replied in unison, "Lovely."

Two young women came down the street with shopping bags in their arms and spotted me at the end of my driveway behind their convertible.

"I do hope my orange traffic cone didn't damage anything under your car when you plowed over it to block my driveway."

They didn't make eye contact; they looked away immediately muttering a feeble, "Sorry."

When they pulled away from the curb, I knew I had a very small window to move my car. I rushed over to Mr. Winston's across the street and backed Bessie into my driveway. Gia pulled up at the same time I was closing the garage door. I put out a new orange cone that would probably be destroyed before Tuesday, and a new sign to be ignored that said, *Please don't block the driveway*. Then I waved goodbye to Grace and Faith and hopped into the Spider.

We were bound for Cold Spring Village to find out what Pauline thought was so urgent that I needed to be there before closing. I sat back on the leather seat and something hard jabbed me in the side. I pulled my purse away from my hip. Two beady eyes glared at me from under bushy white yak hair. The good-luck troll doll was sticking out of my bag giving me the evil eye. Now I had two booths to stop at before six.

CHAPTER 21

Gia and I walked hand in hand towards the Prickled Curiosities tent. I passed the bakery and the ice cream shop and stopped in the middle of the lane, looking around frantically.

Gia watched me with a smile playing on his lips. "What is wrong?"

"She was right here."

"Who was?"

"The swindler who sold me the protection-against-crime-scenes talisman."

I had rooted to the spot where she should have been. Instead of a blue tent selling charms, an orange canopy labeled Curious Cats had sprung up overnight. From the looks of the shelves, the vendor specialized in everything feline. Vintage cat clocks, cat statues, cat lunch boxes, Garfield phones and Felix the Cat race cars. This wasn't what I wanted to find right now. *What am I going to do with this horrid little troll?*

"You want me to buy you that pink panther statue? Maybe he will bring better luck."

"I'm pretty sure that's felt glued onto a light bulb and a soda bottle. I can see the words Dr. Pepper through the paint."

"You could probably make that."

"Henry could probably make that."

From behind us, someone called my name. I looked over my shoulder and spotted Pauline in the lane waving me forward. "Hurry. Someone is looking at the armoire and I can't hold them off for long."

We followed after Grover's pretty little assistant, past the tent that belonged to Whipple's Antique Emporium. The tent had been cleared out and a few bouquets of flowers and a teddy bear sat on the lone folding table. It was all that remained from the grand announcement three days earlier.

A security guard stood in the entryway of Prickled Curiosities. Pauline thanked him for watching the stall and motioned to a mirrored Louis the Sixteenth armoire. "This is what I wanted to show you. It isn't the exact same piece you wanted to bid on, but I thought you might like it. One of our buyers just picked it up from an estate sale in Pennsylvania yesterday. I had him bring it here instead of the shop. Blake will auction it for us next week if you aren't interested."

A plump woman in middle age circled around the armoire, giving it a thorough examination.

Pauline shifted her eyes. "You'd better speak up. I have a feeling about this one."

I walked over to the armoire and opened the door. I stood back in case a body was in there because—fool me once. The armoire was empty and smelled of wood and mothballs. I nodded at Gia, then looked at the tag and my heart missed a pump when I saw the suggested selling price. There was no way I could afford that.

Pauline slipped me a Post-it with a number half the amount written in purple ink. I showed Gia. "What do you think?"

"It is beautiful, and it would be an investment, but it is not my decision."

"It might kill Georgina if I spend that much operating capital."

"Are you trying to talk yourself into it or out?"

I giggled. I handed Pauline the sticky note and nodded.

She grinned and took a sold card over to the armoire and hung it on the knob.

The woman who had been circling, groaned and left the shop. I felt bad for her. I was usually the one in her pink aerobic shoes—leaving disappointed.

Pauline blew out a breath. "Phew. I'm so glad you got here in time."

I gestured to the armoire. "So, this is what you wanted to talk to me about? Not the murder?"

Pauline looked like a deer frozen in headlights. "Yes. Of course. This is a beautiful piece. I know we could get triple that price at auction, but I feel so bad about the other night. It was the least I could do. And my way of saying thank you, for . . . you know."

"It's no problem. I've been a person of interest with the police before, and it's no fun. Have you heard anything from Grover yet?"

Pauline's lip trembled. She flipped her sales receipts to a new page and started filling one out. "No. And I'm so worried. I keep waiting for him to call and tell me he's okay." Her voice broke and a tear slipped down her cheek.

"I hope wherever he is, that he's well." I filled out my part of the sales slip while two attractive women came into the booth. They were interested in a tall Italian piece that was about forty years old and would look great in the bedroom. I wanted to tell them that this piece was priceless, and he was already taken. Still, they flirted and giggled and tossed their hair. Gia was polite. He edged closer to me and drummed his fingers on the table next to mine.

I looked up from my transaction and the women appraised me. When the whispering started, I felt my self-confidence take a jab. I tried to swallow my insecurity. This would be my life with Gia. It wasn't easy dating a man who was so attractive. *If I can't lose weight, maybe I can get him to pudge out some.*

I was reminded of Aunt Ginny's words that no one can make you feel bad about yourself unless you let them. *Don't give anyone that power.*

I handed Pauline my credit card and she rang me up. Gia put his arm around my waist and kissed me on the temple.

Pauline handed me the card. "Can I have it delivered tomorrow?"

"Could you hold it until next Sunday? I can't get it in the room until the current guests check out."

"Of course. I promise to keep it safe."

Hopefully not like the last one. "Pauline? How do you think Auggie ended up in the other armoire?"

Pauline's eyes widened like a camera lens. "I have no idea."

"Are you sure the armoire was empty when you and Grover put it in the storage room Friday night?"

"I'm sure it was, or we would have had a lot more trouble moving it."

That sounds reasonable. "What about the flag?"

Pauline lowered her voice. "Grover took that home with him. He didn't trust it to go in the storage room where he couldn't keep an eye on it. He'd become pretty paranoid about Auggie stealing from him lately."

"So, how'd it get wrapped around Auggie?"

Pauline chewed her lip. "Maybe Grover took it up Saturday morning when Blake opened at ten and . . ." She swallowed hard. "And Auggie's killer grabbed it?"

"Maybe. Do *you* have a key to the storage room?"

She shook her head. "Prickled Curiosities only has one key and Grover holds onto it. They're over a hundred years old. You can't make copies without damaging them."

Gia blew out a breath. "A hundred-year-old key?"

"You're serious?"

She nodded. "There's an antique dead bolt installed on the storage room door. We have one of the brass keys, and Auggie has—or had—one."

The women came up to the table to purchase a box of antique silver spoons and get a better look at Gia, so we said goodbye.

As we were leaving the tent, I whispered, "What kind of security is a hundred-year-old dead bolt?"

Gia grabbed my elbow. "Shh."

I stopped and followed his nod. On the far side of Whipple's empty tent was Blake Adams the auctioneer, and he had June Whipple cornered—his finger jabbing towards her chest. Her face was scarlet, and she looked to be in tears. June slapped Blake across the face, then fled from the tent down the bakery lane. Blake stormed off towards the blacksmith.

I slipped my hand in Gia's. "Yikes. What do you suppose that was about?"

"That was a fight between two people who have slept together."

"What? You can't tell that by watching them."

"Of course, you can. Passion has two sides. You do not get that much hate unless at one time there was love."

"I sure hope that isn't in our future."

He pulled me close and kissed me. "*Cara mia*, my passion for you is not so quickly fleeting."

"It had better not be."

"Come. Let's get a drink before we have to return to crazy."

We walked to the end of the road and down a short path to the restored barn. It was very rustic with an exposed beam ceiling and hewn-oak timber floor. We made our way up to the bar and ordered two sarsaparillas, the house specialty. I wanted to order it like Daffy Duck, but Gia and I haven't dated long enough to pull that out yet.

Blake was sitting at the bar nursing a drink of his own. He was muttering to himself and shaking his head.

Gia gave him a nod and took the seat next to him. "Women, huh?" Gia gave me a wink and I accidentally snorted sarsaparilla foam.

Blake was all in. "How are we supposed to know what they want when they don't know what they want?"

Gia grunted in manly agreement.

Blake threw his palms up. "And God forbid you do something wrong—they'll never forgive you without a notarized witness statement."

Gia nodded. "I saw you arguing with Auggie's sister. She must really be putting you through it."

I bet he doesn't even know her. He was probably coming on to her.

"She's my ex-wife."

Oh. Never mind.

Gia stayed cool. "Really? Auggie was your brother-in-law?"

Blake knocked his drink back and took a swallow. "Yep. Until a year ago."

Gia was being far too subtle. I leaned across him. "Was it Josephine? 'Cause I've had a Josephine and it's not easy."

Blake chuckled. "She's a piece of work alright. The kind of woman who'd star in Nazi training videos. But, no, June and I had bigger issues than just her stepmother."

I really wanted to ask more but it felt incredibly rude to question a near stranger why his marriage failed. *I'll ask Mrs. Davis later.* "Have the police made any advancement in the investigation?"

Blake shook his head. "Not that I know of."

I already knew they hadn't. It would have been all over town by now. "I'm really concerned about Grover Prickle. I hope he isn't hurt somewhere." *Or destroying evidence.*

When he didn't answer I prodded him a little more. "His assistant said she still hasn't seen or heard from him since the night before the auction."

Blake gave us a weird shrug. "I don't know where he

is. But you could check his store. Prickled Curiosities over in West Cape May. He doesn't have any family. If he isn't sick or dead, that's where he'll be."

Gia's pocket vibrated and we both groaned. "I am not going to look at it."

"You have to. What if it's Henry?"

His lips tightened. "We both know it is not Henry." He pulled the phone from his pocket, checked the screen and sighed before answering. "*Ciao,* Momma."

Blake looked across Gia to me and gave me a sympathetic look.

"His mother. She and Josephine would be good friends."

Blake pursed his lips and went back to his drink.

Gia listened for a minute then hung up and jammed his phone in his pocket. "I am sorry, but we have to go. Momma say she is having heart attack. I do not believe her this time, but we should hurry."

Let's not be hasty. I would not say I was hopeful. I wasn't evil. I didn't want her to die. But maybe a near-death experience would remove that stick she had shoved up her Mussolini.

I grabbed my purse and got down from the barstool. "Maybe we can give her some of my kohlrabi and tell her it's a miracle cure."

Gia laughed. "Oh no. You are not getting out of it that easy. I want to see what you come up with to get rid of it."

"Be careful what you wish for. You might end up getting it baked in a cake."

We said goodbye to Blake, then teased each other all the way to the parking lot. We came down the lane to a clearing and I pulled Gia into a tent selling Depression glass and pointed.

June was pinned against a silver BMW, flirting with another man. We could tell by the way his head was moving that the man was talking. Then the man put his hand up and gently curled a lock of June's hair behind her ear.

I whispered. "What is she up to?"

Someone dropped a milk-glass bowl and the man turned in our direction.

I gasped. "Oh no. It's Spencer."

CHAPTER 22

I spent the rest of the evening baking for both the B&B and the coffee shop with Figaro sitting on the counter judging me. He had both stuffed mice the girls had been trying to lure him with under his feet. I was just relieved he'd lost the red scrunchie. I could tell he was hiding from the ladies because he kept looking at the door on the chance they sniffed him out.

I finally carried Figaro up to bed and turned out the light, when a loud thump followed by a crash startled me awake. I checked the time, ten after midnight. Figaro was curled up on the pillow next to me. He cracked one eye open as if to say, *It's your turn*.

Spooky chanting came from outside my door, shocking me upright. I grabbed my robe and threw it on like a cape. When I hurled my bedroom door open, I could see light flickering from one of the spare bedrooms down the hall.

"Come . . . Come to me . . ."

The bedroom door across from me opened and Georgina peeked one side of her face out and hissed, "That better be you making that racket."

I shook my head and listened.

There it was again. "Spirit. Come to us . . ."

"Does that sound like me?" I grabbed the Louisville Slugger I kept by my door and we crept down the hall together. Me in my Daffy Duck shorty pajamas and Georgina two steps behind me in her . . ." What are you wearing?" I hissed.

Georgina's nose shot up in the air. "It's called a sleep sack, if you must know. It's silk, and it's from Paris."

"Well, it looks like a pillowcase with a drawstring around the knees."

I could see she was trying to come up with a smart reply, but we were interrupted by another chant. "This is a safe place. Follow the light . . ."

I threw the door open to the large bedroom. "What in the world are you doing?" Elaine Grabstein was sitting cross-legged in the middle of the floor with all the ladies in the house. Shondra Martins, Grace and Faith Padawowski, Marty Robbins, and Jenna Foubert. They had lit a circle of candles that were dripping wax on my hundred-and-forty-year-old wood floor.

"Oh, sorry, doll. Did we wake ya?"

Georgina snapped rather testily and closed the door behind her. "What do you think?"

Just breathe, Poppy. I flipped the light switch and turned on the ancient glass fixture overhead. I tried to soften my voice. "What are you all doing in here?"

Marty Robbins looked like she was having the time of

her life. Her eyes were twinkling, and she gave me a glee-ful smile. "We're having a séance. Do you want to join us?"

One of the twins nodded and her fluffy white hair bobbed like a dollop of Cool Whip on Jell-O. "We're try-ing to help a lost spirit to cross over."

I was almost speechless. "How did you all get on the third floor?"

Shondra Martins wouldn't look me in the eye, and Jenna Foubert blossomed pink up to her blond scalp. "We took down the rope. I'm sorry."

The other twin wasn't as enthusiastic about their mid-night foray as her sister. She looked a little green. "How did you find us?"

I pointed to the baseball bat down the hall. "My bed-room is literally thirty feet away, and sound travels."

The door opened and Aunt Ginny popped in, breath-less. She was wearing her emerald-green crushed velvet cape and a matching turban she must have dug out of the back of her closet. "Did I miss it? I got the incense, but I can't find the base." She realized I was standing there and tried to hide the fuzzy stick behind her back. "Oh. The fun killer is here."

"Did you approve this?"

She lowered her voice and leaned in to me. "Don't ruin this for me." Then she took a long look at Georgina. "What is that? A pillowcase?"

Georgina wrapped her arms over her chest. "It's a French sleep sack. It's very IN in Paris."

"So is eating horse."

Elaine rocked back and leaned away from the circle. "A presence has arrived."

Aunt Ginny dove on the circle and grabbed Jenna and Marty's hands, dropping the incense at my feet.

Elaine pitched forward. "I hear you, spirit. I know you are trapped. We are here to set you free now."

Georgina narrowed her eyes at the woman with the thick black-rimmed glasses. "This house is not haunted."

Aunt Ginny cocked her head to give me a gleeful smile. I hadn't seen her this excited since the Entenmann truck broke down around the corner and the driver had to give away fifty boxes of raspberry Danish twist.

Elaine's bracelets rattled and she grabbed Marty and a twin's hands and shook them overhead. "Poor little Siobhan, an immigrant servant girl from Ireland, died of smallpox in this house in 1920. Her spirit has been stuck in limbo and I can hear her moaning in pain."

I rolled my eyes on the inside. As far as I knew, no one had ever died in the house except from old age. "I think the moaning you've been hearing is someone not used to manual labor getting ready for bed."

Georgina harrumphed much like Miss Piggy would have done.

The ladies looked at me with pleading in their eyes, except for Elaine who was swaying back and forth, caught up in the spirit world.

"Make sure you blow out the candles, and keep it down, and you can stay. But after tonight, please respect the velvet rope. This floor is off-limits for a reason."

Georgina loosened her drawstring and lifted her sleep sack above her knees and stomped off in her usual snit of complaint. The ladies agreed to my terms and promised to be quiet.

I shut the door behind me and was about to go back to my room when the front doorbell rang. *This better not be another pizza.*

I ran down the stairs and opened the door to find the

Hunan Palace delivery boy holding out an oily bag. "Thirty-six twenty-five, please. You very lucky. We about to close."

I paid him and took the bag, added the amount to Burl Grabstein's bill, and left the sack outside the Purple Emperor Suite in a produce box. *If Elaine doesn't find it soon, I know three cats who will be full of lo mein by morning.*

CHAPTER 23

Goose bumps prickled on my arms as I stared into the abyss of evil. Not just the eyes of evil, but the frizzy yak hair of evil. I knew I had left that crime scene talisman in my purse when I returned home from the police station yesterday, but it had found its way to the kitchen and was sitting on my gluten-free cinnamon bread. "Are you sure you aren't playing a trick on me?"

Joanne flipped a blueberry pancake and snickered. "I don't have time for your childish games. One of us has to make breakfast for ten guests and the staff—and God knows you aren't going to do it."

Who does she think did it before she got here? I opened the junk drawer and swept the troll on top of the takeout menus and bread ties. I slammed the drawer shut, poured myself another cup of coffee, considered Aunt Ginny's stash of Irish Cream, and checked the sausages in the oven. There was nothing to worry about.

Nope, I'm definitely worried.

Thank God for Joanne working the griddle or these guests would have had yogurt and cereal for breakfast this morning. They kept me up half the night trying to convince poor little Siobhan to cross over. I could hear Aunt Ginny's giggles all the way from my room. She didn't believe for one minute that her father ever had an Irish servant girl in the house, but she loved drama like celebrities loved rehab.

Victory stumbled in the back door painted pink with calamine lotion. Her hands were wrapped tightly around something she held out in front of her. "Luik what I feind!"

I sipped my coffee, in carefree oblivion. "What is that?"

She opened her hands, and a giant brown frog blew out his throat and croaked. "*BRROOOAK.*"

"Eis frog!"

Joanne threw her hands in the air and wailed. "Sweet Norma Jean!"

I recoiled. "Eww! Get that outside, Victory."

Victory held the frog out further, sure we were confused. "But eis jus leittle frog."

"*BRROOOAK.*" The frog jumped from Victory's hands and landed in the pancake batter with a splash.

Joanne ran a lap around the island waving her hands over her head. "Getitout—getitout—getitout!"

I recoiled further. "It's in the pancakes! Take that out of here!"

Victory plunged her hand into the bowl and pulled a battered frog from the mix.

"*BRROOOAK.*"

She ran him under cool water. "Aww, now he steicky."

I shooed my hand at her. "Well, get him away from my kitchen."

Victory wrapped her frog in paper towels and removed him from our presence. I cleaned up the mess while Joanne sat in the corner and rocked back and forth muttering about bug eyes and slime.

I snickered. "You're afraid of frogs."

She pointed her whisk at me very ominously. "You shut up!" She picked up the mixing bowl and dumped the batter into the sink to start again.

I was still giggling when the front door chimed, and a ruckus rolled down the hall in a haze of menthol and Coppertone. The biddies had arrived. They rounded the kitchen in one-piece bathing suits and plastic sun visors, their seagrass beach bag ready to fill up with free snacks from Poppy's general store. "Hello, ladies."

Mrs. Davis pushed to the front of the group holding up two envelopes. "Poppy. Look at what arrived at Courtney's house last night. It was delivered to the neighbor by mistake. I told him he had to let me show you."

I put my coffee down and took the offered envelopes. "The Law Offices of Doonan and Mooney." I opened the first and pulled out a crisp white sheet. It was a demand letter from Grover Prickle's lawyer threatening a lawsuit over the ownership of the antique vampire-hunting kit. The other was a letter written by Grover to Courtney.

I know everything. Call off your boy or I'll go to the press. It would be a shame to ruin the reputation of Whipple's Antique Emporium because you can't control your son. Dirty little secrets have ways of leaking out.

I turned the envelopes over to look at the date stamps. They were mailed the day before Auggie was killed.

Aunt Ginny dragged her bleary-eyed self into the kitchen and took the coffee out of my hands. "What's that all about?"

"Grover is insisting he's the rightful owner of the vampire box and he says Auggie stole it from Prickled Curiosities. He's suing for any proceeds that might come from the sale if the auction house doesn't honor his injunction."

Mrs. Davis forked two blueberry pancakes onto one of the heated plates Joanne had waiting next to the stove. "Courtney is just beside himself. Our name is being dragged through the mud."

Joanne tapped the counter and gave me a narrow glare while the biddies heaped up the breakfast she'd been preparing all morning.

I mouthed "Sorry." *At least we have the sausage.*

The timer on the oven rang and I held my breath.

Mrs. Dodson handed me the potholders. "Well, look at that. Just in time."

Joanne smirked that now we both had to start over. "Oh goody."

Mrs. Davis poured a hefty amount of blueberry syrup over her pancakes. "I mean it, Poppy. He needs your help."

I took the sausages out of the oven and set the pan on a rack. "My help? What can I do?"

Three felines appeared in the kitchen with a signed peace treaty and a chorus of meows.

Aunt Ginny was taking the sausages off the paper towels as fast as I could move them over. "You should know how to question someone and get them to spill the truth. You used to work in your late husband's law office."

"Yeah, they don't let you cross-examine the witnesses when you're the receptionist. Besides, no one knows where Grover Prickle is. And I doubt anything would have come from this. These letters from lawyers are usually just a scare tactic. Unless Grover had tangible proof that Auggie had stolen the box, there was nothing he could do. Possession is nine-tenths of the law. And if he did have proof of theft, it's both a lawsuit and a crime."

Mrs. Davis didn't look convinced. "What about the other letter threatening to go to the newspaper with a dirty little secret?"

I started laying another pack of sausage out on the sheet pan for round two in the oven. "Do you know what he was talking about?"

Mrs. Davis shook her head. "No idea. According to Courtney, Auggie was a pillar of Cape May society."

"The newspaper isn't going to just print libelous statements about a small-town antique store owner without evidence. They'd open themselves up to a defamation lawsuit."

Mother Gibson poured herself a cup of coffee. "What about Facebooks and the Tweeters?"

All the biddies and Joanne, who never liked me, looked up with *gotcha* in their eyes.

"Yeees, Grover could launch a social media firestorm against Auggie and Whipple's Antiques. But is that really likely?" I still hadn't climbed all the way out of the one that had been launched against me. Now the only guests I could get who didn't check reviews were ones who sleep-order delivery and hold seances in the attic.

Aunt Ginny pointed her fork at me. "Aha!"

I tried not to trip over the sea of cats spinning and sniffing in ecstasy to get to the oven. "But Auggie is dead and Grover is missing. I kind of think the moment to make good on these threats has passed."

The biddies weren't buying it. They shot off a list of arguments faster than Joanne was flipping pancakes onto a hot plate.

Mrs. Dodson nodded solemnly. "That just means Grover could shift his threats from Auggie to June or Courtney."

"No one knows if Grover's even alive."

Mother Gibson was still working her social media argument. "What if he's lying low until he gets his chance to destroy Whipple Antiques on the Internet? We live in wicked times. A lot of people would boycott them if some ugly secret was revealed. They don't need proof."

I tried to shoo away the cats but Figaro must have told the others that I would eventually cave. "If Grover is found, he'll have enough to worry about with the murder investigation. He'd be the prime suspect."

Aunt Ginny, always a master of manipulation, went straight for my heart. "If he runs loose with this slander, he could ruin Auggie's reputation. Hasn't Courtney been through enough?"

I set the timer for the pan of sausages and tried to back away from the frenzied mob. And the cats. "There are laws to protect the innocent from false accusations."

"What if Auggie isn't totally innocent?" Mrs. Davis's lip trembled. "What if Grover really does know something about Auggie that would bring shame on my family?"

"Then you'd better hope Grover is alive and well. After his fuss at the antique unveiling and that letter in your hands, Courtney could find himself under investigation, and you're holding his motive."

Aunt Ginny kept working me over. "Don't be ridiculous. Courtney couldn't hurt a flea. Grover has probably gone into hiding because he's guilty. Have you thought of that? You could bring him to justice."

I tossed a few cat treats on the floor to spread out the feline riot. "When will you all remember that I'm not the police? Every time I get involved it goes horribly wrong. You would never forgive me if I stumbled onto evidence that Courtney killed Grover because of that lawsuit."

Mrs. Dodson held her head high. "If you could prove it was a crime of passion, he could be acquitted like on that *L.A. Law* show."

We're getting legal advice from TV dramas now. "I don't think judges just forgive crimes of passion. Too many murderers would be walking around. People snap all the time when they're provoked." *At least that's what Amber keeps telling me like it's some kind of threat.*

Mrs. Davis gave me a look that was so pitiful it would put a basset hound to shame. "Poppy, please. Couldn't you just try to find Grover? If you could talk to him, business owner to business owner, I bet he would see reason. You just bought that armoire from his store. He'll listen to you."

"How do you know I bought an armoire?"

Joanne poured out another puddle of batter on the griddle and started to snicker.

Aunt Ginny blushed. "That girl may have called here last night to confirm delivery for next week and I let it slip."

I looked from one old lady to the next, suddenly refusing to make eye contact while they were silently plowing through my blueberry pancakes. "You all knew this all along, didn't you? This is a setup."

Mrs. Davis grinned like the chimpanzee of the week on *Wild Kingdom*. "Maybe you'll find something else nice in Prickled Curiosities to go with the armoire. I could buy it for you."

I felt my resolve melt like the butter on her pancakes. "I'm not making any promises. We don't even know how to find Grover Prickle."

Mrs. Dodson grabbed her cane and hoisted herself to standing. "Maybe you should check with that pretty little girl who works for him. We saw her huddled in the corner with the auctioneer last night at the Cold Spring Village Tavern, didn't we, girls?"

Mrs. Davis nodded excitedly. "She was on her cell phone, and when he went to the bathroom, we heard her say, 'Don't worry, boss. I'll take care of it.'"

I shook my head. "No, I was just there yesterday, and she told me she didn't know where Grover was."

Mother Gibson gave me a rueful grin. "Well then, child, she lied."

CHAPTER 24

"No. I'm staying out of it."

That's what I told the biddies two hours ago. Now Joanne and I were cleaning up from breakfast while Aunt Ginny and her besties made plans to run their own sting on Prickled Curiosities. They were planning a *Mission: Impossible*–style operation they called Strike Force Biddy. I knew I was being manipulated and I just let it happen. I was too tired to fight them. Once we had the guests out of the house, and Georgina was cleaning the bedrooms, I sat the biddies down and told them under no circumstances were they allowed to rappel on grappling hooks into Grover's store from the roof.

Aunt Ginny raised her hands in a shrug. "But what else are we to do? You won't help us."

"You're all being ridiculous. Stop laughing, Joanne. You're just egging them on."

Joanne's expression flattened out. "What? I'm just surprised you're not willing to help the women who've done so much to help you this past year."

The biddies all gave me looks of triumph.

"Medicare doesn't cover dangling from the ceiling on a suspension wire, ladies."

Mrs. Davis gave a thoughtful nod. "Well, if you're there, we could probably just use the front door. After all, you're an established shopper."

Joanne started laughing behind my back again.

"You're all in your bathing suits."

Mrs. Davis pulled a wad of black spandex out of the beach bag. "We came prepared with biker shorts."

Of course you did. "You know I can only fit one of you in Aunt Ginny's Corvette."

"That's fine, dear." Mrs. Dodson lifted and tapped her cane on the kitchen table and a set of keys slid out the top. "You can drive us in my minivan."

Prickled Curiosities was in a hundred-and-fifty-year-old farmhouse that had needed a new paint job since the days when Jimi Hendrix played the national anthem at Woodstock. The ragged chips desperately clinging to the wooden clapboard appeared to be gray, but I suspected even a computer would not be able to decipher what color they had been when they were fresh. The weathered porch was groaning under three rusty metal gliders, several crates of green Coca-Cola bottles, an assortment of washboards, and a butter churn. Embossed metal signs advertising Robin Hood Flour, Blue Label Tomato Ketchup, Pratts Motor Oil, and Moxie Cola covered most of the visual real estate under the warped tin roof.

We entered the building and tried to take in the cornucopia of yesteryear's treasures. Shelves were stacked floor to ceiling with all manner of fascinations. Bird cages and tricycles and mastheads from old whalers hung like stalactites dripping in a cavern of wonders. I had been to a consignment store when I first moved back to South Jersey, but comparing that to Prickled Curiosities was like comparing Morey's Pier to Disney World.

"Okay, ladies, I think it's best if we all stick together . . . Ladies?" I looked behind me. They were gone. The biddies had spread out faster than pink eye at a day care. *This is not gonna end well.*

I tried to find the checkout counter but got distracted in a section of antique kitchen tools. I picked up a fancy-looking wooden paddle-spatula-spoon combo and turned it over in my hands. The tag said it was a spurtle. *What in God's name is a spurtle?* I set it back down and picked up a fancy rolling pin with square pictures of farm animals carved into it.

Aunt Ginny snuck up on my left and jabbed me in the side. "Quit gawking. We aren't here to shop."

"I can't help it. Now that I know a springerle rolling pin exists, I have to have one."

"You can't even eat springerle."

"That isn't going to stop me." I flipped the tag over. Someone had drawn a little dahlia in the upper right corner. Every item on the table had a flower in a corner.

"Can I help you ladies? Oh, it's you."

I fumbled the rolling pin and Aunt Ginny caught it before it rolled off the display table. "Pauline. Hi. You're here. Of course you are, it's your store."

Pauline wound her cinnamon hair into a bun at the

back of her neck and shoved a knitting needle through it. "Well, it isn't exactly my store. I'm just the interim manager. What are you doing here? I thought we settled everything with the armoire at Cold Spring Village yesterday."

We were both taken aback by her icy tone. Aunt Ginny held up the rolling pin. "We want this."

Pauline eyed us without speaking for so long I thought I might have breached some obscure antique store etiquette.

I looked around for a sign that said, "Don't touch anything." I'd been known to miss those even when they were right in front of me. "It is for sale, isn't it?"

Pauline bit her lip and looked over her shoulder. "Everything's for sale. Come on back to the register and I'll get you rung up and on your way."

Aunt Ginny and I passed a silent *What the heck?* between us as we followed her to the back of the store. To my left there was a metallic-sounding crash and a series of accusatory hisses that were much too loud to be whispers. *What's that going to cost me?*

Pauline moved behind a waist-high wooden counter with an antique cash register. Two dozen jars of colorful candy sticks were lined up for sale at ten cents each. There was a display of vintage tins once holding spices and kitchen staples cascading the back wall where a closed door with a curtained window led presumably to a private office or storeroom.

Aunt Ginny handed Pauline the rolling pin. "Quite a place Grover has here."

Pauline fidgeted with the tag. "What? Oh right. It's his life's work."

Aunt Ginny pointed at the tin collection. "I've thrown at least three of each one of those away over the years."

Pauline didn't respond, so I asked her, "Are you okay? You seem kind of edgy."

Over to my right, one of the biddies hissed, "Let me hold it." That was followed by a thud and what sounded like a bowling ball rolling across the floor.

Pauline either gave me a weak smile, or she wanted to throw up. Maybe both. "I'm fine."

"Have you heard from Grover yet?"

"I don't know anything."

Okay. Maybe all redheads are terrible liars.

"I'm sure he's fine." She pressed the keys on the ancient register and the drawer clunked open. "Ten dollars, please."

Aunt Ginny took one for the team. "Oh, I almost forgot. I need a present for a friend of mine. Hold the sale. I'll be right back."

Pauline huffed out a wobbly sigh.

I smiled and shrugged a little. "So, Grover and Auggie didn't get along very well, did they?"

Pauline glanced back at the door behind her. "No, I'm afraid not."

Somewhere behind me, erupted a cascade of tiny cymbals followed by a loud accusation over whose elbow sticks out too far.

"Do you know why they didn't get along?"

She gave me a half-hearted shrug and started to tear up.

Hmm. "Do you know anything about Grover suing Auggie over that vampire-hunting kit?"

"He was?" Pauline dropped her face to her hands. "Oh no. I was afraid of that."

I leaned against the counter and put my chin in my hands so we were eye to eye. "Do you think Auggie was stealing from Grover?"

She shook her head no so violently I was afraid she'd knock her eyes crossed. "Never. Auggie would never steal from anyone."

"Grover told me he was sure Auggie had stolen the vampire box from your store."

Her eyes were downcast. "We've had stock go missing, only later to turn up for sale at Whipple's. But Auggie always had receipts from out-of-town vendors to prove he'd bought everything."

"So, what was Grover's problem then?"

"He was convinced that if Auggie wasn't stealing from him, he was buying stolen goods and selling them."

Behind me was a whooshing sound followed by a thump. "You don't have a cannon, do you?"

Pauline thought for a second. "Not inside."

It's probably fine. "I got the impression that things were bad between Grover and Courtney long before Auggie took over Whipple's Antique Emporium."

"Grover isn't the forgiving sort. Auggie made one mistake and he's never gotten over it."

"What'd he do?"

She waved her hands in front of her face. "I don't want to talk about it."

"I can tell that you liked Auggie. His family is devastated right now. You could really help them make sense out of what happened if you'd tell me." *Not to mention I'd get four nosy biddies off my back.*

Pauline bit her lip and looked to the ceiling. Then she groaned and bounced on the balls of her feet. The knitting needle fell out of her bun and her hair flopped to her shoulders in a swish. "Fine. A few years ago, Courtney found a Revolutionary War–era diary that was supposedly written by Mary Gibbons about an affair she had with George Washington. Auggie had it authenticated, and they were about to sell it for a fortune. Grover suspected there was something off about it, so he convinced Blake to call in his own experts. They determined the diary was a fake and discovered that Auggie had forged the certificate of authenticity."

"Whoa."

"Courtney was shattered. He said he knew nothing about it. He retired right after that. Blake suspended Auggie from the auction house for two years, but June convinced him to let them back in after six months. Now, all of Auggie's authentications have to be done publicly using Blake's experts."

"How many people know about this?"

She shrugged. "Blake didn't tell anyone, to avoid the auction house looking like idiots, but I overheard Grover arguing with him when we were setting up for Cold Spring Village, and it sounded like he was concerned about another forgery."

A movement to my left caught my eye and I spotted Aunt Ginny climbing a stack of blue shelves trying to reach a cluttered display on top. Mother Gibson had her hand on Aunt Ginny's butt to steady her, and at their back was a glass case full of crystal figurines. *Oh my god.* "I'll be right back."

"To the left a little, Lila." Aunt Ginny was dragging a bright red thingamajig towards her, and by the sound of it scraping against the wooden shelf it was going to weigh a ton. "Too far! Back to the right!"

I intercepted them as the base crested the ledge. I stood

on my toes and grabbed the item just as it started to tip towards the floor. "Are you crazy? This is made of iron. You could have been seriously hurt."

All four of the biddies looked at me like I was overreacting.

Aunt Ginny still had her hands on the treasure. "It's a present for Gia."

Mrs. Davis nodded. "To apologize for the dinner party."

I examined what they'd worked off the shelf. It was a cast-iron sphere attached to a box with a drawer. Large wheels were attached on either side and the whole thing was painted red. "What is it?"

Aunt Ginny grinned a full set of pearly whites. "It's an antique coffee grinder."

"Is that what it is?" Mrs. Dodson looked at the grinder like it was the Hope Diamond.

Mrs. Davis helped Aunt Ginny down from the shelf. "Well, yes, Edith. What did you think it was?"

"A garden gnome in a wheelchair."

"Why would Gia want a garden gnome in a wheelchair?" Mother Gibson asked.

Mrs. Dodson looked very unsure of herself. "To remind him of Ginny?"

The biddies laughed all the way to the cash register. Mrs. Davis put her purse on the counter. "Please don't tell my brother I'm shopping from the enemy."

I turned over the price tag. "What is this flower?"

Pauline glanced at the tag. "A poinsettia. That was part of our winter collection. It's my little way to keep track of when items come into the store."

"So, this dahlia on mine?"

She swiped Mrs. Davis's credit card. "That was entered into inventory this summer."

The curtain in the door behind Pauline fluttered and I thought I saw someone watching us. "Who's back there?"

Pauline slammed the drawer to the register shut. "No one's here but me."

I took another look at the office door and then Pauline. She bit her lip.

Hmm. "And you're sure you haven't spoken to your boss since Friday night?"

Pauline blushed scarlet up to her scalp. It was like a redhead lie detector. "Not a peep."

CHAPTER 25

I had to carry the antique coffee grinder to the van. I could barely see past it, so the biddies were leading me with directions. It could have been helpful, except none of their directions were the same. I would have been better off being guided by Tammy Faye Baker. The Pomeranian one, not the wife of the televangelist.

I was a couple more feet away when Mrs. Davis started to cough. She grabbed my elbow and shoved me towards the back of the van. "Mustn't dawdle now. Let's get you home."

"What in the world is wrong with you?"

"Nothing. Don't be silly. Your time is important."

Some days felt like the clowns were running the circus. Every day with the biddies was one of those days. After I pulled out of the Prickled Curiosities parking lot, Mrs. Davis lost all her earlier urgency. She suggested I take them to Wawa to fill up on snacks for the beach. I didn't complain because they weren't raiding my fridge, so I was getting off easy for a change. When they had me drop them at Convention Hall with instructions to go home and park and wait for their communiqué signaling a pickup, I'd reconsidered how lucky I was.

I walked in the front door and stopped short when Figaro ran across the hall, dropped the red scrunchie, and galloped into the library being chased by Sveltelana. I left my purse on the desk, picked up my messages, and he shot out of the library back into the sitting room chased by Cleo. *If nothing else, this week will get those extra pounds off in time for a weigh-in at the vet.*

A text message came in from Gia. **Ti amo, tesoro**. I love you, sweetheart. My heart blew up like a helium balloon.

"What are you grinning like an idiot about?" Joanne stood in the middle of the hall giving me a look that would curdle milk.

Why is she never in a good mood? I put my phone away. "It's nothing. What's wrong with you?"

"Nothing is wrong with me, Buttmunch. But you're about to have a bad day."

"Why? What happened?" *And you're the buttmunch.*

"Well, let's see. The Robbinses are a little irritated because they found Victory asleep in their giant cat carrier. She'd locked herself in trying to see if she fit. The laundry didn't get done because Georgina found a spider in the washer and was afraid to touch it. You have a special order for an allergy-free birthday cake due tomorrow that I forgot to tell you about three days ago. And the cops are looking for you."

I blinked while the wheels turned in my head. "What kind of cake?"

"Chocolate."

Phew. "That's an easy one."

"You'll find a way to screw it up." Joanne turned to the door and gave me a one-finger salute. "I'm out."

Figaro skittered across the hall with Sveltelana literally on his tail, and Joanne hopped to keep from trampling them both. Sveltelana hit Joanne right at the knees and knocked her off balance. Joanne landed on the damp red scrunchie and slid into the coat rack while windmilling her arms, grabbing the London Fog raincoat to steady herself, and pulled the entire contraption down on top of her. A red umbrella hit the floor and popped open with a "*BRROOOAK*" and a terrified frog was sent airborne and landed on Joanne's chest. "*BRROOOAK!*"

Joanne screamed and tried crab-crawling away from it when Victory hobbled down the stairs trailing bandages. "What are you do weith my frog!"

The front door flung open and Grace and Faith Padawowski came in flushed with heat, carrying bags of souvenirs from the kitchen store and Morrow's Nut House. Joanne hurled herself outside through the open door and Victory captured her punch-drunk frog that she had apparently named Anton. "My poor frog babee. I theink he weill be okay."

"*BRROOOAK!*"

Once I could breathe again from laughing, I gave Victory a Tupperware container with a damp paper towel and a Fresca and sent her home with Anton. Then I made myself a cup of coffee and started on all the missing chores.

While the cake was cooling, I made a new bar cookie I'd been thinking about. It was a riff on a millionaire bar. Peanut butter shortbread layered in peanut butter caramel and topped with crunch-coat frozen custard topping. Making it gluten-free was easy. Not eating them all would be harder than squeezing into my skinny jeans.

I'd just finished writing Happy Birthday on the cake in royal icing when I got a 911 text from Aunt Ginny.

You need a cone tell mom new in uterus!

What the heck does that mean? I tapped out a question mark and was answered five minutes later.

Stupid auto corset! You need to come to Thelma's now. It's urgent.

A follow up text arrived soon after.

Bring cookies!

How urgent could this really be if they're demanding snacks? I grabbed my purse and the batch of crunch-coat bars that were still warm, and ran out the door. Mrs. Dodson's van was gone. I don't know when they'd picked it up, but they were very sneaky about it. I never even heard them get the keys off my desk. I hopped in Aunt Ginny's Corvette and drove over to Mrs. Davis's house a few blocks away on Stockton.

In the middle of a row of cookie-cutter gingerbread cottages, Mrs. Davis lived in a slim three-story white number with silver shutters and bright purple trim. Two orchid-colored awnings shaded the hanging white porch swing, and urns of petunias flanked the arched double doors.

The door on the right swung open and Mother Gibson met me with a mischievous grin that let me know skullduggery was afoot. She was fanning herself with a hand of playing cards. "Hello, dear. How nice of you to come."

"I didn't think it was optional."

"That's 'cause you a smart girl."

"What's the emergency?"

"You gonna find out."

Aunt Ginny's voice hollered from down the hall. "Is that Poppy? Did she remember the cookies?"

I had never been inside Mrs. Davis's house before. Every room was a different color, with the curtains and furniture of the room matching the paint in a mono-chrome explosion. I followed Mother Gibson through a cobalt-blue living room, out through a green-apple dining room, and down a tangerine hallway. The kitchen was a snowbank of white except for the ceiling, which was shocking violet.

Mrs. Davis grinned and handed me a green drink in a martini glass. "I know. It's surprising, isn't it?"

I stared at the woman wearing a frilly pink swimsuit coverup. "I don't know why, but I expected a lot of lace and teacups."

She gave me a wink. "Everybody does."

The only thing that was as I expected were the three cats each taking up a different windowsill in the kitchen. One was white, one was black, and one was gray. I had to laugh at the genius of it. I sniffed at the frozen concoction. "What's this?"

Aunt Ginny took the pan of bar cookies from my hand. "Skinny virgin margarita."

Well, that makes one of us.

The biddies were sitting around Mrs. Davis's white kitchen table playing cards. A tray of Bugles and onion dip sat next to them on a snack table. Each lady had five piles of M&M's in front of them.

Mrs. Dodson drummed her fingers on her cards. "I see your plain and I raise you two peanut."

"Too rich for my blood." Aunt Ginny threw her cards down. "Poppy, can you help me to the powder room, please?"

Aunt Ginny had never in her life asked me to help her to the bathroom. Either this was a medical mayday, or a covert mission. From the mischievous gleam in her eye, I figured it was the latter.

"Absolutely." I sipped my frozen drink to brace myself for what was to come and left it on the white marble counter.

I followed Aunt Ginny back through the house. "Are you okay? Is this the emergency? Wow. I have never seen an orange bookcase before. Is that blue table from Morocco? Please tell me there's a pink room somewhere."

Aunt Ginny led me to a fireplace surrounded in glazed cobalt ceramic tiles. Brazenly sitting on the mantel under a discreet museum spotlight was the lapis-and-silver jewelry box that had been at Josephine's house just yesterday.

I looked from the box to Aunt Ginny. She raised her eyebrows. I looked at the box again and back to Aunt Ginny. She raised her eyebrows higher.

"Huh."

"Mm-hmm."

As we walked back through the parlor, Aunt Ginny pushed a door open and flicked on the light.

"Holy cow." I took my phone out and snapped a photo for Gia. The powder room was entirely black marble and polished silver like it was in some swanky nightclub.

Aunt Ginny nodded. "Oh yeah. It was all the talk of the Senior Center Winter Social in 2010."

Back in the kitchen, the curtain was pulled back on Mrs. Davis's heart as her shoulders heaved and she let out a sob. Her sorrow was palpable. Mother Gibson was holding one of her hands and Mrs. Dodson had a hand on her back. Mrs. Davis wiped her eyes.

Aunt Ginny returned to her seat at the table. "Just breathe. One moment at a time."

Mrs. Davis nodded, and held up a deck of cards. Her voice carrying a faint tremble. "You want to be dealt in?"

In that moment I knew everything at my house could wait. Some things were more important than checking email and updating Facebook. I grabbed my skinny virgin margarita and took one of the empty seats. "Sure. I can play a couple hands. But I don't know what you're playing."

Mother Gibson pointed to her stack of M&M's. "Poker. All you need to remember is plain is five, peanut is ten, pretzel is twenty-five, almond is fifty, and peanut butter is a hundred."

I picked up my cards and started to put them in order. "Shouldn't almond be a hundred since they're the biggest?" That was when I got my first warning.

Note to self. Never question peanut butter.

I tried to work the heirloom on the fireplace casually into the conversation. "So . . . how many of those jewelry boxes are there?"

Mrs. Davis shuffled her cards in her hand. "Just the one."

Aunt Ginny and I passed a look between us.

"I could have sworn I saw it at Josephine's the other day."

"Oh, yeah?"

Mrs. Davis's lips were locked tighter than a five-year-old with a birthday wish. I tried a different subject. "I didn't know June used to be married to the auctioneer."

That must have been a secret because the other biddies looked shocked when I mentioned it. Or maybe it was *that* I'd mentioned it.

Mrs. Davis tsked. "Poor June. She has not had an easy go of it. It was a bitter divorce. Blake was the love of her life, but he has an eye for the ladies. She caught him cheating on her under the boardwalk at Mariner's Pier with a topless mermaid."

I looked up from my cards. "What was that again?"

"She was a waitress at The Mermaid Cove in Wildwood. They wear rubber mermaid tails as part of their uniform."

"Isn't that a safety hazard?"

Aunt Ginny threw some M&M's into the pot. "They're impossible to walk in."

I'll ask about that later. "I hate to bring this up, but I saw June with Spencer at Cold Spring Village the other day. They looked cozier than brother and sister-in-law. Is it possible something is going on between them?"

Mrs. Dodson pursed her lips and threw some candy on the pile in the center of the table. "I sure hope not. It isn't worth it to go sneaking around. Too many people get hurt."

Mrs. Davis shook her head and sighed. "Well, if they are, it wouldn't be the first time Spencer cheated. Gimme two cards. Courtney told me Spencer had an affair with the loan officer when he was involved in that ridiculous business with Pudding A Go-Go. Who needs pudding so badly they'd line up at a truck on the side of the freeway to buy it? I'll tell you who—no one. But Tildy forgave him. Again."

Aunt Ginny popped a peanut butter M&M into her mouth. "That Tildy is such a nice girl. Why would Spencer cheat on her? I'll take one card."

Mother Gibson peeked over her cards. "Three, please.

Her momma causes a lot of drama. If Spencer's cheating on her, Josephine will never let it go."

Mrs. Davis checked her cards and held up two fingers. "It was just her and Josephine until she and Courtney got married. Tildy was about twelve, I think."

I had a handful of nothing. "Can I have five?"

Mrs. Dodson gave me a long blink through her eyelashes and dealt me five cards worse than the ones I already had. Then she gave herself two. "Josephine has never believed Spencer is good enough for her Tildy— and she's let him know that many times."

Mother Gibson picked at the Bugles. "That boy is driven to succeed. There's no telling how far along he'd be if not for his shady shortcuts."

Aunt Ginny tossed about three hundred dollars' worth of peanut butter M&M's into her mouth and flipped her cards faceup.

Mrs. Davis turned over three jacks and collected the pot. "Spencer didn't have two nickels to rub together when he married Tildy. I think he thought a big inheritance was coming."

Mrs. Dodson dealt the next hand and called for everyone to ante up. I looked at my stash of chocolate and it had dwindled by half. "What happened to my hundreds?"

The ladies broke into giggles and Mrs. Dodson announced, "Ginny's been eating them since you sat down, girl. Pay attention."

Aunt Ginny gave me a grin. "Well, I can't eat mine. My cards are on fire tonight!" She tossed another hundred dollars into her mouth.

I turned back to Mrs. Davis. "Now that Auggie has passed away, June will inherit everything, won't she?"

Mrs. Davis rearranged the cards in her hand. "She won't inherit the house, but she'll get everything else."

Mother Gibson puckered her lips. "Maybe that's why Spencer's suddenly interested."

"Who inherits the house?" I asked.

"I do, sort of." Mrs. Davis fanned her cards. "Unless June has a son."

Mrs. Dodson reared back. "I thought your father bought you this place as your inheritance when you got married."

"He did. But he also made us promise that the house would always stay in the Whipple family. It was my grandmother's dying wish. It has to pass to a male in the Whipple line. Unless June miraculously has a baby boy, the house goes to my son."

I put one of the peanut M&M's into my mouth, remembered that I was on the keto diet, and spit it back into my hand. "So Tildy inherits nothing?"

Mrs. Davis mashed her lips down. "She can't inherit the house. But everything *in* Courtney's collection goes to whoever Courtney leaves it to."

Aunt Ginny muttered to herself. "And he ain't leaving nothing to Tildy."

"If you were Spencer, and you wanted to inherit that house or something in it, how would you get it?"

Mrs. Davis rolled her eyes up to the ceiling. "I guess he'd have to marry June and get Auggie out of the way."

"Well, if that's his plan, he's halfway there."

CHAPTER 26

The next morning, I came down the main stairs and spotted a yellow slip of paper sticking under the front door. I pulled the door open, and a paper bag slid into the room being dragged by the receipt. It was from the Kebab Kitchen in Ocean Crest. "One chicken souvlaki charged to the Butterfly Wings B and B." Burl was not only sleep-ordering delivery, now he was paying hefty delivery fees. I added the souvlaki to the Grabsteins' bill, took it to the kitchen, and stuck it in the fridge next to a giant bowl of kohlrabi.

Joanne was slicing more tomatoes. "I saw that on the porch this morning, but I wanted you to get the full effect of discovering it for yourself."

"Yeah, thanks for that."

"That can't be safe to eat after sitting out there all night."

"If it were up to me it would go straight into the trash, which is a shame—because these are delicious. But I'm putting it on their bill so Elaine will have to do the honors."

Victory was sitting at the table in a black tankini and bright pink flip-flops, eating a fresh strawberry shortcake parfait. She peeled a strip of dead skin off her arm and dropped it into a small mound of deposited shreds next to her bowl. She frowned. "I am shed my skein."

"That happens when you get badly sunburned." I handed her a paper towel. "Don't leave it on the table. That's gross."

Figaro was sitting in the empty box from yesterday's produce delivery. The contracted one from Robinson's. Not the unwieldy delivery of kohlrabi and tomatoes from Courtney Whipple that was daily vexing me. I watched as Sveltelana scooped some of Figaro's dry food with her giant paw and batted it towards the box. He appraised it and gave it a pat. The giant Maine coon lay down by the bowl and Cleo ran in and swatted the outside of the box approximately where the food had landed. Figaro swatted the box from the inside, then turned his back to the girls.

Joanne layered the tomatoes with fresh basil and mozzarella. "That's been going on all morning."

I was afraid of that. I poured a cup of coffee and set it aside to get the cream. "It's like watching Gia being fawned over by beautiful women when we go out. He shows about as much interest as Figaro does."

Aunt Ginny came into the kitchen on the tail end of the conversation, picked up my cup of coffee, and put two sugars in it. "What are those cats doing?"

I figured she may as well have the cream since she'd

hijacked my cup and I handed her the carton. I took down a new mug for myself. "I believe the ladies are wooing his lordship."

Aunt Ginny stirred cream in her coffee and it made silky swirls in her cup. "Well, they're barking up the wrong tree. I think he's sworn off women since that last one broke his little heart."

I poured myself the last of the coffee and reached for two more packets of stevia. Georgina drug herself into the kitchen and took the mug out of my hands. "Thank God there's coffee. I'm so tired. That young couple asked if I would bring their breakfast up to them. It's like they think they should be waited on hand and foot just because they paid money."

Joanne quirked an eyebrow. "Well . . . you are the maid."

Georgina sneered at Joanne. "I most certainly am not a maid. I'm a business owner who has graciously agreed to help out my daughter-in-law in her time of need. Because I'm a giver, Joanne. I give. It's what I do. Stop laughing at me, Ginny. And for cripes' sake, Victory, that's disgusting!"

Victory rolled just her eyes up to Georgina and continued to peel at her skin. "Eis no my fault. Eit jus come off."

Aunt Ginny went to get a Kleenex to wipe her eyes and I started to make a new pot of coffee while Georgina "the giver" launched into another rant. "This is unacceptable, Victory. Have you no pride in your job? I've seen patches of your scaly dead skin all over the hall this morning. You need to use a loofa. Or a sugar scrub."

Victory gave me a look like she thought Georgina was high on something. She snorted. "I do not have rich lady sugar scrub. I am working for summer only to go to university."

Georgina crossed her arms and made a decree. "You'll just have to wear long sleeves to work today to keep yourself from picking at it."

Victory slurped a forkful of whipped cream off her strawberries. "No way. Eis too hot!"

I poured hot water over my fresh coffee grounds. "Georgina is right."

Georgina puffed in triumph. "See."

"You can't work in that condition. You'll have to take the day off. We can't have you in the guest rooms like this. You're leaving more of a mess than you're cleaning up."

Georgina bristled. "If she has the day off, who will clean the rooms? I only agreed to help because she was incapacitated. She's perfectly fine now. And if she's not here to clean, why is she here at all?"

Victory didn't look up from her parfait. "People like my companee."

Georgina gave Victory a defensive glare. "Well, I've already worked three days in a row."

Aunt Ginny had just returned from drying her eyes, started laughing again, and had to leave the room to get another Kleenex.

I set the timer for four minutes. "A lot of the people who live at the shore don't get a day off from June to September, Georgina."

"That's preposterous. When do they go to brunch, or get a pedicure?"

Joanne snorted and cracked eggs into a frying pan.

Georgina didn't seem to notice the amusement in the

room at her expense. "Getting a pedicure is non-negotiable. It's common courtesy not to wear open-toed shoes if you haven't had your feet done. And there's no way I could go three months without a snail facial. My pores would be huge. I'd be a laughingstock."

Aunt Ginny returned in time to say, "And you'll want to get those roots done. The gray is peeking through."

I gave her a look that said *You're not helping* and turned my attention back to Georgina, who was one tick away from a full-scale tantrum. "Okay, now you're just being dramatic. How many people are going to be close enough to your face to see your pores? But if you don't think you're strong enough to work a full week . . ." *for the first time in your life . . .*

Georgina's mouth twisted into a tight little fist. "I don't think you understand just how hard this job is, Poppy. How many of you have been chambermaids?"

Every one of our hands went up. Georgina began to sputter. "Wha . . . That . . ."

Aunt Ginny snorted. "This is Cape May, Georgina. And except for Victory, most of us grew up here when there were very few options other than chambermaid or waitress, and I've done both." Aunt Ginny flexed her little chicken wing in an attempt to make a bicep. "Working hard all my life is how I got to be in such great shape today."

I bit my lip to keep from commenting. I knew for a fact that just last week Aunt Ginny had pulled a muscle from toweling off getting out of Royce's hot tub. I had to rub essential oils in her shoulder for three days. "Victory will take today off and use a sugar scrub that I will give her. And I guess little old Aunt Ginny will fill in as chambermaid."

We all watched Georgina as her pride went to war with her vanity. "Fine. I'll work, but just for the rest of this week. And I need Friday off because my Itty Bitty Smitty is taking me to dinner. And I get to keep all the tips that come in on Friday—not because I need the money, but it's the principle."

I poured myself some coffee and gave Georgina a solemn nod. "That is very generous of you, Georgina. You truly are a giver."

The doorbell rang, and I went to answer it. Wade and Jenna were coming down the stairs holding hands and making googly eyes at each other. I felt a tug at my heart to go see Gia as soon as I could get away.

I opened the door to find Amber on the front porch. "Hey. Have you ever been a chambermaid?"

"Yep. Three summers between high school and college. Why?"

"Just wondering. Things any better with Sergeant Washington?"

Amber opened her mouth, but I didn't hear what she said because Viola laid on the horn. *BLAAAAAAM!*

"That good, huh?"

Amber sucked her cheek and let it out. "It makes me miss the days of cheerleading with Barbie."

"Wow. Do you want a cup of coffee or something?"

She looked over her shoulder. "I can't. Sergeant Washington does not approve of my investigative methods, so I told her I needed to stop by for just a minute to pick up the addendum to your witness statement."

My eyes rolled back in my head as I tried to remember being asked for an addendum.

"It's not real. Don't worry. I'm gonna tell her your cat shredded it and you'll bring a new one to the station."

Man, I was planning on using that excuse for myself one day. "So, what do you really need?"

"How are things going with the Whipples?"

"I have a mountain of kohlrabi in the kitchen that would suggest Courtney loves me."

Amber pulled out a notebook and flipped through the pages. "I've been going over the witness statements, and many of the alibis are pretty thin. According to Courtney, Auggie arrived home around midnight Saturday and they spoke briefly, then went to bed. No one else in the house saw Auggie that night or the next morning. The security system at Whipple's Antique Emporium was deactivated with Auggie's code at ten after eight later that morning. The next time anyone sees Auggie, he's falling out of the armoire at a few minutes past five p.m. No one at the auction house saw Auggie arrive or enter the storage room where we know the murder took place. The coroner estimates the time of death to between eight thirty and noon. Blake Adams says he was in his office, alone, preparing for the auction. Josephine Whipple and Tildy Jolley said they were shopping together at the baby boutique on the mall, but they can't find any receipts to verify the time. June Whipple says she spent the morning alone at the beach. Courtney Whipple said he was home alone gardening. And Spencer Jolley said he was canvassing the neighborhood to estimate property values. Alone." Amber looked at me with lifted eyebrows.

Viola blew the horn again and I wished I'd taken Amber inside. "Spencer has dreams of running a bed and breakfast. He seems to think it's the pot at the end of the rainbow."

Amber flipped her notebook shut. "Is it now? The next

time you're with the family, see if you can get any more out of them. Be discreet. One friend to another."

"I don't know them *that* well. Why would they tell me anything?"

"Because you're not the police. People let their guard down when they're with friends."

"What about Pauline, Grover's assistant?"

Amber checked her notebook. "She says she was home, alone, getting ready for the auction. She arrived at the auction house at noon for the preview."

Sergeant Washington threw the cruiser door open and began marching our way.

"Won't you get in trouble if I help you?"

"I'm not asking you to investigate. Just listen and report like normal. Be your usual nosy self. Just tell me when you hear something."

"I'll do what I can, but why are you looking at the family when there was so much obvious conflict with Grover Prickle?"

"We need to clear everyone."

Viola stomped up my front steps with her hand on the butt of her holstered gun. "What is going on here? You said you were just picking up an addendum. You know you're not supposed to question this witness without me."

I took a long drink from my coffee. "Why would I be getting questioned at all?"

Viola rocked her head to the side and taunted me like a nine-year-old bully on the playground. "Look at you, little Miss Innocent. We weren't able to pull any fingerprints from the murder weapon or the vampire-hunting kit that didn't belong to the auction house staff or the victim, and the only prints on the armoire were Grover

Prickle's, his assistant's, and yours. Why do you suppose that is?"

"The killer wore gloves?" *I'm going to start wiping down everything I touch from now on.*

Viola tsked. She spun on the balls of her feet and marched back down the steps. "Fenton! We got to check in at the station!"

Amber gave me a grim sigh.

"At least you've got the good cop, bad cop roles figured out."

"Please think about what I said about the family. Especially Josephine."

"Why especially her?"

Amber checked behind her to see how close Viola was. "Because the crime scene techs pulled Josephine's prints off the flag."

CHAPTER 27

"Why in the world would Josephine's fingerprints be on Grover's flag?"

Aunt Ginny shrugged. "She must have been at Cold Spring Village or the antiques auction at some point."

"Yeah, but close enough to touch the competition's prized collectible. Besides, she wouldn't hurt Auggie. He was her stepson. She practically raised him. Right?"

Aunt Ginny shook her head in wonder. "I wouldn't trust Josephine as far as I could throw her. You heard her the other night. She's angry that Courtney doesn't want to leave Tildy anything because she isn't his blood relative. Meanwhile Auggie's living it up, putting stickers with his name all over the stuff he wants to sell when Courtney kicks the bucket."

"True, but she was shopping with Tildy during the auction. June told the cops she was alone on the beach, when she told me she hates the beach and has nothing but bad memories from it."

Joanne pointed a spatula in my face. "Could you please do this after you take my caprese breakfast sandwiches to the dining room?"

Joanne had arranged the toasted squares of fried eggs and tomato with melted mozzarella in a long row and garnished the platter with balsamic vinegar and basil. I carried the platter into the dining room, where the guests were all sitting around the table drinking coffee and chatting about their plans for the day. "How is everyone this morning?"

Marty Robbins put her coffee cup down with a loud *thunk*. "Poppy, is there a place around here to bungee jump?"

Her husband Paul had wild eyes and he shook his head behind her, imploring me to say no.

The giant Maine coon, Sveltelana, jumped into Marty's lap and gave her a nuzzle. It was a lot like the Hulk giving a nose wiggle kiss to a toddler.

The older woman snuggled the cat and breathlessly struggled her back down to the floor. "I promised myself I would enjoy life and take more chances on this trip, and that is what I plan to do."

I was caught between her impassioned request and her husband's obvious terror over it. "I'll check and get back to you."

Before I could escape to the kitchen, Kevin Martins pulled me aside. "I am a man on a mission, and your Yelp review depends on my success."

God help me. "Okay. What is it?" I swallowed hard.

"Where can I find the best cheesesteak on the island?"

His wife Shondra slapped him on the arm. "Kevin! Are you still goin' on about that?"

He gave her a desperate look. "Well, that deli was a sham. I know cheesesteaks. You know I know cheesesteaks, and that was a subpar cheesesteak!"

"Kevin! You don't need no more cheesesteaks!"

He bit his lip and shot her a tense glare. "Woman!"

She threw her hands up. "Oh, my Lord! Just tell him where it is so we can move on from this. I'm havin' scallops tonight, Kevin! Even if I have to leave you here alone to get them."

Kevin grabbed my shoulders. The look he gave me was as serious as if we were on assignment to rescue a kidnapped princess. "Focus. Where is Cape May hiding the cheesesteaks everyone talks about?"

Uh . . . Philadelphia.

The dining room door cracked open and Joanne glared through the crack.

I had to ignore her. This situation I was in felt like life and death. "Well, I hate to tell you this . . ."

Kevin's cheeks slid down to his chin and he looked as though he might cry.

"The best cheesesteaks aren't in Cape May. They're in North Wildwood."

His eyes popped back up and he snapped his fingers at Shondra. "My phone. Where's my phone?"

Shondra handed her husband a cell phone and rolled her eyes at me.

"Okay, where they at?"

"Russo's Market . . ."

Kevin typed the information furiously into his phone. "Yeaaaaah."

Maybe I won't get a one star after all.

Joanne brought in the tray of strawberry shortcake par-faits and sent me a self-pity sigh of pending punishment that I knew from experience was on account of her being peeved that I wasn't helping fast enough.

I promised to make Burl and Elaine a reservation for a horse-and-carriage tour, and chased Figaro out of the empty chair that would have been Jenna's except she was sitting in Wade's lap. Then I made some recommenda-tions for fun excursions for everyone except Wade and Jenna. They were "just staying in" today. They had "just stayed in" every day since they arrived. *Is it their honey-moon and no one told me?* I had a whole honeymoon gift basket I would have left in their room had I known. It seemed too late to ask without being incredibly awkward about the fact that they only surfaced occasionally to get food.

I excused myself to let the guests enjoy their breakfast and face my reprisals in the kitchen. I found my coffee poured down the sink and the pot empty.

Aunt Ginny was sitting at the table with her head rest-ing on her hand, the phone up to her ear. She mouthed, "I'm on hold." I nodded, and asked Victory and Georgina if either of them had been in the Swallowtail Suite yet. We were still missing eight bottles of wine and four wedges of cheese from happy hours. I suspected our young lovers were snatching them and moving them up to their bedroom. They shook their heads no.

I handed Georgina the laundry that I had folded, and sent her to the guest rooms, ordered Victory home to slough her skin in private, and pulled out my recipes for the day. I was making a plum nectarine crisp for breakfast tomorrow, and Gia's shop needed more funnel-cake muffins. The weekend had been especially busy, and they were sold out of everything. Today I was going to make more cotton candy cupcakes, along with some rocky road fudge cakes. I turned to ask Aunt Ginny what the ladies thought of the crunch-coat bars from poker, but she was still on hold.

The side door opened, and someone came in behind a giant produce box. *That better not be Spencer or I'ma knock the bejeezus outta him.*

A tuft of pink bobbed behind the tower of kohlrabi and I rushed to take the box from Mrs. Davis. "Why are you bringing me more vegetables? We haven't eaten the last ones Spencer brought, or the ones before that that Courtney sent over. The guests are starting to notice we've served tomatoes every day."

"I told Courtney you went to Prickled Curiosities to see what you could dig up." Mrs. Davis released her hold on the weight she was struggling under and I set the box on the floor next to the other box. "This is his way of saying thank you."

Joanne and I both groaned. If kohlrabi were cupcakes I wouldn't have to bake for a month.

"Please tell Courtney I'm glad I could help, but I can't take any more. I don't want to hurt his feelings, but none of us are eating it." I looked to Aunt Ginny for backup.

Her ear was still pressed to the phone. She lifted her eyes to mine and realized I was speaking to her. "What?"

"Nothing."

Mrs. Davis picked at the bowl of strawberries. "I just came to see if you've heard anything on Grover. Courtney is so upset he's barely eating. He wants Auggie's killer brought to justice."

"And he's sure that it's Grover Prickle?"

Mrs. Davis shrugged. "Who else could it be? Everyone loved Auggie. No one would hurt him for the world."

And yet, someone did.

"You saw that threat Grover sent the day Auggie died."

"And I saw that Grover knew a dark secret about Auggie. Maybe there's someone we don't even know about who killed Auggie."

Mrs. Davis waved me off. "That's just Grover trying to throw us off the scent. I bet he'd already killed Auggie when he sent that letter. It might just be part of his alibi."

"I will keep my ears open and let you know if I hear anything." *When did I become Homeland Security?*

"Thank you, dear. With Auggie's passing, June has to keep the business going alone. She had to close the store to go to a preview at an estate sale today."

"I would think under the circumstances it would be understandable if she skipped it."

Mrs. Davis shook her head. "Not June. Moss won't grow on that girl. She's up in Stone Harbor all afternoon."

I really don't want to get involved. It's none of my business that she lied to the police about being on the beach.

Mrs. Davis glanced above my head, flinched, and lurched away from me. "Merciful heavens! I think I ruined my Depends."

I followed her eyes to see Figaro sitting on top of the refrigerator in-between the Special K and the Cap'n Crunch. His whiskers twitched nervously when he realized he'd been discovered.

Mrs. Davis fanned her face with her hand. "What's he doing up there?"

"Hiding from suitors."

Mrs. Davis nodded. "Hmm. Some have all the luck."

Joanne handed her a breakfast sandwich and they sat at the island to eat together.

I tried to set out my ingredients for the crisp, but I couldn't concentrate. June's alibi was like a splinter in my heel. I waved my hand to get Aunt Ginny's attention to tell her I needed to run an errand. Her eyes were half open, and she had a slack hold on her mouth. The instrumental Musak version of "Barracuda" tinkling through the phone told me she was still on hold. "Aunt Ginny?"

"Hm? What?"

"Who are you on hold with?"

She blinked and her eyes narrowed. "I don't know."

"Why don't you hang up?"

"'Cause then I'd have to start over."

"But you don't know with who?"

"If I hang up now, I'll never find out."

I pulled my phone out of my pocket and called the best person I knew for running backup. "Hey. Can you break away for a couple hours? I have an estate sale to check out."

CHAPTER 28

I idled at the corner of Washington and Perry, and Sawyer jumped in the car and handed me an iced coffee. "Gia says be careful."

"Why does he think I'm doing something risky?"

"I told him Mrs. Davis was involved."

"That's fair."

"I'm so glad you called. I feel like I haven't seen you in forever. Through the Looking Glass has been swamped all month. What's been going on?"

"Found another body."

"Where?"

Reason one hundred and seventeen why Sawyer is my best friend. She didn't judge me. I filled her in on the events of the past three days and explained why we were making a casual drop-in to visit a suspect at Amber's behest. It took a while to get off the island through the beach traffic, but soon we were on the Garden State Parkway heading for Stone Harbor. Sawyer searched estate sales on her phone, and by the time we crossed the bridge she'd found two. The first one seemed like the word "estate" was pretty ballsy for what would be more accurately termed a tenement eviction sale, but we were very confident that the blond beach house on stilts at the second location was exactly what we were searching for.

I parked next to some decorative nautical pilings and an Estate Sale yard sign with two balloons flapping in the wind at one end of a circular driveway. We shielded our eyes from the afternoon glare and looked beyond the house and sand to the ocean that made up the briny backyard. The foam crept up to the edge of the sand and ran away in a marine version of ding dong ditch. "Wow. Can you imagine having that view every day?"

Sawyer chuckled. "If you could knock down a couple houses and Tiny's Lobster Shack, you *would* have that view every day."

A woman called to me from the side of the balcony overlooking the ocean. "Poppy, is that you?" She was smartly dressed in striped palazzo pants and a fitted white button-down shirt. She removed her wide-brimmed hat with one hand and drank from a glass of champagne in the other and I saw that it was June.

Sawyer pulled her white spaghetti strap up to cover the band of her pink bra. "You didn't tell me there was a dress code."

I ran my hands over my gingham blouse, checking for evidence of the tomato sandwich I'd eaten for breakfast. "I didn't know. I assumed South Jersey casual like everywhere else."

June leaned over the railing. "What are you doing here? I thought this was a preview for dealers only."

"We were just in the neighborhood, and thought we'd stop by to see if we could find anything for the B and B."

She waved us forward. "There are some great pieces in here. Come on up and I'll show you around."

We took the steps to the second-floor deck and the wind whipped our hair back like angry sails on a catamaran. Sawyer went straight to the edge overlooking the Atlantic. "What I wouldn't give to live in a house like this."

June took another sip of her champagne. "I hear it's going on the market next month for ten million."

Sawyer blinked. "But you know the couple blocks' walk to the beach from my condo is good exercise."

I looked from Sawyer to June. "I'm sorry. You two don't know each other. June Whipple, Sawyer Montgomery. Sawyer and I have been friends since grade school. She owns the bookstore on the mall."

They shook hands, then Sawyer nodded toward the house. "Are you finding anything good?"

"I've got my eye on a little something." She crooked her finger and took us inside to the spacious glass living room. She handed us each a color prospectus from a table in the marble foyer. "Don't say anything and don't look too interested, but do you see those chairs over there?"

Sawyer and I peeked over our fliers. "The ugly pink ones?"

June gave us a slight nod. "They're Hepplewhite."

"And that's good?" I asked.

June raised her eyebrows. "Oh, yeah. Are you looking for anything in particular?"

Sawyer and I faced each other. We should have rehearsed on the way up instead of talking about men.

Sawyer bit her lip. "Mmm, maybe a . . . padded headboard?"

Ooh. Good answer. I nodded along. "Yes. For the B and B. I was going to bid on something at the antique auction for one of my guest rooms, but that fell through."

June's eyebrows shot up in interest. "Really? What were you bidding on?"

Sawyer turned her face to mine with panic in her eyes. *Oh. My. God. Don't say armoire.* "Um . . ."

Sawyer was quick thinking, as usual. "A headboard. A French . . . old one . . . made of wood."

I nodded. "Yep, that works. An old wooden headboard at an antique auction."

Sawyer let out her breath and gave me an apologetic shrug.

I could tell that June wasn't convinced but she was gracious anyway. "I wasn't aware that we had any furniture in the auction last week. Well, I hope you find just what you're looking for."

A woman in a yellow summer suit led another couple over to the chairs June had her eye on. I assumed she was the estate manager by the Vanna White way she was spokesmodeling the sale items. I knew I had better get to the real reason I was here before she cornered me and found out I wasn't a dealer and gave me the left foot of fellowship.

"I was surprised you weren't at the auction the other day what with Whipple's vampire-hunting kit up for bid."

June downed her champagne, placed her empty flute on a tray and picked up a full glass. "I told you I have a bad history with Cape May. If I had attended the auction, I'd have to come face-to-face with him."

Sawyer put her hand out and touched June on the arm in a distance hug. "Aww. Your ex?"

June nodded. "You probably don't know this, but he's the owner of the auction house. Blake Adams."

I did my best to feign surprise. "Oh, really?"

"He's a magnificent auctioneer. Seeing him in action is still too painful."

Sawyer's hand covered her heart. "I'm recently divorced myself. My ex, Kurt, had a very narrow definition of what constituted cheating. He was quick to forgive himself for anything short of getting caught."

June crossed her arms in front of her. "A year ago, one of the girls who worked for me said Blake called and I was to meet him under Jumbo's on Mariner's Landing. I thought he was setting up a romantic surprise, but when I walked down the steps to the beach, I caught him with a waitress from the topless bar across the street."

Sawyer and June hugged each other, bonding over their shared betrayal, but something sounded off to me. "Why would he ask you to meet him if he was meeting another woman?"

June wiped a tear from her eye. "What?"

I was worried that I was being insensitive, but I plowed through anyway. "Most cheating husbands work hard to cover their tracks. They don't usually invite their wives to the booty call."

June smoothed her hand down her hip. "I think he wanted out of the marriage but was too weak to face me. So, he forced me into leaving him."

"You know that's a really odd plan, don't you?"

June drank from her champagne. "It wasn't the first time he'd cheated. Blake has always been a flirt. He insisted nothing happened, but a woman knows when her husband is lying."

Sawyer looked at me and nodded emphatically.

"So, if you weren't at the auction, where were you?"

June moved to a floor lamp with a stained-glass shade and examined it. "At Whipple's. Working. This is a knockoff. Nothing special."

"I thought the auction *was* working for you. I know your dad was frantic that Auggie was missing. He said you were both supposed to be on your way."

June threw a dart of irritation at me. "Well, he was wrong. Something came up at the Antique Emporium and I was there all morning sorting it out."

Sawyer tried to smooth over the sudden chill of attitude from June's frosty reply. "I hate it when work emergencies arise, and I have to rush to the bookstore like that. It throws off my whole day."

June gave Sawyer a nod, happy that I was put in my place.

The estate manager came through the dining room towards us. She shook hands with the other couple, and they left through the glass doors to the deck. She smiled at June with dollar signs in her eyes, but a phone rang in the other room. She hurried after it, calling over her shoulder, "I'm sorry. I'm here by myself. I'll be with you in just a moment."

I wasn't sure what I would say to her when she came back. The story of coming to a dealer preview for a single headboard wasn't my best work. I pretended I was perusing the prospectus that laid out each room and the items that were for sale and tried to be casual. "So how is your love life, currently? Got anyone secret hidden away?"

June choked on her champagne. "What? No. Who said there was? Have you heard something?"

"I'd be lying if I said I didn't know about a certain rendezvous."

Sawyer's subtlety was on point as usual. Her mouth dropped open and she gasped. "Ooo-oooh."

June looked frantically from me to Sawyer with wide eyes. She downed the rest of her second glass of champagne. "I don't know how you found out, but please don't tell anyone. Especially not my father."

Huh. I would think she'd be more concerned about Tildy finding out. "I'm not going to be the one to tell him. But are you sure this is right for you? I mean, there are going to be complications to say the least. Thanksgiving will be awkward."

Sawyer's lips rolled in and her eyes bugged out. She was not great with secrets. She didn't even know Courtney and was still in danger of spilling everything to him. She backed away. "I was never here."

June put her empty flute on the table and heaved a sigh. "I don't even know what I'm doing anymore. It was a terrible mistake. I should never have trusted . . ." Her hand trembled and she reached for the bowl of sweet potato chips. "Auggie had my back when we were kids. We were inseparable growing up. Our mother died when we were young, but Auggie and I had each other. I don't know when we grew so far apart that we started keeping secrets. Now it's too late to ask him anything."

I didn't follow most of that. I had a million questions, but the estate manager was heading towards us again. I blew my cheeks out at Sawyer and she followed my eyes.

Sawyer stepped forward to intercept the woman in the yellow suit as she was taking off her jacket. "Hi. I'm hoping you can help me. I'm looking for some Heffalump tables."

The woman was trapped in her sleeves and Sawyer

rushed her back into the dining room she'd just come out of.

I nodded. "What about your ex-husband? What did he think of Auggie?"

June wandered over to a carved sideboard and ran her finger down the edge. "They were friends while we were married, but . . ."

"Not after you were divorced?"

"Something happened before Blake and I separated. Auggie lost a lot of respect for Blake when he caught him with another woman. He hated having to tell me about it. Blake and I were getting ready to move to our dream house. Now it's all ruined."

"I can't imagine what you must have been going through. I heard your dad and Auggie had a fight about the antique store the night before he died. I'm sure that's been hard on him too."

A flicker of horror passed across June's brow. "Dad told you about that?"

Maybe not personally. "Your Aunt Thelma told your dad he could trust me, and he can. You all can."

June picked up a handful of chips. "I can't believe he told you I found an error in the ledger. It was a false alarm. Dad talked to Auggie and found out he'd been taking personal advances. He was going to pay them back. He always did."

"And Auggie had a degree in finance, so he would have known what he was doing? Right?"

June stared at me blankly before nodding. "Right."

"Unless you're worried that Auggie was involved in something underhanded that could have gotten him killed?"

June wouldn't look me in the eyes, and her voice went flat. "Auggie was a gem. No one wanted to hurt him. And the ladies especially loved him. Just ask Pauline. She's been mad for him ever since she came to work for Grover. Have you talked to Pauline?"

"I have, but she didn't say anything about having a relationship with your brother."

"No. I guess she wouldn't. He didn't exactly share her feelings."

"Do you have any idea what Auggie needed the money for? Maybe he was making an investment?"

June shrugged. "I'm sure it was just living expenses. Cash flow must have been poor."

During the high season? "It's amazing that you even caught the withdrawals since you don't do the books."

June flicked her eyes to me and away again. "Before I went on the road to become our buyer, we both took care of the books. We had a check and balance system in place. When I'm home, I still check. Call it a habit."

"When was the last time you spoke with Auggie?"

June ran her finger around the rim of her glass and took another sip. "Friday afternoon. We fought about that stupid French clock again. He said if he could fix the broken second hand it would bring in enough to solve all our money problems for good."

"Were you having money problems?"

June's eyes were looking everywhere except at mine. "Tildy and I aren't exactly raking it in, but I don't know what Auggie was spending all his money on. He still lives at home rent-free. Dad pays for everything. I told him I thought it was time he grew up and took some responsibility. Maybe that would keep his nose out of *my* business for a change."

She cleared her throat and looked away. "The next morning, he was gone before I came down. I never even got to tell him I was sorry I'd brought it up."

The estate coordinator returned, arm in arm with Sawyer, and she was telling Sawyer her life story. It wasn't the first time I'd been caught in that whirlwind. We'd be here all day if I didn't get Sawyer away from her.

"Look at the time. We need to get back to do that thing." I pointed at the glass double doors.

Sawyer nodded. "Yeah, the thing. We should get going. Good luck with your daughter's wisdom teeth."

June gave me an odd look. "What about your headboard?"

"You know, I think I might just shop local instead."

She pulled out a gold-lettered business card and handed it to me. "Come by Whipple's. I'll find you something perfect."

"Right. I guess you are the sole proprietor now."

She raised her glass. "Back in the trenches."

With one hand on the door, I turned around. "Oh, and I like the tan. You look like you've gotten some sun recently."

June made a face like someone had swapped out Perrier for her champagne. "That's bronzer. I stay out of the sun as much as possible."

"Not even to go to the beach while you're here?"

"I'd rather have *my* wisdom teeth removed."

CHAPTER 29

"I'd say June was . . . evasive. She said she was at Whipple's Emporium at the time of the murder. And she kept trying to shift my attention to Grover's assistant, Pauline. Also, you wouldn't believe what they're asking for some ugly pink chairs."

I'd dropped Sawyer back at her bookstore to handle her emergency du jour. Now I was filling Aunt Ginny in on the estate sale and watching a rather disturbing scene unfold in my backyard.

Aunt Ginny pushed her giant white sunglasses up to the top of her head. "I'd believe it. People will throw money at the most ridiculous things."

"Uh-huh."

"You'd be surprised about the offers I've received for Bessie over the years. But then Bessie is a classic Corvette."

"Right."

"Why are you looking at us like that?"

"I'm just trying to figure out how this got started."

Victory held up a frozen daiquiri from her lounge chair on the back patio. "You say take day off."

Aunt Ginny nodded, slurped her daiquiri dry, and handed the empty glass to Royce, who was dressed in tennis whites and had a dish towel draped over his arm.

He put down the palm fronds he was fanning the ladies with and gave them a bow. When he disappeared into the house, I gave Aunt Ginny and Victory a look I hoped would chastise them.

"Just what are you two doing?"

Victory tightened her black bikini string at the hip and reached for her jar of sugar scrub. "He volunteer."

Aunt Ginny nodded and reached for her Evian misting fan. "He said he's doing research for a role in *Julius Caesar*. I'm not going to ruin it for him."

"That explains why you both have so much black eyeliner on."

Victory wiped the sugar scrub off her arm with one of my guest towels. "Eit need to be authentic."

Royce reappeared at the door with two fresh daiquiris.

I lowered my voice to a hiss. "You realize he thinks he's going on stage again. You're taking advantage."

Aunt Ginny waved a hand to shoo me away. "Leave Royce alone. He's having fun."

Royce delivered one daiquiri to Victory, who giggled, then bent over Aunt Ginny's chaise and handed her a fresh drink with an umbrella in it. "Your Majesty."

Aunt Ginny batted her eyes. "Why thank you, Mark Antony. You may fan me."

Royce picked up the palm fronds and began fanning the two women who were lying in the shade on the stone patio.

"I can't believe you all are doing this. And where did you get the fan?"

Royce gave me a wink.

Victory settled back on her lounge and readjusted her sunglasses that matched Aunt Ginny's. "You remember palm by front door?"

"Yes?"

"Eis no more."

I rolled my eyes to the heavens and watched a puffy cloud. *Why am I always surrounded by chaos?*

Aunt Ginny put a finger up and hollered, "Oh, Georgie. Be a dear and bring us some of those grapes I put in the freezer, will you?"

Georgina stood scowling like Mrs. Danvers through the back door overlooking the patio, and I was sure a lock of my hair turned white under her steely glare.

Victory stretched her arms over her head. "And breing beiscit."

Aunt Ginny hollered again. "And the cookies, please!"

Oooh. Who thought this was a good idea? These two were living it up on a movie set and my blood had turned to ice water waiting for the moment Georgina snapped and killed us all in our sleep.

Aunt Ginny slurped her fresh daiquiri. "I told Georgina that Victory was the better maid because she performed the traditional Ukrainian Daphnemoon of afternoon drinks. She said she could do better, and I bet her a hundred dollars she couldn't."

"The Daphnemoon?"

Aunt Ginny nodded.

"As in Daphne Moon from *Frasier*?"

Aunt Ginny nodded and Victory giggled.

Georgina came down the steps, the kitchen door slamming behind her. She held a tray of grapes with one hand and had a bag of Chips Ahoy wedged under her armpit. She stopped next to Victory's chaise and awaited instructions.

Royce, who was more lucid today than I'd given him credit for, pointed his fronds at the redwood side table between the lounge chairs. "Put it there, Miss Brown."

Georgina lifted her arm and let the cookies drop. Then she placed the grapes, clicked her heels together, and gave a small curtsy.

Aunt Ginny and Victory both raised their right hand and gave Georgina a silent corkscrew wave with a nod.

Georgina clicked her heels together again and returned to the house.

Royce and the women burst into laughter when they heard the door slam against the frame, but I knew there would be hell to pay once Georgina thought to google "Daphnemoon."

Georgina had lived a sheltered life of privilege and she could be ridiculously demanding, but I wasn't comfortable with seeing her taken advantage of. I went inside to see if she was really okay with Aunt Ginny ordering her about.

Georgina was wiping daiquiri mix off the counter, the cabinets, and under the range hood. Joanne was dropping cookie dough on a sheet and biting her bottom lip to keep from laughing.

"You forgot to put the lid on the blender, didn't you?"

Georgina growled at me. "You couldn't do any better yourself."

When I first came in here, I'd felt sorry for her. I was over it. I heard a muffled meow and looked around. "Where are the cats?"

Georgina pointed to the laundry room. "I locked them in there. Thanks to the demands of Ginny and that useless chambermaid of yours, that back door has been on a revolving hinge."

I peeked in the laundry room. Cleo and Sveltelana were calmly sitting on the folded guest towels that would now have to be rewashed. Figaro had wedged himself into a shoebox of clothes pins on the second shelf out of their reach. Sveltelana put her head back down on her front paws and closed her eyes. I left the door open a crack so they could get out when they were ready.

Joanne put the pan of cookies in the oven. "The happy hour wine and cheese is ready to be put out and stolen. I've included a plate of sliced tomatoes."

"I'll get it. Fifth time's the charm." I picked up the trays of fruit and cheese and carried them to the library. Marty Robbins was curled up in a blanket on the sofa reading a book. I uncorked two bottles of wine and put the white in an ice bucket. "Reading something good?"

She stretched and gave me a lazy smile. "Mm-hmm. Paul is taking a nap, so I thought I'd catch up on my sci-fi series."

"They both sound like good choices. I could use a nap myself."

Marty grinned. "Did you find anything out about that bungee jump place?"

Oh boy. "I haven't yet. Are you sure that's something you want to do? Paul seemed a bit—hesitant about it."

She hugged her knees to her chest and snickered.

"Paul has a lot more to lose if something goes wrong. But we agreed that this would be a no-holds-barred holiday for us."

I sat on the edge of the wing chair. "You sound like my Aunt Ginny."

"Oh, does she have cancer too?"

"I'm sorry, what?"

Marty tipped her head. "When I was diagnosed with stage four, I decided there was no use waiting for the right time to do the things I'd always wanted to try. I would get my affairs in order, then take the remaining good days I have with reckless abandon."

"Oh, Marty. I'm so sorry. I didn't know."

She waved me off. "Your aunt sounds like a kindred spirit, so I'm afraid I just assumed."

"Well, she has the same philosophy, but without the diagnosis."

Marty laughed. "Good for her. Too many people sit around worrying about what could happen when they could just be living their lives." Marty checked her watch. "Goodness. I have to go wake up Paul if we're going to make that salsa dancing class at the senior center. I hope they won't mind out-of-town guests." She grabbed her book and her blanket and headed up the stairs.

I was awed that she could be so calm. I took out my phone and searched for a bungee tour to tell her about later. Then I texted a message to Mr. Ricardo to be sure to welcome the Robbinses at his salsa class later.

I went to get some fresh ice for the bucket when a knock on the front door caused me to reroute and head back to the foyer. The kohlrabi king had dropped off a secret delivery. A giant basket of vegetables had been left on my porch. I checked the library—wine and cheese still in play—and took the vegetables to the kitchen.

Joanne threw down her potholders. "You have got to be kidding!"

I searched for an empty space for the newest basket. "Maybe we can tell the guests it's a South Jersey delicacy and send each of them home with a bushel."

"Georgie dear!" Aunt Ginny called Georgina to the door again.

"What!" She yelled across the yard.

"Now is that any way to speak to the upstairs when a bet is on the line?"

"What can I do, mum?"

"My misting fan is dry. Bring me the Evian."

Georgina took a bottle of Evian from the fridge, poured it in her glass, refilled the plastic with tap water, and stormed out to the backyard.

Joanne snickered. "I thought for sure you were gonna blow it and tell her they're messing with her."

"I almost did. Then she reminded me why we do stuff like this to her."

Georgina returned and announced she was taking a ten to re-airbrush her foundation, and marched out of the kitchen.

I moved all the kohlrabi into an empty produce box and stuffed it in the corner of the laundry room. Then I gathered up all the baskets and bowls that had brought the avalanche of unwelcomed produce to my house. "I'll be right back. Somebody has to do something about the Whipples."

CHAPTER 30

On my way out the door I looked back to the library, expecting triumph. The wine and cheese were gone. *Come on!* That was the shortest-lived victory ever. The only thing left was the plate of tomatoes.

I drove over to Courtney's, planning what I wanted to say. June had obviously lied to the police about her alibi. She was apparently having an affair with Spencer, eww. And there was a really good chance that Spencer was using her to get his hands on the house to turn it into another B and B. Mostly I wanted to tell Courtney to bless someone else—anyone else—with his kohlrabi.

The front door opened a crack and Courtney's little bird-beak nose poked out followed by his sunken eyes. "Oh, hello."

He looked tired and maybe a little sickly. The lines on his face were deeper than the last time I'd seen him, and they were quoting the poetry of grief. All my ire over the kohlrabi drained faster than Aunt Ginny was going through those daiquiris.

"Hi there. I came by to return your baskets and bowls from the vegetable deliveries."

Courtney opened the door and stepped out. "Are you enjoying them?"

"I can honestly say I've never had a better tomato. And we've been serving them every day. But we don't want to be selfish. I'm sure there are many people who would love to receive some."

"Nah. None of my friends are left around here anymore. And Thelma can't stand kohlrabi. That's why she recommended you. I'm just glad someone is putting it to good use."

If Mrs. Davis wasn't grieving over the loss of her nephew, we'd have words about this. I swung a basket towards the open door. "Do you want me to take them inside for you?"

"That'd be spiffy." Courtney stepped aside and I lugged everything into the foyer.

"Where do you want them?"

"How about the kitchen?"

I walked down the hall to the back and did a double take when I saw Mrs. Davis's jewelry box sitting on the dining room table. *I don't understand what is going on with that, at all.* I put the items in the kitchen and looked around. "Are you home alone?"

Courtney hugged himself and patted his arms. "Oh yes. Josephine and Tildy are off baby shopping, again. They heard about a boutique in Pleasantville. I have no idea where June or Spencer are. Those two have barely been inside since they arrived."

"I guess Spencer doesn't go shopping for baby items with Tildy?"

Courtney spoke through a bitter chuckle. "No. No, he wouldn't. I don't think that baby is ever going to materialize, poor thing."

"How are you holding up? I know it must be very difficult waiting to have the funeral."

Courtney walked to the sink and got two glasses of water. He put one glass in front of me. "It's well water. Not that reverse osmosis garbage." He took a drink and sighed. "I didn't go through anything like this when I buried my first wife, God rest her soul. She was in the ground and laid to rest three days after she died. I don't know what the police are looking for, but I wish they'd get it over with."

"They have to keep the body until they close the investigation."

Courtney pulled out a chair for me and sat down. "Auggie was a good boy. He had his problems—who doesn't. But to be murdered? I just can't make any sense of it."

"June said you and Auggie fought about money the night before the auction."

Courtney didn't meet my eyes. "That we did."

"Do you remember what time that was?"

"I called him around eleven and told him to come home immediately. He stumbled through the door after midnight, smelling of cheap hooch."

"Did Auggie admit he had taken the money?"

Courtney folded his hands in his lap. "He didn't have to. The accounts were not in order. June told me something was wrong, but I didn't want to see it. I'm retired now. It's up to them to work out the business. But she insisted the advances were unreasonable, and she brought the ledger home. Auggie had several large sums listed as purchases for items that were never entered into stock. There's no record of him selling them and they aren't in the storeroom. So, June wanted to know—where did the money go? I should have gotten involved sooner. I didn't know things were so out of control."

"Do you think he might have been embezzling?"

Courtney put his chin in his hands and looked out the window. "There was a time we had no secrets from each other. We were very close."

That's not really an answer.

Courtney gave me a sideways glance. "You know how boys are. I wanted him to settle down. Start a family. We need an heir to the Whipple estate. Now Thelma's boy will get everything. You just can't make your kids be who you want them to be. They have their own ideas and their own lives. You teach them what to do and they still go and mess it up."

I had once heard Georgina give the same speech about my late husband, John. I think it was at our rehearsal dinner. "Did Auggie have a black eye when you saw him Friday night?"

Courtney's eyes rolled to the side like he was searching his memory. "No. No, I don't believe so. But I was so upset with him for coming in drunk and . . . I wasn't really looking for a black eye."

I took a drink of my water. "May I use your restroom, please?"

He jabbed his thumb to the side. "Down the hall."

I knew where it was, but I wanted to get a look in Auggie's bedroom. I crept up the stairs and opened the first door on the right. It was a home office. A large cherry desk sat in the middle of the room. Bookshelves lined the back wall, filled with leather-bound classics and models of sailboats. A painting of a yacht hung over a burgundy leather sofa.

I checked the hall to see if I was being watched, then entered the room. An old-fashioned black leather ledger sat on a camel-colored desk blotter. I paged through it and found a two-thousand-dollar purchase for a chest of war silver. There was a handwritten note in the margin. *Where is this? It's not in stock.*

Over the next five pages, there were three payments made to a vendor called Sugar Sugar for five thousand dollars each.

Sugar Sugar sounds like it could be the name of a horse. Maybe Auggie was gambling? I turned the ledger at an angle and took out my cell phone to snap a picture for Amber.

I flipped another page and a pink slip fluttered to the table.

Dear Auggie, I've covered our tracks. The silver is yours, and so am I, if you want me.

I thought I heard a door shut down the hall and I panicked. I closed the ledger quickly and spun it back into place like I'd found it. A folded letter slid out the side of the blotter.

I was going to stuff it back in, but I saw the words "or else" printed in a heavy font. I picked up a ballpoint pen from the side of the desk and pried the note open. It was a demand for ten thousand dollars for taffy and M&M's. *Dear God, who runs up that kind of bill for candy? Or maybe it's drugs.* I snapped a fast picture with my cell phone and nudged the letter back under the blotter.

I listened at the door for a moment, then opened it and stuck my head out. I knew I had to hurry; no one takes this long to pee without having a prostate problem. I opened the next door down the hall in search of Auggie's room. I needed something that would shed some light on what Auggie could have been involved in.

The room was pale yellow and there were daisies on the bedspread. *This can't be right. Unless Auggie had a hidden dainty side.*

I stepped in and looked around. This wasn't Auggie's room, but I knew exactly whose it was. There were enough baby clothes to start your own boutique. Many things were recently bought from Petit Pois on the mall and still wrapped in tissue paper. Baby Boutique bags were everywhere. Tildy wasn't kidding about shopping. She had a carved wooden cradle and little booties in every size and color.

I felt like someone had punched me in the heart. Pain seared through my chest and I thought I might throw up. I had lived with this same longing for years. It had moved in and made itself at home until one day, I just stopped visiting. I accepted what would never be and the pain slowly faded to the background. Until now.

I ran my hand along delicate rosebuds embroidered onto the hem of a fuzzy pink blanket and a tear dripped from my cheek onto the satin trim. I knew the hole in Tildy's heart and the emptiness in her arms. And her chances got lower every day.

The front door opened, and Josephine called, "We're home." I had to get out of here before I was discovered. I snapped a couple pictures before slipping out of the bedroom and shutting the door. I took the steps as quiet as I could and silently made it to the landing. Courtney came out of the dining room with Josephine and Tildy behind him. "There you are. I thought you fell in."

Josephine narrowed her eyes and looked from me up the stairs. "There's a bathroom on this level."

"I'm so sorry. I'm not feeling well." I put my hand over my stomach. "If you'll excuse me, I should probably get home and take something."

Tildy's eyes were full of concern. "Do you need me to take you?"

"No. I'll be fine. Really." I had to fight hard not to pull her into a hug, but I wasn't supposed to know anything that I knew. I let myself out and ran down the steps to my car. When I backed up, Josephine was still watching me from the front porch. Her expression dark and menacing, her arms folded tightly in front of her like a warrior in bright pink eyeshadow and three necklaces, ready for battle.

CHAPTER 31

I tossed the Chex cereal in melted peanut butter and dairy-free chocolate, and Henry dumped the cup of powdered sugar from over his head, dusting us, the room, and Figaro in a white fog. When I was mixing things together, a piece of cereal dropped to the floor and Figaro was on it like Wayne Gretsky at the blue line.

"Poppy, can I sit on your lap while we watch *Paddington*? I always wanted to do that with a mommy my whole life."

I put the bowl down and scooped Henry into a mama-bear hug so he wouldn't see me tear up. "Of course you can, honey. Let's take the Muddy Buddies to the sunroom and beat Daddy to the remote."

Henry giggled and tore off to the TV room with Figaro on his heels. Figaro was no dummy. He knew wherever a four-year-old ate, smackerals would be easy pickings.

Gia kissed me. "*Paddington* again, huh?"

"Well, we didn't finish it the other night when you were called away for your broken pipe emergency."

Gia slid his eyes to mine with the humble confession of admission that he'd been taken in by a seventy-year-old con artist. "Mm. *Famiglia* . . . I gave my sister Daniela twenty dollars to bring the baby to Momma's tonight. That should buy us a couple hours without *un'emergenza*."

"Have you always been a hopeless optimist?"

He kissed my hand. "Only since you, *cara mia*."

Henry was sitting in the middle of the couch hugging the giant bowl of Muddy Buddies. All three cats were advancing on him like an open can of tuna and he was starting to look a little overwhelmed.

I handed Gia the bowl and Henry crawled into my lap. He snuggled down to watch the movie and laid his head back on my shoulder. I'd never been so happy in all my life.

Gia had originally suggested we go to the Wildwood Boardwalk with Henry tonight. I suggested we stay home away from judging eyes and questioning glances to finish our movie. I didn't want to admit to him that the stares were getting to me. He said I was imagining things, but everywhere we went, scantily clad women watched Gia with lust in their eyes. I was sure they were looking at me, confused as to where Gia's date must be. Like I was some kind of Mrs. Doubtfire chaperone. Gia never pressed me. I knew he didn't like my reasoning. He'd had some choice words for society in general the last time I'd brought it up.

Not that I'm ugly, mind you. I don't want to give you that idea. I'm told I have a very pretty face. A sentiment that never brings the reassurance you might expect.

There's always a giant "but" hanging in the air and it's not the one behind me.

Figaro tapped me on the knee with his fluffy paw. His feet looked like he was wearing gray bedroom slippers.

I gave him my full attention. He sat back, wrapped his tail around his front legs, and gave me a look that I interpreted as, *The child said there was a snack.*

In fact, all three cats had mysteriously moved forward since I'd sat down. Cleo rubbed her face against Figaro's neck. He shrugged her away with some obvious feline contempt and patted me on the knee again. Sveltelana took a step forward with a meow and the other two panicked that she was about to get something they weren't getting and moved forward with her.

I gave them each a small piece of cereal without any chocolate on it. Figaro made a project out of his bite and expected me to hold it steady until he'd licked all the sugar off.

The front door chimed and slammed shut. Aunt Ginny appeared in the hallway outside the sunroom wearing the scowl of doom. Her hair was soaked, and smudges of sand stuck to her cheek and forearm. She was dripping all over the parquet wood floor.

She wrung the hem of her sundress into her yellow beach bag. "I don't want to talk about it."

"I didn't ask."

"There was an incident."

"I can see that."

Aunt Ginny narrowed her eyes and scanned from me to Gia. He kept his eyes straight ahead and I could see the muscle in his cheek working overtime.

Henry was far too innocent and didn't know the warning signs. "Why are you all wet, Aunt Ginny?"

Aunt Ginny was obviously dying for someone to ask her what had happened. "Because Iggy is a terrible director."

Henry nodded and went back to *Paddington*. "Oh."

Aunt Ginny was fuming so hard she had steam rising off her shoulders. "At least Burt Lancaster had someone to warn him."

"I take it you and Royce were on the beach?" I went to the laundry room and opened the dryer for a fresh towel. A large kohlrabi fell to the floor. Someone had shoved a giant box of vegetables inside. I shut the dryer and took her a folded towel covered in cat hair.

Aunt Ginny wrapped the towel around her, tucked it under her arms, picked up her tote bag, and held her head high. "If you must know, there was a *From Here to Eternity* mishap, and I need a new cell phone."

Gia snickered from the couch and I knew it wasn't for the marmalade-covered bear.

Aunt Ginny glided towards her bedroom with all the dignity she could muster, and I mopped up the water and sand that trailed down the hall to the front door.

I was checking my work and considered getting out the Swiffer to do a better job when there was a knock on the front door. *Please don't be vegetables.* I reached for the handle and Georgina flounced down the stairs.

"That's for me. It's my little Smitty."

I stepped aside and Georgina flung the door against me like Mae West entering a saloon. "Hello, stranger."

Smitty removed his Philadelphia Eagles ball cap and grinned. "Heya, slim. Ready to hit the town like two kids on a first date?"

Georgina put a wrist to her forehead and let out a deep

sigh. "Oh, Smitty. I'm so exhausted from scrubbing floors all day."

I tried not to choke. "When did you scrub the floor?"

Georgina kicked at me behind the door. "I don't think I could walk down the steps. Poppy is practically trying to kill me. I've become a regular Cinderella."

Oh, good lord. I hissed at her from behind the door. "You cleaned one room and I had to redo the mirrors, and clean the other rooms."

Smitty cooed at the over-actor. "My poor baby. You want to stay in, and I'll rub your feet?"

I think I'm going to be sick.

Georgina giggled and pulled my handyman into the foyer. She had a sudden burst of energy and led him upstairs—I did not want to think about it.

I started down the hall to the laundry room to throw my now wet, sandy towel in the basket, when one of the twins called me from the steps.

"Poppy?"

I looked down the hall towards the sunroom where snuggles were waiting for me. "What can I do for you . . . ma'am?"

"My sister and I need a wake-up call at six a.m. We're going on a whale-watching tour."

A wake-up call? I supposed it would not be hospitable to suggest they simply use their cell phone like everyone else on the planet. "I will set my alarm and knock on your door at six."

A voice came from a few steps above her around the landing. "Faith! I told you I do not want to get up that early! I'm on vacation."

Oh, okay. This one is Faith.

She hollered up the stairs. "We need to be at the dock

at eight. There is no time for my skin-care regime if we get up too late!"

Grace, the other twin, joined her on the steps. "Poppy. Absolutely do not wake us up at six! We're going at two in the afternoon. Do you understand?"

"Um . . ."

Faith poked her sister in the chest. "You're not the boss of me. Poppy, keep it at six!"

Grace advanced on me, her nostrils flaring. "If you show up at our door one minute before nine a.m., I will sue the pants off you!"

Faith shoved her sister against the wall and my heart caught in my throat. I could not afford a lawsuit if these two old ladies threw themselves down my stairs in a brawl over a wake-up call that I didn't even offer. "We're getting up at six!"

"Ladies, I believe they offer whale tours several times a day. Might I suggest that whichever one of you wants to get up at six for early whale watching simply sets the alarm provided on your nightstand. And whichever wants to sleep late can take an afternoon tour. Then you can compare notes to see who had the better viewing."

The ladies transformed in front of my eyes back into the adorable cherubs who checked in a few days ago. "What a lovely idea, don't you think so, sissy?"

"Oh yes. Delightful. That's exactly what we'll do."

"Okay. Good night then."

They waved over their shoulders as they ascended the steps, chittering excitedly about their plans to see their very own "Shamu" and teasing each other over which one would have the better tour.

I rejoined Gia on the couch. "You would not believe what just happened."

Henry climbed back into my lap and laughed at something in *Paddington*.

Gia took my hand and kissed the back of my knuckles. "We heard." His eyes burned into mine and the heat fanned right up my neck. My breath caught in my chest.

"Have you seen this?" Aunt Ginny marched into the sunroom holding out a newspaper. She'd changed into a pink velour sweat suit that had Babelicious printed over the rear.

I sighed. "No."

She shook the paper in my face since I hadn't taken it from her. "It's an article about that vampire doohickey."

Gia took the paper from Aunt Ginny and she flopped into a leather wing chair next to the couch. Figaro immediately jumped into her lap and hissed at the felines who lay down at Aunt Ginny's feet.

She gave his head a stroke. "You tell them, handsome. Back off, ladies. He shares his catnip with no one."

Gia took out a pair of reading glasses and slid them onto his face. My stomach did a flip and I thought I might swoon, but Henry was with us, so I'd have to swoon another time.

"Interesting. The wooden stake is missing from the picture." Gia looked at Aunt Ginny.

Aunt Ginny shrugged. "Yeah?"

Gia took his reading glasses off and put them away. "This is big deal, *signora*. Either the killer stole the wooden stake sometime on Friday and no one noticed it missing all day, or they got into the auction house after closing and stole it before opening Saturday morning for the interview."

I craned my neck to see the photo. "Auggie left home around eight. If he was killed before Blake opened, how did he get into the auction house? He only had a key to the storage room. And if he was killed between noon and four when the auction house was open to the public, how are there no witnesses?"

Gia folded the paper in half. "I think someone is lying about seeing him. And I would start with Blake Adams."

Aunt Ginny snatched the paper back from Gia. "*Thees ees beeg deal, signora. Abbondanza.*"

I stared openmouthed at Aunt Ginny's exaggerated impersonation of my boyfriend.

Henry giggled. "*Abbondanza!*"

Gia quirked an eyebrow. "Is that supposed to be me?"

Aunt Ginny was still cranked up over her beach disaster. She threw her arms in the air and waved them around, making Figaro jump down and start a bath to wash off her attitude. *"Miya namea ees a Giampaolo Larusso and I ama seenyor smartee pantsa. Ciao!"*

"Aunt Ginny!" I had not seen her this crabby since Royce's sister Fiona hijacked their trip to the Borgata so Royce would stay home and mow the lawn. I didn't know whether to laugh or scold her.

Henry giggled again and waved his arms around. "*Ciao!* I am senior smartee pantses."

Gia crossed his arms over his chest and tried to look stern. "I do not sound like Luigi from Mario Brothers. I am *sofisticato.*"

Aunt Ginny gave him a pert look. "I'm not hearing the difference."

I shook my head. "Maybe you need a spoonful of jelly. Your blood sugar may be too low."

She narrowed her eyes at me and waved the newspaper in a threating way. "Bah! You two are too smart for your own good."

She stormed off and Figaro immediately jumped in her abandoned seat so he could glower at Cleo and Sveltelana.

Gia snickered. "Foo. She is extra feisty tonight."

"I am so sorry about that. I think she's still irritated that Josephine accused her of dyeing her hair this afternoon when they were at Senior Water Aerobics."

"I thought she does dye her hair."

"Yeah, but she doesn't want Josephine to know that."

Cleo jumped into the leather chair and spun around a couple of times before snuggling into Figaro. Fig's ears flattened but he didn't look up.

Gia put his arm around me, and I thought we were moving past the situation. Then he muttered to himself. "*Abbondanza* . . . No one says that."

I patted his knee. "I know."

Sveltelana jumped onto the wing chair and daintily lay down on Fig's leg and Cleo's hindquarters. Cleo clawed the air until she was free enough to breathe and resettle in a new position. Figaro's eyes popped open and he tried to wiggle his way out, but he was trapped under Mount Sveltelana. In the end he just gave up and went to sleep. I was hoping it wasn't the lack of oxygen.

I could hear him purring from under the heap of felines. "You know my cat's in a love triangle."

Gia traced the back of my hand with his finger. He cast Figaro a glance. "Always go with the Italian."

CHAPTER 32

Oliva Larusso must have a direct link either to the psychic network or the Vatican, because Gia's mother can sniff out when we're getting cozy faster than Aunt Ginny can nuke a Pop-Tart. No sooner had the movie ended and Gia had moved a sleeping Henry to the couch when there was a knock on my front door. I didn't have the luxury of ignoring it in case a guest had forgotten their key. But I didn't expect to see Angelo, Gia's shady brother-in-law, standing on my front porch with his hat in his hands doing his best Robert De Niro impersonation.

"Beggin' your pardon, ma'am. I know the hour is late, but Mother Larusso is very worried that she has broken her hip. She requests that Giampaolo come and take her to the hospital."

"Oh my gosh. Did she fall?"

"No, ma'am."

"Was she in an accident?"

"No, ma'am. If you could just get Giampaolo, please."

Gia came down the hall with his cell phone in his hand and a spasm of irritation flew across his face. "Momma is fine. Daniela just text that they are watching *Supermarket Sweep*."

Angelo shifted his feet and crumpled the brim of his hat in his meaty hands. "Please, Giampaolo. Teresa said she won't let me back inside until you go and check on your mother."

Gia said some colorful-sounding things in Italian that I didn't catch. Once I'd reassured him that I would see him tomorrow and gave him a proper kiss goodbye while he made Angelo wait outside on the porch, he collected a sleepy Henry and took off to check on the Godmother, Carmela Corleone herself.

"Hey, doll?" Mrs. Grabstein crept down the stairs with her nose in the air. "Do ya smell that?"

I sniffed. "Smell what?"

"I think I smell smoke."

I sniffed again, this time sniffing my way from room to room. Fig thought we were playing a game and trotted along behind me, wheezing. "I don't smell anything."

Elaine cocked her head and narrowed her eyes. "I don't know . . . How good is ya nose?"

I was starting to panic that another seance was being planned. "It's really good. So are my smoke alarms. I promise you, there is nothing to worry about."

She shrugged. "Okay, doll. I hope ya know whacha doin'. This old house could go up like a bonfire if ya aren't careful."

Elaine disappeared back up the stairs and I suddenly felt very alone. The house changed from full to empty on a dime, and my heart had followed Gia out the door. I cleaned up the sunroom. Bagged the leftover Muddy Buddies for tomorrow's happy hour. Gave all three cats some treats. Washed my coffee cup. Checked the time to see if it was late enough to go to bed yet. I'd killed seven minutes. I spotted the newspaper Aunt Ginny had thrown behind the trash can during her fit. The photo of the vampire-hunting kit was very visibly missing the wooden stake from the open box.

Why the wooden stake? The antique show was a murderer's dream. There were guns, knives, and poisons around every corner. If properly motivated, the killer could have used that giant blacksmith hammer to whack Auggie over the head, but they used a wooden stake through the heart. The hours to the auction house were posted at the end of the article and they didn't close for another forty-five minutes.

I grabbed my purse and my keys and headed for Bessie. There was no traffic going off the island. All the tourists were tucked away at their restaurant reservations, down on the boardwalk, or sitting on the front porch of their B&Bs enjoying the night like half of my guests were doing. I drove into the Adams Galleries parking lot and parked between two other cars that were still there.

I found Blake Adams in the auction room with an older Indian couple. I pulled up one of the folding chairs and waited for him to finish showing the couple a painting of a Union soldier posing on a horse. They finally shook hands and the couple left with his business card. Then Blake came over to speak to me. "Hello again."

I put my hand out. "Poppy. Friend of the Whipples. Niece to the winner of the matador costume."

"I never forget a pretty face." Blake smiled and crossed his arms over his broad chest. He was very fit for a man estimated to be in his early forties. Like a weightlifter, or a boxer.

I tried to imagine him with June, but she seemed so fragile compared to his heft.

"I spoke with you and your husband over at the brewery the other day after that run-in with my ex."

"That's right. I mean except he isn't my husband. He's my boyfriend." Every time I said those words, they felt a little less silly.

Blake's eyebrow shot up and he nodded. "What can I do for you? I was just getting ready to lock up for the night. Looking to have something appraised?"

"No. I just stopped by to see what time you open in the morning."

He grinned. "You could have saved a trip and checked the website. Noon."

"Did you open at noon last Saturday?"

Blake's eyes narrowed slightly. "Yes. We open at noon before every auction to give people a chance to preview the items for sale. Why do you ask?"

"I saw the article about Auggie's vampire-hunting kit in *The Press*. I was wondering when the photograph was taken."

The creases around Blake's eyes softened. "Oh. *The Press* arrived for an interview at ten Saturday morning and Auggie hadn't shown up yet."

"Who was here?"

"I was the only one here. I was in my office going over my notes when they arrived. I didn't want to lose publicity for Whipple's or for the auction house, so I let the photographer take pictures of the box in my office."

"Did you happen to notice the wooden stake was missing?" I handed him the paper.

He sat down hard on the chair in front of me. "Oh my god. I was so preoccupied, I—I didn't notice."

"So, you're sure this picture was taken around ten?"

Blake nodded. "A few minutes after."

"And the box was locked in the storage room until you opened it?"

Blake's expression was blank. Like he was trying to process the information or think up a credible excuse.

"When was the last time you saw Auggie?"

"I told you. Friday night. When he came to lock the box in storage."

"Are you sure the wooden stake was in the box when he locked it up?"

"I'm pretty sure it was. Eighty-five percent sure. We took one last look at the item, then I left him to do his thing. When I came back, the room was locked, and he was gone."

"Who else could have locked the door?"

Blake held up a key ring with a large brass key with fancy scrollwork. "I told you. I have one. Auggie and Grover have the other two. I gave them keys when I bought the auction house. I've never given any other copies out in the twelve years I've been open. There isn't a key maker around who will copy these keys. They're over a hundred years old."

"What about the main door to Adams Galleries? Who has a key to the building?"

"It's an electronic keypad. I'm the only one with the code."

We stared at each other for a beat, letting the implications sink in.

"Did you and Auggie fight the last time you were together?"

Blake cleared his throat and swallowed hard. "No. Not at all. Why do you ask?"

"I was told you didn't get along."

Blake shrugged it off. "What? We did. Who says we didn't?"

"I was told that the relationship had grown cold after you and June separated."

Blake's eyes were looking everywhere but at me.

"Was it because Auggie was angry that you cheated on his sister?"

Blake's eyes went wild. His pupils dilated and he pointed a finger at me. "I did not have an affair! I was set up."

"Found in the arms of a half-naked mermaid is some pretty damning evidence."

His face turned red. Blake kicked a folding chair and said something I wouldn't repeat.

I stood up quickly and fished around in my purse for my keys, to have something to jab at Blake if I needed to defend myself. I pulled out a mini can of Bed Head antifrizz that Blake must have thought was Mace.

He raised both hands in front of his chest and stepped back. "I'm sorry. I'm sorry. Look, I'm still dealing with a lot of stress from that situation and I reacted badly. That whole day causes me to boil over."

I stared at Blake, ready to uncap the Bed Head. "Just what are you trying to tell me?"

"I got a note to meet June at Jumbo's under the boardwalk. It said she had a surprise for me—for our anniversary. But when I arrived, with a red rose, just like she told me, some girl dressed like a mermaid was down there waiting. She had long green hair and a fish tail, and she was crying. She said she'd sprained her ankle and asked me to help her stand. I told her it was probably the stupid rubber tail she was wearing. The next thing I know, she pulls off her top and throws herself into my arms and kisses me."

Blake saw me roll my eyes and he melted onto the next folding chair and dropped his head in his hands. "It's the truth. June showed up at the worst possible moment and said that was the last straw. But I don't even know what the other straws were. Women come on to me all the time. Some of them have made moves on me. I don't return their advances. I love my wife. How is it my fault? June ran off and left me there. I didn't even get to give her the rose. You don't believe me either. I can see it on your face."

"Well, I'm sorry. But it's a ridiculous story. Why would someone set you up to look like you were cheating on your wife?"

"I still have the note locked in my safe." Blake shot from the room.

I wasn't sure if I was supposed to follow him or wait here. I craned my neck to look down the hall where he'd disappeared. *Should I go after him? He'd better not be getting a gun. Or one of those Civil War bayonets. What a stupid weapon. If you're that bad a shot that the enemy can get close enough for you to jab them with a knife, you shouldn't have a gun in the first place. Maybe I should just leave. I don't want to be skewered for trying to help Mrs. Davis.*

Blake appeared from around the corner waving a scrap of paper. "Found it."

He handed it to me. Sure enough, it was just as he described. Of course, he could be psychotic. *Maybe he just wrote this note in his office while I stood here and worried about being stabbed with a gun knife.*

"And this is your wife's handwriting. Right?"

Blake's expression was blank. He lifted his palms. "Everything is text messages and emails nowadays. When do we write each other notes? I didn't really think about it. I guess I just assumed."

Men. "Did you show this to June?"

"She said she caught me red-handed, the note means nothing."

Solid point. "Who would want to break up your marriage?"

Blake turned to get something from the podium, and I snapped a picture of his note with my cell phone. He returned with his iPhone and showed me his lock screen was a picture of him and June holding hands on Sunset Beach. Blake stared wistfully at the photo. "I thought we were happy. We were even planning to move down the coast. Sell everything and get a beach house on the Outer Banks. June must have changed her mind and wanted out."

Blake's story was just as weird as his ex's. They both believed the other one concocted an elaborate scheme to force a breakup. "If she wanted a divorce, why wouldn't she just tell you?"

His expression hardened. "Before we married, Courtney made me sign a prenup saying I would get nothing of theirs if we ever divorced because of adultery. Setting me up to look like I was cheating was one way to make sure I got nothing. That family would rather die than lose any of their precious antiques."

I handed him the note back. "Do you think someone killed Auggie to get their hands on his part of the inheritance?"

Blake screwed his face up in thought. "There's only June, and she wouldn't hurt a fly."

"There's Tildy."

"No, Tildy is the least materialistic person I know. Her husband, however . . ."

"There's Josephine."

He shook his head. "Josephine wouldn't have to kill Auggie to get control. She'd have to kill Courtney. No, if you ask me—it's something darker. Auggie had a problem. He owes some very shady people money. I think one of them tracked him down and when he couldn't pay, they killed him."

"What kind of problem? Gambling?"

"Just check his cell phone apps."

"What about Grover Prickle? Do you think he was jealous enough of that vampire kit that he'd kill Auggie?"

"I don't know. Grover has never struck me as the violent type. He's more the *sit around and complain and shake his fist at kids on the lawn* type. But then anything is possible."

"And Pauline? Were she and Auggie friends?"

Blake snickered under his breath. "Everyone knows Pauline had a crush on Auggie, but he didn't notice she was alive unless he wanted something from her. It was embarrassing really, the way she threw herself at him. And he destroyed her. Poor thing, she's a nice girl. That's what turned him off. Auggie didn't go for nice girls."

CHAPTER 33

I flicked the light on in my bedroom and found three cats snuggled into my pillows. "Don't you two have your own rooms? Why is no one looking for you?"

I tried to shift Sveltelana to the other side of the bed. I gently nudged her away, but she rolled back into place like a lump of bread dough that had over proofed. I went to the other side of the room and yanked the comforter as hard as I could. It flew off the bed and sent the other two cats airborne, but Sveltelana didn't budge. Rooted to the mattress in a magician's tablecloth trick, she blinked at me with amusement. Figaro jumped back on the bed and walked to her side—fascinated with my attempts at extraction. He looked from Sveltelana to me and twitched his whiskers. This was starting to be more trouble than it was worth, so I gave up and crawled into the other side of the bed.

It was weird to still think of it as John's side. I guess it was also kind of weird after a year and a half to still sleep on one side of the bed instead of sprawled out in the middle. I traced his face on our picture on the nightstand. Eventually there would be another man in this bed. Maybe I should switch sides now?

"Fire! Fire!" Mrs. Grabstein's shrill voice sliced through the air moments before the piercing ring of the alarm. I shot off the bed like I'd been bucked from a bull.

I grabbed my cell phone and scooped up Sveltelana like she weighed nothing. Figaro and Cleo didn't need assistance, they'd torn out of the room the moment my legs flailed in the air. Georgina and I practically rolled down the stairs in an avalanche to the second floor.

"What is it? Where's the fire?" I was still holding the Maine coon, who acted like this happened every day in her house. She lay back and reached out a paw to touch the pink foam roller in Grace Padawowski's white hair.

All the guests had congregated on the second-floor landing in their pajamas, or lack thereof in the case of Jenna Foubert, who was wearing something with feathers and sequins. Elaine caught Burl looking and elbowed him in the belly, making him blush the color of his red satin pajamas. "Don't worry, doll. I called the fire department. They're on the way."

"You did what?"

Elaine adjusted her thick glasses. "I told 'em I been smellin' smoke all day they said they'd be right ovah."

The sound of distant sirens getting closer caused my mouth and my heart to drop like a rock.

Aunt Ginny's voice carried up the stairs from the front foyer. "Poppy! Is that you I hear? What in the name of Jeremiah Jehoshaphat is going on? Why is there a fire truck pulling up outside the house? Two fire trucks!"

My voice caught in my throat and the other guests discussed that no one else smelled smoke. They did all think that maybe Jenna should go put on a robe. Everyone except Kevin Martins, but his wife twisted his arm behind his back and said he'd never eat another hoagie as long as she lived if he didn't keep his eyes where they belonged.

Aunt Ginny greeted the firemen like they were guests at her annual VFD soiree. "Why, hello, boys. No, I didn't call you this time. I haven't used that old waffle iron since my niece moved in. You're looking very fit, Dayton. I can't believe you haven't retired yet."

We were commanded to wait outside on the front lawn while they searched the house. Wade grabbed Figaro like a football. Burl picked up Cleo, and we were ushered outside to let the firemen do their jobs. Figaro gave me a panicked look from Wade's arms until Jenna took him and held him like a baby. He relaxed and started to take a bath while she rocked him. *Traitor.*

I still held Sveltelana. She started purring. My back was screaming at me that I'd never lifted so much weight in my life. Marty was hunched over holding her stomach and Paul had his arm around her back. Neither one of them were looking to take the enormous cat from me. I didn't know what else to do so I shifted her up to my shoulder and prayed the firemen would be quick.

Elaine marched back and forth with her arms over her head, calling on Siobhan to watch over the house.

We were doing just fine without Siobhan before tonight.

The neighbors were congregating on their front lawns now. Mr. Winston called me from across the street. "Ho there, Poppy. Everything okay?"

I gave him an embarrassed nod. "We're fine. I'm sure it's a false alarm."

Mr. Winston couldn't hear anything not shouted into his good ear, so Mrs. Pritchard had to translate for him. She cupped her hands and yelled, "It's probably just Ginny making waffles again."

Mr. Winston laughed. "I told her that thing was dangerous. Get you one of them new plastic models, Poppy!"

I gave him a smile and tried to melt into the azaleas. Thank God I had a cat the size of a small child to hide behind. If only it wasn't three thousand degrees under all this fur. The exhaust coming off the fire engines was making me loopy.

Grace and Faith Padawowski were giggling excitedly over by the hose. "Wait until we tell Claude the bed and breakfast caught on fire. He'll be so jealous he missed this."

The Sheinbergs followed the action from down the street. I felt Mrs. Sheinberg tug on the hem of my tank top. "Heya, bubbala. That's a skimpy outfit ya got on theya. What happened? Ginny trying to burn the place down for the insurance?"

I sighed to myself. "I think it's just a misunderstanding. I'm sure they'll give us the all clear soon." *I hope.*

She grabbed a takeout menu tucked under my mailbox flag and fanned herself. "Last time we had this much excitement around here, Ernest Murillo accidentally set off illegal fireworks in his garage. That was in seventy-seven, I think . . . or seventy-eight. Sol! When did Ernest try to blow up the whole block?"

Mr. Sheinberg scratched his chin. "I think it was seventy-two."

Mrs. Sheinberg waved a backhand in his direction. "He don't know."

Kevin Martins came around the side of the house dragging a beach chair through the hostas. His wife, Shondra, hollered at him from the mailbox where she was keeping her distance in case flames burst from the house across the yard. "Kevin! What. Are. You. Doing!"

Kevin stopped dragging the chair. Gave his wife a piercing look. And shook the chair open with one hand. He plopped down and pulled a soda out of his pajama pocket and popped the tab.

Shondra muttered testily beside me. "You know you can't have caffeine this late."

Kevin overheard her and responded just as testily. "It can't keep me awake any worse than the red flashing lights and the sirens."

A new siren joined the nightmare along with blue flashing lights. Mr. Sheinberg cheered. "Whoo-hoo! The fuzz is here. Lookout!"

I felt my bones turn to jelly. *Great.*

The police cruiser pulled up behind the ladder truck and the siren silenced. Amber appeared by my side. "I heard the call on my scanner. Whadya do?"

"I let psychos into the bed and breakfast."

"Is everyone okay?"

"As far as I can tell. They're all out here on the lawn planning their complaints for checkout."

Amber nodded and looked around. Then she looked back at me. "What is that? A baby bear?"

"It's a cat. And it weighs a ton." Sveltelana blinked at me angelically. "No offense."

A little car pulled up and chugged to a stop. It had a lighted delivery car topper advertising Piro's Pizza. A big man in a smock peeled himself out of the car and came up on the lawn holding a brown paper bag with a foot-long cheesesteak wrapped in butcher's paper sticking out of the top. No one spoke, but everyone pointed at Burl Grabstein. Burl blushed and his whiskers bristled pink under the red lights.

Aunt Ginny made a loop around the yard and across the street, greeting everyone like she was on a midnight USO tour. "I know. I didn't hear the smoke alarms go off either. It is a mystery."

I shifted my weight and pulled my cell phone from my pocket. I handed it to Amber. "Look at the pictures."

She thumbed through and made comments. "Where was this?"

"Tildy's room."

"And this?"

"That fell out of the Whipple Emporium accounts ledger. Auggie was receiving threats."

"Do we know from who?"

"Not yet. But he was making some big payouts, and his ex-brother-in-law said to check his cell phone apps. I'd look for gambling sites, personally."

"We don't have his cell. It wasn't on him at the crime scene and the family is having trouble locating it." Amber handed me my phone back. "I'll need copies of these. You should also know that forensics came back. Auggie wasn't on drugs when he died. He had been in at least two fights. A recent one resulting in a black eye, and one several days earlier resulting in a cracked rib and some bruising on his torso."

A single blue light came flashing around the corner and a car with an undercover strobe on the dash parked behind Piro's Pizza.

Amber muttered. "Just what I need."

Viola Washington stomped into my yard and stood in front of us with her hands on her hips, glaring at Amber. "Really."

Eventually the fire marshal came out and asked for someone in charge. Sveltelana and I stepped forward.

"We can't find any fire or smoke of any kind. The only fire hazards were a giant box of turnips in the dryer, and five different hair styling devices plugged into an ancient surge protector on the third floor."

I cut my eyes at Georgina, but she was suddenly focused on the string of her sleep sack.

The fire marshal waved his team to the trucks. "Other than that, you're in the clear." Everyone cheered, but I had a twenty-minute lecture about fire alarms and false emergencies.

Amber snickered. "It's about time that karma caught up to you." She got in the police car and drove away, followed by Sergeant Washington, who no doubt would follow her home.

It was nearly two a.m. Most of the guests were trickling back upstairs. Aunt Ginny had promised a sizable donation to the department fire prevention fundraiser. And I was finally allowed in my house. My back was spasming. I gently put Sveltelana down next to Figaro and stretched. Sveltelana licked Figaro on the ear. He went limp and hit the floor with a thud. Paul grabbed her under the arms and hauled her up to bed. I stared at Figaro for a moment, wondering what we'd be doing right now if we'd stayed put in Virginia. He gave me a look that said we needed to rethink some things.

I locked up for the second time tonight, and turned

around to find Elaine Grabstein standing at the foot of the steps waiting for me.

"That was a close one, doll. Betta safe than sorry I always say."

I forced a smile. *Of course, you don't have to get up in five hours to make breakfast, do you, Elaine?* "Good night, Mrs. Grabstein."

I dragged myself up the stairs. "Come on, Fig. Let's get you a goodnight treat. I'd carry you but I don't have any feeling left in my shoulders."

I rounded the landing to the third floor and the hair stood up on my arms. The blood was hammering in my ears so loudly I couldn't hear myself think. Figaro refused to move any further. The wooden troll doll was standing on the edge of the third-floor banister. Its hair frizzed in a wild arc over piercing black eyes.

Chapter 34

Some days I tried to contort myself out of bed in a fancy enough way to call it yoga. After last night's demonstration of Cape May's finest emergency response services, followed by that creepy talisman scaring the daylights out of me and five hours of fitful sleep, I was calling today's flow *twisted salamander into downward swimming dolphin*. My cool-down salutation was the *cinnamon roll shavasana* with *hot water mudras*. In other words, I flopped out of bed with a twist and rolled to the shower. I was getting really good at it too.

Figaro and I burst through the pantry door into Shangri-la. We had the kitchen to ourselves. It happened so rarely that for a minute it left me confused. "The clocks didn't change, did they? What time is it?" I started the coffee and fed Fig a quiet breakfast of pureed chicken and gravy.

Our peace was as fleeting as a perfect hair day. The

back door whacked open and Joanne trudged into the kitchen stomping her feet. "I heard you set the house on fire last night. What happened, Buttface?"

I put the peach nectarine crisp in the oven to warm. "Elaine Grabstein happened."

Joanne laughed at me under her breath and shook out her apron. "I suppose you forgot to make those quiches for this morning's breakfast."

I felt the little energy I had from the espresso deflate like a bad soufflé. "Oh no."

"Too busy polishing your nails or something?"

"How about this: I make a sheet pan quiche, and after it bakes, we cut it into rounds and serve them on biscuits like little breakfast sandwiches?"

I could tell Joanne was intrigued because she didn't attack me immediately. "I'll top them with hollandaise and call them southern biscuit Benedicts. That just might save the reputation I've been working to build for you all summer."

I was too tired to get annoyed with her. "Alright, sure."

I turned on the eighties station and we worked side by side to put together the tasty little bites. I whipped up a sheet of creamy eggs with ham, Swiss, spinach, and caramelized onions, while Joanne made the delicate little biscuits. While everything baked, I whisked together the cinnamon cream sauce for the crisp.

I had just put on a giant pot of blanched tomatoes from Courtney's garden to make tomato jam and free up the dryer for today's laundry when Aunt Ginny padded into the kitchen dressed in a Cape May Fire Department T-shirt and capris. She looked in the oven for the coming attractions.

I handed Aunt Ginny the cream. "Where'd you get that T-shirt?"

She looked down at her chest. "I've had this old thing for ages. One of the firemen left it here and I never returned it."

Joanne raised an eyebrow and shook her head. "When will you learn not to ask?"

It was unusually quiet in the dining room this morning. Everyone was still a little drowsy from the late night. Victory arrived while I was filling the coffee carafes for the guests. She helped Joanne plate the breakfast biscuits while I took out the cobbler and cinnamon cream sauce. We left everyone happily and silently digging in and retreated to the safety of the kitchen.

I had just joined Aunt Ginny and Victory at the banquette to eat my keto breakfast biscuit when all hell broke loose on the other side of the door.

I was on my feet with the first crash, but Joanne beat me to the dining room before the screams began. She flew back into the kitchen and said two words I never wanted to hear again. "Call 911."

Burl Grabstein lay on the floor next to half a biscuit, clutching his chest. I put a pillow under his head and said a silent prayer. *Lord, please don't let Santa die at my house. I would never recover from that.*

Aunt Ginny patted Elaine's hand and reassured her that everything would be alright. The other guests moved back to give Burl some air. Figaro jumped up in Burl's chair to see what he'd left on his plate since he clearly wouldn't be needing it now, and Joanne swatted him away. We knew the ambulance had arrived when the sirens whined to a stop.

Burl was assessed by the rescue squad and loaded onto a stretcher for transport to the emergency room. All the guests lined the hall and gave quiet words of encouragement as Burl was wheeled out the door. Even Figaro allowed Cleo to rub her face against his, just this once.

Elaine had twisted a hole into one of my cloth napkins. She reached for me, trembling. "Poppy, could ya go to the hospital with Burl? I don't want him to be alone and I'm too shook up to drive right now."

I put my arm around her shoulder, my irritation from the night before on pause. "Why don't you go with your husband? I can bring your car up to you later."

She whimpered and patted her chest. "I'm way too scared for that. What if he senses my fear? I don't want to send him into the light. Maybe I should stay here and wait for ya to call and let me know it's safe to come up." A fat tear slid down her cheek.

Joanne stepped forward. "Why don't you go ahead? I can drive Mrs. Grabstein to the hospital as soon as she calms down."

I looked into Elaine's thick glasses at her spidery lashes and red, watery eyes. Her lip quivered.

"Okay. I'll see you up there soon."

Elaine patted me on the hand and sniffled. "Good. Good. I'll go get ready."

I grabbed my keys and headed to Cape May Court House, the county seat where the hospital was located. At least this time I got to park in the visitors' lot instead of the emergency bay. If I showed up here any more often, they'd have to give me an ID badge.

The emergency room waiting area smelled of disinfectant and Fritos. Rows of easy-to-clean vinyl chairs were occupied by patients with sunburns, food poisoning, broken bones, and one woman holding a baby that would not stop crying. Two televisions hung on opposite sides of the room—one playing something called *Yo Gabba Gabba!* that looked like it was created after a night of heavy drug use, and the other played the news, which had been known to cause heavy drug use. I had to wait in the front lobby by reception while Burl was sent back for tests.

I was surfing Pinterest for recipe ideas on my phone from a blue vinyl couch when I overheard, "Delivery for Grover Prickle," spoken behind me. A florist had arrived with a vase of sunflowers. The old man working reception let his glasses slide down his nose as he typed the query into the computer. A very long two minutes later, he gave the florist driver the room number. He wrote it on the delivery card, and they put the vase aside for someone to deliver to the room later.

Grover Prickle is here? By name? Not John Doe. He's not missing? Amber could have mentioned that last night while she was looking at my recon pictures. After all this time, the information still only flowed in one direction unless I pushed.

Burl was in good hands with those tests. And they were not going to be quick hands. I had time to pop up to Grover's room and offer my well wishes. If he mentioned where he'd been for the last few days, and what he was doing during Auggie's murder, at least I would have something to tell Mrs. Davis.

I bought the world's most expensive balloon in the hospital gift shop and tried to look like someone who was supposed to be here. The elevator doors opened on Grover's floor and I passed a nurses' station and followed the signs to his room.

The hospital was a good place to be if you were going to have a heart attack. Such as maybe because you suffered a little fright coming at you down the hall. I was thankful for that when my heart skipped a beat. Because as soon as I turned the corner, the last person I expected to see came out of Grover Prickle's room. "Hi, Josephine. What are you doing here?"

CHAPTER 35

"**A**re you following me? Does Thelma know? You aren't going to tell anybody, are you?"

I wasn't sure how Josephine had managed to steal back that fancy jewelry box from Mrs. Davis so many times, because the woman had absolutely no covert skills at all.

Josephine spluttered several more things without making a lot of sense, but the guilt was written all over her face.

"I take it Courtney doesn't know you're here."

Josephine's neck blossomed the same fuchsia as her zigzag leggings. "I don't know what you're talking about."

"Why are you visiting your husband's enemy? And how did you know he was here?"

Josephine pulled herself up to her full height plus the

extra seven inches from her teased-up platinum hair. "Don't be ridiculous. I'm not visiting Grover Prickle. I'm a candy striper."

Josephine ran towards the elevator, her fuchsia hoop earrings clacking against her lime-green choker necklace. She jabbed furiously at the call buttons while looking back at me. When the doors opened, she dove into the elevator. "Watch out!"

A young woman, with an identical overpriced balloon to mine, tripped out of the elevator and growled at the oldest living candy striper that she should be more careful.

I gave a tentative knock on the door.

A raspy male voice croaked, "Come in."

Grover Prickle sat against a stack of pillows. An IV was taped to his left hand and several machines stood nearby to give the occasional beep of concern. The son of anarchy was looking a little more feeble and bushy than when I'd seen him at Cold Spring Village. But even though he was sitting in a hospital bed hooked up to a heart monitor, he'd taken the time to spruce up for company and put on a leather vest and a gray Irish flat cap.

"Hi. I don't know if you remember me, but I was at the antique show."

Grover stared at me blankly, then his eyes focused and he nodded. "I remember."

"I don't want to bother you, I just wanted to check in and see how you were feeling." I casually looked around the stark room. There was no evidence that any visitors had been here other than the lingering smell of Giorgio perfume mixing with the Lysol. I put my arm out and offered the balloon I'd originally only bought as a cover story. It bobbed under the air vent, awkward and alone.

Grover pointed his IV hand at an orange chair by his bedside. "Mighty kind of ya. Have a seat."

"Are you sure?"

He shrugged. "What else am I gonna do?"

I tied the balloon to his tray table and settled myself into the hard plastic. It immediately suctioned itself to my backside and formed a seal. *Well, now I know exactly how wide my hips are when I sit down. A half an inch smaller than this chair.* "I went to Prickled Curiosities the other day. You have a beautiful store."

Grover gave me a wan smile. "Thanks. I'm the fourth Prickle to run the Curiosities. My great-great-grandfather was born in that house. And his son, my great-grandfather, turned it into Prickled Curiosities."

"That's amazing. My father's family has owned a house in Cape May for generations. I wonder if our ancestors were friends."

Grover gave me a tiny shrug and winced slightly. "Hard to say. But it was a small community a hundred years ago, so they probably knew each other. Now I'm the last. No family to carry on when I'm gone."

"I've been worried. When you didn't show up for the auction, we all wondered what had happened to you."

He adjusted one of the leads that disappeared under his vest. "If this is about the armoire . . ."

I rocked forward and the chair made a *fwaap* sound against my butt. "No. It's not about the armoire." *At least not in the way you think.* "How did you end up in here?"

"I'm not exactly sure. I left Blake's after putting my auction items in storage and went to my shop to lock the regimental flag in the safe. A nice pre-bid offer had come in from a collector in Jacksonville. He was flying in just for the event and there was no way I was going to trust Blake's 'secure' storage room with something so valuable."

I nodded. "Understandable."

"I had a glass of port to unwind, and when I went to open the safe, someone hit me over the head. I woke up in the emergency room in the worst pain of my life, and I fought in Vietnam."

"How'd you get to the hospital?"

"I have no idea, but it saved my life. Doctors gave me an MRI to check for a brain bleed and they found two of my arteries were blocked. I was a heart attack just waiting to happen. They did emergency surgery to put a stent in. I was out the whole weekend."

"I'm glad you're okay. You were really lucky they found it in time. Do you have any idea who attacked you?"

One of the machines to the right of me beeped.

He looked at me with wide eyes. "I was attacked?"

"Um, that's what you said."

"By who?"

"I don't know. Do you know who called the ambulance?"

He wouldn't meet my gaze. "I don't know."

"And somehow the flag ended up at the auction house."

His pulse rate was rising quickly.

Grover smoothed down the tape surrounding the IV needle in his hand. "Did it?"

I was getting concerned. "Has Pauline been in to see you?"

"She was here Monday morning. When I woke up

Sunday night, the first thing I did was call her. Poor thing was terrified. Thought I was dead in a ditch somewhere. I was so embarrassed about the whole incident that I told Pauline not to tell anyone. She's a good girl. She's all I've got."

"Well, she told someone. I saw Josephine leaving as I was coming in."

Grover smiled and laid his head back against the pillow. "Pheenie was caught, huh? I heard she cornered Pauline in the shop Monday afternoon and wheedled it out of her. Pheenie can be quite terrifying when she wants something."

"I didn't realize the two of you were friends, what with the things you said to me about Whipple's and the lawsuit and all."

Grover cut his eyes to mine. "The lawsuit's just business. And, well, I've known Josephine longer than Courtney has. Some would say I've been carrying the proverbial torch."

I tried to lean forward in my chair, but I could feel it sucking me back down like an octopus pulling me to my death. "Aww. What happened?"

He looked away and shrugged. "It doesn't matter." He was quiet so long I thought the subject was closed. Then he said, "She used to come into my shop when Matilda was a wee shy little thing. She was raising the girl on her own and didn't have a pot to pee in. I always kept my eye out for things I knew she'd like, and I'd keep them in the back room and sell them to her at cost."

"That was sweet."

He clicked his cheek with a tiny shrug. "We went out a few times. I finally worked up the courage to ask her to go away with me for the weekend. Took her to Dixon's

Auction in Crumpton, Maryland, so she could get a silver tureen appraised."

Uh-oh.

"That's where she met Courtney. He'd been in Cape May running Whipple's for twenty years and she goes and meets him in Maryland on our romantic retreat."

Oof. "I'm sorry."

"She chose not to drive home with me. Said she wanted to ride in Courtney's Z28."

"No wonder you were angry with the Whipples. Is that why the lawsuit?"

Grover looked at his hands. "That was a scare tactic. I wanted Auggie to admit he stole the box from my store. I told you—you can't trust him. He's just like his father. They'll do anything to get what they want. He's been cheating his own sister out of her inheritance."

Does Grover not know that Auggie is dead? Should I tell him? Why didn't Josephine tell him? "Are you sure?"

Grover nodded and one of his machines beeped again. "Overheard Auggie and Blake arguing at Cold Spring Village the afternoon of that pompous display. Auggie said June was lying to her father about the money to make him look bad so she'd get controlling interest in Whipple's."

"Do you believe him?"

Grover yawned. "Not as far as I can throw him, and right now, that's not far. I don't know what all's going on, but the truth is going to be with whatever the other guy says. You can't trust a Whipple for a minute."

"Your letter to Courtney said you knew a dirty little secret about Auggie. What are you planning to do with the information now?"

Grover smiled. "That's between me and Auggie and Pauline. He darn near broke her heart. The girl can barely stand to look at him without running from the room."

"Um, Grover? You did hear about Auggie, didn't you?"

"Hear what?"

My cell phone buzzed in my pocket and vibrated the chair. The sound echoed like I had a hive of bees in my butt and scared us both half to death. Which wasn't good for Grover. His heart monitor jumped, and the alarm sounded. A nurse ran in and adjusted his leads, then insinuated I should leave so he should get some rest.

"I have to go now anyway." The beehive was a message from the emergency room nurse that the doctor needs to speak to me. I peeled myself out and the chair made a soft *thwpppp* sound before clattering to the floor. A wave of heat hit me in the face.

The nurse ignored me and adjusted Grover's IV bag.

Grover held up a hand and gave me a little wave. "Thanks for the visit. Hey, if you see Pauline, tell her to call me. I haven't seen that girl in days."

"You just said she was here Monday morning."

Grover's black eyebrows plummeted. "She was?"

The nurse put her hand on my shoulder.

I said goodbye to Grover, and she walked me out. "Is he doing okay?" I asked.

She gave me a nod. "I can't tell you anything specific because of HIPAA, but generally speaking—when a patient comes in with a brain injury, you can't always rely on their memory to be accurate. They tend to repress trauma. Whatever they remember today, could be different tomorrow."

CHAPTER 36

"You have gas?"

Burl shrugged and his eyes crinkled at the corners. "Probably from the midnight cheesesteak."

The doctor adjusted his stethoscope. "The good news is he can go home now. I've given your father a prescription for over the counter Gas-X."

I glanced at Burl and he winked.

"I'll make sure *my father* gets that picked up right away."

While Burl was discharged and wheeled to the front door, I went to get the car. He was so excited when he saw the Corvette pull up that he popped out of the wheelchair like a jack-in-the-box. "Whoo-whee."

I got him settled in the passenger seat and called Jo-anne. She was halfway to the hospital with Elaine, who'd had to change outfits three times and consult the spirits before leaving the house. "We're on our way home, so why don't you turn around and wait for us there?"

I could tell Joanne wanted to say something about that, but she was being professional with a visitor in her truck, so she just gave me the silent treatment and hung up.

I wanted to avoid the heavier traffic on the Garden State Parkway, so we took Route 9, which runs parallel to the highway. Burl tried to get me to stop at Rita's Italian Ice for frozen custard. When that didn't work, he put in a bid for Mack's for a slice to go.

"No way, mister. I'm taking you right back to the Butterfly Wings. Elaine has been worried sick."

As I was driving past Duckie's Farm stand, I noticed a white Lincoln parked out front with the license plate that said COMPOST. *Josephine.* I didn't slam on the brakes and careen into a 180-degree U-turn in the middle of the road—no matter what Burl says. I put on my turn signal and when the road was clear, gently turned around. Especially if Aunt Ginny asks.

Burl clutched the dashboard with both hands. "Where are you going? I need to get home. I almost died."

I pulled up behind the Lincoln and put the car in park. "I don't think gas is fatal. And I'll only be a minute."

Burl's knuckles were white in stark contrast to the glow rising up his neck. "You're not getting more tomatoes, are you?"

"No. I'll leave the air-conditioning on and you can stay here. Just try to relax."

Burl let go of the dashboard and farted. His eyes crinkled at the corners. "Oops."

I reached over and rolled my window down an inch. "I'll be right back."

I was totally wrong. Josephine was not at the red wooden farm stand. That distinction belonged to the woman holding a bushel basket full of kohlrabi, trying to convince the lady behind the counter that it was a donation. June pushed the basket closer to the register. "You don't have to pay us. Just take it with our blessing."

The lady shook her head and pushed the basket back towards June. "I can't sell them. Almost no one knows what they are."

"Well, we can't keep them. No one in my house will eat it. We don't like kohlrabi. Just tell people they're turnips."

My mouth dropped open and I felt my blood pressure begin to rise. The lady at the counter looked around June. "Can I get you anything?"

June turned to offer me a kohlrabi. "We have these lovely . . . Oh. Poppy. What are you doing here?"

I was so irritated; I couldn't stop myself from being a little snarky. "First of all, I live here. I go all over the place. And second . . . I'm here for the rice puddin'."

The lady behind the counter nodded. "How many?"

The last thing I needed was rice pudding. *But since I'm here* . . . I held up two fingers and she went to get the containers from the fridge. I gave June an attempt at a smile. I wanted to take every single kohlrabi and throw them at the Lincoln. *I can't believe they've been shoving these off to my house and they don't even like them.* "I'm surprised to see you here. I thought that was Courtney's car."

June looked behind me. "Oh, it is. But Dad was at a garden club meeting this morning, so Josephine borrowed my car to run an errand and hasn't come back yet."

She borrowed it to sneak around and visit Grover Prickle in the hospital is more like it. "I spoke to Blake last night."

June shifted the basket over to the register again. "About what?"

"He said Auggie never showed up for his ten a.m. interview with the newspaper last Saturday."

June pushed her Chanel sunglasses to the top of her head. "I wouldn't know anything about that. Auggie made all those arrangements himself. Dad and I were left completely out of it."

"It's a shame no one got to talk to Auggie before he left the house."

She grabbed a copy of the *Shoppe* guide on the counter and thumbed through it. "Well, except for Spencer."

"Spencer spoke to Auggie?"

June nodded. "My bedroom is above the kitchen. I heard them argue about that stupid bed and breakfast idea while I was getting ready for an early meeting. There was no way in a million years that Auggie was ever going to let that happen. I had to turn on my hair dryer to drown them out."

The farm stand lady brought the rice pudding to the register and rang me up. I paid for the pudding and stepped aside to sniff the late-season strawberries while I waited for June to accept defeat and walk away.

The woman pushed the basket back to June. She told her again that they could not sell the kohlrabi, so June snatched up the bushel basket and marched it out to the car.

I followed while looking across the parking lot to check on Burl. He gave me a little wave.

"I understand that Auggie had been taking some very large cash withdrawals. That was way more than just living expenses."

"What business is it of yours?" June opened the back door of the Lincoln and took out a brown paper bag.

"I just thought you should know that I had a talk with someone this morning who heard Auggie tell Blake that you made it all up."

Her head whipped around to face me. "He what?!"

I nodded. "Auggie was telling people that you were trying to get control of Whipple's for yourself."

June looked off into the distance for a few seconds. "I confronted Auggie about the ten-thousand-dollar cash withdrawal two weeks ago and he assured me he had everything under control. He said he was going to deposit it back the next morning like usual. He never did."

"You must have been furious."

"You bet I was furious. Whipple's is my livelihood too. Auggie was treating it like his personal trust fund."

"What do you think he was using the money for?"

June squinted against the afternoon sun. "I don't know. But I think Dad knew, and he's been covering for Auggie just like he always does."

"I saw records for sugar and taffy and M&Ms. Do you think those are codes for racehorses?"

June shrugged and took her purse off the front seat. She dug around until she found a Sharpie. "I don't know. Gambling isn't Auggie's style. But then there used to be a time I didn't think embezzling was Auggie's style either. Blake used to say that Auggie had secrets I was better not knowing. We had an unspoken agreement. As long as he put the money back, I wouldn't ask what it was for." June took the Sharpie and wrote FREE TURNIPS on the paper bag. Then she stuck the bushel of kohlrabi with the paper bag sign on the side of the road.

I waited for her to come back to the car. "What about drugs?"

June dropped her sunglasses from the top of her head to shield her eyes. "If Auggie was on drugs, he knew how to hide it well."

I need to get Burl home before the car runs out of gas. Preferably before Burl fills it for me. "I should probably tell you that Gia and I saw you with Spencer at Cold Spring Village. Just be careful, okay. I really like Tildy and I don't want to see her get hurt, but I don't want to see you get hurt either and I'm not sure Spencer isn't just after your money."

June narrowed her eyes and stared at me a moment. Then she threw her head back and laughed. "You think I'm with Spencer? That cheap little wannabe?"

"You're not?"

"He's been hounding me to be a silent partner in his bed and breakfast scheme. Which means he wants me to give him money for a house I already own and convince my dad that he should control it. And the silent means I'm not allowed to say anything about the way he runs it."

"Why Courtney's house? Why not buy another property to turn into a B and B?"

"Spencer doesn't have any money. He's been trying to get that house since the first time Tildy brought him home. He comes from a poor family outside of Philly, and he thought Tildy was his ticket to the good life." She snickered. "He didn't know Tildy comes from nothing. Josephine was a penniless single mom when she met

Dad. All she's ever had to her name is that silver soup tureen. When we were growing up, Auggie and I were convinced she stole it from the guy she used to nanny for."

The Corvette horn sounded, and Burl waved to me from the driver's seat.

Hmm. That's not good. I looked back at June. "Then why does Tildy stay with him?"

"She wants a baby. She lost one a few years ago and she hasn't gotten pregnant since."

"I didn't realize she'd been pregnant before. What happened?"

"You've seen Spencer's temper. He's been known to snap because she bought a five-dollar box of brownies. She's not allowed to make a move without his permission. We've never actually seen him lay a hand on her, but no one just runs into doors and falls down that often."

"You think he's abusive?"

June gave me a look that said *What do you think?*

The crunch of tires on gravel nearby caused me to turn my head. Burl was slowly crawling the Corvette closer to me. From the look on his face, you'd think he was the lead car at the Indianapolis 500. "I gotta go."

June opened the driver's door of the Lincoln. "Keep what I said between us, please. I don't want it getting back to Josephine. She has ways of making life miserable if she thinks you're spreading rumors about Tildy. She once shaved all my Barbies' heads because I said Tildy's haircut made her look like a boy. You have no idea what lengths she'll go to for her daughter."

I opened the door and Burl farted again. I waved my hand for him to get out and switch sides. I waited for things to air out, then got in the Corvette and closed the door. June pulled out of the parking lot ahead of me and waved in the rearview mirror.

If she's not sneaking around with Spencer, who did she think I was talking about at the estate sale?

CHAPTER 37

W hen I pulled up in front of the house, some of the guests were waiting on the front porch to welcome Burl home. "It looks like you have a fan club."

They applauded gassy Santa, and everyone told him they were glad he didn't die. Except Elaine, who punched him in the arm. "That is it for you, mista! Give me ya phone. I'm sleeping with it under my pilla from now on." Elaine burst into tears.

Burl grinned and pulled her into a bear hug.

"Pssssst."

At first, I thought the sound was Burl. He was killing me on the way home. I didn't think he needed that Gas-X after all. Then I followed the sound around the porch to the left side of the house. Mother Gibson's head peeked around the corner and she crooked her finger to me.

I bet this is what it's like to know a tsunami is coming and you can't get out of the way in time.

I casually edged my way past the porch swing and the rocking chairs, and found the biddies huddled together on the side by the kitchen. Gorgeous smells from Mrs. Pritchard's rose garden wafted up to tickle my nose. "What are you four up to?"

Mrs. Davis stepped forward. "We need you."

Mrs. Dodson gave me a grave nod. "For a rescue and retrieval mission."

I looked into their faces, one at a time. "Is this about the jewelry box?"

Mrs. Davis's face took on a stony expression. "That woman had the nerve to come into my house and steal it while I was in the tub."

"What do you think I can do about it?"

Mrs. Davis picked up her pocketbook from the outdoor coffee table and tucked it under her arm. "We're getting it back."

Mother Gibson grinned. "You're the distraction."

Oh Lord.

Aunt Ginny took my arm and started walking me towards the driveway. "Just get in the house and keep Josephine busy."

"What if the box is in my sight?"

Mrs. Dodson tsked me. "Then move to another room out of eyeshot."

"Is eyeshot even a thing?"

Mrs. Davis took me by the hand and led me down the front steps. "Ginny is taking the Corvette, Lila is driving me and the girls in the church van, and you can take Edith's minivan." She gave my hand a pat. "Okay?"

"Why do we need so many cars?"

She rubbed the back of my hand like she was trying to soothe me. "We'll leave in three different directions in case Josephine realizes we've got the box and comes after us. She won't know which car it's in."

"I think you're overthinking this."

They weren't listening. They were herding me towards the blue minivan double-parked across the street.

Mrs. Dodson dropped a set of keys in my hand. "Think of this as your chance to ask Courtney what he was doing at Prickled Curiosities Monday afternoon when we bought that coffee grinder."

I stopped moving forward. "He was there?"

Mother Gibson shook her head at me. "Child. Didn't you see the Lincoln when Thelma was rushing you into the van?"

Mrs. Davis's face softened. "Oh, heh. I didn't realize you all knew that was Courtney's car."

Mrs. Dodson tapped her cane on the ground. "For God's sake, Thelma. Who else has a license plate dedicated to rotting vegetable peels?"

I looked into the eyes of the silly biddy with the pink hair. "Why didn't you tell me this sooner?"

She gave me an innocent look and a one-shoulder shrug. "I didn't want you to think Courtney was involved in Grover's disappearance."

I'm not convinced he wasn't. I'm also not convinced he was the one at Prickled Curiosities. The biddies abandoned me, and each went to their designated vehicles. I climbed into Mrs. Dodson's minivan and moved the seat backward about six inches. Then I moved the "I brake for Bingo" card that hung from the rearview mirror, and against my better judgment, followed the tiny redhead in the Corvette that blew through the stop sign.

* * *

I parked on the side street and watched the three ladies hop out of the church van and bob and weave up to the house using two azaleas and a trash can as cover. Aunt Ginny pulled into the driveway and honked the horn.

Courtney came through the gate like he had the day I'd visited, and Aunt Ginny followed him through to the garden. The biddies used an intricate set of hand and eye signals to tell me they were going to stay in the bushes until I was inside. I hope.

I walked up the front steps and Josephine threw the door open. She stepped to me and lowered her voice. "You never saw me today. Understand?"

I nodded. "I can keep your secret. If you can answer my questions."

Her eyes narrowed and she tilted her head to the side and gave me a once-over.

"Was that you in the back of Grover's shop the day I was there with Aunt Ginny?"

She gave me a nod. "It might have been."

"What were you doing there?"

She pushed the door with her butt and held it open. "I'm not having this conversation where I don't know who's listening."

I entered the house, scanning unsuccessfully for the jewelry box, and followed her to the back library where the French clock was sitting on the mantel. Josephine took a seat on the chaise in the corner. "*If* I was there, I was trying to get information from that girl on where Mr. Prickle might be."

"Do you visit him a lot?"

Her eyes flashed a mixture of anger and fear. "Are you the morality police?"

"You'd rather I ask Courtney?"

She bit her bottom lip while she considered me. "Occasionally. If he has something in stock he wants to show me. As one collector to another. That's all!"

"I'm not here to judge you, Josephine."

Her cool demeanor cracked, and she snapped at me like a truck stop waitress. "Then whaddayou want!"

"I want to know how well you know Grover Prickle."

Josephine clutched her long strand of black beads and ran them through her fingers. She sat back against the chaise. "Not well at all."

"There's not a history to speak of?"

She shrugged and gave her head a tiny shake. "None whatsoever. I only know he has an antique store around here that competes unsuccessfully with ours."

I stared at the older woman, stunned that she would lie so easily to my face. "I was under the impression that the two of you might be old friends. You were awfully concerned about him to go visit him in the hospital." *And maybe get your stories straight.*

She lifted her chin, defiantly. "I thought he might have killed my dear son and wanted to check his alibi. Is it so hard to believe a mother wouldn't be concerned?"

A cell phone rang somewhere on Josephine's person. She felt around the upper half of her body until she found it and fished it out of her blouse. She checked the screen and answered. "Hello?" She listened for a moment then narrowed her eyes at me. Standing to her feet, she pointed in my face. "Stay right there!" It was not a request.

Even though she left the room I could still hear her side of the conversation. "Why didn't you call me with this sooner? It's too late for that."

I looked towards the doorway she'd run out of and she leaned back until she saw me, then snapped forward again. "I'll handle it."

Josephine came back into the library and perched on the edge of the chaise, examining my face. "Why are you really here nosing into things that are none of your business?"

What's a nice way to say I want to know if you helped Grover kill Auggie so he could get revenge on Courtney and rekindle your romance?

I was prevented from saying anything, because Aunt Ginny's voice carried through the kitchen door. "Can I get a glass of water, Courtney?"

Josephine jumped to her feet. "Virginia!" She ran to the kitchen to confront Aunt Ginny and I grabbed her cell phone to see who had just called her. Josephine had some kind of pattern lock to get into her phone. Her screen was so dirty I was able to follow the obvious Z and got in the first time.

"I did not invite you inside, Virginia."

"Courtney did. And water is free. You know you've always been cheap, Josephine. It's not a good look on a woman of your age."

Phone. Recent calls. Pauline Milford. *Josephine's last call was from Pauline?*

Josephine called out the side door, "Courtney! I need you to come here please!"

I threw the phone back on the chaise where she'd dropped it and hopped back to my seat.

Aunt Ginny stuck her head into the library and gave me a thumbs-up.

What does that mean? Are we done?

She started heading through the kitchen towards the

front door with both Courtney and Josephine in tow. "I know where I'm not wanted, but I never expected anything so low from you, Courtney. We've known each other all our lives."

I started to follow the kerfuffle to the front door, but I was ambushed in the breakfast nook. Mrs. Davis popped out of the butler's pantry and shoved the jewelry box into my hands.

"Go! Now! Out through the garden."

I tried to shove the box back into her hands. "What, me? No way! Josephine'll call the cops on me."

"No, she won't, now get moving. You still have both of your original hips and you don't have arthritis in your feet yet. We'll meet you back at the B and B." She threw the screen door open and pushed me out into the garden. I spun around and tried to get back into the house, but she'd shut the kitchen door and I heard the *thunk* of a dead bolt.

Oh my god. Are you kidding me! My heart lurched in my chest. I was so terrified I would get caught stealing this priceless antique that the blood in my veins was coursing to the sound of AC/DC's "Highway to Hell."

I stumbled down the steps, clutching the box to my chest, scanning the yard for Whipples. I hopped over a patch of kohlrabi and eggplant, then dodged through trellises of tomatoes. I tripped over a rock and grabbed a bean pole to keep from going down. The sprinklers came on and I jumped through the spray, praying I wouldn't slip and fall on the delicate antique. I ducked under the arch of a climbing rose, ran to the garden gate, and slid to a stop face-to-face with Madeleine Humphries coming out of Courtney's shed carrying a bucket marked fertilizer.

I was frozen with humiliation, and desperate to escape.

She looked at the jewelry box in my hands, then up to my face with a smug sniff of condescension.

I made a point to look at the bucket of granules she was holding, then back to her face with some commentary of my own. "Don't judge me, hypocrite."

Her face fell a bit and she appeared a touch sheepish. With a glance to the house, she grabbed my arm and dragged me through the garden gate to the alley beyond. "I'm just trying to prove that Courtney's been using banned fertilizer. I wrote letters telling the garden show committee that I know he's a fraud, but they refuse to investigate."

I was barely listening to her. My ears were peeled for police sirens. I clutched the jewelry box tighter. "What are you talking about?"

"I heard them." She shifted her eyes to the back of the house. "Courtney and Josephine were arguing because she finally discovered he's been cheating."

Fifty feet to freedom. "What exactly did you hear?"

"I heard Josephine tell Courtney that she discovered his dirty little secret. Then Courtney yelled at Josephine that she had no right to make any changes without his permission. He didn't want *them* to find out or they would start taking everything away."

"Who would start taking what?" *Oh my god, lady, just spit it out!*

She shrugged. "The garden committee. He must have been afraid they'd take back his blue ribbons. Why else would Josephine say that it wasn't fair, and that someone else deserves them?"

"Someone like who?"

Madeleine Humphries looked up her pinched nose at me. "I don't know, but she said she was going to see that they got them if it was the last thing she lived to do."

I sighed. And looked at the crazy woman in front of me with her bucket of what smelled like something she scraped off the bottom of a shoe. *I don't have time for this.* I took a step backwards from her and waited to see what she would do.

She took a tentative step back away from me.

We gave each other a look of understanding. Nobody sees. Nobody knows. We took off in our opposite directions without another word.

I sprinted down the side path to the parked minivan. The biddies were waiting for me in the rhododendrons.

Mrs. Dodson opened the sliding side door for me and yelled to the others, "Scatter!"

I gently placed the jewelry box on the floor behind the seat. It had survived wars, a peasant uprising, and a transatlantic journey in a flour sack. There was no way on God's green earth that I wanted to be the one to break it schlepping it four blocks in a Dodge Caravan. I drove home as gently as I could.

I ran up on the curb, threw the minivan in park, gingerly took the box to the kitchen, and cried in relief when it was safely placed on the center of the table.

"What's that?"

My heart leapt to my throat and I smacked at Joanne. "Don't sneak up on me!" I took a couple gulps of air and headed for the coffee beans. "It belongs to Mrs. Davis. I hope. Or her brother. In which case she's an accessory."

Joanne eyed me suspiciously and turned on the burner under the teapot.

The front door chimed, and Aunt Ginny flew down the

hall. "I'm being followed. Someone's after me! What do we do?"

"What do you mean, someone's following you?"

"Some guy has been on my tail since the Washington Street Mall. I tried to shake him, but it's like he has a tracking device on me. I think Josephine must have hired him. Where's my shotgun?"

The door chimed again, and the rest of the biddies hobbled into the kitchen, gasping and wheezing.

Mrs. Davis doubled over and held her side. "For the love of God, Ginny. Do you have a fire to get to?"

Mrs. Dodson leaned hard on her cane and sucked air before she could speak. "We've been trying to get your attention for four blocks."

Aunt Ginny wouldn't meet anyone's eyes. "What color is the church van?"

Mother Gibson wagged her finger. "The way you were driving I thought someone was after us. Ethel nearly sprained her neck watching the rear window. I had to floor it over the speed bumps just to keep up with you."

Aunt Ginny faced the biddies with seething indignation. "I thought we were all going to take separate routes to throw Josephine off the scent."

Mrs. Davis stood upright and cocked her head to the side. "I forgot about that. When Josephine threw that ceramic rabbit at the Corvette, I just wanted to get the heck out of there before she called the fuzz."

Mrs. Dodson leaned against the counter. "Good thing she's got a bad arm."

Joanne laughed. "You've all been in a car chase with yourselves."

I dumped the coffee beans into the grinder and looked at the ladies each in turn. "We need to talk."

CHAPTER 38

I took my coffee to the dining room and joined the biddies at the table. They were pensive, so they could tell something was wrong. "You know I love each one of you."

Four heads bobbed.

"But today was unacceptable. I'm never doing anything like that again." I turned to Mrs. Davis. "If you get caught taking that jewelry box from your brother's house, it's an argument. If I get caught—it's a robbery. And it's a felony. I could go to jail. Do you understand?"

She started to give me an excuse, but seeing the look on my face, she nodded and bit her lip.

"No more guilting me into crazy schemes you know you'd never do without my involvement."

The ladies wouldn't look me in the eye, so I knew I'd made my point. I also knew it would last about as long as it took me to drink this coffee. "Okay. Now I need to ask you something about Josephine."

Mrs. Davis turned her palms up. "Sure. Anything."

"What happened to her first husband?"

The biddies glanced around the table shrugging at one another. Mother Gibson pulled a four-pack of Yoo-hoos out of her giant purse and passed them around.

Mrs. Davis shook her Yoo-hoo. "She was never married as far as I know."

"Then who's Tildy's father?"

Mrs. Davis shrugged. "I don't know. I'm not sure *she* knows. A lot of things happened in the seventies that we never spoke about after."

Aunt Ginny opened the buffet drawer and grabbed a fistful of Cow Tales. She threw the caramel sticks into the center of the table to share. "And Josephine wasn't a spring chicken when she had Tildy. An accidental pregnancy might have been her last chance to have a child."

Mrs. Davis twisted the cap off her chocolate drink. "Why do you ask?"

"I was thinking about that whole argument at the dinner party. Josephine was so upset about Tildy not being in Courtney's will. I just wonder if she found a way to make sure Tildy inherits something."

"By killing Auggie?" Mrs. Dodson's eyebrows arched into her teased hairline. "Doesn't that seem extreme to you?"

"Murder always seems extreme to me. It only makes sense to the killers."

Mrs. Davis ripped the paper off her caramel. "I can't stand my sister-in-law, but I don't think she's a killer. If she was, she would have done me in years ago to get that jewelry box. Besides, Courtney is not exactly at death's door for the kids to be murdering each other over an inheritance that won't come for twenty years. Josephine has plenty of time to talk some sense into him. And if they ever get that grandchild, that will change everything."

Aunt Ginny took a drink of her Yoo-hoo. "I could see Josephine being a murderer."

Mother Gibson yanked the wrapper off her Cow Tale and flung it at Aunt Ginny.

Aunt Ginny looked from Mother Gibson to Mrs. Dodson. "You didn't see the crazed way she went after Auggie and June for tagging stuff around the house."

I tried to imagine how Josephine and Grover would have done it. Grover could have gone back into the auction house and stolen the stake after Auggie left the box in storage. Then Josephine could have conked him over the head back at his store and called an ambulance. Then she lured Auggie to the auction house sometime in the night or early the next morning. Killed him, used Grover's keys to lock him in the storage room . . . but how did she get in the auction house without Blake's help? No. It's almost there but something still isn't right.

I took a sip of my coffee and wished it was Yoo-hoo. "Did any of you take pictures of that vampire-hunting kit Friday night before the antique show was shut down?"

All four biddies pulled phones out of their purses and started the long process of trying to remember how to access their photos. Eventually they each set a phone in front of me with a clear shot of the vampire kit. The wooden stake was visible in each frame, even the one where a furious Grover had his finger pointing at Auggie's red face, and Blake held his hand up to stop the crowd from taking pictures.

Mother Gibson pointed to her screen. "That was when the police came, and everyone was sent home. Anyone could have taken something from the box in that disorder."

I awoke to the sound of a chickadee singing good morning. We didn't have a rogue delivery last night, so Elaine must have hidden Burl's cell phone. Kevin didn't sleep-Shazam himself around the house. And there were no appearances of Siobhan or her afterlife posse.

I gave Figaro a head fluff. "It was good night, wasn't it?"

He gave my hand a whisker bonk and purred.

"Maybe things will be quiet today. We deserve an easy day for a change, don't we, baby?"

I got out of bed and stretched. I had enough time to do a nice yoga flow and a shower before I had to make breakfast. I looked at the clock. And the bed. And my closet. Something was giving me a sense of unease. Maybe it was because we weren't used to easy mornings during tourist season.

Figaro's head reeled towards the bedroom door and his ears pinned flat. He shot off the bed and pulled the door open with his paw before flying down the hall.

Muffled voices rose to my ears and I could feel my peace shrivel like celery in the back of the fridge. The voices weren't coming from inside the house, they were out front. I pulled my curtain aside and looked down in the yard. A year of my life slipped away. There was a body lying on the front lawn.

With blood pounding in my ears, I pulled on a pair of jeans and a yoga tank, stepped into my flip-flops and ran down the main stairs.

All the guests were in the yard, surrounding the victim who appeared to be stabbed. Paul and Marty were fully dressed and casually drinking coffee from the bagel store around the corner.

Elaine Grabstein was still in her bathrobe. She pointed at the body. "I think I have that same feather boa."

Kevin Martins squatted down and examined the entry wound. He looked up at Shondra. "That reminds me, your father would love a new hunting knife for his birthday."

One of the twins nudged the body with her foot. "Whoever did it, did a good job."

I was horrified. I couldn't believe their lack of outrage. *What do these people watch on television?* "Did anyone call for an ambulance?"

Wade Foubert looked at me over his shoulder. "You don't need an ambulance."

Elaine waved me over. "Come'ere, doll, I think someone's playing a trick on ya."

I crept closer and realized the body was made of papier-mâché. Someone had either tried to sculpt a lady vampire, or this was supposed to be me. Although she looked more like Stella, "the Man-Eater from Manayunk" of *Saturday Night Dead* fame. There was a wooden stake made from a shaved-down antique spurtle sticking out of her ample chest.

Burl tapped me on the shoulder. "There's a note."

Pinned to her stretchy low-cut nylon dress, was a warning. *Mind your own business or you're next!*

Aunt Ginny hollered from the front porch. "What's going on out there?"

Shondra called back, "You gotta mess a trouble here, Mrs. Frankowski."

Aunt Ginny came down the steps and bent over the body. "Who is that? Is that the night hostess for them B movies?"

I sighed. "I think it's supposed to be me."

Aunt Ginny put on a brave face for our guests. "What a clever advertisement for one of Cape May's next kitschy events. You are all welcome to come back in the spring for vampire week."

I couldn't take my eyes off the sawed-off wooden spurtle. "That isn't a thing."

"Oh, Poppy. You're such a kidder." She pulled my arm to get me upright and gritted her teeth. "It will be, after I get off the phone with the chamber of commerce."

I reached for my back pocket out of habit. I'd come downstairs in such a rush I'd left my phone inside. "Don't touch anything, please. I'm going to go call the police." And while I'm at it, I should probably call a Realtor to see what I can get for the house since this is probably the final straw for the Butterfly Wings. We'll have fewer guests than the El Dorado Motel. *I wonder if Spencer wants to buy us.*

I ran up to my room to grab my cell phone and dialed Amber's number. She answered on the second ring with a tone sharp enough to slice tomatoes. "What's wrong, McAllister?"

"I thought we were past that."

She cleared her throat.

Oh. "Would you rather I call the emergency line, so Sergeant Washington doesn't have a fit?"

"Too late. What do you need?"

"Do the police have the vampire-hunting kit in evidence?"

"Yes, why?"

"Someone just left a papier-mâché death threat on my front lawn, and she has a wooden stake through her heart."

I was met with silence.

"Then now's probably not a good time to tell you that the second layer of the kit is missing the revolver."

Chapter 39

The police cruiser screamed to a stop at the end of my driveway. Sergeant Washington climbed out of the passenger side with a slam and a whistle. "See, now this here's gonna be a paperwork nightmare."

Amber scanned the disarray until she found me sitting on the front step. "McAllister! What the literal hell! I told you to keep a low profile."

I'd given up all hope an hour ago. I looked the little blond cop in the eye, which was easier now that I was sitting down. "I haven't told a soul."

My guests were huddled around the "body," scarfing down bagels that Paul and Marty had ordered for everyone.

Joanne had arrived for work, scanned the carnage on the front lawn, and said, "Nope." Then got in her car and peeled out.

Georgina was lured out of her room on the third floor

by the growing ruckus but immediately disappeared back inside and slammed the door.

Neighbors noticed the loitering and spilled outside to see if they were missing a yard sale. That attracted the tourists who were looking for parking spots to investigate what might have been a pop-up party. Suddenly the hottest ticket in town was on my front yard with a sawed-off wooden spurtle in the chest.

Aunt Ginny had crime scene tape that she'd stolen from the Senior Center Theater incident, and she strung it up between the big tree and the bird feeder. Now she was charging ten dollars a head for pictures with the death threat.

Amber removed her sunglasses. "Please tell me no one has touched the evidence."

"I lost sight of it for a few minutes when I broke down and cried a little, so I can't make any promises."

A local news van pulled to a stop at my mailbox and a camera crew jumped out and started hauling around a bunch of cables and battery packs. A slim brunette in a blue dress was getting mic'd up. She bent over the yellow tape to examine the body. "Hey, that looks like Stella."

Georgina threw the front door open. She was dressed in an emerald silk evening gown and opera gloves that she'd found in the attic. "Good morning, everyone. Tours of the Murder House will begin at ten. Interested guests can sign up with myself, part owner of McAllister Mansion—or Victoryna, the French maid."

I craned my neck to see what nonsense was happening on the porch, and Victory jiggled out from behind Georgina dressed in the sexy maid costume Aunt Ginny had given her to wear her first day on the job. "*Bonjour, mes amis*. Who want to hear about wine tour murder?"

Aunt Ginny pursed her lips and with her eyes half closed, gave Georgina a slow nod of admiration.

Georgina clapped her hands in self-congratulations.

Amber fiddled with the handcuffs dangling from her belt. "We have to put a stop to this, now." She raised her voice. "Ladies and gentlemen."

That was the last thing anyone heard because about twenty people rushed the porch and started shouting their names at Georgina to get on one of the tours.

Gia pulled into the driveway in his silver sports car and he and Cameron climbed out. They were carrying takeout containers of coffee and muffins. Gia found me fighting tears of relief and gave me a sad grin.

He blew off Viola's command to stay back. "I heard there was dead body in the yard of a B and B around the corner and the owner was waiting for the police. I had a feeling it would be here. I brought breakfast for your guests just in case."

"I'm so glad to see you." I threw my arms around his neck.

Cameron held up the cardboard containers of coffee. "Where is the best place for these?"

I had a yard full of tourists. Every neighbor was either on Mr. Winston's front porch or sitting in Mrs. Pritchard's yard in lawn chairs like a parade was coming by. Another police car pulled up behind the news van. "God forbid we interrupt the nine o'clock tour, so how about on the dining room sideboard."

He nodded and went to work.

Gia put the boxes of muffins on the arm of an Adirondack chair and pulled me into a better hug. "Oh, Bella. What happened?"

"I pissed off another homicidal maniac."

Cameron came back out to grab the boxes of muffins. "You know there are three cats lined up in the window over there?"

I nodded. "Yep."

"One of them just fell over."

I sighed. "That's Figaro."

Amber was down by the . . . vampire dummy? Paper Stella? I didn't know what we were calling it. She put her arm out and curled her fingers for me to come to her.

Now? With the cameras out there? I shook my head.

Amber's eyes got big and her mouth set in a tight line. She curled again with more attitude.

I looked at the news van and pulled my sport tank up on my shoulder and let it snap into place.

Amber rolled her eyes and held up five fingers.

I ran into the house and took the stairs in the pantry to the third floor. I dragged a brush through my hair and wiped the mascara from under my eyes. Then I put on a sun dress and lipstick and went back to the front yard.

Amber gave me a droll look when I appeared on the front porch. To my relief, the news crew didn't even notice me. They were too busy interviewing Aunt Ginny— the encyclopedia of all things South Jersey crime related. *That's gonna come back to bite me later.*

Two officers I didn't recognize were across the street talking to the Sheinbergs.

Gia kissed my temple. "Do you want me to stay? I can send Cameron to the shop."

I squeezed his hand. "Yes."

He squeezed mine back. "Okay. I will be right here."

I joined Amber on the lawn.

Before she could speak, Viola appeared by her side. "Good lord, what did you do?"

"Nothing. I've only had conversations with people."

Viola's manicured eyebrows shot up to her braids. "Is this usually the kind of thing that happens when you have conversations?"

Amber and I answered in unison. "Yes."

Viola puckered her lips and looked around the yard shaking her head. "Well, this is unacceptable."

Amber took out her notebook and pen. "Sergeant Washington, could you . . ."

"Nope. I'm staying right here with you. I wanna hear everything Miss McAllister has to say. Captain's orders."

Amber let out a jumbo sigh. She gripped the pen until her knuckles were white.

I filled them in on the events of the morning and every person I'd spoken to over the last two days. I conveniently left out stealing that jewelry box and committing grand larceny at the behest of four senior citizens. "Grover's in the hospital—but I guess you knew that. Josephine Whipple and he were once lovers. Now maybe they're accomplices. Tildy is addicted to buying things for a baby she may never have, with inheritance money she will probably never get, and her husband is going door to door begging residents to let him turn their house into a bed and breakfast. Auggie was into something so shameful, no one will talk about it. But he owed money to someone dangerous enough to kill him for it. And it seems like the first priority with everyone in the Whipple family is to protect the heirlooms at any cost."

Amber's radio crackled that the crime scene techs were running late because a trailer carrying a Jet Ski broke off an SUV and caused a pileup on the parkway. She put away her notebook and turned to Sergeant Washington. "I need you to bag and tag the evidence. If we wait for CSI to get here, half of Cape May will have touched it."

Viola cracked her neck and sighed, but she went to the police cruiser and pulled a black tackle box from the trunk.

I looked at the handmade victim on the lawn. "Do you have any ideas who could have done this?"

Amber took her phone and snapped a couple photos of the death threat. "It's not sophisticated. Like it was made in a classroom. And it doesn't look like it was made recently. My gut tells me it came from a thrift shop or one of the two antique stores. Maybe part of a display."

"That's a good suspicion if someone in the Whipple family or Grover Prickle killed Auggie. But what about the mystery thug everyone keeps bringing up?"

Amber shook her head. "It could have come from the auction house in that storage room. I'll check with Blake Adams to see if this is missing."

Viola put on rubber gloves and slid the dummy into a plastic garbage bag. I turned my back to her and whispered to Amber. "Who called the ambulance for Grover?"

She glanced at Sergeant Washington. "It was anonymous, but it was a woman's voice. Why? What are you thinking?"

"It's just too convenient. A Good Samaritan just happened to be on a midnight stroll wandering around West Cape May and finds Grover Prickle unconscious in the back of his antique store? It might be nothing. Or it might be the best alibi ever."

"What's going on? Are you having a yard sale?" Spencer walked up behind us holding a giant metal colander full of kohlrabi. The white Lincoln was parked across the street.

I pointed at the vegetables and yelled, "No! Take them back! I refuse to take any more of your space turnips. They're like Tribbles multiplying all over my house. And I heard you all don't even like them."

Spencer held the colander with one hand and adjusted his glasses with the other. "We thought *you* liked them."

"You've given me a dozen baskets in ten days. I haven't even had time to try them. No more."

Spencer shifted the colander in Amber's direction.

Boy, was that barking up the wrong tree. If it didn't come in cellophane or from the Wawa deli, Amber wasn't interested in it.

"Mr. Jolley, what are you doing here?"

Spencer looked like the kid not paying attention in class who just got called on to do long division. "I came to talk to Poppy about the Innkeepers Association. Is this a bad time?"

There must have been thirty people in my front yard, including two police cars and a channel three news van. I stared at Spencer with new concern that he was suffering from chronic ignorance. "Seriously?"

Sergeant Washington finished packing the evidence into the police car. She wandered around shooing people off the property. "Go on home now. You can watch it all on You Tube later."

The reporter moved the cameraman up to Amber. "Officer, can we ask a few questions?"

"No."

"Just five minutes."

"No."

Amber closed her book and put it in her pocket. "We're done here. We'll have an official report for the blotter later. You can check there." She turned her back to the reporters and crossed her arms over her chest. "I don't want you involved anymore, McAllister. You've done enough. I want you to stay away from the Whipples and their competitor. Got it?"

"Sure. Uh-huh." *Not on your life. Now it's personal.* Someone threatened to stab me this morning. If Amber thought I was going to sit around on my hands and wait for it to happen, she didn't know me at all.

CHAPTER 40

While the news crew was fleecing the neighborhood for dirt, I escaped to the porch and joined Gia. He was sitting back on the swing, one ankle crossed over his knee. "The muffins are gone."

"Darn it." I snuggled into him and felt some of my tension drain away.

He reached over to the table next to him. "But I was able to save you one."

I grinned and gave him a kiss. "Thank you." I ripped the paper off and ate it in four bites. It was almost noon, and this was the first thing I'd eaten all day.

"Your guests are all inside having second breakfast and taking questions from the tour groups. You want me to make you some coffee?"

"Not yet. Stay with me for right now."

Spencer walked up to the porch, sans kohlrabi. He put his hands up in surrender. "I'm sorry. Tildy says I'm being a pest. I'm just trying to get a business off the ground."

I was too worn out from the morning's ordeal to fight him off anymore. "Does Courtney want to turn his house into a B and B?"

Spencer shrugged. "Not yet, but I'm working on it."

"Why? You said you have an investor, why not buy another property and start there with less drama?"

"Because Courtney's house is free money. Courtney and Josephine aren't coming up anymore after this summer, so it's the perfect time."

Gia rubbed lazy circles into my shoulder. "How do you know that?"

Spencer took a seat on the chair across from the swing. "Tildy told me. This is their last hurrah. Now Auggie's gone, and June doesn't want to live in the house. What else are they going to do with it?"

I yawned. The ceiling fans on the porch were lulling me to sleep. Drama had pulled the plug on my adrenaline and it was circling the drain. "Why aren't they coming back?"

He shrugged. "Too old, I guess. It's a long trip. And that garden is a full-time job. Josephine thinks it's too much for Courtney at his age."

Gia rocked the porch swing gently. "How old is he?"

Spencer leaned back in his chair. "He'll be seventy-five. Josephine just turned seventy."

Gia chuckled. "That is not really old, Spencer. My mother is sixty-five and she runs a restaurant on the mall."

That's not all she runs.

Spencer shrugged and gave his head a little shake.

I yawned again. "What does your investor think?"

Spencer took his glasses off and cleaned them with his shirt. He put them back on and sighed. "I haven't exactly locked that down. I've been trying to convince a silent partner with a ton of alimony to back me. She doesn't even have to be hands-on or ever come down. Tildy and I will live there. I want to name it the Coastal Pearl."

Gia asked, "Is that what you were talking to June about in the Cold Spring Village parking lot?"

Spencer shifted in his seat like he was sitting on a bag of marbles. "How did you know about that? Did June tell you? Because I was only propositioning her to be business partners. She took it the wrong way."

Gia chuckled under his breath as he got up and disappeared into the house.

I watched him through the side window. Some of the women in the tour group flocked to his side before he made it through the dining room. "Is this what Tildy wants to do? Leave her job, move here, and run a bed and breakfast?"

"Tildy will be happy when I'm happy. She doesn't care where we live as long as she gets to have a baby."

"How old is Tildy?"

"Thirty-nine."

"Spencer, if you want to start a family, Tildy doesn't have a lot of time for you to launch a business and get it successful."

Spencer leaned forward on his chair. "I have to prove to her family that I can work hard and make my own way in life if they're ever going to accept me. I saw how things went with June's husband. Blake was always snooping around, appraising everything. Whispering to Courtney how much he could get for this and that. Auggie said Blake planned to strip the house of antiques once Courtney died. Blake even tried to get Courtney to assign him power of attorney to protect Courtney's assets in case he got sick."

"Maybe he was just trying to take care of them."

Spencer's lip curled at the corner. "When Blake takes care of you there are dollar signs in his eyes. Auggie was the only one standing in his way because June couldn't see him for what he was. If it wasn't for Auggie, Blake would have auctioned off half the house the minute Courtney and Josephine decided to move to Florida full time."

"What did Auggie do?"

"He started following Blake to see what he was up to. Discovered the guy was cheating on June." Spencer sat back with a satisfied look on his face. "Once he told his sister what was going on, she kicked Blake out that same night. That shifted the balance of power back where it belonged."

"Where does the balance of power belong?"

"With the men of the family."

I snorted. "I didn't realize Auggie had that much influence over June. When was the last time you spoke to him?"

Spencer lay back with his arms behind his head. "Saturday morning before he left for Adams Galleries. I wanted to talk to him one more time about letting me and Tildy convert the house into a B and B before I went canvassing the neighborhood. It's a really great opportunity and I knew he would want in if he just took a moment to think about it. He was almost on board, but he had some emergency to go deal with and couldn't talk right then."

Gia returned with the French press and three mugs. I wanted to throw him down right there. He gave me a grin and handed me two packs of stevia from his pocket.

I poured the coffee and turned my attention back to Spencer. "What kind of emergency?"

"I dunno. Auggie was a very private person. If he didn't want you to know what he was up to, you weren't going to find out."

Spencer's cell phone rang, and he checked the screen. He stepped off the porch to answer it. "What? I told you not to bother me today. I'm finally getting somewhere. Yes, I'm here. What's all over the news?" He looked around the yard then looked my way in surprise.

Gia and I each held up a hand and gave him a wave.

Gia snickered. "You can see the blood drain from his face all the way up here. He really does not know how to read a room."

I laughed. "Unless he's faking it. Isn't it serial killers who return to the scene of the crime so they can watch the aftermath?"

Suddenly it wasn't funny anymore.

CHAPTER 41

Spencer had all the earmarks of being psychotic. He was a smooth talker, he believed everything he said was the truth, even after you proved him wrong, and I'd seen his wicked temper up close more than once. I wasn't bucking for a third time.

It was Gia who finally got through to Spencer that it was time to leave me to manage the B&B. He took one for the team and asked Spencer to give him a ride to La Dolce Vita, just to get him off the property.

I felt a migraine coming on. If Spencer was to be believed, Blake had been after the family fortune for years and Auggie was the only one standing in his way. And Courtney was convinced Grover Prickle was out to destroy him. He didn't even know his wife was sneaking around visiting his biggest rival.

The news van rolled out in search of corruption or kittens—whichever would bring in the biggest ratings at five p.m. With nothing left to see, the neighbors went back to their TV dramas and afternoon strolls and we were left with just the people looking for Murder House Tours. Somehow that group was growing in spite of the rest of the circus calming down. The last time I checked, Elaine Grabstein was giving a talk in the library about poor little Siobhan dying of smallpox and being trapped in the attic, and Aunt Ginny was taking names for tomorrow's waitlist. *How in the world are they spreading this around?*

The twins grabbed my arm as I came through the dining room with my coffee cup, both of them giggling and excited. They had names on their T-shirts today. One read *You gotta have Faith*. "We're organizing the ghost tour for later. This is so much fun."

Her sister in the *You gotta have Grace* said, "So much better than jigsaw puzzles."

"I'm so glad you're enjoying yourselves." *I gotta get outta here before I get sucked into a dramatic reenactment of Siobhan's last day.*

I found Aunt Ginny with a group of ten in the pantry, showing them the hidden Prohibition trap door. She had her tour captivated with tales of being on house arrest. I pulled her aside to tell her I was running an errand. "I need to talk to June Whipple."

She spoke in a stage whisper. "She's not at home. Thelma just called. Everyone must be out. She was worried about Courtney."

I spotted a lady examining a jar of our fruit in raspberry cordial on the pantry shelf and had to ask her to please stop caressing my peaches. "I'm going over to their antique store to see if she's there."

I grabbed my purse and left the house with a backwards wave to Victoryna the French Maid lining up the two o'clock tour. I had lost all control of the staff long ago.

I pulled out the card June had given me days earlier for the address to Whipple's Antique Emporium. I plugged it into my GPS and headed for Cape May Point—the most southern tip of New Jersey, where the Delaware Bay smacks the Atlantic Ocean in the face.

Driving inland through the sleepy residential neighborhood, I passed a cute little church, and circled partway around the park. There I found Whipple's in a long wood-paneled building. A beautiful hand-painted sign spelled out Whipple's Antique Emporium, est. 1918 in scroll work down the roof line. A bushel basket of kohlrabi sat by the front door with a sign that said FREE TURNIPS.

A little bell chimed when I entered the store. The first room was like walking into a craft store where all the crafts had been completed for you. Hand-painted plates, decorative wooden plaques, framed embroidery, woven baskets. Further in, there was a whole row of shoes and handbags next to a rack of vintage clothes. A section of vinyl records ran floor to ceiling by the doorway into the kitchen cornucopia of antique casserole dishes, plates, glass, tin, and all manner of wooden spoons. The window display was a dressmaker's dummy with a vintage wedding ensemble. I couldn't imagine something as tacky as a papier mâché mannequin stuffed in the elegant tableau next to the tuxedo. I sneezed twice.

"Oh my gosh, it's you." I followed Tildy's voice to my left. She was staring at me from behind a vintage jewelry display. "Are you okay? It's all over the news. That was terrible what someone did."

I waved my hand. "I'm fine." *Nothing a few years of hypnotherapy won't cure.*

"What are you doing all the way out here?"

I grabbed a first edition *Joy of Cooking* from a stack of books and took it to the counter. "Just browsing. What are you doing here? Have you been enlisted?"

Tildy shrugged. "June had an estate auction in Deptford, so Mom was asked to watch the store today until she can hire someone full time. I just came along to keep her company."

I put the book on the glass and looked at the cameos. "Are you having fun?"

She wrinkled her nose. "It's very musty."

I spotted a beautiful silver brush and mirror set in the jewelry case next to an ivory pin. "Ooh, what's that?"

Tildy opened the case and pulled the drawer out. "Isn't it beautiful? I found it in a box in the storeroom under a stack of old newspapers. It's already tagged, so Mom said I should bring it out."

She flipped over the tag and I gasped. There was a distinctive little dahlia scrawled in the upper right corner.

"What's the matter?"

I looked into those big brown eyes behind her glasses. "What? Nothing. It's just so . . . expensive."

She looked at the price. "This says it's Victorian silver. Maybe that's why it costs so much."

I nodded and stared at that little flower, a thousand thoughts running through my head. "I'm surprised you're not out shopping."

Tildy gave me a rueful grin. "I have enough baby items to outfit a small village. I'll have to donate all of it if I can't get pregnant."

I looked at the price tag in my book. No flower. "Have you seen a fertility doctor?"

"Not yet. I was able to get pregnant on my own before, but I'm older now and I might have more trouble, so we'll see."

I said a prayer that what I was about to ask wouldn't be offensive but would open a door to her safety. "What happened the last time?"

She shrugged, but there was more pain in that shrug than in a roomful of tears. "I lost her. It just wasn't meant to be."

"I'm so sorry. I had a miscarriage when I was younger. It was the most painful thing I've ever been through."

"Did you try again?"

"No. I had complications that forced a hysterectomy. But I could adopt one day."

A tight frown wobbled into place. "Spencer has refused to consider adoption as a possibility."

Aye yi yi. "But you and Spencer are . . . happy? Right? He's . . . good to you?"

I wasn't convinced by the blank eyes behind her nod.

"He works a lot. He has big dreams, and he wants to take care of me in a grand way. But I've told him I don't need a big house and fancy things. I just need love."

I tried to swallow but it caught in my throat and I kind of croaked like Victory's frog. "If he ever hurts you, you know there are people you could call for help. The National Domestic Violence Hotline is 1-800-799-SAFE. Plus, I only live five minutes away and I have a dozen cops on speed dial."

She gave me a soft grin. "Thank you, but that isn't necessary. He has a temper, but it doesn't usually come my way."

Okay, well, I tried. Sometimes you can't help people until they're desperate. Then again, maybe June lied to me and Tildy has nothing to be desperate about. "Spencer came by to see me today."

Tildy groaned. "He said he might. I hope he wasn't rude."

No more than usual. "He had some more questions about running a bed and breakfast. Is that something *you* want to do?"

"If it will make him happy. But I don't think Courtney will ever go for it. Spencer has been on him every minute he's been around since the dinner party. He's begged, he's bargained, he's reasoned. Courtney is unpersuadable. I've never seen Spencer so possessed to make something happen before. He's determined to start that bed and breakfast."

I turned over a crystal candy dish to see the tag. No flower. "He said your mom and Courtney aren't coming up after this summer."

Tildy's eyes grew panicked behind her glasses. She looked over her shoulder and her voiced dropped a few decibels. "He shouldn't have said that. No one is supposed to know."

"Why not?"

"Mom and Courtney were worried that June and Auggie would start taking things out of the house if they knew it was the last time they'd be up."

"Okay, but they'll eventually get those things, right? Why be tormented about gifting them early?"

Tildy looked tired. Like the weight of living with so much bickering was wearing on her. "Courtney has always been obsessed with protecting his grandmother's legacy. Only a male born in the Whipple bloodline can inherit the house and the heirlooms. My God, it's like *Game of Thrones* over there. I don't think he can bring himself to face reality that the likelihood of that happening is like one in a million now that . . ." Her voice trailed off and she busied her hands with a tray of perfumes.

"Now that Blake and June are divorced?"

"I wish they could have worked things out. Blake was good for June."

"I'd heard Blake was trying to seize control of the estate."

Tildy sniffed a blue bottle and jerked it away from her nose. "That's what Auggie said, but I never saw any evidence of that. June was furious that Auggie would even accuse Blake, but then Blake was caught cheating again . . ."

"He had cheated before?"

"He got emotionally involved with a woman at the auction house. He said he broke it off before it became physical, but Auggie said he caught them in the act. June didn't know who to believe and I told Spencer we needed to stay out of it."

I picked up one of the perfume bottles. No flower. "How did Spencer and Auggie get along?"

Tildy squeezed the pump on a perfume atomizer and sniffed. "We didn't see him that often. Only when we came up for visits or holidays. He was a good brother, but he could be very cruel sometimes. Especially about money." Her voice broke and a fat tear rolled to the corner of her eye. "I can't believe he's gone."

Josephine came from a back room carrying a faded Holly Hobbie doll. "I knew it was back there. Oh, Poppy. What can we do for you?"

I held up the *Joy of Cooking* and Josephine scowled

that she'd have to wait on me. She handed the doll to Tildy. "Darling, go put this with my things in the car. I don't want it to go home with you until it's been washed in hot water."

Tildy took the cloth doll and gave me an apologetic look. She disappeared into the back room her mother had just come from.

Josephine reached over the counter in a flash and grabbed my wrist. "What do you want!"

I was so startled I almost lost my coffee. I should have peed before I left home. I didn't have a chance to come up with a good answer and I felt no joy with my cookbook.

Josephine was leaping to conclusions like an Olympic hurdler. "I don't want you coming in here and harassing my daughter. She's been through enough."

"I wasn't." I held up the *Joy of Cooking*. "I just want this book."

Josephine snatched the book from my hands. "She's still mourning her stepbrother, crying for him every day—not like he ever did a thing for her or deserved her grieving over him."

She punched the numbers onto a point-of-sale iPad and kept muttering angrily to no one in particular. "The boy was disturbed. It was shameful what he was doing. And always hanging out down at that topless mermaid bar. It darn near killed his father to find out."

"What was he doing?" *Please don't pummel me with the* Joy of Cooking.

Josephine gave me a look that could freeze hot dogs on the grill. "You're not going to hear it from me. My husband is a saint, but his first wife had two of the greediest, most materialistic, selfish children I've ever seen."

"June seems lovely." *Why did I just say that?*

The point of sale forgotten, Josephine leaned against the counter to shriek at me some more. "Let me tell you something. June acts like a saint, but she is just as selfish as her brother was. While we were down in Florida, she forged her brother's name on a transfer of ownership to become the sole proprietor of Whipple's. Courtney had to come up two weeks early to straighten it all out with the lawyers."

"Why would she do that?"

Josephine punched in the last number on the price. "Greed. Five dollars and thirty cents."

I fished my credit card out of my wallet and Josephine nearly had a meltdown that I didn't have exact change. She tried several times to swipe my card before I convinced her to try plugging the chip into the slot.

I tried to imagine this woman having the finesse to sneak into Mrs. Davis's house and rob her repeatedly, but I came up empty. "Can I ask you something?"

She narrowed her purple-lidded eyes at me. "What?"

"How do you keep breaking into your sister-in-law's house to get that jewelry box back?"

She dropped the cookbook into a plastic ACME bag and shoved it at me. "I don't break in. I use my key."

I had to remember to close my mouth. "You have a key to Mrs. Davis's house?"

"I've had a key for twenty years. She's never changed the locks."

I tried to absorb that information while I wove back through the store to the front. *This is kind of shame on Mrs. Davis, if you ask me.*

My eyes were drawn to the window display I'd seen on the way in. There was a row of hanging plants in knotted rope hangers beside the wedding dress. A spider plant lay broken on a rag rug inside the display. A crisscross pattern was burned into the faded plastic pot on the window shelf. I held up my phone and snapped a picture of it.

I called back to Josephine. "You know you have a broken pot and a pile of dirt up here in the front window?"

She hollered back to me. "It's June's problem now. She's the sole proprietor of Whipple's, just like she wanted."

CHAPTER 42

Josephine always unsettled me. She was spring-loaded with a hair trigger. Courtney was such a nice man. How did he end up married to the three faces of Eve? And I could not get that dahlia out of my mind. Maybe Auggie bought the silver brush and mirror from Prickled Curiosities at an auction. But why would he do that? You can't make money reselling antiques unless you buy wholesale. That's why June shopped at estate sales.

I was on autopilot. Bessie must have understood my dilemma and before I knew it the car pulled onto the crushed-clamshell parking lot at Prickled Curiosities. Never one to argue with a sentient convertible, I made my way through the main showroom, flipping tags on every item as I passed them. *Tulip. Tulip. Dahlia. Poinsettia. Tulip. Dahlia.*

"Well, hello again. You must be following me." Grover leaned on an ebony-handled walking stick. His trousers were baggy, and a sweater hung loosely around his shoulders.

"Mr. Prickle? I'm surprised to see you out of the hospital. Are you feeling better?"

Grover tilted his head and fluttered his eyes. "I think they figured this was as good as I was going to get, so they let me go."

"I guess by now you've heard about Auggie."

His eyebrows dipped together. "What about Auggie?"

Pauline hustled out of the back room with a steaming mug in her hand. "Okay now, that's enough about that. You are supposed to be resting. Not coming back to work. Now I made you some tea, drink this and you'll feel better." She looked at me and mouthed, "I've told him six times."

"I'm tired of being in bed. There's nothing good on TV at that hospital. Can you believe they don't have *Masterpiece*? But something called *Pimp My Ride* comes on four times a day. Concussion or no, I had to get out."

Pauline fussed over him and gave him the mug. "Well, I wish you would go home. I can handle things here."

He gave her a paternal little nod. "I know you can. What can we do for you . . ."

Pauline filled in the rest. "Poppy."

I looked around the giant store. It was starkly different from Courtney's showroom. If everything were professionally spread out and displayed, this would fill four Whipple's Emporiums. It was one busty papier mâché mannequin away from being an episode of *American Pickers*. "Actually, I had a question about the price tags. The little flowers you put in the corners to symbolize the season of acquisition—is that an antique store standard or just something you do here?"

Pauline was hovering at Grover's side even though there were customers waiting at the register.

Grover sipped his tea. He nudged his mug towards Pauline. "That's the girl's idea. She's the clever one."

That's what I thought. "She is very clever. Well, that's all I wanted. But while I'm here, I was interested in a silver brush and mirror set. Maybe something from the eighteen hundreds?"

Pauline's eyes widened and she started to perspire across her lip.

Grover shook his head. "We had one in stock, but it disappeared a couple months ago. I've got a private investigator tracking down some of the items that have gone missing. He's looking into a stolen vampire-hunting kit, if you can believe it. I think Auggie's been forging receipts. I can put your name down if I come across another."

I waved him off. "No, that's alright. I'll keep looking. One's bound to turn up very, very soon. It's probably in someone's front display by their register right now."

Pauline took two quick steps to me and tucked her arm in mine. "You know what we do have though? There is an oil lamp in the front room with your name on it. I'll show you. Go sit in the back and put your feet up, Grover."

Pauline practically dragged me to a tiny front room full of antique copper. Everything was tarnished and there was a metallic tang in the air. She let go of my arm and threw it to the side. "What are you really doing here?"

I turned on her fast and put my back against a shelf of genie lamps, pepper grinders, and candlesticks. "I know what you and Auggie were doing."

"I don't know what you're talking about."

I pulled out my phone and scrolled through my photos until I found the picture of the note from Auggie's ledger. 'The silver is yours and so am I.' Sound familiar?"

Pauline's cheeks turned splotchy like she'd been slapped.

"Your price tag is still on the silver set with the dahlia in the corner. You think the police can't trace that back to you?"

Pauline burst into tears. "I didn't mean to hurt him. It was an accident. He was supposed to go home."

"What? Who, Auggie?"

She flicked an irritated look my way. "No. Grover. I thought you said you knew what happened."

"I know you've been stealing things from your boss's storeroom and giving them to Auggie to resell at his store."

She waved her hands in front of her face. "No. Not stealing. Selling. I've been selling things to Auggie." Her voice trailed off. "At cost."

"And the vampire-hunting kit. How did you expect to hide that one?"

"Auggie said he had a buyer lined up. He wasn't supposed to take it to the Cold Spring Village Antique Show and put it in the auction in front of everyone. He paid me more than Grover bought it for in Boston, so I thought I was doing my boss a favor. I swear, I will make it up to him."

"Then why does Grover think it was stolen?"

Her lip trembled. "Because I've been doing it behind his back, after hours, and later recording the sales as random objects from stock that don't exist. I know it was wrong and I'm ashamed, but Auggie was so handsome and . . . I just wanted him to like me."

Oh, foolish girl. I wanted to shake her and tell her to snap out of it. "We've all been there."

Pauline sniffled. "I told Auggie how I felt, but he said he could never be interested in me that way. I was too Maryanne and not enough Ginger." She started to weep. "I don't even know what that means."

"Did you kill Auggie because he rejected you?"

Pauline's eyes grew ridiculously big. "No. No, I could never hurt Auggie. I loved him. I hoped he'd eventually break up with his girlfriend and maybe he'd give me a chance."

"His girlfriend? Who's that?"

"I don't know her. I accidentally walked in on Auggie video chatting with her in his storeroom when I took him the silver set."

Judging from the scarlet that crept up Pauline's neck, I had a feeling she didn't catch Auggie *chatting.* "What were they talking about?" *Oh wow. Yeah, they were not talking. She won't even look me in the eye.*

"Well, I left pretty fast. I did hear her say Auggie needed to give her more money; she sounded foreign. Auggie asked her to be patient while he worked out how to get more."

"I see." *Maybe this is one of the girls at the Mermaid Cove.* "Well, if you didn't kill him, what did you mean when you said you didn't mean to hurt him? He was supposed to go home?"

Pauline's lip started to tremble again. "I can't tell you."

"Sure, I understand. I'll go ask Grover."

Pauline flung herself between me and the doorway. "No! Please. He can't know."

"Girl, what did you do?"

Pauline looked out into the main showroom. She looked back at me and started to cry. "I thought he was a burglar."

Oh no.

"He was supposed to go home."

"You attacked Grover?"

She nodded and tears fell to the floor. "I was fixing the ledger to say we'd sold an antique radio so I could record what Auggie had given me for the vampire kit. We have six radios in stock, Grover would never know. Then I heard someone in the office. The lights were off, but I could see them trying to open the safe. I panicked. Grover had a cast-iron skillet on his desk."

I felt my stomach try to come out of my throat. "Oh my god."

Pauline started to weep. "I thought I killed him. I didn't know what to do, so I called Auggie. He checked Grover and said he was barely alive and told me everything would be okay if I just stayed cool. We could make it look like a robbery. He had me call an ambulance from the rotary phone but told me not to give my name—then get out and go straight home."

"Okay. And what was his part in this?"

Pauline wiped her eyes on the hem of her shirt. "He said we had to hide the flag. If the cops found it, they'd know it wasn't a robbery because the flag was in the news that it was worth a lot of money. Grover was counting on the sale of that flag to pay his taxes. A high-dollar collector was flying in just for this auction to bid on it." She started to cry harder. "I might have just killed Grover, but if he pulled through, he'd never forgive me for losing that sale. I begged Auggie to get that flag into the auction. He said he could sneak it into the storage room Saturday morning before the auction house opened."

"How was he planning on getting in there?"

"He had a meeting at nine."

"With who?"

"Blake Adams, the auctioneer."

CHAPTER 43

Why was Auggie meeting with Blake at nine a.m. on the morning he died? And why has Blake never mentioned it? He said the last time he saw Auggie was Friday night. Did someone kill Auggie before the meeting with his former brother-in-law? Or did Blake kill Auggie after all? One thing I did know was that I had to visit this mermaid bar for myself. I checked the time. Almost four p.m. Happy hour.

I stopped at the house to make sure there were no emergencies, considering we were overrun with crazies on the lawn all morning. The screen door shut behind me and I started past the library. Sveltelana was standing on the coffee table over the happy hour tray. A giant wedge of pepper jack cheese stuffed in her mouth. "Oh, my Lord! Bad kitty!"

She jumped down and disappeared under the couch. I got down on my hands and knees and shone the flashlight on my phone under the skirt. Her golden eyes hit me like white lasers and she had chowed through a significant portion of pepper jack like a Weight Watchers dropout after a bad weigh in. There was a curve of red wax from the round of gouda three days ago cowering in the back corner.

"Sveltelana, you cheese thief! You aren't going to fit in your crate when you have to leave. You'd better give me a good review after the fifty dollars of cheddar you swiped this week."

I sat upright and saw the grapes were as yet untouched. The wine, however. Already missing. *Unbelievable.*

I looked back under the couch. "Where are you taking the wine?"

Sveltelana stood over the remaining pieces of cheese, daring me to reach for them while she licked her chops.

I turned off my flashlight and considered my options. Then I dialed Sawyer. I might as well do something I could control for a change.

"Hey."

"I need to go to a topless mermaid bar."

"Cool."

"Wanna go with?"

Sawyer spoke to someone in the bookstore, then came back and said, "Yeah. Come get me."

"Oh, Sawyer?"

"Yeah?"

"Ah, don't tell Gia about this one. I don't think I want him to know there's a bar in Wildwood where you can see topless women."

A few minutes later I picked her up at the usual spot. The first thing she did was yell at me.

"Why didn't you tell me you had a death threat?! I had

to hear about it from my ex-husband of all people. Who, by the way, says tell Gwennifer at the hostess stand hello for him." Sawyer slid me a look and a huff.

I tried not to laugh. "Of course, Kurt would be on a first-name basis at a nudie bar. We should have asked his advice days ago. And I'm sorry. It was a long morning filled with the deafening sound of failure."

"Failure? Why?"

"Let's just say I won't be getting Innkeeper of the Year."

Sawyer pulled her cell phone out of a turquoise leather satchel. "Just wait till I get my hands on Ben. You would think living with a cop would get me inside information when my best friend is threatened by a murderer, but no. There are no perks in that department!"

"What about uh . . . the other . . . departments?"

Sawyer grinned. "Oh no, there are lots of perks in those departments."

By the time we got off the island and over the bridge to Wildwood, I had told Sawyer all about the morning's drama, including Lady Georgina of the McAllister Mansion working the system, Spencer's latest turnip drop, and my terrifying trip to Whipple's Antique Emporium. "All the men in that family are either monsters or angels depending on the time of day and who you ask. The only thing anyone agrees on is that the others are greedy and trying to get their hands on Courtney's valuables."

"So why are we going to the Mermaid Cove?"

"Auggie was into something seedy that might have gotten him killed. This is the seediest place I've heard about and it keeps coming up in conversation—so it seems like a good place to ask questions. Blake was caught rubbing up against one of the waitresses. He's either a cheater, or the victim of a weird bait and switch meant to kick him out of the family fortune. If I'm wrong, at least we can get some half-price shrimp cocktail."

The Mermaid Cove was in the heart of Wildwood next to a tattoo shack and a ten-dollar-an-hour parking lot. The windowless blue cement building had two competing points of allure. The neon mermaid with the clamshells that flickered on and off her glowing orange boobs, and the overflowing dumpster next to the ramp leading up to the boardwalk.

Sawyer's nose crinkled when we got close enough to smell the excitement. "Well, this is delightful. That rat looks like he's having a good time."

"How much do you think he paid for parking?"

I pulled between the yellow poles to enter the parking lot, and a four-hundred-pound Polynesian man eventually tore himself away from his concave lawn chair to take my money. He waddled over in stretched-out Nike flip-flops, a pair of OP board shorts, and a Gold's Gym muscle shirt.

"Nice ride, lady."

"We should only be an hour."

He handed me a ticket for my window and looked around the parking lot. "There's an opening on the other side of that truck against a rusty chain. You want me to park it?"

I gave him my best smile. "That's okay, I got it." I parked and locked up, took a few photos of the car on all sides, handed him my keys, and we went to find a way in.

The Mermaid Cove was exactly what you'd expect, if you expected fake pearls hanging from the ceiling and one entire wall to be a saltwater fish tank. A woman wearing an iridescent rubber mermaid tail sat on a pink pillow in a giant open oyster shell. She wore a bikini top made out of two D-sized clamshells.

"Hi. I'm Gwennifer. Welcome to the Mermaid Cove. Just the two of you?"

Sawyer stared at the woman's clamshells and sighed. "Kurt says hello."

I pulled out my cell phone and found one of the pictures from Cold Spring Village. I turned it to show the busty Venus. "Do you recognize this man?"

She looked closely. "That's Auggie. He's one of Miranda's regulars. He isn't in trouble again, is he?"

I put my phone away. "Well, you could say that. What kind of trouble was he in before?"

Gwennifer adjusted her straps. "Some guy was in here looking for him a couple weeks ago. Said Auggie and he had business dealings to discuss. When we wouldn't let him inside, he started shouting up the place. Calling Auggie to come out and face him."

"Did Auggie come out?"

She nodded and her spidery black wig shifted slightly on her head. She pulled it back into place. "I know he didn't want to. The guy was not here to sell cookies. But I think Miranda was getting nervous, so Auggie came out and went off with the guy."

Her wig shifted again, and Sawyer fished around her purse and pulled out a bobby pin. "Here. When was this?"

Gwennifer took the offered pin. "Oh, thanks." She slid it across the top of her wig. "Saturday before last. It's our second busiest night after Wednesday half-price margaritas."

I looked at the calendar on my phone. *That Saturday*

was the night before the garden party at Courtney's. "Did you see Auggie after that?"

Gwennifer gave her head a little shake. "No. I went home early. My three-year-old started throwing up and my husband couldn't handle it. But you could ask Miranda. If Auggie came back, he sat at her station."

Gwennifer waved a merman with oiled-up muscles and a trident over and told him who we were looking for. He led us to the back, towards a table by a plastic coral reef.

Sawyer whispered in my ear. "I may have misjudged this place."

The customers were mostly men and the room smelled like deep-fried shrimp. A pink-haired mermaid teetered by, carrying a plate of calamari. I sent a quick text to Amber while we waited for Auggie's waitress.

A minute later, a green-haired mermaid on stilettos took small steps towards us and placed cocktail napkins on the table. "I'm Miranda. Would you like to start with some oysters tonight?"

"Not yet. We were hoping you could answer a couple questions for us."

Sawyer looked down at her fins. "How are you walking in that?"

She turned to show us the back. "I ripped out the seam up to the knee."

I showed her the same picture I'd showed Gwennifer. "Do you know this man?"

Miranda took my phone with her long pearl-encrusted fingernails. "That's Auggie. I read in the paper that he'd been killed."

"How well did you know him?" I took my phone back and looked for another picture.

Miranda checked behind her, then pulled out a chair and angled herself onto it. "Auggie was one of my favorite customers. His picture's on the spotlight wall over there with the other regulars who ate an entire seafood tower in one sitting. He came in every week before he went to talk to his girlfriend. I can't believe what happened to him. I just saw him at Cold Spring Village when he debuted that Dracula box."

I went over to the wall of Polaroids. Auggie's picture was dead center with his arm around our waitress, giving the camera thumbs-up. It was dated last May. I snapped a picture of it with my cell phone and came back to the table. "Who was his girlfriend?"

Miranda unstrapped her shoe and rubbed her ankle. "Some chick he met online, I think. Cookie? Candy? Something like that."

"Taffy?"

She rolled her foot in circles out in front of her. "That sounds right."

"Can you tell me about the night the man came for Auggie last week?"

"What a nightmare that was. He was saying the most awful things. Threatening to kill Auggie if he didn't pay what he owed. Auggie was very charismatic. He could charm you into doing all kinds of things you wouldn't normally do. None of us believed he'd be mixed up with a creep like that."

"What did the guy look like?"

She tossed her hair over her shoulder. "I don't know. I never left this room. If anyone saw him, it'd be Gwennifer or Ricky, the guy who brought you back."

I showed Miranda the picture of Blake Adams. "How about this guy?"

Miranda looked at the picture then flicked her eyes to me. Her shoulders drooped with her smile. "Him I'll never forget. I'm still ashamed of what I let Auggie talk me into. When I saw the look on his wife's face. And the way he ran after her, begging her to believe that he loved her. I couldn't work the rest of my shift. I went home sick."

"Why'd you do it?"

"Auggie paid me two hundred dollars to meet a guy with a rose under the boardwalk in my work uniform. All I was supposed to do was take off my shells and throw myself into his arms when the blonde came down the steps, and let her see us together. I thought it was like a bachelor party prank and we'd all get a good laugh. Later he told me the blonde was his sister and his brother-in-law was greedy and trying to rob him of his inheritance. I told Auggie I refused to get involved in any more of his schemes, whether I'm late on rent or not."

I held up the picture of Blake again. "Did he ever come here looking for you?"

"Not until last Friday night. But he didn't find me. I hid in the kitchen and the other girls covered for me until he left."

"Do you know what he wanted?"

"I'm sure he was here to rip into me about how I wrecked his marriage. I don't know how he found me."

Sawyer played with the lemon in her water. "Probably the mermaid tail. I'm surprised it took him as long as it did."

Miranda re-strapped her shoe. "Auggie swore he'd never tell him who I was. I waited for Auggie to come in last weekend so I could warn him that his brother-in-law had found me, but he never made it."

"Miranda!"

A dark-skinned man in black jeans and a black golf shirt jerked his head to the side for our waitress to get back to work. "Uh-oh. I've been caught. Are you sure I can't get you a drink? Onion rings are half-price for another hour."

I want all the onion rings. A battle raged in my mind, but I'd been so diligent. "No, thank you. We're good." My stomach growled. *But the onion rings.*

Sawyer had been looking around, examining the other mermaids. "What exactly do you all do here? Other than serve drinks and bar food in those getups?"

Miranda adjusted her shell strap. "Every hour on the hour Ricky plays 'Under the Sea' from *The Little Mermaid* and we dance. When we get to the finale, we take our shells off."

Sawyer's jaw slid south in shock.

I took a sip of my water. "Walt Disney would be so proud."

Miranda gave us a rueful nod. "It pays the bills better than teaching third grade."

The lights turned to strobes and the music cued up. The men were starting to whoop, and waitresses were heading towards the fish tank wall.

Miranda adjusted her shells. "That's my cue."

She headed over to join the other mermaids, and Sawyer jumped to her feet. "Well, I'm ready to go if you are."

My cell phone dinged that my answer text had arrived. I left a twenty on the table and we went back out to see Gwennifer.

"You weren't in there long. The dance is about to start."

Sawyer gave an involuntary shudder. "Sorry to miss that."

I gave her a grin. "You can always perform the matinee at home. I have the DVD."

She gave a sideways glance at Gwennifer. "I'll have to dig out my shells."

I tapped on my screen and stretched the photo that had come in from Amber. I showed it to the mermaid hostess. "Is this the man who came threatening Auggie two Saturdays ago?"

She squinted at the picture. Her eyes flicked up to mine and she squirmed in her shell. "I don't know. It could be."

"Thanks. Good luck with the three-year-old."

We left the Cove, and the humidity wrapped its hands around our throats the minute we were outside. An oily breeze wafted down from the Curley's Fries stand on the boardwalk and reminded me of the onion rings. My stomach rumbled. A mechanical grinding sound up on the boardwalk headed in our direction. "Watch the tram car, please."

Sawyer wiped her forehead. "Was that helpful?"

"I don't know yet." I dialed Amber and she answered on the first ring.

"Was it him?"

"Either she's not sure, or she's not talking."

CHAPTER 44

I dropped Sawyer back at her bookstore for the last couple hours of the day. I had planned on stopping in to
visit Gia, until I spotted his mother in the front window of
La Dolce Vita drinking a coffee. I didn't realize Aunt
Ginny's old whitewalls would leave skid marks down the
road—but now I know.

The first thing I noticed was that the house smelled
lemony fresh. I could even see my reflection in the parquet floors, they were buffed to such a high shine. I found
Aunt Ginny in the kitchen eating a tomato sandwich.
"Where've you been?"

I took my gluten-free bread from the freezer and
popped two slices in the toaster. "I had to get away for a
bit and clear my head."

"Uh-huh. Did you go to Whipple's or Prickled?"

I sawed off two gorgeous ruby slices of Courtney's

tomatoes. "Both. Mrs. Davis is right, Josephine's a psycho."

Aunt Ginny raised her glass of tea in my direction. "Thanks for catching up."

"Who cleaned the kitchen? It looks amazing."

Aunt Ginny shrugged. "Georgina."

"She's been holding out on me."

Figaro's head raised above the kitchen table to his eye level and a gray fluffy paw patted the triangle on Aunt Ginny's plate.

She looked at the feline. "Boy, what did I tell you about that?"

The gray head slowly descended out of view.

I spread mayonnaise on my toast and layered on the tomatoes. "I'm surprised the other two cats aren't in here as well."

"Just wait." Aunt Ginny raised an eyebrow in my direction and took a bite of her triangle.

I took my sandwich to the table to join her and was greeted with a *swat swat swat* on my ankle. I looked under the seat and Cleo's green eyes blinked back at me. "There's number two."

Aunt Ginny rolled her eyes towards the window.

I picked up half my sandwich and followed her gaze. Sveltelana had wedged herself into an old breadbox on the windowsill. She was smooshed into a tight loaf and I worried we'd have to butter up the Jaws of Life to get her out again. "What time did Georgina and Victory stop giving tours?"

"About two. They have a bunch set up for tomorrow though."

"Good Lord, how do people keep finding us?"

Aunt Ginny shrugged. "Probably the video."

I savored my sandwich with just the right amount of salt and pepper. And the tomatoes were perfect. "What video?"

Aunt Ginny dabbed the corners of her mouth daintily with a cloth napkin and turned her cell phone to face me. She tapped the screen and a video started to play of her interview on the lawn in front of the Butterfly Wings Bed and Breakfast shingle.

"The dummy on the lawn's not a real person. It's papier mâché. Oh no, it's not my niece's fault that she keeps getting targeted by a bunch of weirdos. Poppy tried a wooden troll doll to ward off evil, but it don't help none."

Then the drums started beating.

My mouth went dry as Aunt Ginny's voice was looped to an Auto-Tune.

"It's not her fault. Oh no, it's not her fault. It's not her fault the wooden troll doll don't help none."

A guitar came in with a melody.

"The dummy on the lawn's not real.
The dummy on the lawn's not real.
My niece just finds dead people everywhere."

A choir started singing backup vocals.

"The dummy on the lawn's not real.
The dummy on the lawn's not real.
She's not real and my niece was cursed by a bogus psychic.
The dummy on the lawn's not real.
The dummy on the lawn's not real.
It's not her fault the wooden troll don't help none.
Poppy was targeted by a bunch of weirdos."

The tomato slid out of my sandwich and landed on the

plate with a splat. I looked across the table at Aunt Ginny, but she wouldn't meet my eyes.

She gave me a little shrug. "It's probably not that bad."

"There have been over fifty thousand views since this afternoon."

"Maybe it will bring in more business."

"That's what I'm afraid of."

Aunt Ginny turned her emerald eyes on me. "Are you mad?"

It was like kicking a puppy. "No. I'm not mad. I don't think I can show my face at the Innkeepers Association after this, but I'm not mad."

"Are the police any closer to finding out who killed Auggie?"

"I don't think so. If they were, we wouldn't have received a papier mâché victim with an antique spurtle in the chest as a warning."

"You know they sell those spurtles at Prickled Curiosities. They were on the table with your rolling pin."

"I know. But they sell them at Whipple's too. I saw them today with a bunch of wooden spoons."

A gray paw resurfaced on my side of the table and snatched a hunk of my fallen tomato.

"Hey!" I looked at the naughty feline under the table. He sniffed at the tomato then turned his nose up and walked away. "Serves you right, you little thief."

Aunt Ginny took her plate to the sink. "What are we going to do?"

"I'm going to give Blake Adams a visit tonight to see what he does when I show him a picture of the woman who, with Auggie, ruined his life."

"Can I come with you?"

I could tell by the look on her face that she was feeling bad about the viral interview. It was going to bring every nutjob on the East Coast to our door and we were already over the limit. "Go get your purse."

I finished my sandwich and took my plate to the sink with hers. I grabbed my cell phone and keys and noticed the landline was off the hook. "What's happening there?"

"It's been ringing all day. I probably shouldn't have given my interview next to the vacancy sign. Also, I should probably tell you, we have a hundred and eighty-six messages."

CHAPTER 45

The door to Adams Galleries was locked but the lights were on inside. "They don't close for another hour."

Aunt Ginny banged on the door with her fist. "We know you're in there, Blake! Open up or face my wrath! What are you hiding?! Why are you looking at me like that?"

I held up my cell phone. "I thought we'd call. Not bang the door down."

The door swung open, and Blake looked ready to tell off whoever had been going wolverine on it. Then he saw little old Aunt Ginny and straightened up. "Ladies."

I gave him my biggest we're-not-here-to-investigate smile. "Can we come in?"

He stood aside and swept his arm across the threshold. "I was just appraising a Confederate button in my office."

The large auction room was dark, and the only light appeared to be coming from down the hall.

Blake closed the door behind us to keep the fraction of cool air inside. "Perhaps you don't realize this, but my hours, outside of auction days, are by appointment only."

I was about to apologize, but Aunt Ginny launched into Blake with a ferocity usually only seen on *The Biggest Loser*. "Well, you should have thought about that before you killed dear little Auggie. He was a good boy even if he did spend his father's money like a hotel heiress. How dare you!"

Blake's back was against the wall and his hands were over his head. The fright in his eyes was enough to put most people off, but not Aunt Ginny.

She lifted her pocketbook to whack him and I grabbed her wrist. She rolled her eyes to mine. "What?"

"What are you doing?"

"Aren't we here to knock him to kingdom come?"

"No."

She put her arm down. "Then why did you bring me for backup?"

"I brought you because I thought you wanted to get out of the house and stretch your legs."

Blake looked from me to Aunt Ginny. He nodded as if to encourage her that exercise was a sound idea.

Aunt Ginny lowered her voice. "Didn't he kill Auggie?"

I cleared my throat. "I don't know. We're here to ask him some questions."

Her mouth formed an O. "So, you might still need that backup before we leave."

I kept my expression passive and nodded. "Let's put a pin in that."

Blake relaxed his shoulders but kept his eyes on Aunt Ginny. "I didn't kill my brother-in-law."

"We know you had a meeting with him at nine a.m. the day he died. And you lied to the police about it."

Blake rubbed his hand over his head and groaned. "Why don't you come to my office."

Aunt Ginny pointed a finger in his face. "Okay, but don't even think about doing anything shifty. I know how to kill a man with a nail file."

He took a quick step back. "I promise."

We followed him down the hall past a set of restrooms. His office was at the very end on the left. I pointed to the door across the hall on my right. "Is that the storage room?"

"That's it."

Aunt Ginny butted in front of me. "Can we see it? Or are you hiding another body in there?"

Blake pulled out a key ring with a large brass key with fancy scrollwork. The lock was ornate. Formed in a diamond pattern with scroll work on the top and bottom that matched the pattern on the key.

Aunt Ginny squinted and leaned in to look at the brass. "That's a pretty fancy lock for a security system. Why didn't you go with one of them high-tech numbers?"

Blake shrugged. "It was here when I bought the auction house when the last auctioneer retired. It's a stunning example of Victorian craftsmanship and it's over a hundred years old. I don't dare remove it and risk damaging the metal."

I held up a finger. "Wait. You're not the original owner?"

Blake put the key in the lock and shook his head. "I bought the auction house from Tom Jensen. He was a friend of Courtney's. It was Courtney who introduced us." The key turned with a *thunk*, and Blake opened the door to expose a large room. He switched on a light just inside. Fluorescent bulbs woke slowly and flickered to a dim glow. The room held a few pieces of furniture, a rolled-up oriental rug, a life-sized pink-and-silver pony from a carousel, and a few boxes labeled Prickled in black marker. There was a blue tape divide down the center of the room. "The police have already been through here and they didn't find anything."

Aunt Ginny took a step inside. "How much are you asking for that big horse?"

I pulled her arm and extricated her before she went in any deeper. "That's the last thing we need."

She muttered some sass under her breath. "The last thing we need is more kohlrabi."

Blake led us across the hall to an office that would have been spacious if it were not so cluttered. It looked as though everything that had not sold at Cold Spring Village had ended up here to be appraised. Several weapons were on the windowsill next to a stack of old books on an antique three-legged table. A large wardrobe sat behind a walnut desk that was spotless. Only a gooseneck lamp and a magnifying glass graced the top, next to a brass button on a red square of velvet.

Blake wheeled around in a burgundy leather chair to face us. He indicated the two black chairs with curved arms in front of the desk. "Ask what you will, I have nothing to hide."

"Why'd you lie to the police about seeing Auggie the morning he died?"

"Ask me something else."

Aunt Ginny opened her purse and started digging around. "Where's my nail file?"

Blake gripped his desk. "I'm sorry. I just can't tell you that."

I took out my cell phone and pulled up the photo of Auggie with Miranda at the Mermaid Cove. I turned the phone to show Blake.

He leaned across the desk, squinting at my screen. I knew the moment he'd worked out what he was looking at because the blood drained from his face. "Where did you find that?"

"I think you know where. When did you realize Auggie had set you up?"

Blake wouldn't take his eyes off the picture. "When I saw that on the wall under the spotlight. I saw her earlier that day, you know—the girl with the green hair. At Cold Spring Village, after Auggie got the vampire kit authenticated. I almost didn't recognize her with normal clothes on. But then she went to Auggie's booth and they were laughing and hugging like they were friends. Auggie told her he'd be in later and to save him his regular seat. I wanted to confront her right there by the ice cream parlor."

"Why didn't you?"

"Grover Prickle brought that demand letter from his attorney saying he'd filed a civil suit against Whipple's over ownership rights to the vampire kit. He and Auggie started shouting at each other and escalating their threats until Cold Spring Village called the police and closed the show early. By the time I was finished smoothing over all their juvenile embarrassment, the girl was gone."

Aunt Ginny looked at the photo on my phone. "I remember her. We were both trying to buy a chain-mail corset by the blacksmith. She said that green hair was a rinse. So that's the floozy June caught you with on the beach?"

Blake chewed his bottom lip. "I came to my office and

googled 'mermaids and Mariner's Pier' and found the Cove. So, after Auggie put his things in the room across the hall and left, I locked up and drove straight there. I wanted to see for myself if she was the woman who destroyed my marriage."

I set my phone down. "What was your plan for when you found her?"

"To ask her why she did it and see if I could get her to tell June the truth. June wouldn't listen to me, but maybe she'd listen to the woman she thought I was cheating with."

Aunt Ginny reached out and grabbed a saber from the windowsill. She jabbed it at a stuffed jackalope. "Did you find her?"

"I knew I had the right place as soon as I walked in; it was definitely Auggie's style. But she wasn't there. The bouncer said it was her day off. When I saw the Polaroid of her with Auggie on the back wall, dated two years earlier, I didn't want to believe it. What had he done to me?"

I took the sword away from Aunt Ginny. "Did you call him?"

"You bet I called him. I didn't care that it was after eleven. He owed me some answers. He picked up right away, but he sounded weird. He was out of breath and distracted, like he was moving furniture. He said he was in the middle of some emergency. I told him we needed to talk, and we agreed for him to be here at nine before his interview with the paper."

"What time did he show up?"

"About twenty till. I told him I knew what he'd done." Blake pulled out his own cell phone and swiped his screen until he pulled up the same photo of Miranda and Auggie that I'd taken. "I showed him this. And I asked him why. He just grinned at me with that smug look. Can you believe that? He poisoned my wife against me, wrecked my marriage, and he refused to give me a straight answer. The only thing Auggie would say was that I was a dead-beat, and he had a responsibility to protect the Whipple legacy."

Aunt Ginny picked up a heavy glass paperweight on the corner of a small table and shook it. "Protect the family legacy from what?"

Blake put his phone down on his desk blotter. "From anyone who wasn't a Whipple. Especially me. He said I'd put ideas in his father's head about power of attorney and he knew I was trying to get my hands on the family fortune."

I took the paperweight from Aunt Ginny and put it on the other side of the desk. "I take it from the black eye he had that you decked him for saying that."

Blake grinned. "Oh, I let him have it. I'd wanted to knock that condescending look off his face for years. I plowed him right in the face and kicked him out. I told him I didn't want to see him again until the auction."

"What time was that?"

"About nine."

"Did you go lock the door behind him when he left?"

"No. I never left my office."

Aunt Ginny rubbed her hand over a gold-embossed leather-bound book, and some of the gold foil rubbed off on her fingers. "What'd you do for the next hour?"

Blake's eyes shifted around the room. "Nothing. I just sat in here, thinking."

I handed Aunt Ginny a Kleenex and gave Blake a level stare. "Except you weren't alone, were you?"

Aunt Ginny wiped the gold off her fingertips. "Ooh."

Blake looked from her to me. "I don't know what you're talking about."

"You didn't call Auggie in here just to *ask* him if he'd set you up. You already had your proof. You had June in here so she could overhear his confession. She told me she had an early meeting she was getting ready for on Saturday before Auggie left the house. And we know something happened for her not to make it to the auction. She lied to the police that she was on the beach alone, but she was in here with you, wasn't she? Listening from that big chest maybe?"

Aunt Ginny smacked a stack of reference books. "Did the two of you kill Auggie together?"

"No! Oh my god, of course we didn't kill Auggie." Blake drummed his fingers on the desk and looked around the room. I was glad that curved sword wasn't within his reach.

"Why didn't you just tell the police you and June were in here together? You could have given each other alibis."

"Because the truth makes us look more suspicious. We've had a very ugly, public divorce. June doesn't even come to the auctions anymore, and everyone on staff will back that up. How are we supposed to convince the police—who already suspect her of killing her brother because she's just become the sole heir of the Whipple estate—that she was hiding in a cabinet to overhear her brother admit to convincing a topless waitress to stage an affair? That just makes us both look suspicious. And if the police find out she left my office for a few minutes and was out of my sight, she'd be arrested on the spot. It's better if they think she was nowhere near here. And we didn't kill Auggie. We were busy . . . discussing things."

Aunt Ginny snickered. "I bet you were discussing them on top of that big desk that's so clean."

Blake let a tiny grin slip only for a second. "Anyway, I never locked the front door, and . . . there was too much noise to hear if anyone came in while we were . . . talking. I was trying to convince June to come back to me. I know she still loves me, but she refuses to believe I wasn't cheating on her. Since I couldn't get Auggie to confess to setting me up, no matter what I do to prove myself, June won't let go of the past. And thanks to Auggie, Courtney believes I was trying to rob him blind. He's threatened to disown June if she comes anywhere near me for something not antique related. I've never wanted any of Courtney's things. If you ask me, they've been a curse. That clock he's always fussing over—he's terrified to let it out of his sight. Searching for his grandmother's letters hidden somewhere in the house, that jewelry box Josephine is paranoid will get stolen, they're too obsessed with losing their things to enjoy them."

"If you were in here with June, where was Auggie?"

Blake's eyes were wide, and he turned up his hands. "I thought he'd left for his interview with the paper. I have no idea how he ended up dead in the armoire."

Aunt Ginny stood. "Excuse me for just a moment. I need the ladies' room." She disappeared out the door.

I should have been more worried, but I was finally getting somewhere. "You had a strong motive to kill Auggie. He broke up your marriage."

"What am I, an idiot? Murdering her brother would push June further away. It won't bring her back. And anyone could have come in here while the front door was unlocked."

"But not anyone could lock the storage room door when they were done. Are you absolutely sure it wasn't you, out of habit?"

"I'm positive. June and I were interrupted when *The Atlantic City Press* arrived at ten for their interview. Auggie was supposed to meet them at Cold Spring Village and he never showed. We didn't want to lose the free publicity, so June went to the storage room to get the vampire-hunting kit, and when it was locked, she had to come back to get my key to open it."

Or to lock up after herself.

Aunt Ginny stuck her head into the room. "Hey. We gotta go."

"Why?"

She looked at Blake and crooked her head towards the front door. "I don't want to miss Jimmy Fallon."

Since when? I stood and collected my purse. "One last thing. Are you missing a papier mâché mannequin?"

Blake's eyebrows knit together. "I told the cops earlier. I've never seen anything like that in my auction house. But it sounds like something Grover would use in his front window."

Aunt Ginny grabbed my wrist and jerked me down the hall to the front door. "Hurry up."

"What are you so worked up about?"

She looked past me towards Blake's office. "I found Auggie's phone."

CHAPTER 46

"What do you mean, you found Auggie's phone?" Aunt Ginny held up the black iPhone and waved it in front of my face.

I pulled out of the Adams Galleries parking lot and onto Shore Road. "How do you know it's his?"

"Who else would lose a cell phone under an old radiator in that storage room?"

I spun my head to look at her.

She grinned. "I had Blake so flustered he forgot to lock the door after he showed us the room. No one suspects an old lady with a weak bladder. It must have fallen out of Auggie's pocket in a struggle."

"Well, what's on it?"

"I don't know. It won't turn on."

"And now your fingerprints are all over it." My cell phone dinged, and I fished around my purse until I found it. I had a text message from Gia. **What are you doing?**

I handed the phone to Aunt Ginny "Please tell him I'm on my way home."

She dumped Auggie's iPhone into my purse, then took about as much time as Beethoven needed to compose a symphony to craft my response to Gia. We were almost home when my phone dinged again.

Aunt Ginny checked the screen. "He wants us to go to the shop. He's making us special coffees."

"Oh. Okay." I turned at the Washington Street Mall and cruised down the alley behind La Dolce Vita.

We found a meter that still had seventeen minutes on it. Aunt Ginny went nuts. She'd walk an extra block for free meter time. "There! Park there!"

Gia met us at the back door. "There is my beautiful lady." He pulled me into an embrace and kissed me deeply.

Aunt Ginny pushed past us into the kitchen. "What am I? Liverwurst? How about a 'hello, gorgeous' for Ginny?"

Gia snickered. He ran his hand down my back. "I hear you want me to make you something fancy?"

"What?"

"That is what you said in your message."

"Aunt Ginny!"

Aunt Ginny cackled, up ahead of us.

Gia ran his fingers through the back of my hair and drew me closer. "I should have known. I am very happy you are here." He checked that we were alone and kissed me until one of us couldn't take any more and we had to join the others in the dining room.

Henry was sitting on one of the marshmallow-colored leather stools at the bar, but he was transfixed by the game in front of him. Sierra restocked cups and lids on the shelves behind the bar and Cameron was wiping down the tables. He was singing, "*The dummy on the lawn's not real. The dummy on the lawn's not real.*"

I was thankful Aunt Ginny was too interested in what Henry was doing to notice.

"What's that doohickey?"

"iPad."

"What are you doing there?"

"Playing *Crossy Road*."

"What's that crazy thing?"

"Chicken." Henry's concentration was tight. I'm not sure he even knew I was there. "He has to get across the road without getting splatted. See?"

Aunt Ginny watched for a minute. "What's that?"

"A river."

Aunt Ginny made a face that this was the deal breaker for her. "Well, good Lord, who puts a river in the middle of the road? No wonder he can't get across."

The video game was making chicken clucks and horn sounds and Henry was clucking along with it. "*Buk buk buk.*"

Gia kissed me on the temple. "How about a keto peanut butter cocoa?"

"Yes, please. Aren't you closing soon?"

"Forty-five minutes. I was hoping you would come home with me. We could watch a movie."

The game went, "*Bkaaah!*" and Aunt Ginny and Henry laughed like it was the funniest thing in the world.

Aunt Ginny hoisted herself onto the stool next to Henry. "He got splatted."

"I have to take Mary Poppins here home first. We've just come from the auction house. Aunt Ginny found Auggie's iPhone."

Gia got out a jar of peanut butter from the cabinet. "Did you find anything good?"

"No. It's dead. I'll have to give it to Amber in the morning."

Sierra popped up from behind the counter. "What kind of iPhone is it?"

I shrugged. "I dunno. It's in my purse. But I wouldn't touch it if I were you. It's bad enough Aunt Ginny's fingerprints are on it."

I waited for some sass from the bar, but Aunt Ginny was too busy clucking along with the chicken.

Sierra pulled on some plastic food service gloves and opened my purse to face her. "May I?"

I nodded. "Sure."

She pulled out the wooden troll doll, shrieked and dropped it. "My God, what is that?!"

I felt my heart make a similar reaction to Henry's chicken getting splatted. I picked up the wooden doll that I knew I had left on the desk in my bedroom. "Aunt Ginny! Are you playing a joke on me with this thing?"

Aunt Ginny barely glanced up from the iPad. "I don't know what you're talking about. Whoa, a train!"

Cameron pointed at the troll and half laughed, half sang, "It's not her fault 'cause her wooden troll don't help none."

Gia laughed, and set a hot cocoa in front of Aunt Ginny and then one in front of me. "Bella, I am sure someone is having fun with you."

Behind me, Aunt Ginny yelled, "Lily pad!"

Henry yelled back, "Aaah!"

Sierra reached into my bag and pulled out the black iPhone. "No problem. Cameron, you have an iPhone, don't you?"

Cameron joined her behind the bar and tossed his rag into a bucket of sanitizer. "Not that old. Hold on."

While he left to retrieve the charger, I sipped my cocoa. "Oh, that's good. It almost makes up for the evil death troll that mocks me."

I went to hurl the wooden troll doll into the trash can behind the bar and Sierra screamed. "Don't leave that here. We'll all be cursed."

Gia took the troll from my hands. He put it on the shelf behind the sink. "Now you are safe."

I kept one eye on the frizzy white yak hair. Next to me Henry's game went "*Bkaaah!*"

Cameron returned with a brown messenger bag and handed Sierra the charger. She plugged it in under the bar and the phone lit up. "We're gonna need the password."

"Yeah, I don't have that."

Sierra and Cameron launched into a discussion that I understood very little of. I just sipped my cocoa and watched it unfold.

Cameron nodded at the phone. "Try 1234."

Sierra pushed the buttons. "That didn't work."

"We have to reset it."

"You'll lose all the data."

"Not if we back it up."

"How you gonna do that?"

Cameron grinned. "I have tricks you don't know about."

"Like what? Recovery software?"

"Maybe."

"He'd have to have iTunes."

"Dude, everybody got iTunes. It's like a virus. Relax." Cameron took out his laptop and pulled on a pair of gloves. Then he attached the cable between the two devices. He typed some things into the computer while Sierra hovered over his shoulder.

"Where'd you get this program?"

Cameron gave her a smug grin. "Can't tell you that."

Sierra's look was more amusement than irritation. "You're a dork."

Gia and I noticed at the same time and passed a silent message between us. *It's getting interesting.*

I filled up the pastry case while Gia did an inventory of coffee syrups and brought out a bag of roasted beans. We were eventually able to lock the front door and turn the sign around to closed. Henry was keeping Aunt Ginny occupied, and Sierra and Cameron were still babysitting the computer, so we left the kids to their hacking and escaped into the kitchen.

As soon as we were out of sight, Gia was all over me. "I miss you."

I giggled into his neck. "You just saw me this morning."

"That was forever ago, and Spencer was there. I don't like being away from you."

"I don't like it either. Want to know what happens when you're not around?" I took my phone out of my pocket and hit play on Aunt Ginny's Auto-Tune interview.

Gia laughed out loud. "I have been hearing that all day. Everyone is playing it. I had no idea what it was."

"It's my newest vexation."

Gia pulled me close. "Aww. Come here, *cara mia.*"

Things were getting delightfully snuggly when Sierra yelled, "We got it!"

Gia made a face. "We need to go away from here. Alone. Maybe Antarctica."

I gave him a quick peck. "I would love that."

We went out into the dining room where the kids stood behind Cameron's laptop. Sierra was beaming. "He did it. Cameron downloaded all this guy's data."

"You're kidding?!"

Sierra flashed us a megawatt smile. "Cameron backed up everything on the iPhone to his laptop."

Gia and I went over to the laptop to see what had come up. Even Aunt Ginny left *Crossy Road* to see what secrets Auggie had been hiding.

Cameron stood back and blew out his breath. "Whoa. Dude was into some janx."

I pointed to a row of colorful icons. One of them was called Sugar Sugar. "What are these, Cameron?"

Cameron flicked his eyes to Henry to be sure he was still distracted by his game. He lowered his voice. "These are apps for watching cam girls."

Aunt Ginny slid him some side eye. "What the devil is a cam girl?"

Cameron cleared his throat and looked at Sierra.

Sierra had a dozen emotions cross her face before she spoke in a whisper. "Cam girls are sex workers who perform live on the Internet through web cameras."

Cameron took another run at it while he continued to click around the backup of Auggie's phone. "It's like back in the day when guys would call one-nine-hundred numbers and listen to some woman talk dirty to them. Only now, they can see her too. And she gets naked if you give her money."

Sierra narrowed her eyes at him. "How do you know so much about it?"

"I have never done it. But guys talk and . . ." He

pointed at the computer screen. "And this guy spent a fortune on it."

I pointed to an icon that said Taffy. "What's that one?"

Cameron shrugged. "I've never heard of that one."

He clicked on the square and a prefilled password appeared. He hit enter and a screen opened up. A dark-haired woman in sexy underwear was lying on a bed. She turned to the screen and spoke in an accent similar to Victory's. "Auggie, is that you?"

We were all frozen into place, not sure if we were watching a video or speaking to someone live.

"Auggie, who are all those people?"

I waved. "Uh, hi. Are you Taffy?"

The girl looked wary like she might disconnect us. "Who are you?"

"I'm a friend of Auggie's."

"Is he okay? He missed many appointment. Did something happen?"

Aunt Ginny found her voice. "No, dear. He's not okay. He's dead."

The girl on the screen started to whimper. "No. My poor Augustus."

I pulled up the photo of Mitchel Maloney that Amber had sent me when I was at the Mermaid Cove. "Taffy, do you know this man?"

Her face got really close to the camera and she nodded. "Eis my manager."

Aunt Ginny whispered, "Manager?"

Sierra whispered back, "Pimp."

I looked back at the girl who couldn't be more than twenty. "Do you know why your manager would be threatening Auggie?"

She shook her head no, but there was fear in her eyes. "I know nothing."

Aunt Ginny spoke so soothingly that the girl relaxed. "Your manager is dead too, so he won't find out you spoke to us."

The girl looked into the lens and tapped her camera. "Are you sure? Eis not recording?"

I held up my phone again. "I only know Mitchel Maloney washed up under the pier almost two weeks ago. He had been strangled with a macramé plant hanger. It's like a fancy rope with lots of knots."

Taffy's eyes brightened. "Eis dead? He discovered Auggie was going to take me away. We were to meet as soon as Auggie send me money. But every time Auggie send money, Mr. Maloney take it."

Gia took a breath and wouldn't look directly at the laptop. "Where are you right now? What country?"

"I am in United States, New York. I come for good job with lawyer, but Mr. Maloney pick me up and say I owe him money and I not leave until I work it off."

I texted Amber that I needed to talk to her right away. "Do you think Mr. Maloney came to New Jersey to threaten Auggie?"

The girl nodded. "He came to make Auggie pay. He has recordings of Auggie during our sessions. He was going to make them public if Auggie did not give him ten thousand dollars."

Aunt Ginny moved closer to the camera. "Are you safe? Are you being held against your will?"

The girl looked terrified. "Mr. Maloney eis really dead? I don't know where to go. If the others find out Maloney does not come back they will make me stay. I just want to go home."

The screen went black and no one moved. Gia shook his head. "No. We have to do something."

Aunt Ginny wrung her hands and swayed back and forth. "Do you think Amber could help?"

"I've already texted her that we need to talk. They know Mitchel Maloney was from Yonkers. Maybe they can connect with Taffy and find where she's being held."

Gia sighed. "Was Auggie being blackmailed? Or *stupido*?"

Cameron answered, "Probably both."

Aunt Ginny turned her sad eyes on me.

"Do you think that's who killed Auggie? That Maloney fella?"

I shook my head. "No. He couldn't have."

"Why not?"

"Because Auggie had already killed him before he got the chance."

CHAPTER 47

"How are you so sure Auggie killed that guy?" Aunt Ginny rummaged through the pastry case and took out a crunch-coat bar.

"Follow the evidence. Mitchel Maloney was threatening Auggie. Witnesses saw them together the night before he washed up under the pier. Then there's Auggie's cracked rib a few days before he was murdered. And how many places do you know of that are missing a macramé plant hanger?"

Gia handed Aunt Ginny a plate. "It must have been self-defense."

Aunt Ginny shrugged. "I guess you never know what you're capable of until you're desperate and your back's against the wall."

We sat in silence for a few minutes. We were all in a somber mood after the video call. We wanted to help Taffy but didn't know how.

A sharp rap on the door shook us out of our stupor. Amber had arrived with Officer Viola. She took one look at Cameron's laptop and launched into praise about how clever and smart we were to save her hours of work from getting her IT department to get the data themselves. *Yeah. In my dreams.* What really happened was a thirty-minute lecture/rant over how irresponsible we were to tamper with evidence.

Amber paced back and forth. "Do you have any idea what would have happened if you'd erased that data?"

I opened my mouth to try to answer and Officer Viola cut me off. "Of all the moronic moves, this one takes the cake. I hope your behind gets sued."

"By who?"

Amber didn't wait for Viola to answer. "How am I supposed to trust you when you pull idiot stunts like this?" Amber passed me a thumb drive and half an eye roll.

Officer Viola took out her notebook. "I'm getting statements from everyone to document this ludicrous display of ineptitude."

Amber gave her partner an approving look. "Excellent idea, Sergeant Washington."

I stood and excused myself, but neither of them were really paying attention to me. They were too busy complaining about every decision I'd ever made. Although I think Amber only meant about half of her reprimands. I suspected the other half was for Viola's benefit. "I'll just see if Cameron can get you that data."

I went through to the kitchen to hand over the thumb drive and caught Sierra and Cameron in a hefty lip lock. Sierra had the boy bent over backwards on my counter space.

"Hey!"

Sierra glanced at me without breaking contact from Cameron.

"That has to wait until the cops leave. They want that data, and Sergeant Washington wants to yell at you for a few minutes." I handed Cameron the thumb drive. "And they want the phone and the data we downloaded."

Cameron took the drive. "Okay, geez. You'd think we'd get a thank-you or something."

I laughed. "Yeah. I'm still waiting for a thank-you for figuring out who killed the cheerleader. Don't hold your breath."

Sergeant Washington was interviewing Aunt Ginny, who was being her usual cooperative self.

"We were trying to break level twenty."

Henry nodded. "She kept getting splatted."

Aunt Ginny tapped Sergeant Washington's notepad. "Write that down."

Amber eyed Viola and sidled up to me. She nodded at the laptop. "This wasn't your best idea, you know. But good work."

"Thanks. You and I both know I'm not capable of cracking into that cell phone on my own, but I'd rather keep everyone else's name out of the report."

Amber looked at Viola. "We'll see how it goes."

"What are you going to do about Taffy? Can we help her? It sounds like Mitchel Maloney was holding her against her will and forcing her to do horrifying things for money."

"Captain Kieran has contacts at the Bureau of Justice. They can look into the situation and find out what was really happening with Taffy and Mitchel Maloney. They're going to try to reach out through the same app that you stumbled into and see if the girl can give them any more information. In the meantime, we're still trying to catch Auggie's killer. Can you try to lay low for a couple of days? Hang out with your man. Bake some muffins?"

I grinned. "I'll do my best."

When the berating was finished and the evidence collected, we were all ready to escape the coffee shop.

Gia was so upset after seeing what Auggie was involved in on the Internet that he took Henry's iPad and told him electronics were bad for him and he needed to read a book. So, I was enlisted to read *Dragons Love Tacos* for the umpteenth time. Gia loaded Henry into the car for home and I promised I was right behind them. But first I took Aunt Ginny back to the B&B and dropped her off.

Elaine Grabstein was holding a candlelight vigil with the other ladies on the front lawn. They'd gotten wind about Auggie's passing and my misfortune of being on the scene when they read the comments left on the viral video.

Mrs. Grabstein hailed me as I pulled into the driveway. "There is a bad energy with this house. I can do a cleansing for ya if you'd like?"

"Oh? What would be involved with that?"

"I could burn some sage."

"Pass. I'm still on probation with the fire department."

"We could set up some crystals around the house and invite positive energy using aromatherapy."

"Figaro would have a fit. And he's bad enough when there are no crystals and no aromas. What else you got?"

"I could contact the spirit world and ask the presence to leave."

"Bingo. Let me know how that works out."

She waved as I backed out of the driveway. Aunt Ginny was already lighting a candle and picking a spot on the lawn to vigil with the other guests. I suspected she just wanted a distraction from seeing Taffy.

I drove to Gia's house and parked across the street. As soon as I shut the car door, all the safety lights went off around the duplex like someone had flipped a master switch. The upstairs light flicked back on and Gia appeared on the landing with Henry, already in pajamas.

I wasn't in the house more than five minutes before the downstairs neighbor was banging on their ceiling. Gia took out his phone and made a call in Italian while I tucked Henry in and read him his book. Then three more.

By the time Gia came in to join us, Henry was sound asleep.

Gia took my hand and led me into the living room to the sofa. "I finally have you all to myself, *amore mio*." He pulled me into his lap and nuzzled my neck. There was a sharp banging on the front door. I flopped over to the seat next to him while Gia went off in a rant, and threw the door open.

Officer Consuelos was standing on the landing. "Gia. Poppy. I'm so sorry to bother you so late."

Gia leaned against the door. "What is the problem, Officer?"

I jumped to my feet. "What's the matter? Did they burn the house down this time? Is it Aunt Ginny?"

Ben Consuelos was no stranger to Aunt Ginny's antics. Or getting bested by them. He grinned. "Not that I know of. I'm here because the neighbor downstairs is complaining about the noise."

"Wha—How is that possible? All I've done is read bedtime stories to a four-year-old."

Gia started to shut the door. "Thank you. We will be quiet as the church mice for rest of the night."

Speak for yourself.

Ben put his hand up to stop the door. "I'm sorry. There is also a complaint about a Corvette across the street. It has a dead registration. That would be yours?" He looked across the room right at me. "When was it last renewed?"

"I don't know. It's Aunt Ginny's. But who would complain about that?"

The muscles in Gia's jaw clenched. "I am sorry, Bella."

Ben made a face. "The neighbor downstairs reported it."

"Who is the neighbor downstairs?"

Gia took my hand. "My sister Teresa."

Oh great. Momma junior.

Ben gave me a small head shake. "I'm sure the car is just an oversight. I'm giving you a warning. Keep it off the road until you bring the registration current."

"How will I get home?"

Gia ran his hand down my back. "You can stay."

Ben smiled. "I'll let you drive it home."

Gia shot a glare at Officer Consuelos.

He chuckled. "Unless you want me to tow it away for you?"

"No. I'd better go." I grabbed my purse.

Officer Consuelos grinned at Gia. "I'm sorry, man."

I tried to give Gia a peck on the cheek, but he caught me and kissed me deep enough that Ben turned his back to us for a moment of privacy.

"*Cara mia*, are you sure?"

I was a little breathless. "If I don't go now, I might never leave."

"Would that be so bad?"

My resolve melted and I was about to put my purse back on the counter. Then the banging on the ceiling started again and Teresa's voice punctured through the drywall. "You're both sinners!"

"Yeah, I gotta go."

CHAPTER 48

Something startled me awake in the wee hours of the morning. I opened my eyes to look for the time and a ghostly figure was hovering over my bed. I threw my pillow at it. "Gah! Siobhan?!"

"Relax, doll. It's me. I think we got a prowlah."

"What?"

"A prowlah."

"Why are you in my room, Elaine?"

"I heard a noise outside. It sounds like a man cryin'."

I'm going to have to apologize to the biddies for every time I said they were pests. "Are you sure it's not Siobhan?"

"Yeah. I'm telling ya. I heard something. Also, I think you need betta security. Anyone could walk in here while ya sleeping."

"Yes. Thank you for bringing that to my attention. Why don't you go back to bed now?"

"Okay, doll. I'll see ya in a couple howas."

Elaine left me stewing in my irritation. Figaro had grown immune to her antics. He was lying on the pillow next to me pretending to be asleep. I reached over to get my phone off the nightstand and wrapped my hand around the wooden troll doll. "Gah!" I threw it into my sitting room, where it landed behind the love seat. I grabbed my phone and saw that it was almost five a.m.

I texted Smitty. **I need a pet door and a dead bolt. ASAP!**

Lying in the dark, listening to Figaro wheeze, I considered where I wanted my life to be in five years. Also, in two hours. Both scenarios included a lot more Gia and a lot less Elaine and yak-haired good luck charms. *Great.* Now *I* hear someone crying.

My cell phone woke me to the sounds of *gnyuck, gnyuck, gnyuck*. Smitty had replied to my text. **You got it boss**. I'd fallen back to sleep for almost an hour. I thought I heard someone banging on the front door. Figaro's ears flattened and he turned his head to look over my shoulder towards the window. "So, I'm not imagining that?" *If this is some nut case here because of that Auto-Tune interview, I'm going to sue news channel three.*

I lifted my window a crack.

"Jenna! Jenna, come out!"

I threw the sheet off and pulled on a pair of leggings. Yesterday I was caught half-dressed. I wouldn't make that mistake again. I grabbed a peacock-blue summer blouse and whipped it over my head.

"Jenna! I know you're in there!"

I went down the stairs at a leisurely pace. Everyone was already awake anyway. The guests were congregated in the foyer and sitting room, mugging all the window space. Jenna Foubert was leaning into the coat rack, one arm hugging her body, holding the other elbow. Her eyes were puffy. Wade was pacing back and forth from the sitting room to the library.

Georgina held up her cell phone. "Do I need to call the police or not?"

The twins had taken position on the couch in front of the bay window. "He's looking up to the second floor now. Oh, I think he's leaving. Nope. Just getting a better view of the second-floor windows. He is definitely still crying."

Aunt Ginny padded down the hall in a feathery peach dressing robe. "Is someone locked out?"

I looked at Jenna. "What is going on out there?"

She wiped a tear away. "That's Frank."

I reached for the door handle. "Okay, who is Frank and why is he yelling at my house?"

Wade stopped pacing and faced me with a sigh.

Jenna half whispered, "Frank is my husband."

I looked at Aunt Ginny. She sighed. *Tourist season in Cape May.* There was nothing in the Innkeeper Handbook to address this situation.

Shondra Martins squealed. "Ooh, girl . . . he's coming back to the door!"

There was more pounding. "Jenna!"

Georgina started pushing buttons. "I'm calling the police. That little blond cop will know what to do."

I took the phone away from Georgina and looked back at Jenna, who was now wrapped in Wade's arms. "Is Frank violent?"

She shook her head. "No. He only puts energy into his video games. I don't know how he found me. I told him I was at a training seminar in Chicago."

Kevin Martins grunted. "I think he's on to you. I was in the kitchen at five a.m. and he was laying on the swing, moaning." He glanced at me. "I owe you some lunch-meat."

Elaine snapped her fingers. "I told you I heard crying."

I turned the lock. "What do you want me do? The whole neighborhood will be over here soon."

Jenna nodded. "I need to talk to him."

Wade squared his shoulders.

Paul and Marty scooted across the foyer and took positions in the sitting room next to Burl on the couch, where they could still see the front door when I opened it.

A very doughy Frank stood on my doormat and faced me. His eyes were bloodshot, his Moosehead Lager T-shirt was frumpled and stretched. "I'm looking for Jenna Mason?"

I turned my palm out to the side in Wade and Jenna's direction. Frank stepped into the house and handed me a white paper bag from the Magnolia Room. "This was on the porch. I'm sorry, but I ate the fried chicken."

"Thank you." I waved to Mrs. Pritchard, who was watering the top corner of her yard that had a view of my doorway.

Frank reached for Jenna. "What are you doing here? I saw you on a viral video about the dummy on the lawn. You're supposed to be training."

Jenna looked at her hands.

Frank looked at Jenna's hands. "Where's your wedding ring?" Frank took one look at Wade and ran out of words.

Aunt Ginny stepped forward. "Why don't you come into the library where you can talk things out in private?"

Frank nodded and headed across the hall. Jenna followed and Wade sat at the bottom of the stairs.

Georgina bent to face Wade. "Still having fun?"

As soon as Aunt Ginny shut the large walnut door, the rest of the guests launched into a Maury Povich–style discussion about the scandal in the library.

Joanne opened the front door and stopped short. She looked into the room across the hall, then at the closed library. "Do I want to know?"

Aunt Ginny took her by the elbow. "You definitely don't. But I'm gonna tell you everything anyway while we get the coffee on."

I gave Cleo a pat on my way past my desk. She'd made herself a bed in the middle of my paperwork. We busied ourselves in the kitchen making kohlrabi fritters and a Denver omelet casserole, but each one of us had our ears tuned to the front of the house.

Georgina came back from refilling the coffee urn in the dining room. "They're still at it. Elaine Grabstein said the little fella went from crying to yelling and back to crying."

Aunt Ginny topped the fruit parfaits with a last scoop of yogurt. "They must be getting close to being done. Which man do you think will be leaving?"

The oven timer went off and I took the casserole out. "I'll just be glad when it's over. I'm past my limit on stress. I hope next week's guests are coming in from a convent."

Aunt Ginny decorated each parfait with a mint leaf. "What do you have to be stressed about? Your man loves you to death."

"My man's sister is trying to get me arrested. Speaking of which, where is the registration for your car?"

Aunt Ginny shrugged. "I have no idea. All my husbands took care of that sort of thing."

"Aunt Ginny, your last husband has been gone for forty years. Are you telling me you haven't renewed your registration in that long?"

She snickered. "You better check your facts, I'm pretty sure a registration is like a driver's license. Once you get it it's good forever."

We all stopped what we were doing and stared at her.

Joanne dropped an egg on the floor. "Are you saying you've never renewed your driver's license?"

Aunt Ginny licked yogurt off her hand. "What's the big deal?"

I didn't believe her. "Let me see it."

"Fine. It's in my wallet." Aunt Ginny retrieved her purse and dug through her wallet while Victory and Georgina whispered something to each other. She pulled out a paper card and handed it to me with pompous satisfaction. "There you are, smarty pants. It was right where I said it would be. Are you okay? Poppy Blossom?"

"Aunt Ginny, your license expired the year I was born. You've been driving illegally."

Aunt Ginny snatched the card from my hand. "If the cops in this town don't have better things to do than arrest a seventy-year-old woman—"

Georgina added under her breath, "Eighty-two."

"For driving with a license that is slightly expired—"

Joanne wiped up the egg. "Forty years ago."

"Then God help me, we're paying them too much."

Victory giggled and peeled another kohlrabi for Joanne. "There eis plenty of murder to keep them beesee."

Aunt Ginny shoved the card back in her wallet. "Exactly. Why haven't they arrested Grover for Auggie's murder yet? They know where to find him. He's at Burdette Tomlin."

"It's Cape Regional now, and he's out. I saw him yesterday."

Aunt Ginny scowled. "What do you mean, he's out? They're just going to let him go free?"

"He has an airtight alibi, seeing as how he was in surgery when Auggie was killed. Amber said he was cleared as a suspect days ago."

Joanne was shredding kohlrabi into a mixing bowl with eggs and spices. "I think the sister did it."

I turned on the burner under the big skillet. "Why would June kill Auggie?"

Joanne mixed the ingredients together and started patting them into discs. "So she doesn't have to split the inheritance."

Georgina checked on the dining room to see if the guests were ready for us yet. She shook her head. "Wouldn't you kill the person leaving the inheritance, to collect it?"

Victory sliced scallions in tiny little hoops. "Eit eis never too early to keill your seiblings so you no share inheritance when death come. Eit look less suspicious that way."

I took the temperature of the pan with an infrared thermometer. "You're saying June could be playing the long game? Kill Auggie now, and when Courtney dies in fifteen to twenty years, she'll be set?"

Aunt Ginny laughed. "Unless Josephine gets her hands on that money first."

I took the discs Joanne had made and laid them in the shiny oil in the pan. There was something feral about Josephine's protection of her adult daughter. "Josephine is desperate to leave something to Tildy."

Joanne lifted one of the discs to check the bottom. "Desperate people do dangerous things. They don't always plan, they just react."

I set up a sheet pan with a wire rack for the finished fritters. "I have to go warn Courtney about Auggie's cell phone. I don't want him to be blindsided when the police ask him about those apps. Maybe I'll take him a few jars of tomato jam."

Joanne flipped the rest of the fritters to let the other sides crisp up. "Alright, but we need to get to the restaurant supply early, before the new stuff is picked over."

"What are you talking about?"

She scowled at me. "I told you we need a couple more cases of mason jars for the rest of the tomato jam. I left you a Post-it note on your desk."

"I haven't seen any notes from you."

Cleo ran past with three Post-it notes stuck to her slick black fur.

"Alright, fine. But I have to get back to make some more crunch-coat bars for Gia for the weekend."

Joanne moved the finished fritters to the rack to cool. "I don't want to spend one moment with you longer than I have to. You invite trouble like the cheerleaders used to invite jocks under the bleachers. It's amazing no one has killed *you* yet."

"Well, it's not for lack of trying."

CHAPTER 49

We drove over to Courtney's in tense irritation. Joanne was still angry because Paul Robbins said her *latkes* were "off." We'd made two dozen kohlrabi fritters and all but one were still on the plate when Joanne cleared from breakfast. Elaine Grabstein gave my shoulder a pat and said, "Better luck tomorrow, hon."

Frank went home and Wade ate breakfast with the other guests like nothing unusual had happened. Around the time the dishes were being cleared away, Jenna appeared in the dining room, red eyed and a little embarrassed, looking for coffee.

Joanne handed me my car keys. Not one for breaking tradition, she took her earlier disappointment out on me. "We are running late."

"I could just give you my credit card for the restaurant supply and you could drive yourself."

"That would have been good to offer two hours ago."

I pulled in front of Courtney's house. He was out front deadheading roses from the looks of it. I grabbed the basket with two jars of tomato jam. "I'll be as fast as I can."

Joanne stared out the passenger window. "I'll see you in an hour."

Courtney took off his gardening hat and wiped his brow with the back of his gloved hand. "Hello there. What brings you by?"

"I just wanted to give you this as a thank-you."

He held up the basket. "Tomato jam. Wait till Josephine gets a look at this."

"Where is Josephine?"

He snickered. "She's over at Thelma's stealing the jewelry box back."

"You know they've been stealing it from each other?"

He gave me a sly little smile. "It keeps them young. The box is Thelma's. I've made sure it's in my will, just in case Josephine tries anything funny after I'm gone. She already tried to forge my signature on some will changes, but you're a witness. If there's ever a question about that jewelry box, it belongs to my sister."

"Every time that box showed up in your house, I thought I was imagining it. It was on the mantel the day we brought you the cherry pie, and I know Mrs. Davis had it in my house the night of the dinner party."

Courtney chuckled. "Josephine filched it Saturday morning while my sister was at the beach doing cheese gong or something."

"I thought Josephine was baby shopping with Tildy Saturday morning."

Courtney's eyebrows pinched together, and he shook his head. "I'm pretty sure Tildy went shopping alone. She was back before Josephine. She bought out half the baby store."

Did they lie to me or is he confused? The horn blared and Joanne tapped her finger on her wrist.

"My—Joanne is getting antsy. I need to tell you something."

"Uh-oh. That sounds serious."

"It is. I wanted you to hear it from me before the police come by."

Courtney indicated the porch steps and we sat together.

"We found Auggie's cell phone in Blake's storage room, and we were able to get into it to see his apps."

Courtney's face fell. "Oh. So, you know."

Are we talking about the same thing? "You know about the . . . ?"

"The pornography girls? Yes. Cam girls, as Auggie called them. You teach your kids right and wrong, but once they grow up, you can't control what they do anymore. Even when they make bad decisions and get mixed up with the wrong people, you still want all their dreams to come true. I guess some dreams just weren't meant to be."

"How long have you known about his . . . activities?"

"A few months. One of the girl's bosses was pressuring Auggie to send money or he'd make some shameful video public and ruin the Whipple name. I didn't want to know the details. My father started Whipple Antiques. How could I let some low-life thug destroy it because my son made a mistake? I gave him an advance to pay the man off. He told me it was over. But last week, June came to me and said Auggie had taken several more advances to pay for his habit. I sat them both down together and made Auggie sign over his shares of Whipple Antiques to his sister."

"When was that?"

"The night before . . . Friday night, when Auggie came home after the antique show."

"I thought June was in bed when he got home."

"No, that was a bit of an exaggeration on my part. Trying to protect her. She knew I wanted to get things wrapped up quickly. We couldn't trust her brother anymore, he wasn't thinking clearly. Auggie was livid. We fought and he said some awful things. But what could I do? I told June she'd have to safeguard the estate so creditors couldn't come after her if Auggie owed them money. She'd tried to warn me in the spring that her brother was sinking the business, but I didn't listen. I blocked the business transfer and put everything right back in limbo again. I didn't realize things had gotten as dire as they had."

Courtney's voice choked up and he looked away from me. "I'm scared June might have taken matters into her own hands and gone too far."

"You think she killed her brother?"

Courtney wouldn't answer me directly. "I should have taken control of the situation sooner. I've been so desperate to protect the Whipple family legacy that I've made some terrible decisions in the here and now. I'm afraid my kids will pay for my mistakes."

"If June killed Auggie, where'd she get the key to lock the storage room when she was done?"

Courtney fanned himself with his hat.

"Do you think Blake let her use his? Or is there something you haven't told me?"

Courtney stretched his legs and leaned back against

the step. He glanced at me and looked away immediately. "I've had a key since Tom Jensen ran the auction house. Heck, I installed the lock."

"So, there are four keys."

"We only gave Blake three copies. I kept one for myself, just in case. When Blake bought the place from Tom, he made a big pompous announcement to Grover and me that he had a brilliant idea to use his spare room for pre-auction storage. Tom and I had been using it for a decade. He presented each of us with a copy of the key to the dead bolt like it was the key to the city. He was so full of himself I didn't tell him I already had one. I gave my copy to Auggie while he was apprenticing with me. Kids today always think they invented good ideas. Like you never learned anything before they came along."

"Where's the key now?"

"On my key chain. With all my other keys."

Like the car key? That everyone in this family borrows.

"I should have let June and Auggie work out the finances instead of getting involved. I'm too tired to fight them anymore." Courtney looked at the back of his hands and let out a wobbly sigh. "It's too late anyway. They'll know soon enough. I'm sick. The doctor didn't give me a great prognosis. This trip was supposed to be our last hurrah. I'll be in surgery as soon as I get home to Florida."

"Oh, Courtney. I'm so sorry."

"We haven't told the kids. I didn't want them fighting over the stuff in front of me. Maybe that's foolish."

"So, none of them know?"

Courtney shook his head. He let out a sigh that turned into a sob in this throat. "Only Josephine knows. When we leave in a few weeks, I'll be saying goodbye to this old house for the last time."

CHAPTER 50

"That was nowhere near an hour, Joanne."

"In this heat it might as well have been a week. You're lucky I didn't have a stroke. You don't have workers' comp, do you?"

"Of course, I do." *I'm almost positive.* "As soon as I get home, I will call my insurance agent and find out for sure." *Right after I renew the registration on this car we're driving illegally.*

"Are you lost, Buttmunch? The restaurant supply store is the other way."

"We're making a slight detour."

"What for? You're not getting your nails done, are you?"

I glanced at my ragged cuticles. *That's not a bad idea.* I took note of the mileage on the odometer and wondered how many times it had gone around zero. "The Washington Street Mall is a block away from Courtney's house. I want to see how far away Mrs. Davis's house is."

"Why?"

"This whole time I'd believed that Tildy and Josephine were together at the baby store when Auggie was killed. Courtney just told me his wife was committing B and E at the time."

"So?"

"So, they both lied about their alibi. Why would they do that?"

"Maybe they thought their lives were none of your business. I know that's how I feel."

I pulled the car out and headed towards Stockton. "Maybe. But whoever drove the Lincoln the morning of the auction had the key to lock Auggie in the storage room after they killed him. Spencer said he was canvassing the neighborhood, Tildy was supposed to be shopping for baby clothes, and now I find out Josephine was stealing the jewelry box. That makes three people, two cars, and only one key. So someone had to walk."

Joanne rolled her eyes at me. "The entire strip is two miles long. They all could have walked."

"Not all the way to Cold Spring Village they couldn't." We rolled past the row of painted ladies and the odometer had barely clicked half a mile. "Josephine had to hoof it a mile round trip if she walked to Mrs. Davis's house to steal that jewelry box."

"That answers nothing. They could all be lying."

I turned the car around and went back the way we came.

Joanne released an impatient grunt. "And this little jaunt only proves that any one of them *could have* walked. It doesn't tell you if they actually went where they said. For all you know the three of them stayed together, stole the box, stabbed Auggie at the auction house, then went out to breakfast. Courtney is old. You can't trust his memory. Have you even asked the baby-store staff who came in?"

"I know someone's been there. There are fifty bags from Petit Pois in Tildy's room."

"Did you see a receipt with a day and time?"

"I did not."

Joanne huffed like I'd said we were going on a meditation retreat. "Maybe. And follow me here. Maybe you should check with the store."

I had one nerve left and she was playing it like Eddie Van Halen. "Maybe, you know, I should let the police handle it."

"Yeah? Then why are we back at the mall?"

I parked around the corner from Petit Pois. "Because I don't like being lied to. And as soon as I can prove Tildy and Josephine were shopping for baby clothes, I can have a clear conscience that neither one of them killed Auggie. Can you stay here with the car running so I don't have to feed the meter?"

Joanne opened her door and got out. "I'm not sitting in the car one more minute while you prance around some store."

Fine. Whatever. I locked the car and dropped a quarter in the meter. Joanne and I walked around the block to the door of Petit Pois. I put my hand on the doorknob and took it off again. I cracked my neck and shook my arms out. I slowed my breathing to try and make my heart rate relax. I hadn't been in a baby boutique in thirty years. *You can do this.*

Joanne grunted. "For God's sake, what are you doing?"

I didn't feel like explaining to her why this was so hard for me. "I'm working up to it. Give me a minute."

"Do you need me to sing you 'Eye of the Tiger' or

something? Let's get this over with." Joanne reached past me and yanked the door open with a jingle from above.

A cold blast of air hit me between the eyes and Joanne nudge-shoved me into the store. The room smelled of baby powder and cotton candy and made me feel like I was watching that commercial where the dad is talking to the little girl in the driver's seat and she ages before your eyes. I swallowed hard and scanned the frilly lace and fuzzy blankets.

Just as I'd spotted the front counter with the cashier in a butter-yellow blouse stocking stuffed elephants, Joanne gave me another nudge-shove. "Get in there already. We're blocking the door."

I hissed back at her. "Well, I told you to wait in the car."

The lady looked up and smiled. "Good afternoon, ladies. What can I help you find?"

I swallowed my heart back down to my chest and forced myself forward. A sign next to the register read "When Are You Due?" I sucked in a mouthful of air-conditioning and tried not to choke. "Hi."

The lady smiled back. "Hi."

Joanne drummed her fingers on the counter. "What are we looking for Butt—*Poppy*?"

"Right. Hi. I'm looking for something for a friend."

Joanne huffed under her breath. "Obviously."

I tried to ignore her. "She's been in here a lot this week with her mother. So, I'm not sure what she doesn't already have."

The lady nodded and moved a pink stuffed elephant from one side of the counter to a basket on the other side. "I can't divulge any private information about our clientele. You understand."

"Of course. I understand. I own the Butterfly Wings B and B here in town and we have the same policy."

"Oh, I didn't realize you were a local." The lady leaned in with a gleam in her eye. "Tourist season is about to drive me to drink. The other day, I had a woman who wanted to return a toddler bathing suit. There was sand in the crotch. I told her it wasn't a rental."

I groused a little to let her know we were compatriots. "I have a sleep disorder, a couple having an affair, a woman who's convinced I have a ghost, and a cat who's been stealing the happy hour cheese."

She huffed with a tsk chaser and shook her head. "How far along is your friend? Let's start there."

"She isn't pregnant yet, but she may have looked like she was. She wears very flowy dresses."

"Okay. Anything else that would stand out?"

"Her mother wears a lot of jewelry. Even if it doesn't go together."

The lady smiled. "I know exactly who you're talking about. They spent a ton in here the other day."

I felt my shoulders relax. "Oh good. Do you remember when that was?"

"Friday afternoon. I think they bought one of every-thing, then the poor girl's credit card didn't work. She had to call the bank while she was here to find out why it wouldn't go through."

Something squeaked behind me and I caught Joanne playing with a little orange duck. She knew she'd been caught and dropped it like it had burned her hand.

The lady continued. "The dear thing. I overheard her conversation with the bank. People are never private when they think it's a bank mistake, you know. They get real quiet when they find out they're overdrawn. Well, she got into a tiff with her mother when she hung up, because her husband had emptied the account without telling her. She wanted to put everything back, but her mother refused. She pulled out an American Express black card and wanted to buy it all."

I reached out and touched the pink elephant trunk with the tip of my finger. "That sounds like them. I saw a ton of bags from here in her room the other day, so her mother must have spent a small fortune."

The lady behind the counter leaned in closer. "No. The girl refused. I let her put it all on hold. The poor little thing started to cry and promised she'd come back the next day with cash."

"Wait, when did you say they were here?"

"Friday afternoon."

"Not Saturday morning?"

The lady shook her head. "Definitely Friday. Nina called out and I was here alone. They shopped for hours."

"And then they came back Saturday morning to pick everything up?"

"Your friend did, yeah."

The bell over the door jingled.

"She was alone?"

"Yeah, and she was in a hurry too. Even though she could barely hold everything."

"What time was this?"

"Right after we opened. Maybe ten thirty?"

Joanne grabbed my arm. "We gotta go."

"Was she walking, do you know?"

"I have no idea. But if she did walk, it couldn't have been far. I don't know how she would have made it home with all those bags."

Joanne tugged my dress. "Now."

I spun around to be sure she saw my irritation when I asked her what was so important that she was pestering me at a crucial moment, and I found myself looking right into the eyes of Tim, my high school sweetheart who I'd broken up with. Twice. Gigi, his perky little chef friend stood next to him, hugging a blue striped baby blanket.

CHAPTER 51

Tim's eyes shot down to my belly, and my eyes refused to obey me and drifted over to Gigi's midsection. She had a tiny little pooch. I mentally counted back four and a half months to the day I told Tim I didn't think we belonged together. *How long does a pooch take to form?*

Joanne tapped her wrist. "We're late. We gotta get to that appointment now!"

My face flushed and fight-or-flight kicked in with my default setting—run away. Joanne threw the door open and I ran out so fast I didn't have time to cry.

It wasn't fair. I'd wanted a baby more than anything in the world. On the morning John and I booked a flight to China to pick up the daughter we were adopting, the oncologist called and robbed me of everything that was important. That one bitter moment was like a rusty saw slowly slicing through my heart, year after year.

Joanne poked me in the back. "Just go."

We got caught in a crowd of tourists waiting to cross the street and had to weave through them. Like a pack of slow-moving sardines, they descended on the mall for fudge and lemonade and to complain that there were too many people here.

The air was thick with humanity and pineapple suntan lotion. It squeezed the oxygen from my lungs and made my brain go fuzzy. We hopped into the car and I started her up, having no plan other than to get away. Once I was out of the mall parking, I started to calm down.

Joanne acted like she'd missed the last ten minutes of my life completely. "That backs up Courtney's story that Tildy was shopping alone. But it still doesn't tell you who had the Lincoln. Too bad there isn't a way to check Spencer's story."

I swung the car into a parking lot and turned around. "There is. If they're home."

"If who's home?"

"Spencer showed me a picture of that purple house on Hughes with the tower room in the front. He said he talked to the owner about buying it."

"Is it for sale?"

"No. So they'd probably remember him." I drove down the beautiful tree-lined street that had prompted some famous paintings for its depiction of small-town life, and pulled against the curb across the street.

Joanne marched up the steps and rapped the knocker.

A girl of about seven opened the door and said, "Hi."

That was followed by "Charlaine! What have I told you?" And a woman who I presumed to be Charlaine's mother thew the door open wider and stepped onto the porch. "Can I help you?"

I gave her a warm smile. "Hi there. I own the Butterfly Wings Bed and Breakfast around the corner."

The woman nodded. "Oh." Then her eyes widened, her expression fell, and her voice dropped an octave. "Oh." She moved her daughter behind her and pulled the door a little tighter against her.

Joanne snickered at my discomfort.

I cleared my throat and trudged onward. "We were just wondering, did a man come by a few days ago and offer to buy your house?"

"Yes, but I told him we weren't selling."

She started to close the door and I rushed my words. "No, of course you're not. It's just that, he's been seen around the neighborhood all week taking pictures."

She nodded, interest piqued.

"And we were wondering if you happened to notice if he was on foot or driving a big white car?"

The woman shook her head. "He wasn't on foot. In fact, he knocked over our trash can because he was taking pictures while he was driving and not paying attention to where he was going."

Charlaine squeezed out onto the porch in front of her mother. "His car is brown. And noisy."

I bent down to her eye level. "How was it noisy?"

She pointed to a car parked in front of her house. "That thing that sticks out was dragging in the road."

The woman put her hand on the girl's shoulder. "She means the exhaust pipe."

I stood to my full height. "But the car was definitely brown?"

They both nodded. The woman said, "He was so suspicious, I took a picture of him in case we'd need it later to identify him."

Joanne brightened. "Can we see it?"

She left the doorway while her daughter repeated everything we'd just been told. She'd make a great court reporter one day. When the woman returned, she showed us a blurry picture of some idiot driving a brown car, his head and arm hanging out the window with his cell phone in his hand.

Yep. That was definitely Spencer. "Thanks. That helps."

She put her phone away and told me, "Sure. And good luck with the death threat. I'm sure it's not your fault."

"Thanks."

Heading back down the sidewalk, Joanne snickered and sang under her breath. "The dummy on the lawn's not real."

We climbed into my car and pulled away. I drove back towards the Washington Street Mall and racked my brain. "I guess that means either Tildy or Josephine had the Lincoln. But how do we find out which one?"

I stopped at a light and waited for a crowd of people to cross the street. "Maybe I should just forget about it. Let Amber figure it out on her own."

Joanne pointed out the front window. "Or you could just ask her."

I followed the direction she was looking. Tildy was crossing the street and heading towards the baby store. "Again? How much baby stuff does one person need?"

The light was green, but I had to wait for about twenty more people to cross on the red because they didn't want to wait. Then I pulled behind the row of shops and started the search for parking. It took me two laps and a strong hover behind a car with Pennsylvania tags before I could get a meter.

We hopped out and entered the throng of tourists on the brick-paved mall, keeping one eye open for Tim and Gigi. I did not have the emotional strength to run into them again.

I turned the corner to get away from the crush and ran into the person I'd thought this whole time was a kindred spirit. "Tildy, just the person I'm looking for."

Tildy had a messenger back slung across her body and she held a lone Petit Pois bag in one hand and a ring of keys in the other. I stared at the brass scroll work on the antique key she slowly closed her hand around. She smiled but it didn't reach her eyes. "Oh, hi, Poppy. You caught me. I'm just visiting my favorite store one more time."

"There was something I wanted to ask you about your visit here Saturday morning."

"Oh?"

"I know Spencer had your car that morning, checking out the neighborhood. Did you have the Lincoln when you picked up your things from the baby store?"

"Why do you ask?" Her eyes bore into mine, searching. Looking for judgment or contempt.

"I'm curious about that key you're holding. It looks familiar."

She clutched the key tighter, curling her fingers around the antique brass, trying to make it disappear. But it was too late. I couldn't unsee it.

Tildy licked her lips and her breathing sped up like a trapped animal looking for a path of escape.

Joanne made an *uh-oh* humming sound under her breath.

I felt my heart sink. She couldn't talk her way out of

that guilty look. "Oh, Tildy. Why'd you have to be driving the Lincoln today?"

Tildy bit her lip and looked at Joanne. Her eyes darted left and right, then she took off running down the little alley behind the bathrooms.

"Tildy, wait!" I ran after her.

She zigzagged through the lot like she'd forgotten where she parked. Then she crossed the street into the Rotary Park, straight for the bandstand.

Joanne ran after me. "What is she gonna do, drown herself in the fountain?"

I hollered at Joanne, "Go get some help!"

Tildy darted around a bench and dodged a couple eating ice cream on the lawn. She ran through the bandstand and tried to exit the park from the back, but the sidewalk was blocked.

"Tildy! I just want to talk."

She doubled back into the bandstand. With nowhere to go, she fell to her knees and started to cry. "I know you know. I can see it in your eyes."

I dropped to a squat. "You have to stop running and turn yourself in."

Tildy's face dropped to her hands. "You don't understand. I didn't mean to hurt him. I just wanted to talk."

I settled to my knees in front of her. "What happened?"

"Spencer found the secret account that I'd set up to have fertility treatments, and cleaned it out. He said Auggie had asked for seed money to prove he was serious about turning the house into a bed and breakfast, and we could finally start our family when it was off the ground. Then Saturday morning I overheard Auggie laughing at Spencer, saying he would never agree to such a stupid plan. He mocked him for all his failed businesses. Spencer was furious and he demanded Auggie give him the money back, but he refused. He said he didn't have it anymore and it was a good lesson for Spencer in bad investments."

"You must have been devastated."

"Spencer flew out of the house in a rage and drove off. I took Mom's car and followed Auggie, thinking he might listen to me. We're family. At least, we're supposed to be. I followed him to Whipple's and sat in the parking lot while trying to figure out what I would say. Before I could work up my nerve to go inside and confront him, he came back out and got in his car again. I should have gone home, but I followed him over to Adams Galleries. I drove around the block a couple times before I could work up the courage to park. I don't even know what I was going to say.

"When I got inside, he was down the hall yelling at Blake. They were in an office and Blake was accusing Auggie of ruining his marriage."

"What did Auggie say to that?"

Tildy wiped her eyes with the hem of her blouse. "Auggie just laughed at Blake that he'd never get his hands on the clock. Then Auggie came out of Blake's office holding his eye and slammed the door. I told him I needed to talk to him, but he said he didn't have time for *poor Tildy*. He had to take care of something *important.*

"He went in a room that had all kinds of junk in it, with an old key like the one on Courtney's key chain, and went inside. I followed him and begged him to listen to me. The bed and breakfast would benefit the whole family. And it's better than the house sitting empty. He wouldn't even have to move out. We could work around him. At least give us back our money if nothing else."

Tildy's lip trembled and her eyes stared past me. "He laughed in my face and said that that would never happen as long as he was alive. He's always had a mean streak, but he'd never been so cruel to me before. He opened an armoire and took out this big wooden box and said he had an important interview coming and he was furious with Blake for hitting him in the face before the photographers arrived."

She looked at her hands. "I couldn't believe that was what he was the most upset about. He had no compassion for what I was going through, or how he was hurting Courtney with the scandal, or how he had treated Blake and June. Then he told me I would never have a baby with Spencer and maybe the universe was telling me that I shouldn't be a mother. I would just ruin that kid the way Josephine ruined me."

Tildy started sobbing and I had to blink back my own tears.

"I snapped. I grabbed the sharp wooden stick in the box and stabbed Auggie. I didn't mean to kill him. I was just so angry. I wanted to hurt him the way he was hurting all of us. He—he bent over. And he—he was bleeding. It was coming through his shirt so fast. He looked at me with blood on his hands like he couldn't believe what I'd done. I grabbed an old flag that was folded nearby and tried to stop the bleeding but there was too much."

Her voice caught and she hiccupped. "Then Auggie fell backwards into the armoire and he wasn't moving. His eyes were still open, but he wasn't breathing. He was dead. I panicked and stuffed him the rest of the way into the armoire. I knew I had to get out of there before Blake came out of his office.

"I used my blouse to wipe off the stake and the armoire and I closed him in. Out in the hallway, I could hear Blake was with a woman. I shut the door as quietly as I could and used Courtney's key to lock the room. Then I ran. I don't know what I was going to do. I just wanted to get away. I can still see the blood." She dropped her face to her hands and cried.

"Oh, Tildy. You've made such a mess of things."

Her nostrils flared and her eyes went wild. "You have no idea what I'm going through. This is my last chance to have a baby. Spencer's always waiting for his big break with his get-rich-quick schemes and his radical business plans. Well, I'm done waiting." She reached into her purse and pulled out the silver revolver and pointed it at me.

"Whoa! Okay. Calm down." *Where is Joanne with that help?* "Look, I get it. June doesn't want kids. Auggie was having sex with Internet prostitutes. Spencer is living in a fantasy world waiting for his ship to come in. And somehow, you're the one who's overlooked. It isn't fair."

"You better believe it isn't fair. I never wanted Courtney's money or the house, but he treats me like I'm worthless because I'm not his real daughter. He may as well spit in my face."

"I agree with you. Now put the gun down. That thing is so old it probably doesn't even work."

With a shaky hand she pointed the revolver to the sky and fired off a shot.

A terrified blue jay fled the nest for safety and the park cleared out of its handful of patrons. I looked up to see if a seagull or banner plane was plummeting my way.

Tildy doubled down and aimed at me again. "I knew it was a matter of time before someone figured out what had happened. And you just kept coming around asking questions. So, I'm prepared. You're not going to stop me. Mom and I have an appointment with a fertility clinic that has donor DNA. We're leaving this afternoon for New York. I'm having a baby."

"I know you think that's a good idea. But do you really want to be on the run from the police for the rest of your life?"

"I'm empty inside. I need someone to love." Tildy's arm dropped, and she started to weep.

I inched closer. "I know what you're going through. But this isn't the answer."

I put my hand on the revolver and Tildy let it go. I took it from her and tossed it a few feet away into the grass. I put my arms around her and let her cry on my shoulder.

"I didn't mean to do it."

"I know."

CHAPTER 52

I'd never been so relieved to hear Amber's voice hollering at me.

"McAllister! Did you touch that gun? What have I told you about getting your fingerprints on the evidence? What were you thinking?"

"That I didn't want to get sepsis from being shot with a hundred-year-old vampire bullet."

Sergeant Washington handcuffed Tildy and clicked her tongue. "I get it now. You're obviously the secret to Fenton's success."

I grinned at Amber, who I swear almost sprained her neck spinning her head around. "No! Uh-uh."

The mocha-skinned cop put her hands on her hips. "And I see why you been leaving out a few details on your reports, Fenton. 'Cause if I wasn't with you every time this hot mess stepped her foot in it, I wouldn't have believed it."

I stretched my hip to work out the cramp I'd gotten from sitting on the concrete. What started as indignation ended as more of whine. "Hey! I'm not a hot mess."

Amber was ranting to her partner. "We didn't have a crime spree in Cape May until she moved back to town. Why am I the one getting all the flack for putting the perps behind bars?"

Sergeant Washington started leading Tildy to the back of the cruiser and gave Amber a look that said, *Not listening—don't care.*

Gia flew into the park and we locked eyes. He closed the distance between us and pulled me into his arms. "I was so worried when I hear you were here and there were shots. Are you okay, *cara mia*?"

"I'm fine. But that blue jay will never be the same."

He turned to Amber. "What do I have to do to get her a bulletproof vest?"

Amber snorted. "I've already tried."

"Will you two relax? I don't need a flak jacket. Dear God. Tildy was never going to shoot me. I don't even think she meant to kill Auggie."

Amber raised an eyebrow. "Do you have any idea what it takes to stab someone in the chest with a sharp wooden stake?"

"About thirty years of emotional abuse."

Gia's cell phone rang. He groaned and he pulled it out and checked the screen. "*Si?*"

I braced myself for the excuse of the day. *We've had flood, fire, and fake heart attack. I wonder if it's time for the frogs and locusts?*

His eyes narrowed and he spat out a string of Italian that included the words Teresa, *ristorante*, and *cinque minuti.* Then he clicked his phone off and shoved it in his pocket. "This ends now."

Gia insisted he wasn't letting me out of his sight. I thought he was very sweet, but—I was safer now than I'd been for the past two weeks. At least until Josephine found out what had happened. Then I might need to hire a security detail.

We walked over to Momma's restaurant, Mia Famiglia. Gia breezed past the hostess and three waiters who parted like the Red Sea to get out of his way. He pushed through the double doors into the kitchen and all activity stopped.

Gia's older sister, Teresa, blew into the kitchen on a storm cloud, followed by her husband, Angelo, who was twisting a Phillies cap in his hands. They slinked over to stand with Gia's mother and faced us with defiance.

I half hid behind Gia. The anger rolled off of him in a wave. I'd never seen him like this. Two of the line cooks ducked out back to take five and get out of the line of fire.

Gia's hands flew out in an X like an umpire calling out. "No, Momma. No. *Starai bene.* You are fine. No more calls. *Niente più emergenze false.* Poppy is *mia famiglia. La amo.* And Teresa, this butting in is finished. *Questo è finito, Momma!*" He held up his cell phone and dropped it in a pot of boiling pasta.

Momma swallowed hard but she did not give me stink eye for a change. Teresa looked like she was digging her heels in. She opened her mouth to speak, but Momma put her hand on her arm and she silenced.

Gia took my hand and led me back through the kitchen door. The three waiters who stepped aside when we entered, scattered from the doorway when we burst through.

I had to quicken my step to keep up. "Wow. How long do you think that will last?"

We walked out the front door and Gia pulled me into his arms. "My family will not bother us again." He kissed me deeply. "But now Aunt Ginny and I both need new cell phones."

We walked back to the car and Gia drove me home. Joanne was waiting for me on the porch. "You locked my cell phone in your car. I had to try three stores before someone would let me call the police. The last store made me buy something first." She handed me a SpongeBob wind-up toy the size of a bar of soap and a four-dollar receipt. "I need to expense this."

I don't think I could rely on Joanne to save me from a spitball.

Aunt Ginny wrapped her little arms around me. "I'm just glad you're safe. I never imagined in a million years that sweet little Tildy could be a killer. Of all the whack-adoos we've run into, she was my favorite."

"I really wanted her to be innocent."

Aunt Ginny petted my hand like I was her fur cape. "Then it was for the inheritance after all."

"No. It was for a baby. I couldn't find a reason for urgency that anyone would kill Auggie over an inheritance that could be twenty years away. The only urgency came from Tildy's desire to be pregnant. Courtney's dying. He said he only told Josephine, but we know whatever Josephine knows—Tildy knows. So, the window was closing on Spencer's bed and breakfast plans, and Tildy's chances of getting pregnant were shrinking. June and Auggie would have sold that house and everything in it before the casket was in the ground. Tildy was desperate to give Spencer what he wanted so they could start a family, and she was furious with him for spending the money she'd saved for fertility treatments, but it was Auggie's cruelty that pushed her over the edge."

The front door opened, and Burl poked his head out. "Oh, hello. I um . . . I can't find the plate of grapes you've been leaving out for me every day at four."

"The plate of grapes?" *Was Burl the only one coming down to happy hour after the wine and cheese were gone?*

Burl's eyes crinkled to slits. "Most people leave plates of cookies at bedtime, but I like the grapes better."

Gia snickered. "It is almost five. Father Christmas has happy hour at four."

I smiled at Santa. *Might as well.* "Give me a couple minutes to get it set up." *If Burl thought I was leaving these grapes just for him all week, why didn't he leave me any presents?*

Gia sat in the library entertaining Burl while I went to the kitchen. Georgina and Victory were sitting at the table drinking tall glasses of iced tea and playing rummy. I went to the refrigerator and took out the bowl of grapes and a wedge of Jarlsberg. "Shouldn't one of you be cleaning something?"

Georgina grinned at Victory. "We're all finished for the day."

I noticed the copper range was gleaming in the afternoon sun. Even my powder-pink espresso machine was clean and ready for a new shot. "It's looked great in here the past couple of days. You really pulled through for me this week, Georgina. I know cleaning is way out of your wheelhouse, but I'm impressed that you stepped up. And you did it so well."

Georgina fluttered her eyelashes. "I don't know what you're going on about. I know how to do things. Besides, it was no trouble at all—just this once."

I was slicing the cheese into thin strips that were harder to steal than a hunk, when the pantry door popped open and a Latina in a gray dress popped out with a bucketful of wine bottles. "Feenesh, Miss Georgie."

Georgina waved her hand like she was swatting a mosquito. "*Shh-shhht.*"

The woman backed into the pantry and shut the door.

"Wasn't that Marta?"

Georgina raised her eyes to mine. "Who?"

"Your maid?"

Georgina shuffled her cards. "You'll have to be more specific. I've had at least three Martas."

The door opened a crack. "Miss Georgie, I have to go home now. I'll miss the ferry."

Victory popped a grape into her mouth and gave me a grin.

Georgina spoke through gritted teeth. "I told you I'd put you in a hotel for another night and you can go home tomorrow."

A voice came through the door. "I have to make deener."

I piled the grapes up in little bunches on the tray. "Marta?"

"Jes?"

"What room were all the wine bottles in?"

"Miss Georgie's. Ein the hamper."

Georgina cleared her throat and threw a dirty look towards the pantry.

"Thank you, Marta."

"Welcome."

I threw some shade *Miss Georgie*'s way. "Georgina. What the heck?!"

Georgina dropped her cards to the table. "What? You're always complaining that you don't have any money. I'm just trying to show you that it's frivolous expenses like these that add up. Did any of the guests complain that there was no wine? No. And just think of all the money I saved you this week by not serving it."

The pantry responded. "The red wines are all empty."

"Marta!" Georgina swept her cards into her hand and shot me a look. "You still saved on all the chardonnay. Besides, I didn't get a paycheck. And Marta didn't cost you a dime. I paid her expenses out of my share of the house tour money."

I picked up the happy hour tray. "Please let her out of the pantry."

The pantry responded. "*Gracias.*"

I took the fruit and cheese to the library and set it out for happy hour. I kept my eyes peeled for Sveltelana the cheese thief. I handed Gia the bottle of red to open while I fluffed the pillows.

The Martins wandered down the stairs dressed for dinner, eyeing the coffee table. "Is that the happy hour mentioned on your website? We thought that was a myth."

Sveltelana prowled into the room and kept to the perimeter. I gave her a look that I hope she took as a warning to leave the cheese alone. "It gets pounced on faster than anyone could imagine."

CHAPTER 53

I turned off the alarm on my phone and did a corkscrew stretch. My shoulder popped into place with a loud crack. *Hmm. That's new. If I had insurance, I would get that checked.* Nothing could ruin my day. No one was after me to keep silent. The cops wouldn't be on my doorstep because they had the killer in custody. And best of all, the guests were checking out today. No more midnight seances or Shazam-ing down the steps. Two hours of bliss was waiting for me this afternoon as soon as I finished that blog post on running a B&B at the shore. A scratching sound against my door brought me out of my reverie.

I opened it a crack and Cleo pushed her face through, looking for Figaro. Fig's ears flattened and he looked away. Cleo slinked over to the bed and hopped up to the covers with a dainty *fwump*. She tried to nuzzle Figaro and he half resisted, half rolled over in silent protest. Cleo curled up next to him and licked his ear. He lurched away from her and settled his face back to his paws with one eye open, watching the green-eyed kitty through an orange slit.

I pulled out my mat and started a yoga flow. In the middle of a pigeon pose, my door received a head butt and flung open all the way. Sveltelana entered the room like Matilda the Hun entering the ring. Her whiskers twitched and she lifted her nose to sniff the air. She trundled over to check out what I was doing on my mat and found very creative ways to get under my face no matter what position I was in. While I was in chair pose, she flopped to the floor on her side with a thud.

"You did not just do a Figaro death scene."

Sveltelana purred and stretched her paw to play with my hair while I stroked her belly. Figaro had found his spine and a new appreciation for the big girl. He jumped down to sit on the edge of my mat and check her out ringside. She turned her golden eyes to him and gave a see-what-you've-been-missing-out-on blink.

Figaro came closer and head bonked in Sveltelana's direction. He didn't actually make contact, but the intention was clear. Cleo peered over the edge of the bed, her tail flicking angrily. Figaro disappeared into the closet for a moment. He returned with the red scrunchie, now dirty and ripped, and dropped it next to Sveltelana. She reached out a paw to swat it. When Figaro flopped next to the Maine coon, Cleo jumped down and left the room. She paused in the doorway and kicked her back feet out one at a time like she was shaking the dust off.

I gave Figaro a rub under his chin. "Good for you, baby. It's always better to go for common interests over society's misguided rules about physical beauty." *Whoa.* I suddenly realized it was the same with Gia. When we were together, we could talk for hours. Some nights we have. Everything was brand-new and yet it was like we'd known each other for years. Maybe that was why he wouldn't rather have some slinky young thing like a Cleo.

As Figaro gave a nuzzle to the chunky Maine coon, I thought about how much time I'd spent obsessing about my weight when no one else was. Why was it such a big deal to me? No one was shaming me for being fluffy. Well, except for Georgina. And that spoke far more about her self-esteem than mine. I thought everyone was judging me, but I was the one who broke every situation down in terms of fat or thin. I was the shallow one. Just because I'd started living my life and not hiding in my room, I hadn't fully accepted that I could be loved just for being me. Gia had been trying to show me that from the beginning. I hadn't given him enough credit and I planned to let him know just how I felt about that.

I ran through my morning routine to get to the kitchen and get this day started and this week ended. The last breakfast of the week was being presented for this particular set of guests. Aloha pineapple pancakes with coconut syrup and toasted macadamia nuts. Because *aloha* also means goodbye.

I approached the door to the steps leading down to the pantry. With my hand on the doorknob, I paused. Something was moving on the other side of the door. It was scurrying. *Figaro, if this is a mouse, you are in so much trouble, mister.*

I nudged the door open a crack and spotted Aunt

Ginny. She had the troll doll, and she was tying a pink ribbon around the white yak hair, giving it a ponytail. She giggled to herself and I pulled the door shut.

What had I just seen? That evil little troll. And I don't mean the wooden one. Aunt Ginny had been scaring the stuffing out of me all week with that thing.

When I heard her snickering disappear down the stairway, I opened the door and took in the fullness of what she had done. She'd left it at the top of the landing, lying down like a murder victim next to a piece of crime scene tape. *She has to be punished.*

I picked it up and took it to my room. I colored the hair with an orange sharpie and wound it into a beehive. Then I fashioned a red and white gingham bikini out of a handkerchief. I went down the stairs and stuffed it into Aunt Ginny's box of Cap'n Crunch. *I'll teach you to mess with me, old woman.*

Joanne had bagged up five gift bags full of kohlrabi and spread a packet of cookies over the top of each one. "Maybe they won't go through it until they're on the road."

"We can hope." I tried not to look right at Joanne. It was hard to take her seriously when she was dressed head to toe in bright purple and her T-shirt was an enormous face.

"Quit staring at me." Joanne flipped two pancakes onto the warming tray.

"I'm sorry. I just—What is it? A Teletubbie?"

She poured a scoop of batter onto the griddle. "If you must know, it's Grimace. From McDonald's. And I think you spend way too much time focused on my clothes and too little on your own."

"What's wrong with my baby-doll blouse? It has little yellow roses on it."

Victory wrapped around the door frame and lugged herself into the kitchen under a dark cloud. She sniffled. Aunt Ginny came in right behind her and Victory started to cry again.

Aunt Ginny gave her a hug and patted her on the back. "Now, now. It isn't that bad."

I filled the carafe with fresh coffee and prepared to take it to the dining room. "What's going on? Georgina left yesterday to take Marta home, so you'll get all the checkout tips for yourself."

Aunt Ginny sighed. "Victory just found out she has to return to the Ukraine two weeks sooner."

"Oh no. Why?"

Victory gave me the most pitiful look. "My class for nuclear energy eis start early."

I felt a surprising drop in my mood. She was the world's worst chambermaid, but I was just getting used to finding her asleep in the linen closet. "We will all miss you terribly." I gathered Victory into a hug.

Aunt Ginny wiped her eye with the back of her hand. "After you get your degree you need to come back and visit us. As a guest. As long as you're not radioactive."

Victory nodded. "I weill. Promeese."

A knock on the dining room side of the kitchen door pulled our attention across the room. Joanne smacked her lips and gave me a snarl. "I'm not about to answer that."

"Is that any way for Grimace to be?" *I wish other people were going to the Ukraine in two weeks.* I pushed the door open to find Elaine Grabstein.

"Hey, doll. We gotta get on the road right after breakfast, but I just wanted to let ya know that I've put a call in to *Paranormal Pathfinders*. That's a ghost-huntin' show, in case ya don't know."

"A call for what?"

"For a paranormal investigation for ya. You know ya under some kinda of spiritual gray cloud here. I can sense it all around ya. Anyway—I told them all about hows you keep findin' murder victims and people are threatening ya an' all. They might be callin'."

Oh sweet Jesus. I glanced at the mantel clock in the dining room. Ten till nine. Two hours to go. "Thank you for the heads-up, Mrs. Grabstein."

"Of course, doll. Burl and I had a wonderful time. Best vacation we ever had."

"I'm so glad."

"The only mar on an otherwise perfect stay was that fire business, but I know you'll take a little off our bill to cover the inconvenience."

"Wait, what fire business?"

"Ya know. The fire alarm and standing in the yard in our stocking feet at midnight. I think everyone should get a few bucks off, don't you?"

Holy Cocoa Puffs! "Elaine, *you* called the fire department. *You* created the false alarm."

She patted my hand. "Ya don't have to thank me. Say it with a discount."

I was getting light-headed from my brain cells jumping around in hysteria. "I'll have the coffee right out."

On the other side of the kitchen door, Aunt Ginny screamed. "Yahh! What the crap! Poppy! And why is it wearing my bathing suit?!"

I grinned to myself. *Revenge is sweet.*

Joanne was on the phone. She cut her eyes to me. "Uh-huh. I'll let her know. Yep. We'll be on the lookout for it." She hung up the receiver.

"Lookout for what?"

Joanne slid a mug in my direction. "Why don't you have your coffee first?"

"Why? Who was that?"

"That was a call for lost and found. Apparently one of your past guests left something here that they brought home from Paris and they want to know if you can return it."

I picked up the coffee and braced myself. "What is it?"

"The red scrunchie."

EPIL●GUE

A couple weeks later, another group of guests had arrived and gone, and a new group had arrived and settled in. We were back to normal. If you consider normal wading through eight hundred messages on the phone, and emails wanting rooms and tours of the murder house.

Amber had come by earlier to let me know that agents from the FBI Child Exploitation and Human Trafficking Task Force had found Taffy through Auggie's app. They were able to get her and six other girls out from where they were being held and into a safe house.

Officer Viola told me that the medical examiner was able to match Auggie's DNA to Mitchel Maloney's defensive wounds, so that was officially a closed case and I needed to mind my own business and stop bothering them about it.

I'd been reading reviews at the front desk from the last group all week, and I was pleasantly surprised by their reports. SantaBaby1 raved about the immersive activities they got to take part in, like the murder house tour. Got-Faith? referred to our free guest participation events. RobbinsHood rated the delightful attic séance as five-star. And RedskinsFam said that even though the week was a total cluster, you wouldn't find another vacation quite like it. And the cheesesteak recommendations were "on point."

"It's here! It's here!" Aunt Ginny sped to the front door and threw it open.

One of the auction aides from Adams Galleries held out a long cardboard box. "Mr. Adams said to tell you he would have delivered it himself, but he was running late for the memorial service. He'll see you all there."

Aunt Ginny took the box and giggled all the way down the hall like a mad scientist.

Gia stood in the library and struggled to adjust his tie without a mirror. "She is going to put it on, isn't she?"

"Oh, absolutely. A hundred percent." I took over for him and folded the pale blue silk, which matched his eyes, into a Windsor knot.

Henry bounded down the hall with Figaro chasing his trailing shoelace. "Can we have chicken nuggets for dinner?"

I squatted down and tied his shoe. "Right after the memorial."

Gia added, "After we leave the memorial."

I glanced at him. "When the memorial is finished."

Gia cocked his head and patted his tie. "When we are finished with the memorial."

I stood to face him. "You know we're not saying the same thing."

Gia winked.

I wasn't sure if I should kiss him or strangle him. "So how are we going to do this? Are you going to make three trips to get us all there?"

Henry covered his mouth with both of his hands and tried to hold back a giggle that came out like blowing raspberries.

I looked from him to Gia, who was way more pleased with himself than I thought he had a right to be. "What are you two up to?"

Gia nodded towards the door. "See for yourself."

I opened the front door. Sitting in the driveway was a brand-new sporty blue sedan. "Is that yours?"

Gia ran his hand down my back. "Mm-hmm."

"What happened to your sports car?"

"I sold it. There are three of us now."

A warmth spread up my body and circled my heart.

He looked into my eyes and kissed me. "Do not worry. It is Maserati. Still Italian."

Henry exploded into giggles. He was bouncing on the balls of his feet. "I kept a secret! Daddy paid me two dollars not to tell you."

I gave Gia a look of mock horror. "You bribed a child?"

"*Si*. And I regret nothing."

The sound of *shkkkkt shkkkt* coming down the hall made us all turn and look.

"What do you think?" Aunt Ginny had squeezed into the black and gold *traje de luces*. She had the rosebud cape draped over one shoulder. She sucked her stomach in and adjusted the waistband. "Matadors must have to keep very thin."

Henry's eyes filled his thick lenses. "Are you gonna fight a bull, Aunt Ginny?"

Aunt Ginny pulled at the black silk that was a little tight in the seat. "I might. Let's see how long it takes Josephine to serve the food."

Courtney had set the sitting room up as a shrine to Auggie. A giant framed portrait sat on an easel in front of the window. Gentle music played lightly in the background. Sympathy arrangements tastefully dotted the room along with boxes of tissues. The largest one was from Prickled Curiosities.

Mrs. Davis sat next to her brother on the couch and patted his knee. Courtney rose when I entered. Making a couple unsteady steps towards me, he took my hand. "I'm so grateful for what you've done for me."

I glanced at Mrs. Davis. "Your sister has been very good to me since I've come back. I'm glad I could help her family. I'm just sorry it went this way."

Courtney squeezed my hand. "Thelma tried telling me for years that I coddled Auggie and ignored Tildy. I wouldn't listen. So worried about the next generation to carry the Whipple name, I neglected the ones who were here. I've held on to things far too tightly when I should have spent that time and energy with my kids—all of them."

"I'm sure you'll make the most of the time you have left."

His hands dropped to his side. "None of us realized how much Tildy was hurting. I don't know how the girl got herself into such a fix, but we're doing all we can to help her. I've already called my lawyer and set up a trust for Tildy's defense. The legal team is still trying to decide between making a plea for voluntary manslaughter due to emotional distress, or temporary insanity."

"Does Tildy want to plead temporary insanity?"

Courtney let a bitter chuckle slip through his lips. "Well, she may not have a choice."

Mrs. Dodson and Mother Gibson came in the front door. Mother Gibson caught my eye and lifted a shawl off a tray of salami, cheese, and crackers. She set it on the coffee table next to a statue and gave me a nod. Mrs. Dodson was right behind her. She took a jar of olives from her purse and opened it next to the cheese plate. She gave me a thumbs-up and the two ladies sidestepped into the hall, trying to look innocent.

June and Blake were ten feet apart at the other end of the room with their backs to each other. An invisible forcefield of unresolved tension surrounded the divorced couple.

Gia handed me a lemonade and I steeled my spine to breech the perimeter of their resentment bubble. June was dressed in an elegant black sheath dress and holding a fizzy water. "Hey there."

June made a heavy sigh. "Hello."

"Where's Josephine?"

June chuckled. "She took a couple Valium and now she's sleeping it off. She's boycotting the memorial for Tildy's sake, and because of your presence here."

"My presence? What did I do?"

"Apparently you are the reason her daughter's life is being ruined. She's been ranting about it all day. She said you couldn't keep your nose out of it, even after Josephine sent you some harmless warning out of something she found in our storeroom."

Son of a biscuit.

When I didn't say anything, June added, "If it's any consolation, I feel sorry for you. You were just in the wrong place at the wrong time and all."

I felt sorry for me too. "Well. Since my nose is already in it, I did have something I wanted to show you."

June set her bottle of water on a coaster. "What's that?"

I took out my phone and pulled up the picture of the note Blake received to meet June under the boardwalk. "Do you recognize this?"

June's eyes flashed with anger. "Blake told me about it when he tried to convince me he was being framed. But he had no proof to back it up."

I swiped my screen left until I found what I wanted. "How about this?"

June examined the photo. "Those are the entries Auggie made in the sales ledger when he was skimming money for his booty calls. So?"

"The handwriting is the same." I swiped back and forth. "Auggie wrote the note."

June's eyes widened. She looked over her shoulder at Blake. "He was telling the truth. Auggie did set him up." The next thing I knew she was in his arms.

Gia brought Henry over to stand by my side. "That went well."

"See. Sometimes it's good when I stick my nose into people's business."

Gia put his hand in mine.

A clatter in the hall caught everyone's attention and Josephine stumbled into the room clutching the jewelry box to her chest.

Gia muttered in Italian. "We are leaving soon, Piccolo. Stay close."

Henry reached up and took my other hand.

"My daughter, Tildy, can't be here tonight, but I want you all to see what she wasn't allowed to have because she isn't a Whipple."

Courtney struggled to his feet. "Josephine! What are you doing?"

Josephine had a wild look in her eyes. "What I should have done years ago."

I whispered to Gia, "I hope someone films this. It could help Tildy's insanity defense. Power of genetics and all."

Josephine lifted the box to her shoulder height, preparing to throw it, and Mrs. Davis lunged at her.

"That is a priceless family heirloom. Don't you dare try to destroy it because you're angry."

Courtney grabbed for the box and got his hands around it. "This was my grandmother's most precious possession. You can't treat it like this!" Courtney yanked the box out of both the women's hands. Something inside sounded like it broke loose and made a soft *thump* against the side. Everyone grew quiet and Courtney gently shook the box. *Thump.*

With a wild gleam in his eye, he placed the box on the coffee table next to the cheese plate and started pulling every drawer and unhooking every latch until they were all open. He sat back, perplexed. "There's nothing there."

Mrs. Davis gingerly lifted the box and gave it a tiny shake side to side. *Thump thump.*

Courtney turned the box upside down and Mrs. Davis gave it a light rap on the bottom. *Ting.* "It's a false bottom."

Courtney feverishly ran his hands over every inch of

the jewelry box while the room gave him their rapt attention. "It must be. There's only this little 'C' carved into the plate. I'd always thought it was an artist mark from the craftsman, but maybe it's a keyhole."

I could barely breathe there was so much anticipation everywhere, except with Blake and June, who were celebrating their reunion at the back of the room. Blake put his hand on June's belly and looked into her eyes. June nodded yes and they kissed.

Their discussion the day of the auction must have gone better than we thought. I hope Mrs. Davis's son isn't going to be too disappointed.

Mrs. Davis touched the "C". "What kind of key would unlock something like that?"

"Um."

All eyes turned to me.

"I think I might know."

The biddies squealed and Aunt Ginny pulled at the seat of her pants.

Mrs. Davis grabbed my arm and shook it. "What do you know?"

I looked to Courtney. "I might know where the key is. With your permission, I'll be right back."

He stared at me openmouthed for a moment, then shook himself and waved me on. "Go!"

I left the sitting room and headed down to the library off the kitchen. It was right there in front of them the whole time. Hanging from the French clock, in a *dramatic corkscrew of ebony* according to Auggie, the broken second hand. I gently removed it from the post where it was dangling, and turned around, to see everyone in the house standing right behind me. "Oh. I thought you would all wait in the other room."

Courtney's face was euphoric. It was a little like watching Sméagol get his hands on the one ring.

I handed him the second hand and he ran through the house holding it over his head and giggling with joy.

The key fit perfectly into the little C-shaped hole, and Courtney looked at Mrs. Davis. "The jewelry box belongs to you, Thelma. Why don't you do the honors?"

Mrs. Davis reached for the key and turned three full revolutions until it made a click. The bottom panel lifted up from the base and inside was a single sealed envelope tied in faded blue ribbon that had been glued to the base. Mrs. Davis took the envelope in her hands. "This is it. This is what we've been searching for our whole lives."

Courtney looked at the envelope in awed reverence. "Our grandmother's legacy, Thel. After all this time, we'll finally get to read the love letters Grandad sent during the war."

Aunt Ginny whispered, "I thought there'd be more."

I gave her a little nod.

Mrs. Davis handed her brother the prize. "I've waited all my life to hear about their grand romance."

With trembling fingers, Courtney took out a single page and started to read.

My dearest family, I hope that I am long gone before any of you find these my final words. You have all heard me speak of the great love of my life, William Loughton Whipple. Your grandfather and maybe even your great-grandfather, if my missive stays hidden as I hope it will. The truth is William Whipple was a drunk and a brawler. He hit me and near put me in hospital many a time. How I longed to be rid of his foul temper. I thought the war

*would be my sanctuary, but alas, William deserted,
bringing shame on us all. When the draft board
came looking to collect my husband for service, I
told them he had already reported to Camp Dix.
Then I made him a good roast and poured plenty of
fine whiskey. When William had imbibed enough to
be long asleep, I slit his throat straight through
with a piano wire and buried him in a shallow
grave in the backyard. I planted a crop of tomatoes
over him to keep the townsfolk from asking
unwanted questions. I do not ask for your forgive-
ness, as I would do it again if I were afforded the
opportunity. I only ask that you never sell the
house to keep my secret hidden.*

Aunt Ginny covered her mouth with her hand and bent over. Mrs. Davis wrapped her arms around her stomach and groaned. Josephine threw her head back and laughed, happier than I'd seen her in the short time I'd known her.

I knew Courtney was wishing that secret had died with his saintly grandmother.

Gia squeezed my hand. "Time to go."

Henry scrunched up his face to mine. "What's going on? Why is everyone getting sick?"

I grabbed my purse and Henry's hand. "They had some award-winning produce that isn't agreeing with them."

Gia chuckled. "Should we go home and watch a movie?"

I looked from Henry to Gia and smiled. "No. Why don't we get our bathing suits on and take our chicken nuggets to the beach?"

Henry started bouncing. "Yes! Yes! The beach!"

Gia stared into my eyes. "Do you know how much I love you?"

I kissed him. "Mm-hmm. I have an idea."

I took one last look at the chaos unfolding behind us. Gia quirked a grin. "Bella, what are you smiling about?"

"The lady next door is going to be thrilled."

RECIPES

Banana Saltwater Taffy Muffins

Yield 12 muffins

Ingredients:
2 teaspoons baking powder
¼ teaspoon baking soda
½ teaspoon xanthan gum (if not included in your gluten-free flour)
½ teaspoon salt
1¾ cups gluten-free flour
8 tablespoons butter, softened
½ cup sugar
1 teaspoon vanilla
2 large eggs
1½ cups mashed, very ripe bananas (about 2 large bananas)
12 pieces saltwater taffy about 1" long. Or 6 pieces of 2" taffy broken in half.

Instructions:

Preheat the oven to 375°F. Grease a 12-cup muffin pan or line the pan with papers.

Whisk together the baking powder, baking soda, xanthan gum if using, salt, and gluten-free flour. Set aside.

Beat together the soft butter, sugar, and vanilla.

Beat the eggs into the butter one at a time, scraping the bottom and sides of the bowl between additions. Add mashed banana and combine well.

Add the dry ingredients to the bowl in three parts, scraping the bottom and sides of the bowl one or two times during this process.

Scoop the batter into the prepared pan about ¾ full. Plunge a short piece of saltwater taffy into each cup until fully submerged, but not all the way to the bottom. Let the batter cover the top of the taffy. The batter may rise above the level of each cup; that's fine.

Bake the muffins for 22 to 25 minutes, until golden, and the middle springs back when lightly touched. Remove from the oven and let rest for 5 minutes before removing from the pan. Like all gluten-free breads, these are best served warm and fresh.

Unicorn Cotton Candy CuppyCakes

Yield 12 cupcakes

Ingredients:
Unicorn Cakes:
1¼ cups gluten-free flour blend
½ tsp xanthan gum (if not included in your flour blend)
¼ teaspoon salt
1½ teaspoons baking powder
½ cup canola oil (or neutral oil of choice)
¾ cups granulated sugar
1 Tablespoon vanilla extract
2 large eggs, room temperature
½ cup milk
½ cup rainbow jimmies

Light and fluffy buttercream:
½ cup unsalted butter, softened
1⅓ cup powdered sugar, sifted
Pinch salt
½ teaspoon orange blossom extract
Cotton candy—whichever flavors you want. You don't
    need a lot of any one flavor.

Instructions:

Preheat oven to 350°F. Position rack in center of oven.
Grease a 12-cup muffin tin or line with papers.

In a medium bowl, combine gluten-free flour, xanthan
gum (if it is not already in your flour blend), salt, and
baking powder. Set aside.

In another medium bowl combine oil, sugar, and vanilla. Add eggs and beat with an electric mixer at medium speed for one minute until fluffy.

Add the flour mixture to the egg mixture and combine until it starts to come together. Then add the milk. Combine thoroughly.

Fold in the rainbow jimmies.

Spoon batter evenly into paper liners or a greased muffin tin. Bake for 18–22 minutes or until a toothpick inserted in the center comes out clean.

Let cakes cool for 15 minutes on the counter, then remove to a storage container with a lid resting on the top—but not snapped tight to let cool completely. This will keep them moist.

In the bowl of a stand mixer, add softened butter and whip with your wire whisk until fluffy. Add powdered sugar a spoonful at a time and continue to fluff with the whisk. The goal of the frosting is to give something for the cotton candy to stick to. We don't want it to be overly sweet. About a cup and a third of the powdered sugar is all you should need. Adjust if you feel you want a little more sweetness. If your frosting is too soft, try chilling it for twenty minutes then whipping it some more. Add salt and orange blossom extract and whip to combine.

Frost your cupcakes with a light spread of the buttercream. The frosting is the glue for the cotton candy. The cotton candy is the real spotlight here. Pull tufts of different flavors of cotton candy and stick to the frosting. These hold up very well in the refrigerator as long as you don't store them warm and give them plenty of headspace in the container so nothing lies against the cotton candy.

Strawberry Funnel Cake Muffins

Yield: 12 cupcakes

  Gluten-free Muffins

Ingredients:
1¼ cups gluten-free flour blend
½ tsp xanthan gum (if not included in your flour blend)
¼ teaspoon salt
1½ teaspoons baking powder
½ cup canola oil (or neutral oil of choice)
¾ cups granulated sugar
1 Tablespoon vanilla extract
2 large eggs room temperature
½ cup milk

Strawberry jam
Gluten-free funnel cakes—recipe below
Powdered sugar

Instructions for Muffins:
  Preheat oven to 350°F. Position rack in center of oven. Grease a 12-cup muffin tin or line with papers.

  In a medium bowl, combine gluten-free flour, xanthan gum (if it is not already in your flour blend), salt, and baking powder. Set aside.

  In another medium bowl combine oil, sugar, and vanilla. Add eggs and beat with an electric mixer at medium speed for one minute until fluffy.

  Add the flour mixture to the egg mixture and combine until it starts to come together. Then add the milk. Combine thoroughly.

Spoon batter evenly into paper liners or a greased muffin tin. Bake for 18–22 minutes or until a toothpick inserted in the center comes out clean.

Let cakes cool for 15 minutes on the counter, then remove to a storage container with a lid resting on the top—but not snapped tight to let cool completely. This will keep them moist. Scoop out the center top of the muffin and fill with strawberry jam.

Gluten-Free Funnel Cakes

Ingredients:
$\frac{1}{2}$ cup gluten-free flour
$\frac{1}{2}$ teaspoon baking powder
pinch salt
$\frac{1}{4}$ teaspoon cinnamon
1 Tablespoon sugar
1 egg
$\frac{1}{2}$ teaspoon pure vanilla extract
$\frac{1}{2}$ cup plus 1 Tablespoon milk
Mild oil for frying (sunflower, safflower, non-GMO
    canola, vegetable oil)

You will also need:
Deep fry thermometer
Wire rack over a paper towel–lined cookie sheet for draining
Pastry bag, gallon-size ziplock bag, or squeeze bottle with a small hole in the spout for pouring the batter

Instructions for Funnel Cakes:
I like using a squirt bottle to add the batter to the hot oil, but in a pinch you can add your batter to a ziplock bag and cut a tiny bit of the corner off to make a small hole.

Fill a heavy pot or deep fryer with oil up to at least 3 inches deep. I like using a small saucepan because it takes less oil to get to 3 inches deep. Heat oil to 350°F.

In a medium bowl, add flour, baking powder, salt, cinnamon, and sugar and whisk together.

Whisk together the milk, egg, and vanilla. Then stir into the bowl with dry ingredients.

Whisk until combined and lump-free. The batter should be the consistency of thin pancake batter and be able to squeeze out of your bottle.

When the oil has come to temperature, drizzle the batter into the oil in figure eight and circle swirly designs the size of a golf ball. The dough will puff and expand to the circumference about the size of a baseball.

Cook until the underside of the funnel cake is lightly browned, then flip to cook the other side. The total cook time should be around 1–2 minutes, depending on how thick your batter is when squeezed out.

Use a slotted spatula or a wire spider to flip and remove the cooked funnel cakes and deposit them on a wire rack over a paper towel-lined cookie sheet to cool while making remaining funnel cakes.

When slightly cooled, place a funnel cake on top of a strawberry-jam-filled muffin. Drizzle with more strawberry jam and sprinkle with confectioner's sugar and serve. These are best the day they are made.

Peanut Butter Fudge Cakes

Yield 12 cupcakes

Ingredients:

Cupcakes:
1¼ cups gluten-free flour blend
½ tsp xanthan gum (if not included in your flour blend)
¼ teaspoon salt
1½ teaspoons baking powder
½ cup canola oil (or neutral oil of choice)
¾ cups granulated sugar
1 Tablespoon vanilla extract
2 large eggs, room temperature
½ cup milk

Frosting:
2 sticks butter, divided and softened
½ cup smooth peanut butter
16 oz. confectioners' sugar
1 teaspoon salt
1 teaspoon vanilla

To add later:
½ cup cocoa
¼ cup heavy cream

Instructions:

Cupcakes:
Preheat oven to 350°F. Position rack in center of oven. Grease a 12-cup muffin tin or line with papers.

In a medium bowl, combine gluten-free flour, xanthan

gum (if it is not already in your flour blend), salt, and baking powder. Set aside.

In another medium bowl combine oil, sugar, and vanilla. Add eggs and beat with an electric mixer at medium speed for one minute until fluffy.

Add the flour mixture to the egg mixture and combine until it starts to come together. Then add the milk. Combine thoroughly.

Spoon batter evenly into paper liners or a greased muffin tin. Bake for 18–22 minutes or until a toothpick inserted in the center comes out clean.

Let cakes cool for 15 minutes on the counter, then remove to a storage container with a lid resting on the top—but not snapped tight to let cool completely. This will keep them moist.

Frosting:

First, make peanut butter fudge.

In a microwave-proof glass bowl (or over a double boiler), melt together one of the sticks of butter, ½ cup smooth peanut butter, 16 oz. confectioners' sugar, and 1 teaspoon salt. Stir to combine. Heat for another minute if necessary, to melt some more. Stir to see where you are on getting the ingredients to make a smooth, silky mixture. When completely melted together and smooth, add 1 teaspoon vanilla and combine well. Set aside to cool.

Turn the fudge into filling.

When the fudge is cool, using a hand mixer, beat it with the other stick of butter. This will whip it up to a peanut butter filling. (Note: You won't use all of this to fill the cupcakes. You'll end up with at least half of it left over to finish with the cocoa and cream for frosting.)

With a small spoon or melon baller, scoop out a little hole in the top of each cupcake. Fill a pastry bag with about ¼ of the peanut butter filling. Fill each hole with peanut butter filling.

Turn the filling into frosting.

Add ½ cup of unsweetened cocoa to the leftover peanut butter filling. Whip it with your mixer into frosting, adding just enough of the 1/4 cup of cream to get it to the right consistency. You may not need all of it.

When the frosting has whipped up light and fluffy, add to a clean pastry bag and pipe onto the tops of the cupcakes.

Alternatively, you could just spread it over the cupcakes with a knife if you aren't trying to be fancy.

Caramel Apple, Candy Corn Cupcakes

Yield 12 cupcakes

Note: Make the Caramel Sauce several hours before you make everything else. It needs to cool completely before turning it into buttercream.

Ingredients:
Apple Pie Filling:
2 apples
6 Tablespoons butter
3 Tablespoons sugar
½ teaspoon apple pie spice

Cupcakes:
1¼ cups gluten-free flour blend
½ tsp xanthan gum (if not included in your flour blend)
¼ teaspoon salt
1½ teaspoons baking powder
½ cup canola oil (or neutral oil of choice)
¾ cups granulated sugar
1 Tablespoon vanilla extract
2 large eggs, room temperature
½ cup milk

  Caramel butter cream—recipe follows
  Kettle corn (I prefer the lightly sweet if you can find it)
  Caramel sauce—recipe follows

Instructions:
  Make the apple pie filling.
  Peel, core, and chop apples into small cubes. Add but-

ter to a frying pan over medium heat. Fry apples until soft and cooked through. You don't want them to brown necessarily, so you may need to adjust your heat down to low if they are getting crisp. Once the apples are soft, add sugar and spice and cook for another minute until the flavors are throughout. Taste your apples to make sure they have enough sugar and spice to your liking. If they need more of one or the other, adjust accordingly. Set the apples aside to cool completely.

Make the cupcakes.

Preheat oven to 350°F. Position rack in center of oven. Grease a 12-cup muffin tin or line with papers.

In a medium bowl, combine gluten-free flour, xanthan gum (if it is not already in your flour blend), salt, and baking powder. Set aside.

In another medium bowl combine oil, sugar, and vanilla. Add eggs and beat with an electric mixer at medium speed for one minute until fluffy.

Add the flour mixture to the egg mixture and combine until it starts to come together. Then add the milk. Combine thoroughly.

Spoon a little bit of batter into paper liners or a greased muffin tin no more than halfway full. Add a tablespoon of apple pie filling over the batter. Add more cupcake batter on top of the apples. Bake for 18–22 minutes or until a toothpick inserted in the center comes out clean.

Let cakes cool for 15 minutes on the counter, then remove to a storage container with a lid resting on the top—but not snapped tight to let cool completely. This will keep them moist. Top with caramel buttercream and kettle corn. Drizzle with caramel sauce. Recipes follow.

Caramel Sauce

Ingredients:
1 cup granulated sugar
6 Tablespoons salted butter, softened
½ cup heavy cream, at room temperature
Heavy pinch salt

Instructions:
Heat granulated sugar in a heavy-duty saucepan over medium heat. Do not stir. You can swirl and tilt the pan if you have to. Sugar will melt into an amber-colored liquid. Be careful not to burn it. If you have trouble getting the sugar to melt, or you form clumps, add some water. Once the sugar has melted, let it boil for a minute to boil off the water you added.

Once the sugar is completely melted, immediately stir in the butter until combined. It will bubble and spit but just keep whisking the heck out of it. It will settle down and come together. Return to heat and cook for 1 minute without stirring.

Very slowly stir in ½ cup of heavy cream. It may bubble and spit again, just keep whisking. After all the heavy cream has been added, stop whisking and allow the caramel to boil for 1 minute. Remove from the heat and add your pinch of salt. Let it cool completely. You'll reserve about ¼ of this for the caramel drizzle, and ¾ of this for the caramel frosting, recipe below.

Caramel Frosting

Ingredients:
$\frac{3}{4}$ of the cooled caramel sauce from above
1 cup of unsalted butter (2 sticks)
Pinch salt
$1\frac{1}{3}$ cup confectioners' sugar

Instructions:
In the bowl of your stand mixer, with the wire whisk attached, whip the cooled caramel sauce to loosen it up. Add the softened butter and whip again to combine. It may be a little lumpy-looking, as these two things don't naturally want to come together. Add your pinch of salt, then add the confectioners' sugar a little at a time. Continue to whip the frosting until it becomes smooth and fluffy. We aren't adding a lot of confectioners' sugar because we don't want to overwhelm the cupcakes with sweetness. This will make a light, fluffy frosting to act as glue for the kettle corn.

Frost your cupcakes with enough frosting for the kettle corn to adhere to, then roll the top of the cupcake in the lightly sweet kettle corn. You may need to move the kettle corn around to cover the top of the cupcake completely. Finish the cupcakes by drizzling over the remaining $\frac{1}{4}$ cup of caramel sauce.

Crunch Coat Bars

Yield 24 bars

Ingredients:
Peanut Butter Shortbread Crust:
2¼ cups gluten-free flour
½ cup peanut butter powder
½ teaspoon salt
1 cup unsalted butter, softened
⅓ cup sugar
⅓ cup light brown sugar, packed
1 large egg yolk
1 teaspoon vanilla extract

Peanut Butter Caramel:
½ cup sugar
1 cup heavy cream
⅓ cup creamy peanut butter
1 cup crunch coat topping
(or ¾ cup peanut brittle chopped very fine mixed with
   ¼ cup rainbow jimmies)

Instructions:
   Preheat oven to 350°F and line an 8x8 baking pan with parchment paper.
   Combine gluten-free flour, peanut butter powder, and salt. Set aside.
   Using an electric mixer, beat butter and sugars until light and fluffy.
   Add egg yolk and vanilla extract and beat until well combined, pausing to scrape down the sides.
   Add flour mixture to the egg mixture and mix until a

crumbly dough forms.

Scoop dough into prepared pan and evenly press dough into the bottom of the pan. You may need to use an offset spatula to spread it out.

Bake at 350°F for 20–25 minutes. Edges should be lightly golden brown. Set aside and let cool.

Make the caramel.

In a dry heavy saucepan cook sugar over moderate heat, without stirring, until it begins to melt. Continue cooking sugar, without stirring, swirling the pan, until a deep golden amber. Remove pan from heat and add cream all at once (caramel will bubble and steam). Return pan to heat and simmer, stirring, until caramel is dissolved. Whisk in the peanut butter and simmer, stirring, until smooth. Pour over the baked crust. Let cool for about an hour, then top the caramel with crunch coat topping. Let cool in the refrigerator or overnight. Cut into bars and serve chilled.

Kohlrabi Carrot Fritters with Avocado Cream

You knew I'd have to include a kohlrabi recipe after all the hoopla over them. But here's the thing: I can't stand kohlrabi. My next-door neighbor when I was a kid had a garden and they grew a ton of kohlrabi. They kept "blessing" us with their produce and we didn't know what to do with it. So, when looking for a kohlrabi recipe, I thought we should use one from the experts. Thank you to Sonja and Alex Overhiser of *A Couple Cooks* for letting me borrow their recipe for kohlrabi carrot fritters.

With permission by Sonja & Alex Overhiser

Yield 8 fritters

Ingredients:
For the kohlrabi fritters:
2 kohlrabi
1 carrot
1 egg
¼ teaspoon kosher salt
¼ teaspoon cayenne
½ cup grapeseed or vegetable oil (enough for ¼-inch depth in a large skillet)

For the avocado cream:
½ avocado
¼ cup plain yogurt
½ lemon
¼ teaspoon kosher salt
Green onions (for garnish)

Instructions:

Cut the leaves off the kohlrabi and peel the bulb. Peel 1 carrot. Shred the vegetables in a food processor, or by hand using a grater. Squeeze the shredded vegetables in a tea cloth (or with your hands) to remove moisture, then add to a medium bowl with the egg, kosher salt, and cayenne. Mix to combine.

Place the oil in a large skillet (enough for $\frac{1}{4}$-inch depth). Heat the oil over medium high heat, then place small patties of the fritter mixture into the oil. Fry on one side until browned, then fry on the other side. Remove and place on a plate lined with a paper towel to drain excess oil.

For the dipping sauce: Remove the avocado pit and scoop out the flesh with a spoon. In a small bowl, mix the avocado, plain yogurt, lemon juice, and kosher salt to make the avocado cream (or blend the ingredients together in a food processor).

To serve, slice the green onions. Serve fritters with avocado cream and green onions. Note: These fritters are best eaten warm the day of making; they don't save well. Like anything made with avocado, the avocado cream sauce will become brown after exposure to air. Make sure to cover the surface with plastic wrap when storing.

Find it online: https://www.acouplecooks.com/kohrabi-fritters-with-avocado/

Acknowledgments

A special thanks to author and friend Tina Kashian for letting me use her fictional Jersey Shore Kebab Kitchen for Burl to order his midnight souvlaki from.

If you want to stay up to date on all my news, or you're looking for advice from Figaro's column, sign up for the newsletter on my website. Libbykleinbooks.com

Connect with Us

Visit us online at
KensingtonBooks.com
to read more from your favorite authors, see books
by series, view reading group guides, and more.

for sneak peeks, chances to win books and prize packs,
and to share your thoughts with other readers.

facebook.com/kensingtonpublishing
twitter.com/kensingtonbooks

Tell us what you think!

To share your thoughts, submit a review,
or sign up for our eNewsletters, please visit:
KensingtonBooks.com/TellUs.